W9-BRC-084

DC SUPER HERO GIRLS ™

HITS AND MYTHS

an original
graphic novel

WRITTEN BY
Shea Fontana

ART BY
Yancey Labat

COLORS BY
Monica Kubina

LETTERING BY
Janice Chiang

SUPERGIRL BASED ON THE CHARACTERS CREATED BY
JERRY SIEGEL AND JOE SHUSTER. BY SPECIAL ARRANGEMENT WITH THE JERRY SIEGEL FAMILY.

MARIE JAVINS Editor
BRITTANY HOLZHERR Assistant Editor
STEVE COOK Design Director - Books
AMIE BROCKWAY-METCALF Publication Design

BOB HARRAS Senior VP - Editor-in-Chief, DC Comics

DIANE NELSON President
DAN DiDIO Publisher
JIM LEE Publisher
GEOFF JOHNS President & Chief Creative Officer
AMIT DESAI Executive VP - Business & Marketing Strategy,
Direct to Consumer & Global Franchise Management
SAM ADES Senior VP - Direct to Consumer
BOBBIE CHASE VP - Talent Development
MARK CHIARELLO Senior VP - Art, Design & Collected Editions
JOHN CUNNINGHAM Senior VP - Sales & Trade Marketing
ANNE DEPIES Senior VP - Business Strategy, Finance & Administration
DON FALLETTI VP - Manufacturing Operations
LAWRENCE GANEM VP - Editorial Administration & Talent Relations
ALISON GILL Senior VP - Manufacturing & Operations
HANK KANALZ Senior VP - Editorial Strategy & Administration
JAY KOGAN VP - Legal Affairs
THOMAS LOFTUS VP - Business Affairs
JACK MAHAN VP - Business Affairs
NICK J. NAPOLITANO VP - Manufacturing Administration
EDDIE SCANNELL VP - Consumer Marketing
COURTNEY SIMMONS Senior VP - Publicity & Communications
JIM (SKI) SOKOLOWSKI VP - Comic Book Specialty Sales & Trade Marketing
NANCY SPEARS VP - Mass, Book, Digital Sales & Trade Marketing

DC SUPER HERO GIRLS: HITS AND MYTHS. November, 2016. Published by DC Comics,
2900 W. Alameda Avenue, Burbank, CA 91505. GST # is R125921072. Copyright © 2016 DC Comics. All Rights Reserved.
All characters featured in this issue, the distinctive likenesses thereof and related elements are trademarks of DC Comics.
The stories, characters and incidents mentioned in this publication are entirely fictional. DC Comics does not read or accept
unsolicited submissions of ideas, stories or artwork. This book is manufactured at a facility holding chain-of-custody
certification. This paper is made with sustainably managed North American fiber. For Advertising and Custom Publishing
contact dccomicsadvertising@dccomics.com. For details on DC Comics Ratings, visit dccomics.com/go/ratings.
Printed by Transcontinental Interglobe, Beauceville, QC, Canada. 12/9/16. Second Printing. ISBN: 978-1-4012-6761-2

TABLE OF CONTENTS

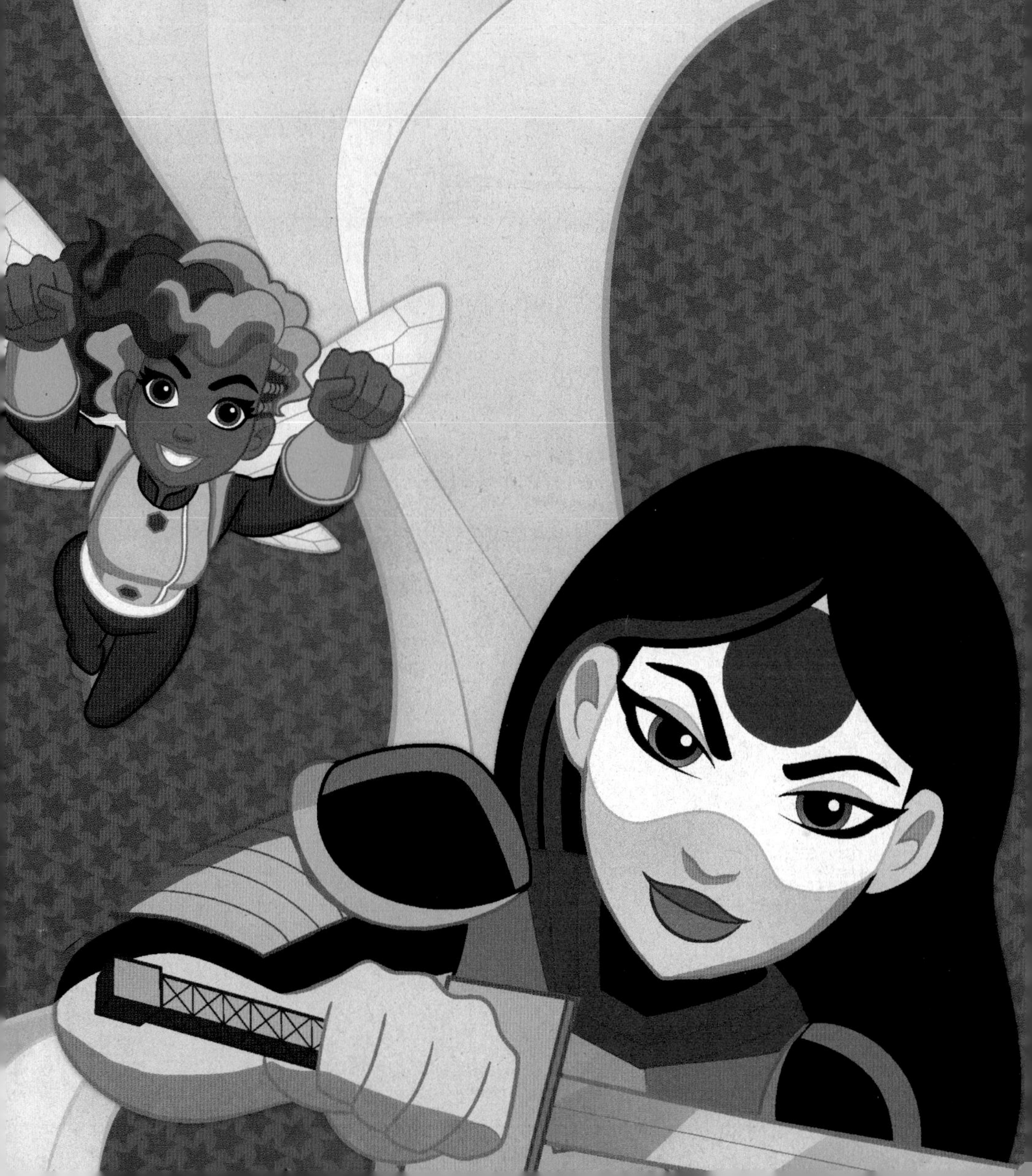

ROLL

SUPER HERO HIGH SCHOOL

WONDER WOMAN

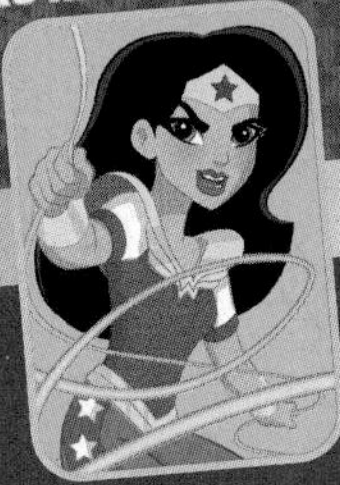

SUPERPOWERS
Super-strength, flight, near-invincibility, super-athleticism

SUPER HERO HIGH SCHOOL

SUPERGIRL

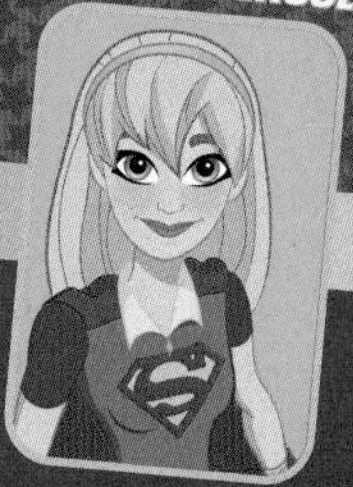

SUPERPOWERS
Super-strength, flight, invincibility, super-hearing, heat vision, x-ray vision

SUPER HERO HIGH SCHOOL

BATGIRL

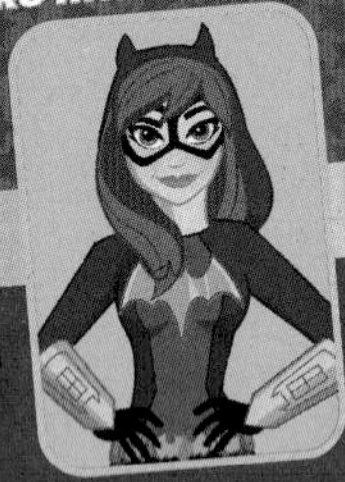

SUPERPOWERS
Computer genius, expert martial artist, photographic memory, legendary detective skills

SUPER HERO HIGH SCHOOL

BUMBLEBEE

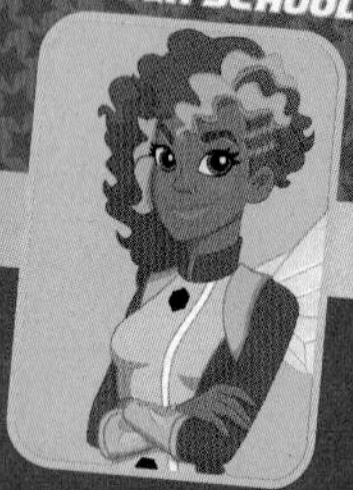

SUPERPOWERS
Enhanced strength, flight, ability to shrink, projects stinger blasts

SUPER HERO HIGH SCHOOL

POISON IVY

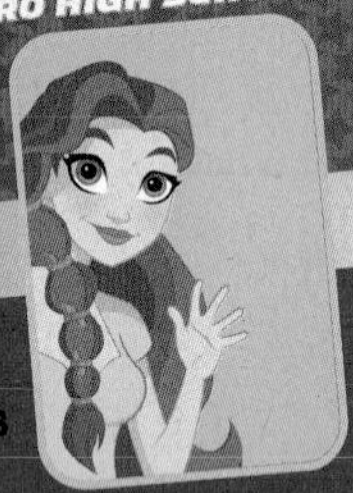

SUPERPOWERS
Genius-level intellect, summons and controls plants

SUPER HERO HIGH SCHOOL

HARLEY QUINN

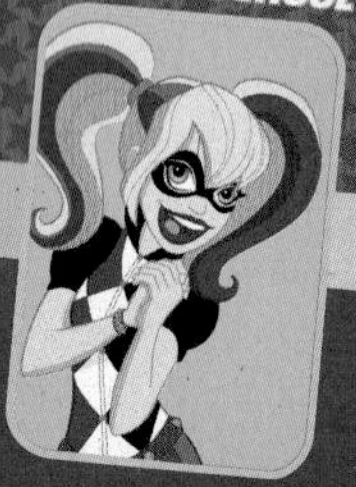

SUPERPOWERS
Expert gymnast, acrobat, quick-witted class clown

SUPER HERO HIGH SCHOOL

KATANA

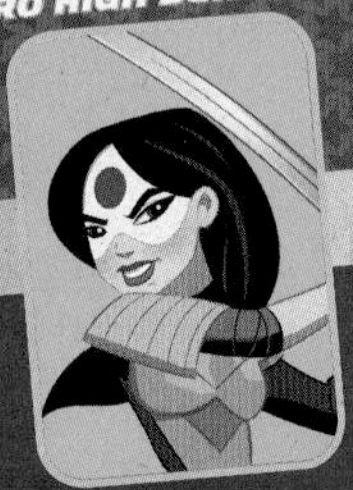

SUPERPOWERS
Superior sword-fighter, expert martial artist, advanced stealth skills

SUPER HERO HIGH SCHOOL

BEAST BOY

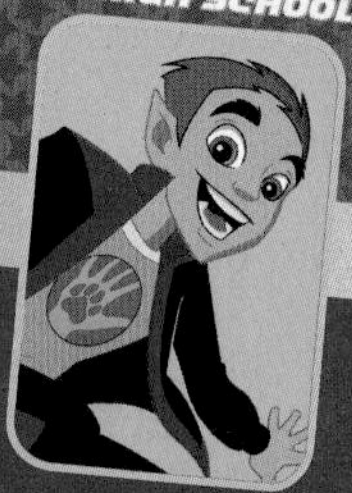

SUPERPOWERS
Shape-shifts into any animal form, world-class slacker

SUPER HERO HIGH SCHOOL

CHEETAH

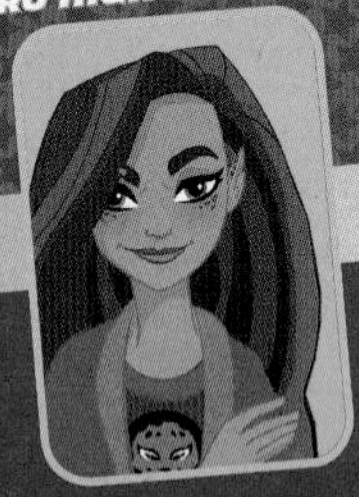

SUPERPOWERS
Agility, speed, sharp reflexes, even sharper claws

CALL

SUPER HERO HIGH SCHOOL

SILVER BANSHEE

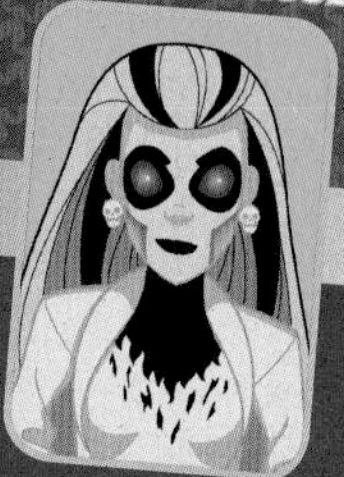

SUPERPOWERS
Supernatural destructive scream, accelerated healing, flight

SUPER HERO HIGH SCHOOL

FLASH

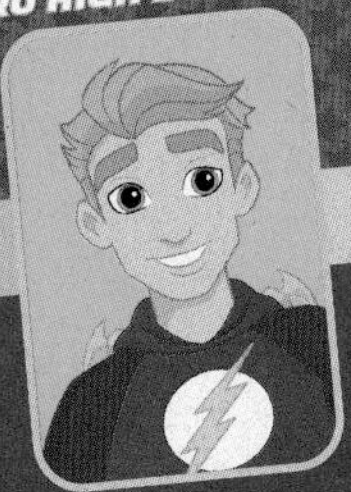

SUPERPOWERS
Super-speed, vibrates his molecules through walls, detective skills

SUPER HERO HIGH SCHOOL

RAVAGER

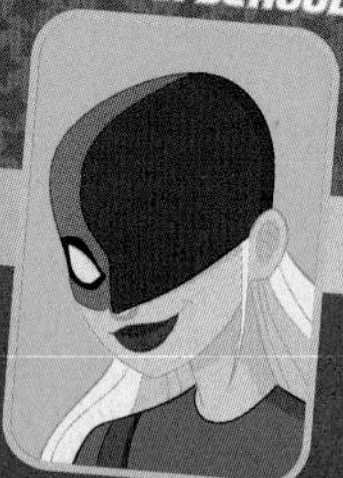

SUPERPOWERS
Advanced hand-to-hand combat, double-swords expert

SUPER HERO HIGH SCHOOL

HAWKGIRL

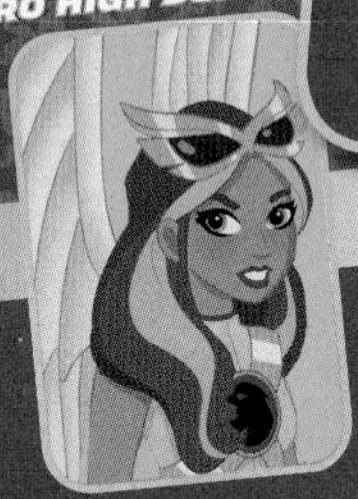

SUPERPOWERS
Flight, super detective skills, weapons expert

SUPER HERO HIGH SCHOOL

MISS MARTIAN

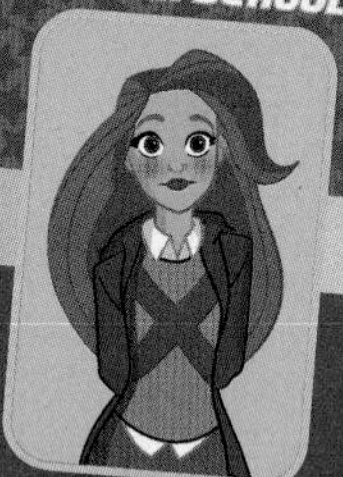

SUPERPOWERS
Flight, shape-shifting, mind-reading, invisibility, super-strength

SUPER HERO HIGH SCHOOL

AMANDA WALLER

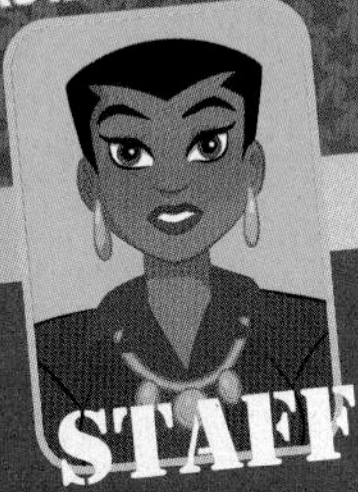

Principal, mentor, stern but fair

STAFF

SUPER HERO HIGH SCHOOL

GORILLA GRODD

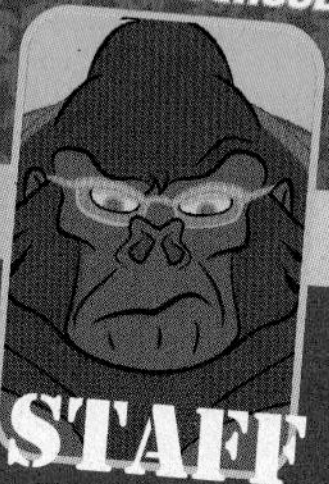

Vice Principal, mind-control powers, in charge of detention

STAFF

SUPER HERO HIGH SCHOOL

ETRIGAN

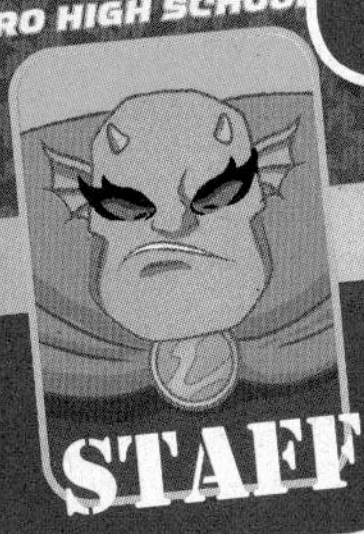

Professor of Poetry, not just *A* demon, *The* Demon!

STAFF

SUPER HERO HIGH SCHOOL

JUNE MOONE

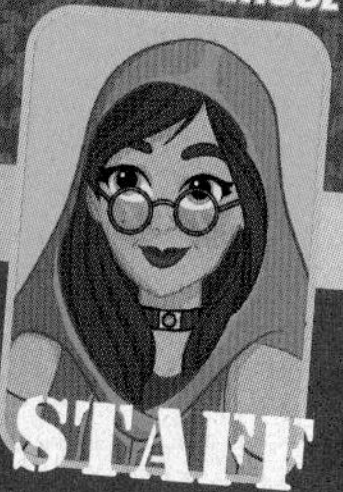

Professor of Art, magical enchantress

STAFF

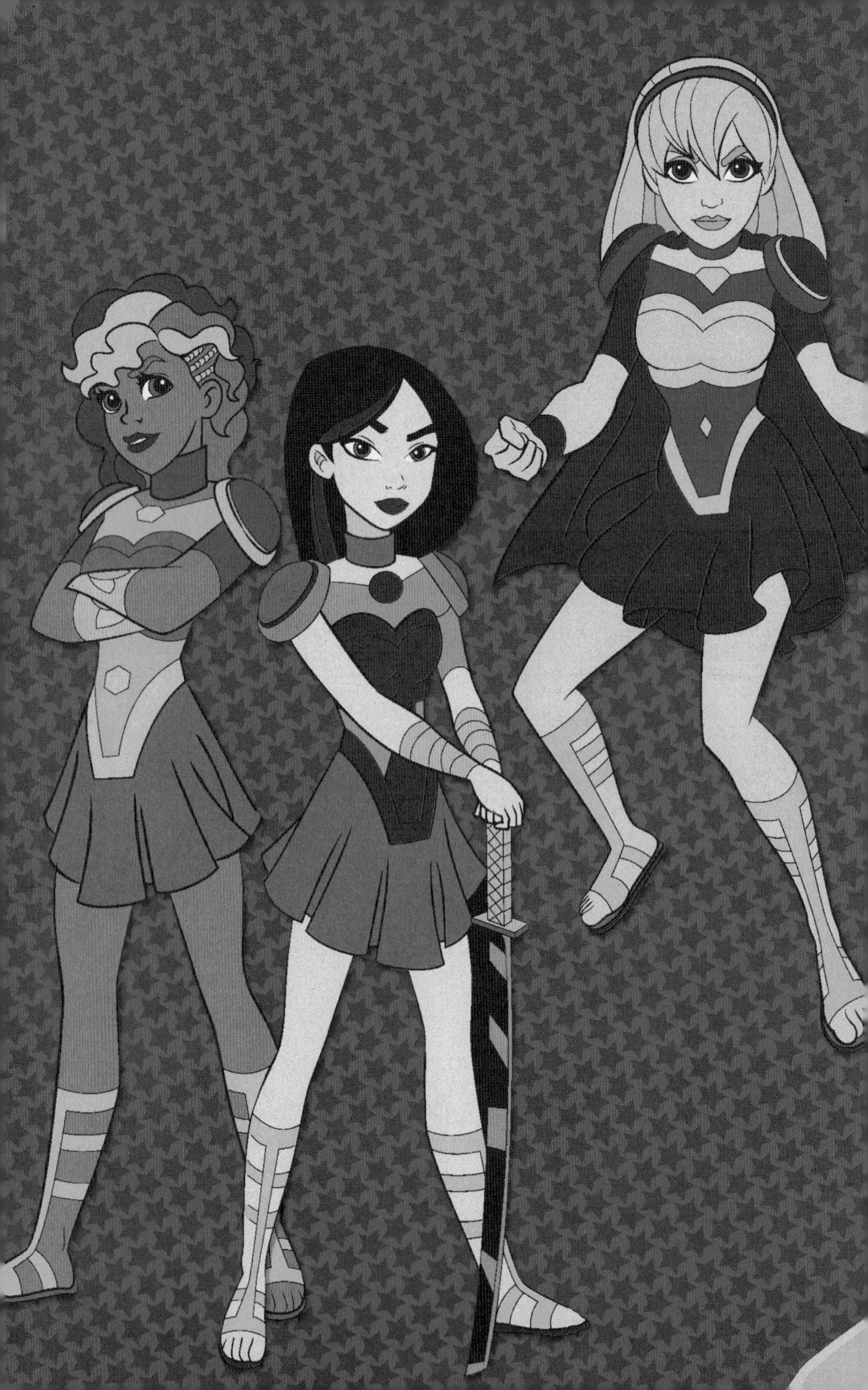

CHAPTER ONE
THE JOURNEY

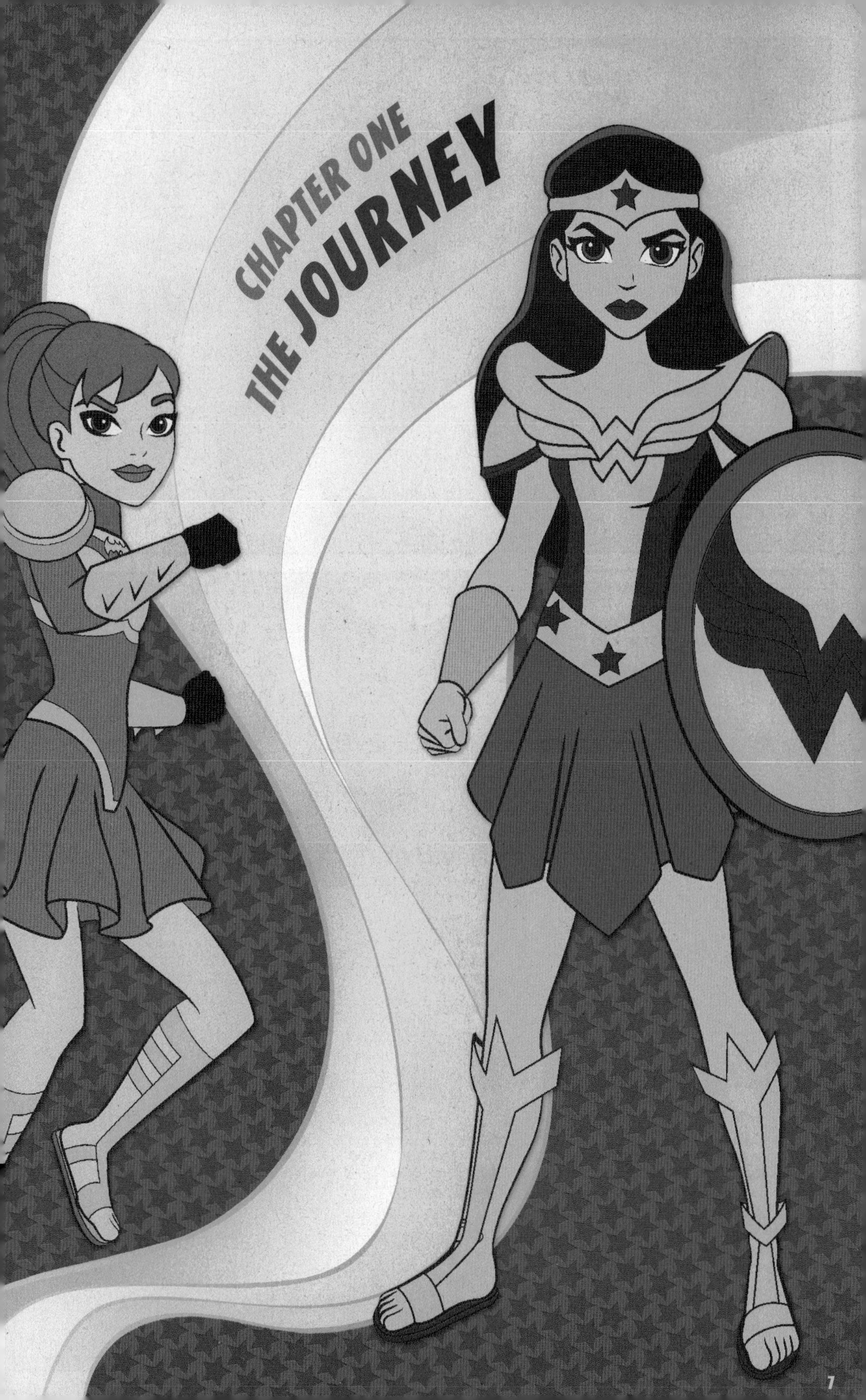

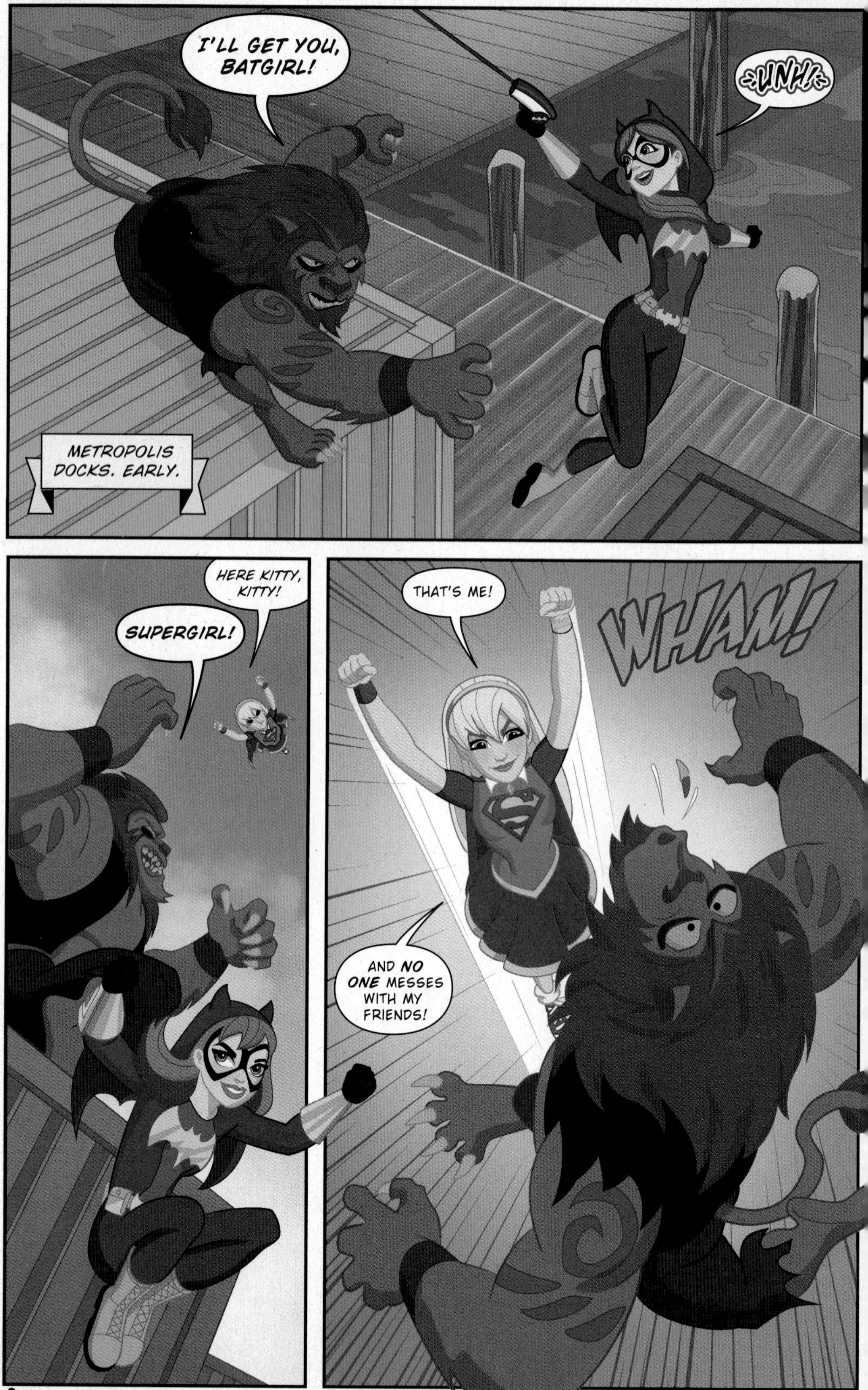
I'LL GET YOU, BATGIRL!
UNH!
METROPOLIS DOCKS. EARLY.
HERE KITTY, KITTY!
SUPERGIRL!
THAT'S ME!
WHAM!
AND NO ONE MESSES WITH MY FRIENDS!

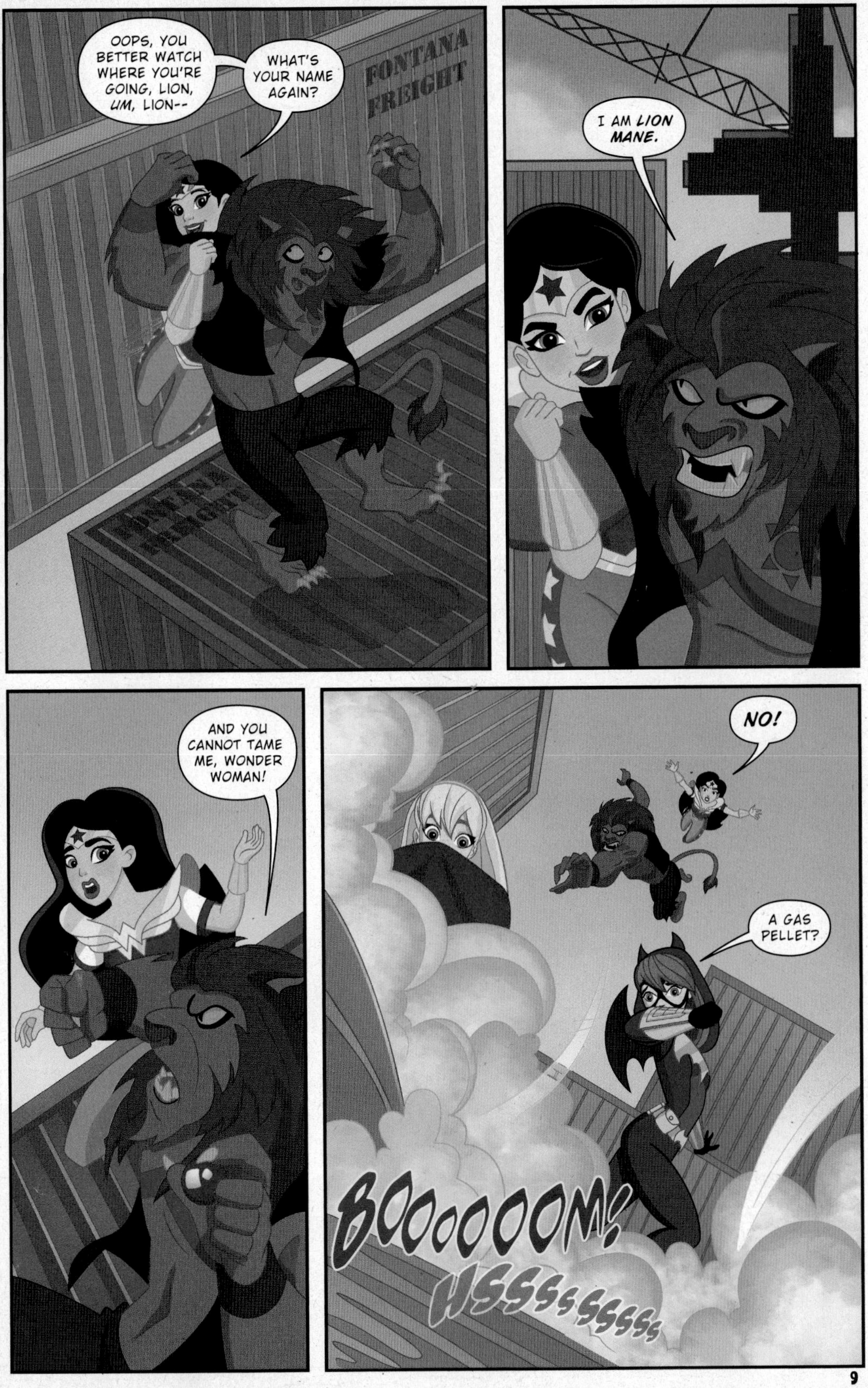
OOPS, YOU BETTER WATCH WHERE YOU'RE GOING, LION, UM, LION--
WHAT'S YOUR NAME AGAIN?
FONTANA FREIGHT
FONTANA FREIGHT
I AM LION MANE.
AND YOU CANNOT TAME ME, WONDER WOMAN!
NO!
A GAS PELLET?
BOOOOOOM!
HSSSSSSSSS

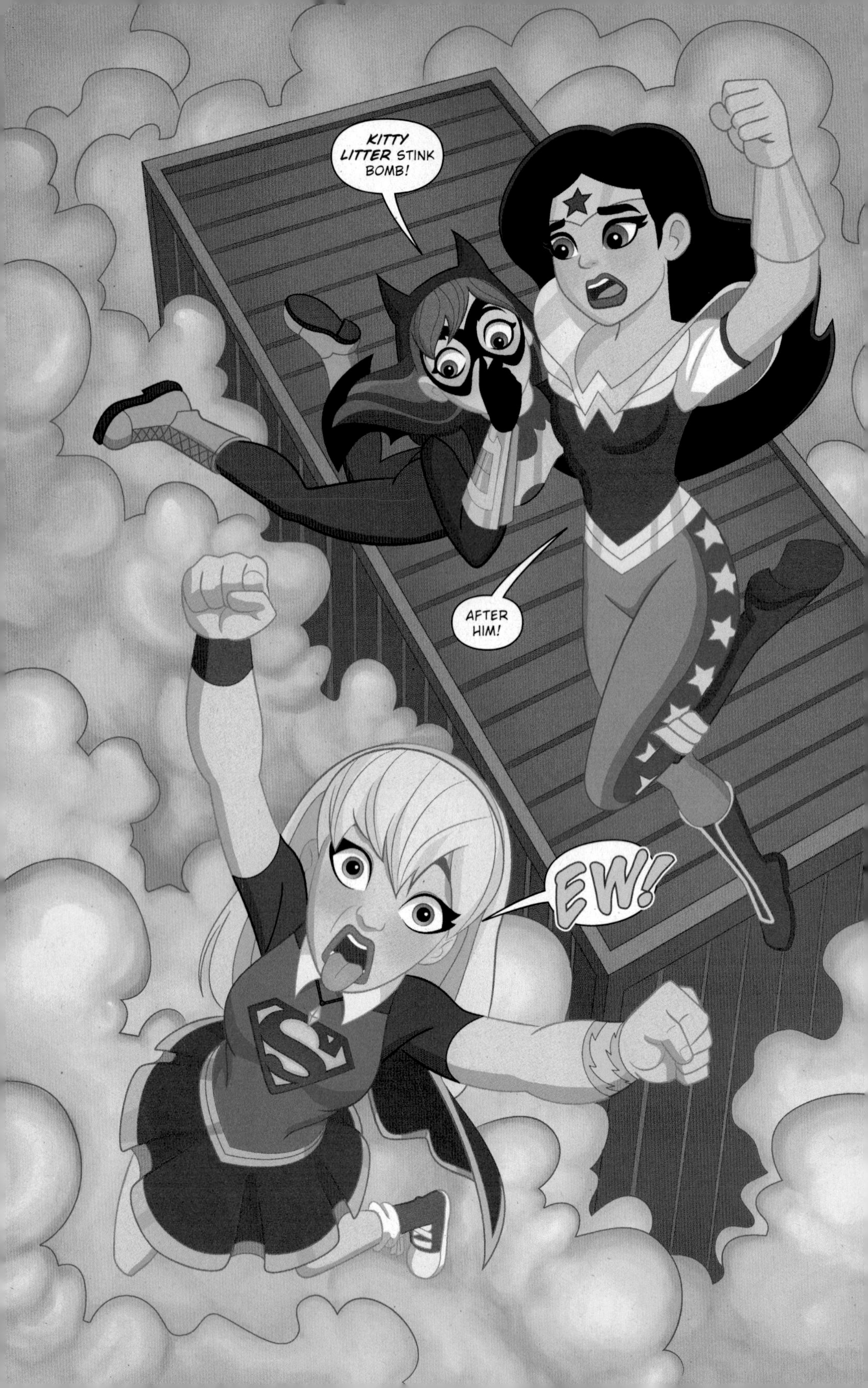
KITTY LITTER STINK BOMB!
AFTER HIM!
EW!

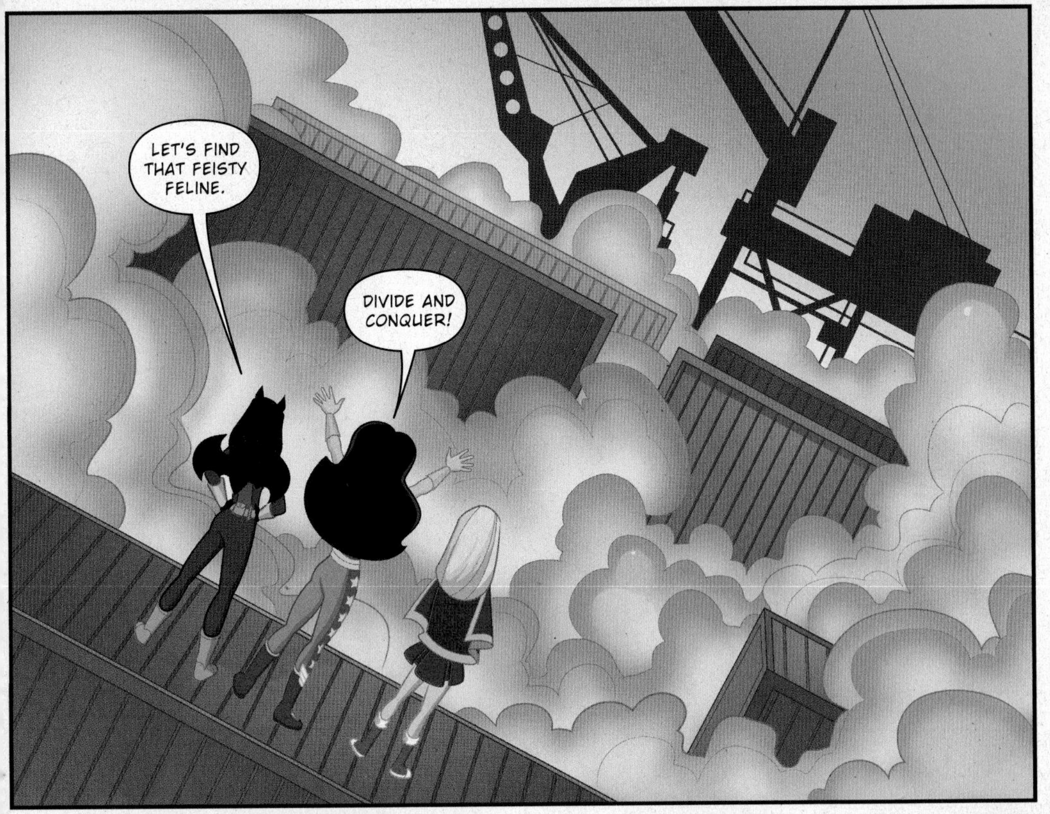
LET'S FIND THAT FEISTY FELINE.
DIVIDE AND CONQUER!

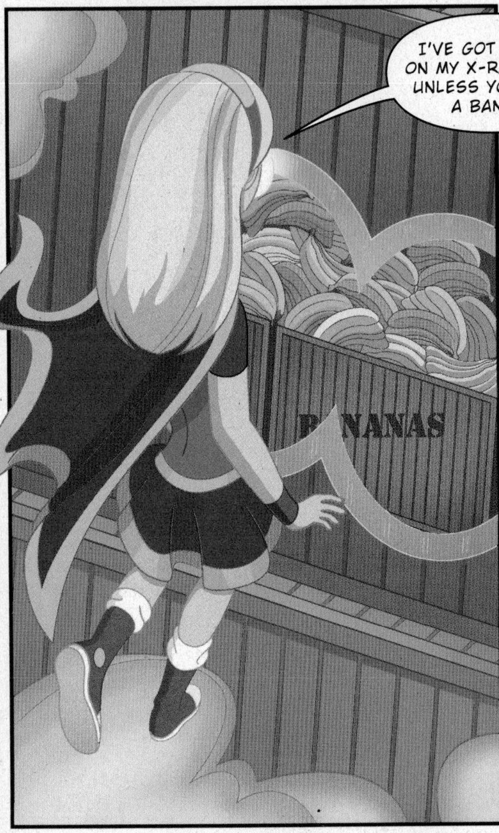
I'VE GOT NOTHING ON MY X-RAY VISION. UNLESS YOU WANT A BANANA.
NANAS

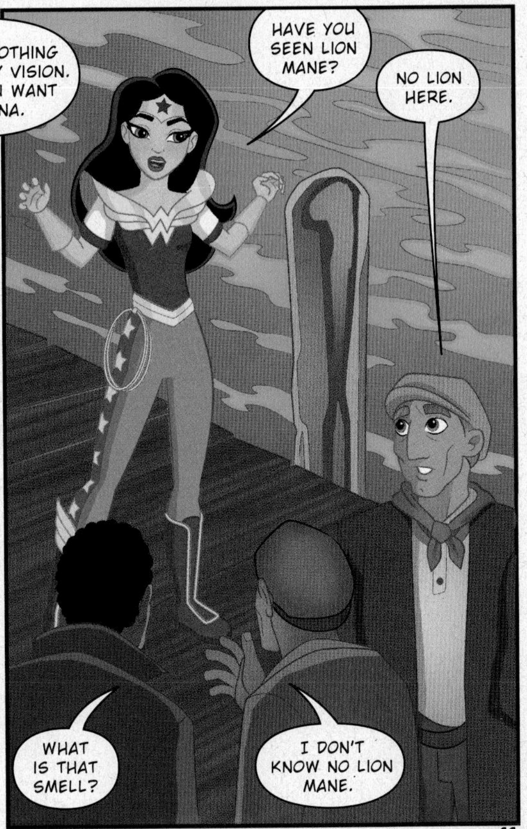
HAVE YOU SEEN LION MANE?
NO LION HERE.
WHAT IS THAT SMELL?
I DON'T KNOW NO LION MANE.

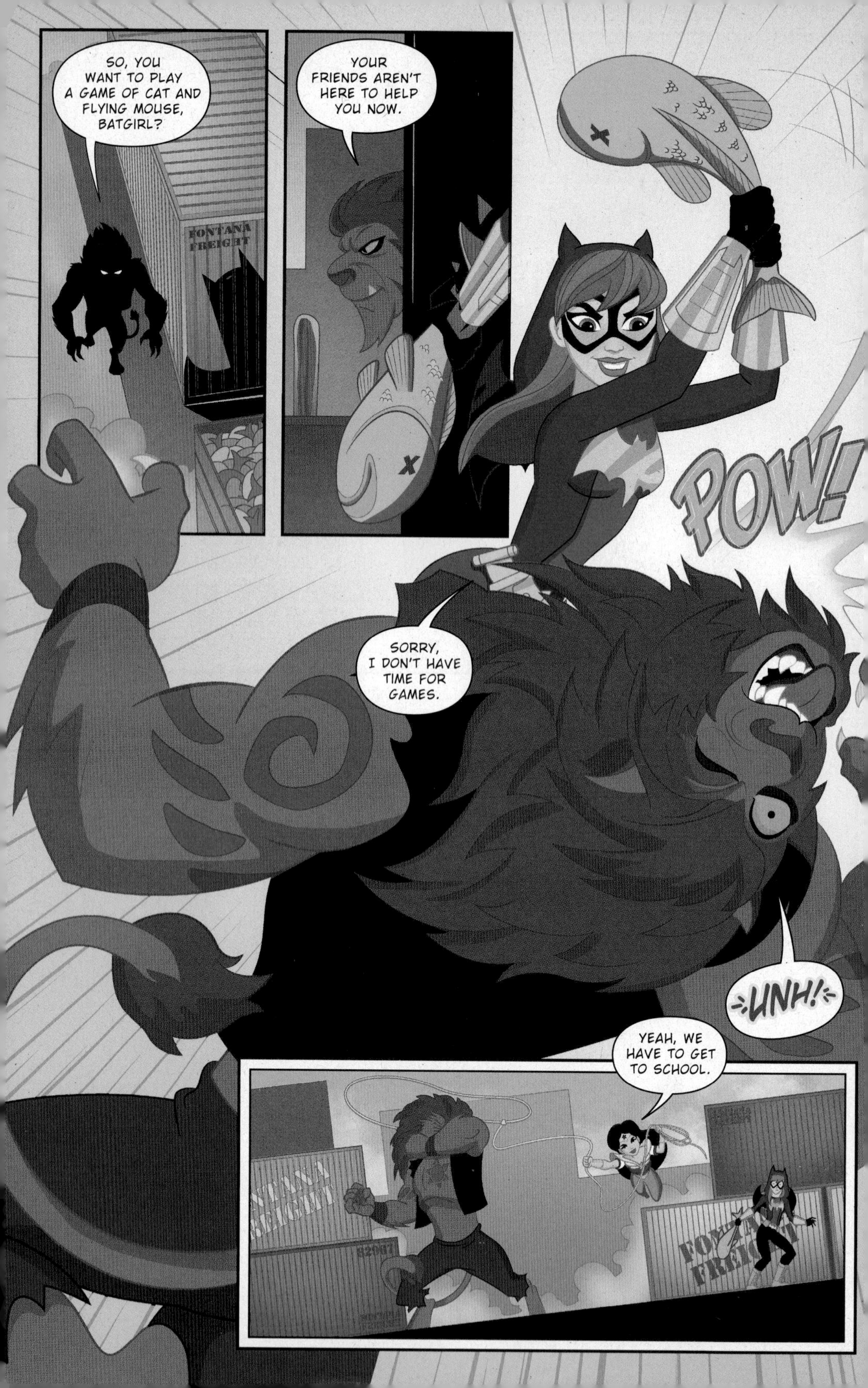
SO, YOU WANT TO PLAY A GAME OF CAT AND FLYING MOUSE, BATGIRL?
YOUR FRIENDS AREN'T HERE TO HELP YOU NOW.
FONTANA FREIGHT
POW!
SORRY, I DON'T HAVE TIME FOR GAMES.
UNH!
YEAH, WE HAVE TO GET TO SCHOOL.
FONTANA FREIGHT

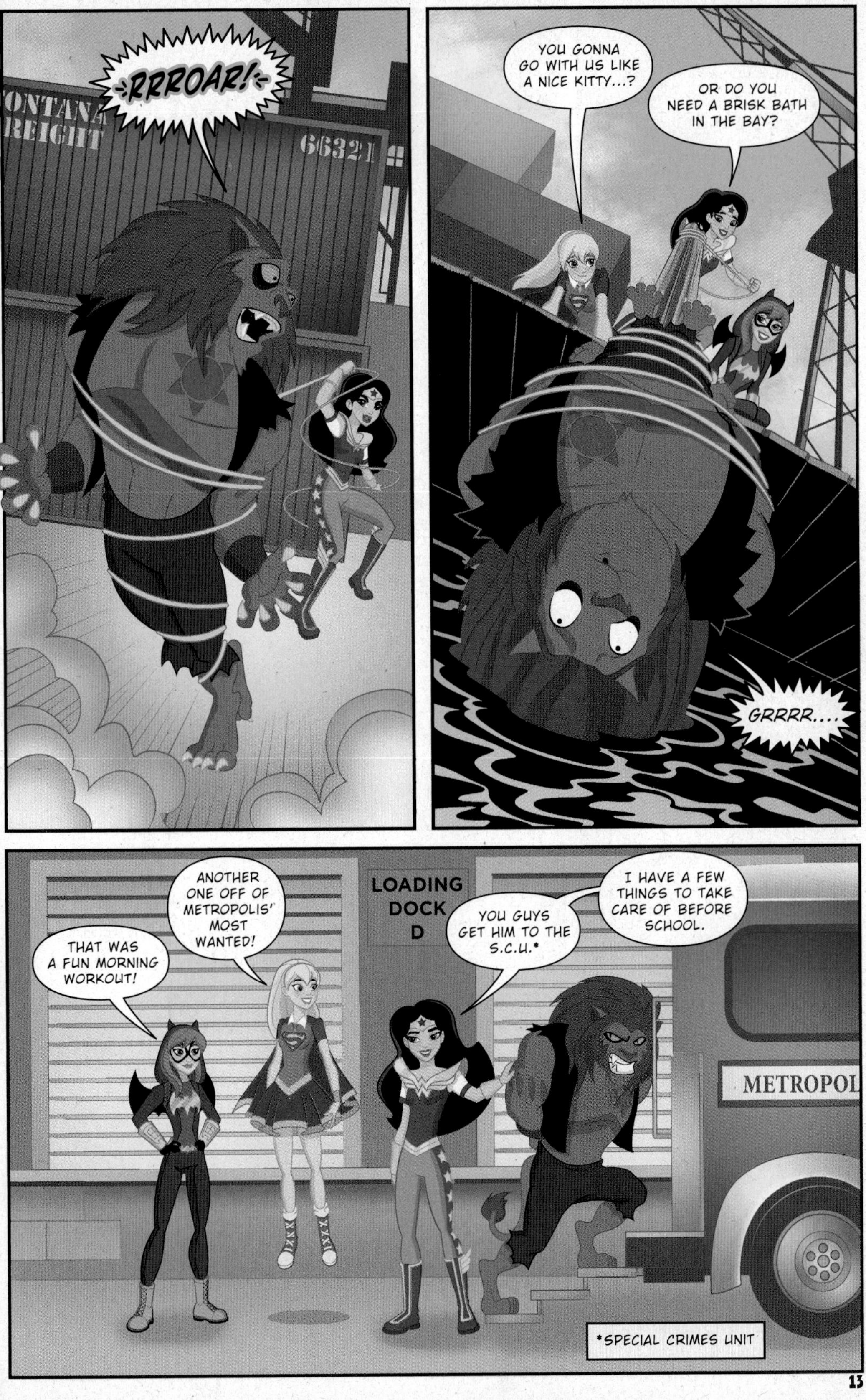
RRROAR!
ONTANA
REIGHT
66321
YOU GONNA GO WITH US LIKE A NICE KITTY...?
OR DO YOU NEED A BRISK BATH IN THE BAY?
GRRRR....
LOADING DOCK D
THAT WAS A FUN MORNING WORKOUT!
ANOTHER ONE OFF OF METROPOLIS' MOST WANTED!
YOU GUYS GET HIM TO THE S.C.U.*
I HAVE A FEW THINGS TO TAKE CARE OF BEFORE SCHOOL.
METROPOL
*SPECIAL CRIMES UNIT

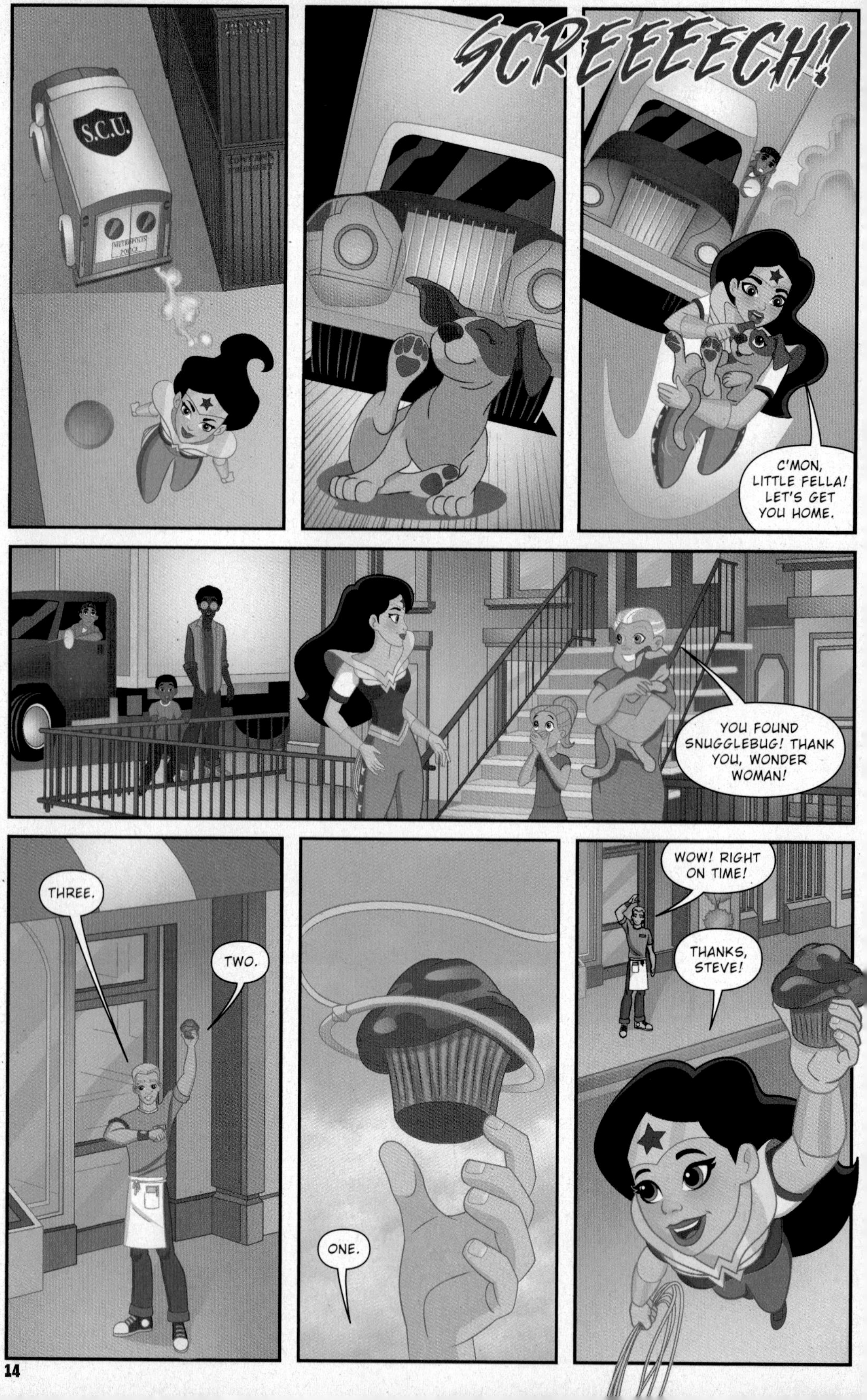
S.C.U.
SCREEEEECH!
C'MON, LITTLE FELLA! LET'S GET YOU HOME.
YOU FOUND SNUGGLEBUG! THANK YOU, WONDER WOMAN!
THREE.
TWO.
ONE.
WOW! RIGHT ON TIME!
THANKS, STEVE!

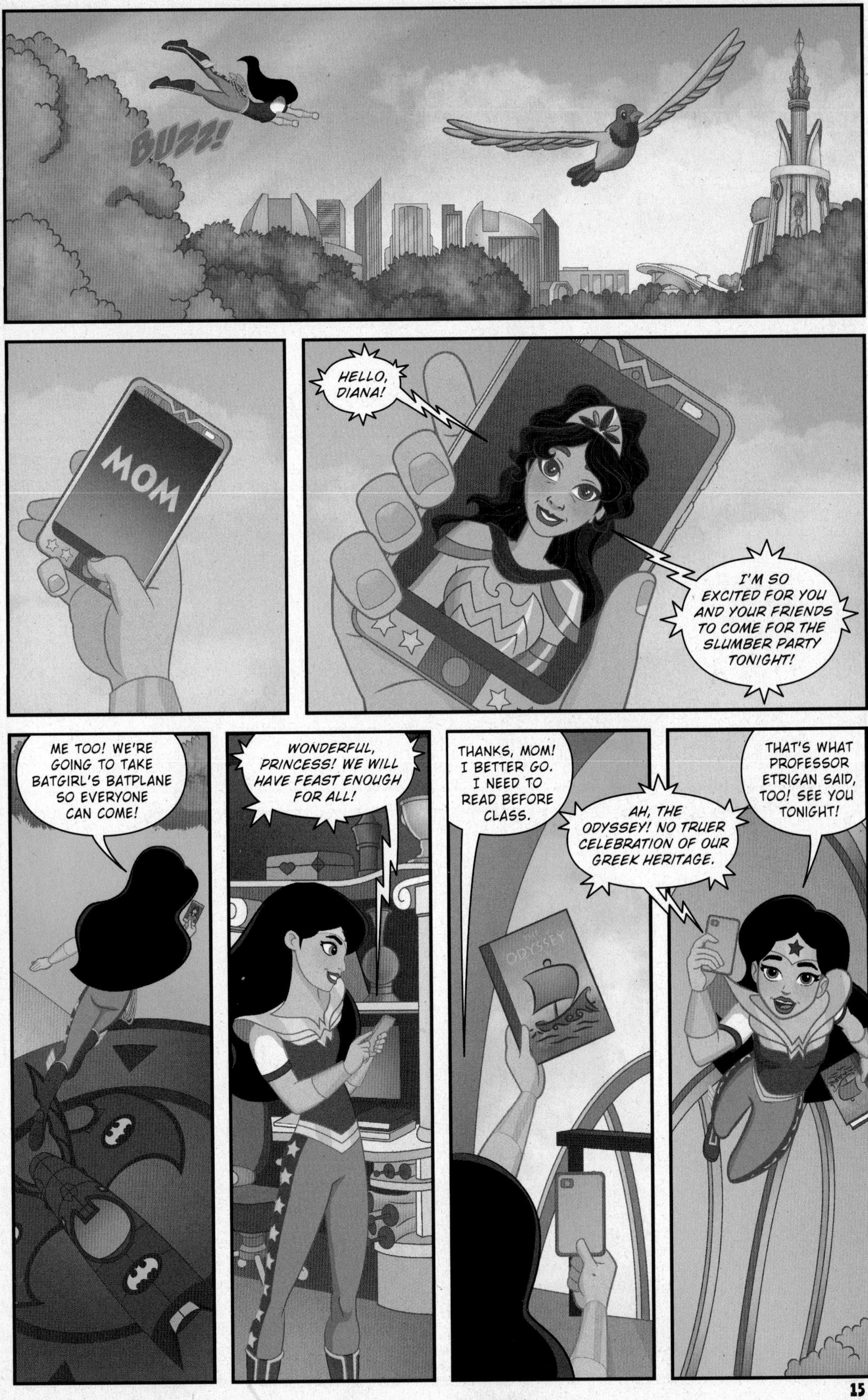
BUZZ!
MOM
HELLO, DIANA!
I'M SO EXCITED FOR YOU AND YOUR FRIENDS TO COME FOR THE SLUMBER PARTY TONIGHT!
ME TOO! WE'RE GOING TO TAKE BATGIRL'S BATPLANE SO EVERYONE CAN COME!
WONDERFUL, PRINCESS! WE WILL HAVE FEAST ENOUGH FOR ALL!
THANKS, MOM! I BETTER GO. I NEED TO READ BEFORE CLASS.
AH, THE ODYSSEY! NO TRUER CELEBRATION OF OUR GREEK HERITAGE.
THE ODYSSEY
THAT'S WHAT PROFESSOR ETRIGAN SAID, TOO! SEE YOU TONIGHT!

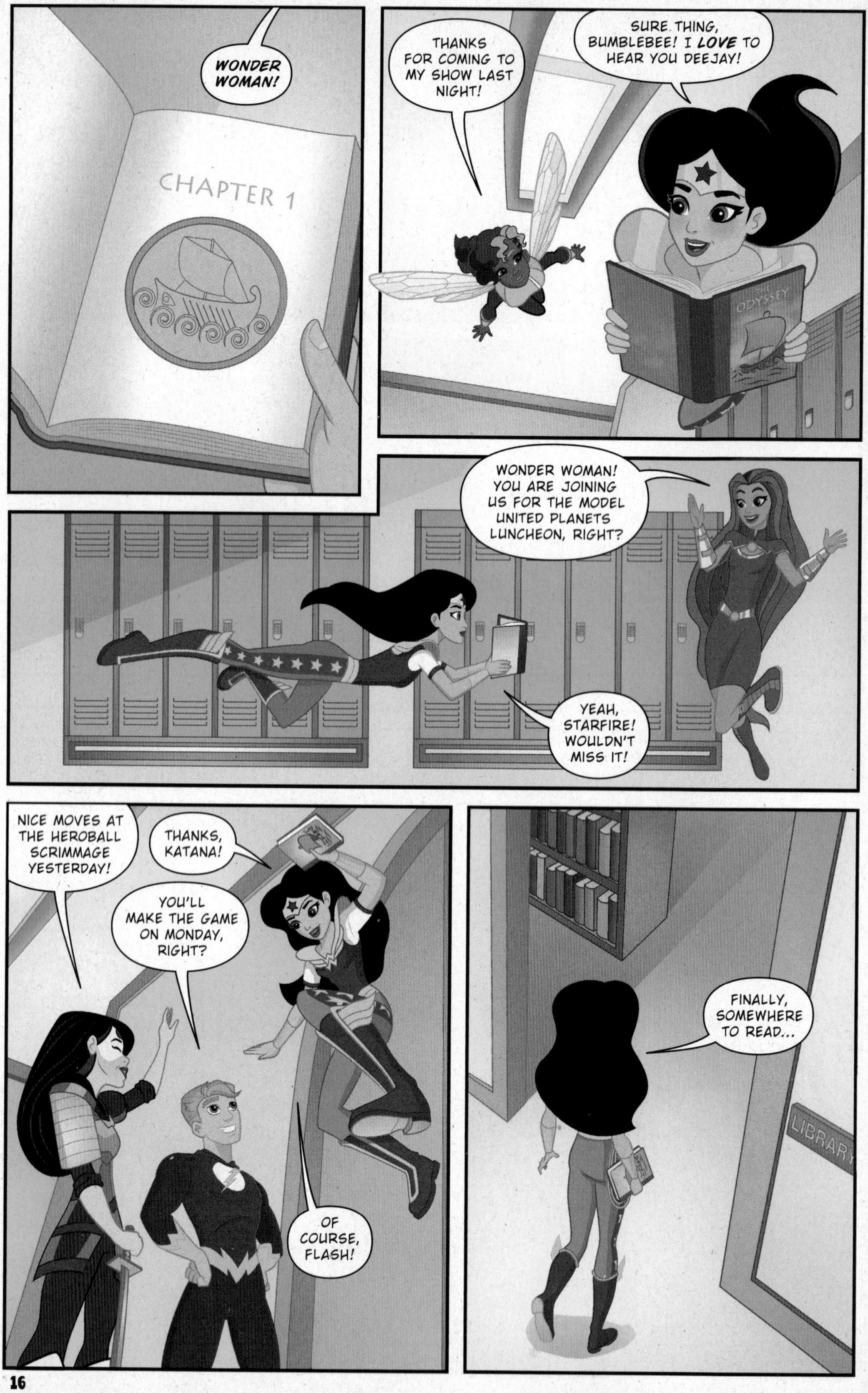
WONDER WOMAN!
CHAPTER 1
THANKS FOR COMING TO MY SHOW LAST NIGHT!
SURE THING, BUMBLEBEE! I LOVE TO HEAR YOU DEEJAY!
THE ODYSSEY
WONDER WOMAN! YOU ARE JOINING US FOR THE MODEL UNITED PLANETS LUNCHEON, RIGHT?
YEAH, STARFIRE! WOULDN'T MISS IT!
NICE MOVES AT THE HEROBALL SCRIMMAGE YESTERDAY!
THANKS, KATANA!
YOU'LL MAKE THE GAME ON MONDAY, RIGHT?
OF COURSE, FLASH!
FINALLY, SOMEWHERE TO READ...
LIBRARY

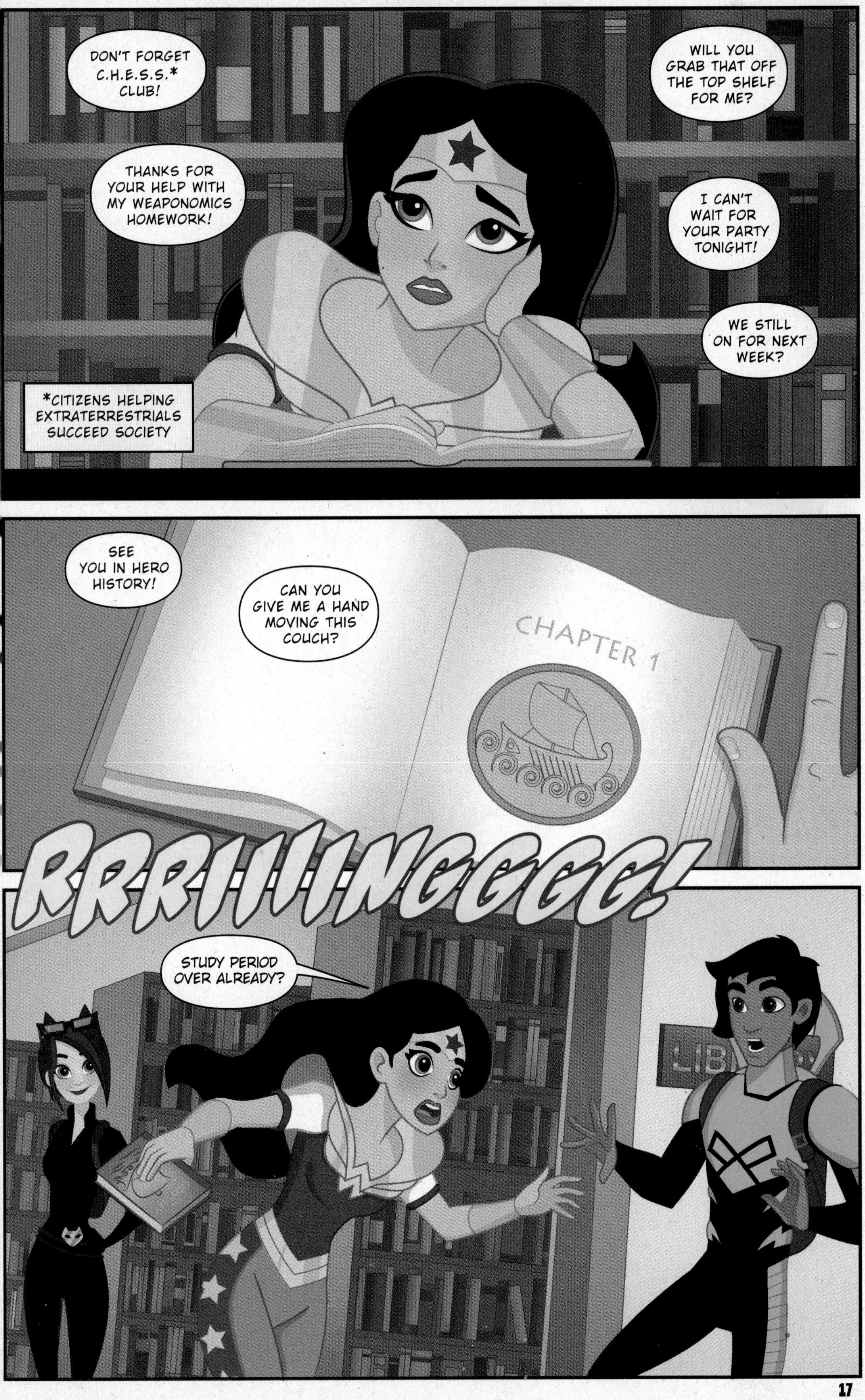
DON'T FORGET C.H.E.S.S.* CLUB!
WILL YOU GRAB THAT OFF THE TOP SHELF FOR ME?
THANKS FOR YOUR HELP WITH MY WEAPONOMICS HOMEWORK!
I CAN'T WAIT FOR YOUR PARTY TONIGHT!
WE STILL ON FOR NEXT WEEK?
*CITIZENS HELPING EXTRATERRESTRIALS SUCCEED SOCIETY
SEE YOU IN HERO HISTORY!
CAN YOU GIVE ME A HAND MOVING THIS COUCH?
CHAPTER 1
RRRIIIINGGGG!
STUDY PERIOD OVER ALREADY?

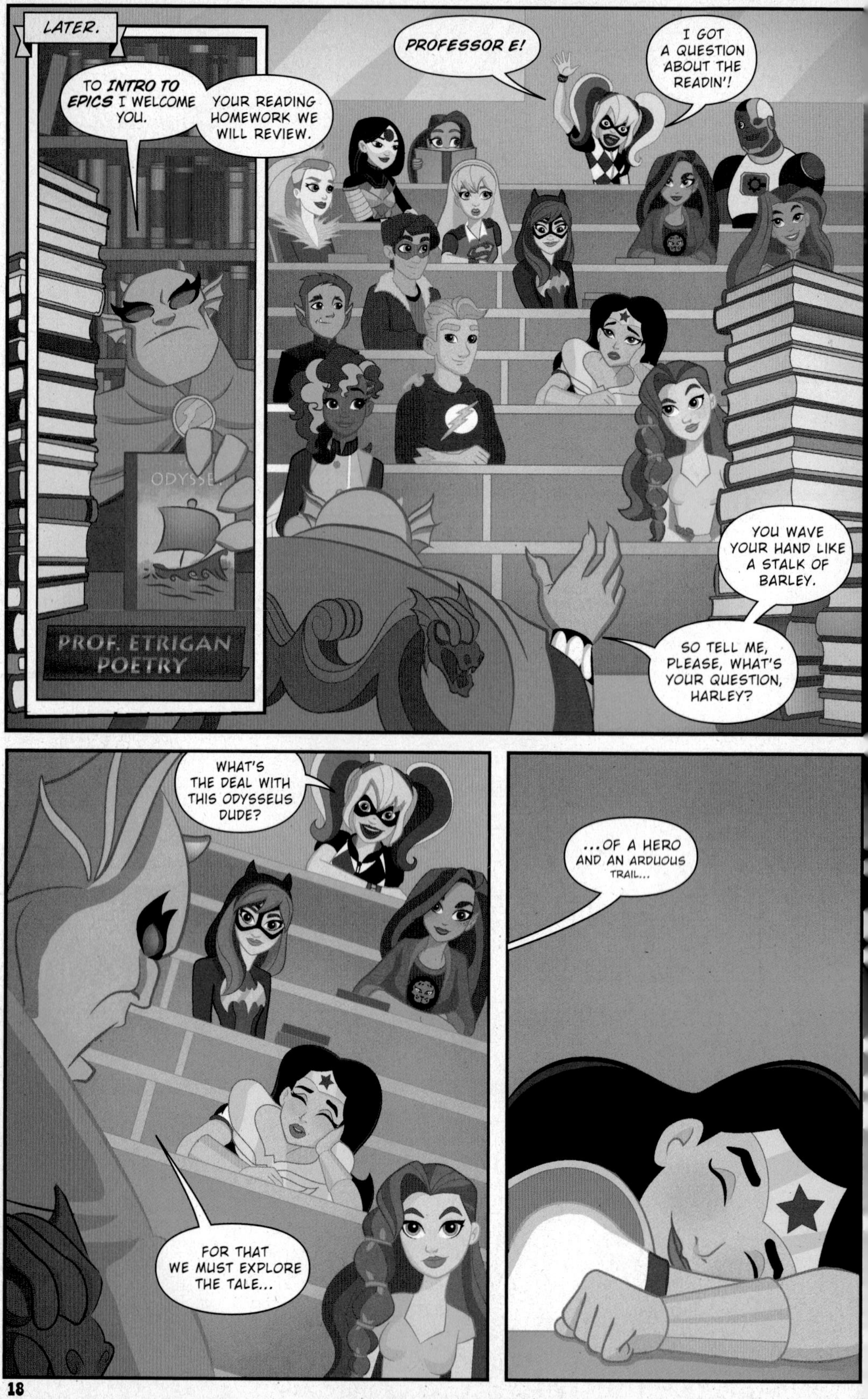
LATER.
TO INTRO TO EPICS I WELCOME YOU.
YOUR READING HOMEWORK WE WILL REVIEW.
PROFESSOR E!
I GOT A QUESTION ABOUT THE READIN'!
ODYSSEY
PROF. ETRIGAN POETRY
YOU WAVE YOUR HAND LIKE A STALK OF BARLEY.
SO TELL ME, PLEASE, WHAT'S YOUR QUESTION, HARLEY?
WHAT'S THE DEAL WITH THIS ODYSSEUS DUDE?
FOR THAT WE MUST EXPLORE THE TALE...
...OF A HERO AND AN ARDUOUS TRAIL...

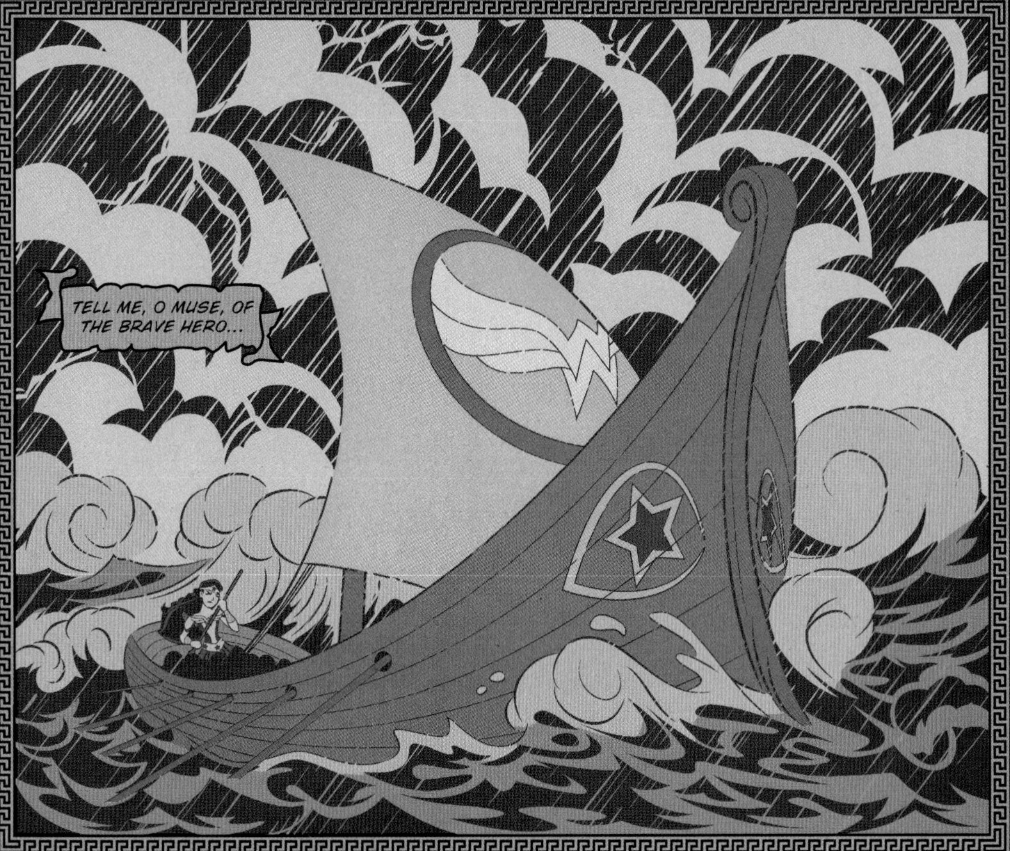
TELL ME, O MUSE, OF THE BRAVE HERO...

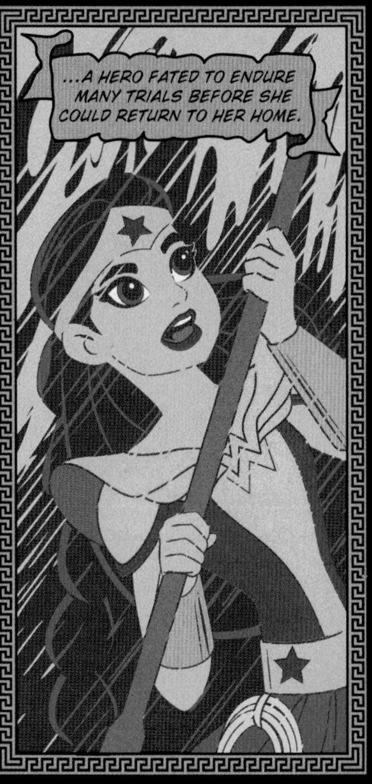
...A HERO FATED TO ENDURE MANY TRIALS BEFORE SHE COULD RETURN TO HER HOME.

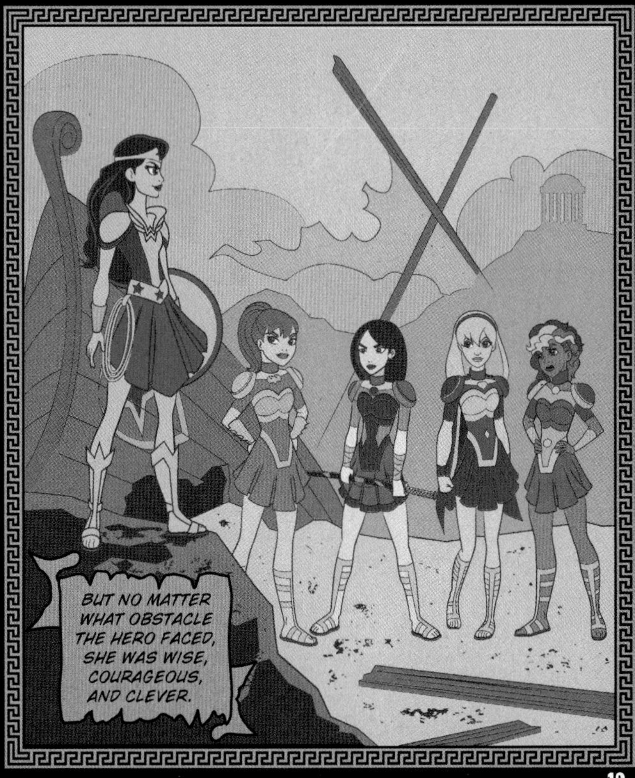
BUT NO MATTER WHAT OBSTACLE THE HERO FACED, SHE WAS WISE, COURAGEOUS, AND CLEVER.

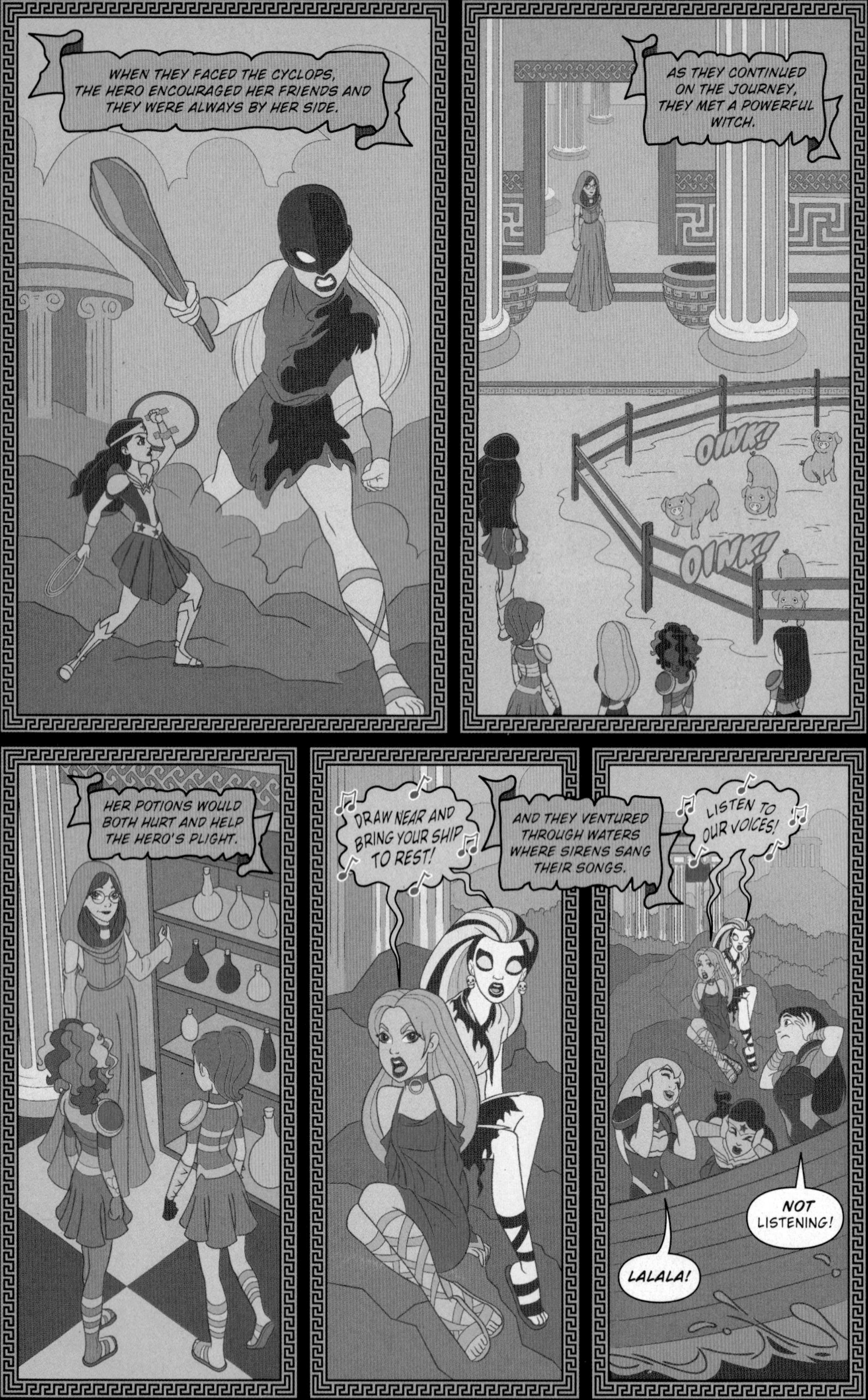
WHEN THEY FACED THE CYCLOPS, THE HERO ENCOURAGED HER FRIENDS AND THEY WERE ALWAYS BY HER SIDE.
AS THEY CONTINUED ON THE JOURNEY, THEY MET A POWERFUL WITCH.
OINK!
OINK!
HER POTIONS WOULD BOTH HURT AND HELP THE HERO'S PLIGHT.
DRAW NEAR AND BRING YOUR SHIP TO REST!
AND THEY VENTURED THROUGH WATERS WHERE SIRENS SANG THEIR SONGS.
LISTEN TO OUR VOICES!
NOT LISTENING!
LALALA!

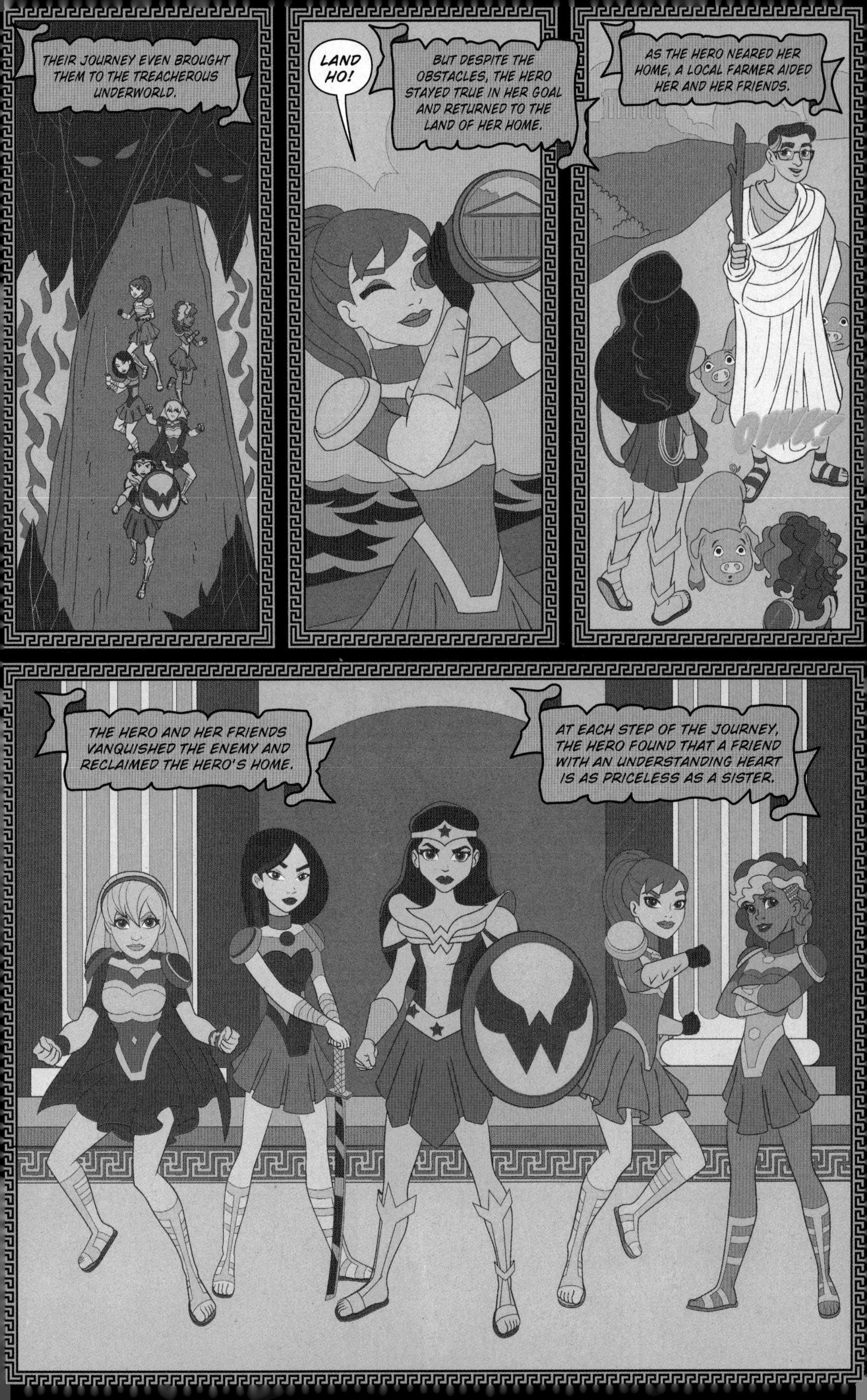
THEIR JOURNEY EVEN BROUGHT THEM TO THE TREACHEROUS UNDERWORLD.
LAND HO!
BUT DESPITE THE OBSTACLES, THE HERO STAYED TRUE IN HER GOAL AND RETURNED TO THE LAND OF HER HOME.
AS THE HERO NEARED HER HOME, A LOCAL FARMER AIDED HER AND HER FRIENDS.
OINK!
THE HERO AND HER FRIENDS VANQUISHED THE ENEMY AND RECLAIMED THE HERO'S HOME.
AT EACH STEP OF THE JOURNEY, THE HERO FOUND THAT A FRIEND WITH AN UNDERSTANDING HEART IS AS PRICELESS AS A SISTER.

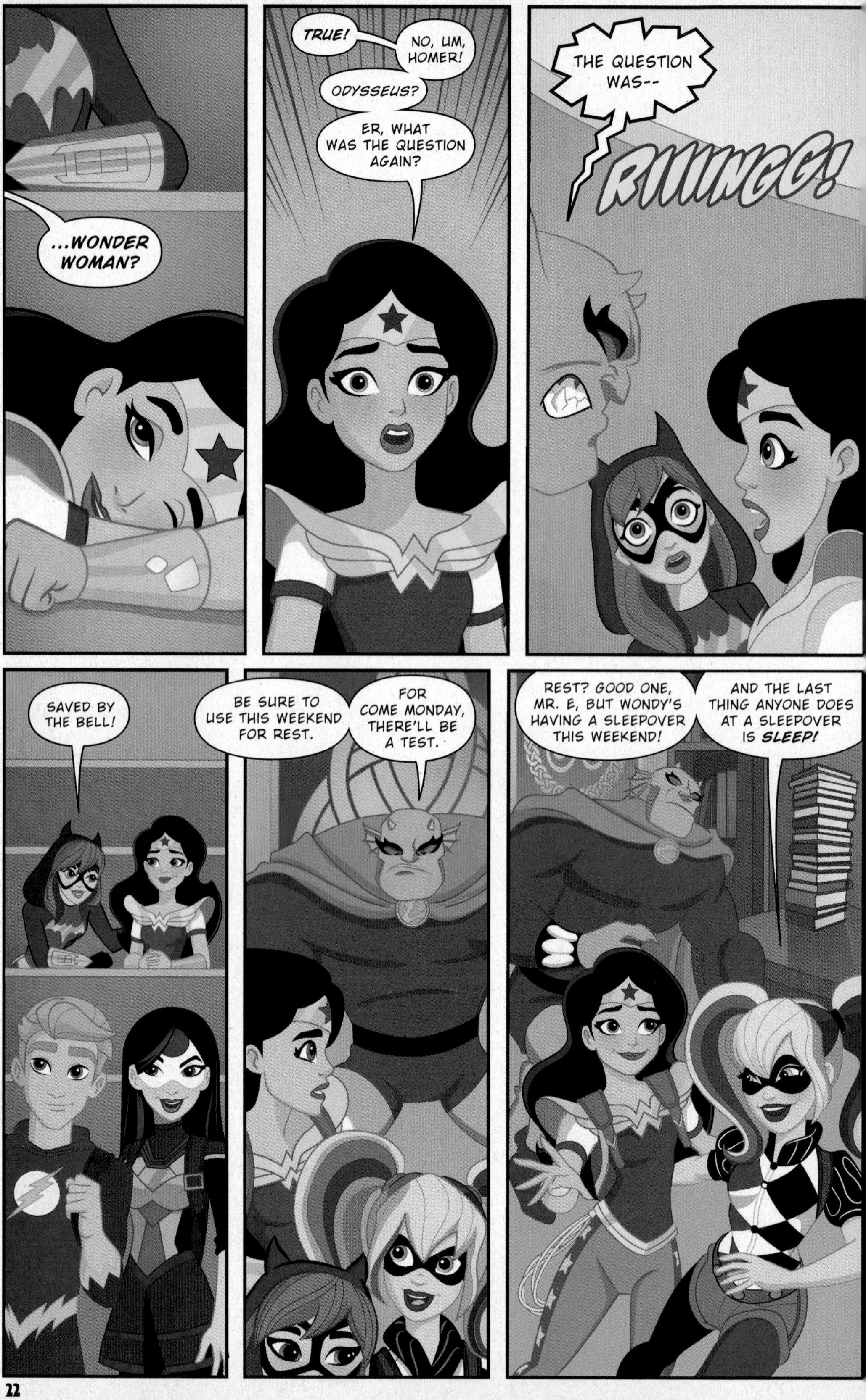
...WONDER WOMAN?
TRUE!
NO, UM, HOMER!
ODYSSEUS?
ER, WHAT WAS THE QUESTION AGAIN?
THE QUESTION WAS--
RIIINGG!
SAVED BY THE BELL!
BE SURE TO USE THIS WEEKEND FOR REST.
FOR COME MONDAY, THERE'LL BE A TEST.
REST? GOOD ONE, MR. E, BUT WONDY'S HAVING A SLEEPOVER THIS WEEKEND!
AND THE LAST THING ANYONE DOES AT A SLEEPOVER IS SLEEP!

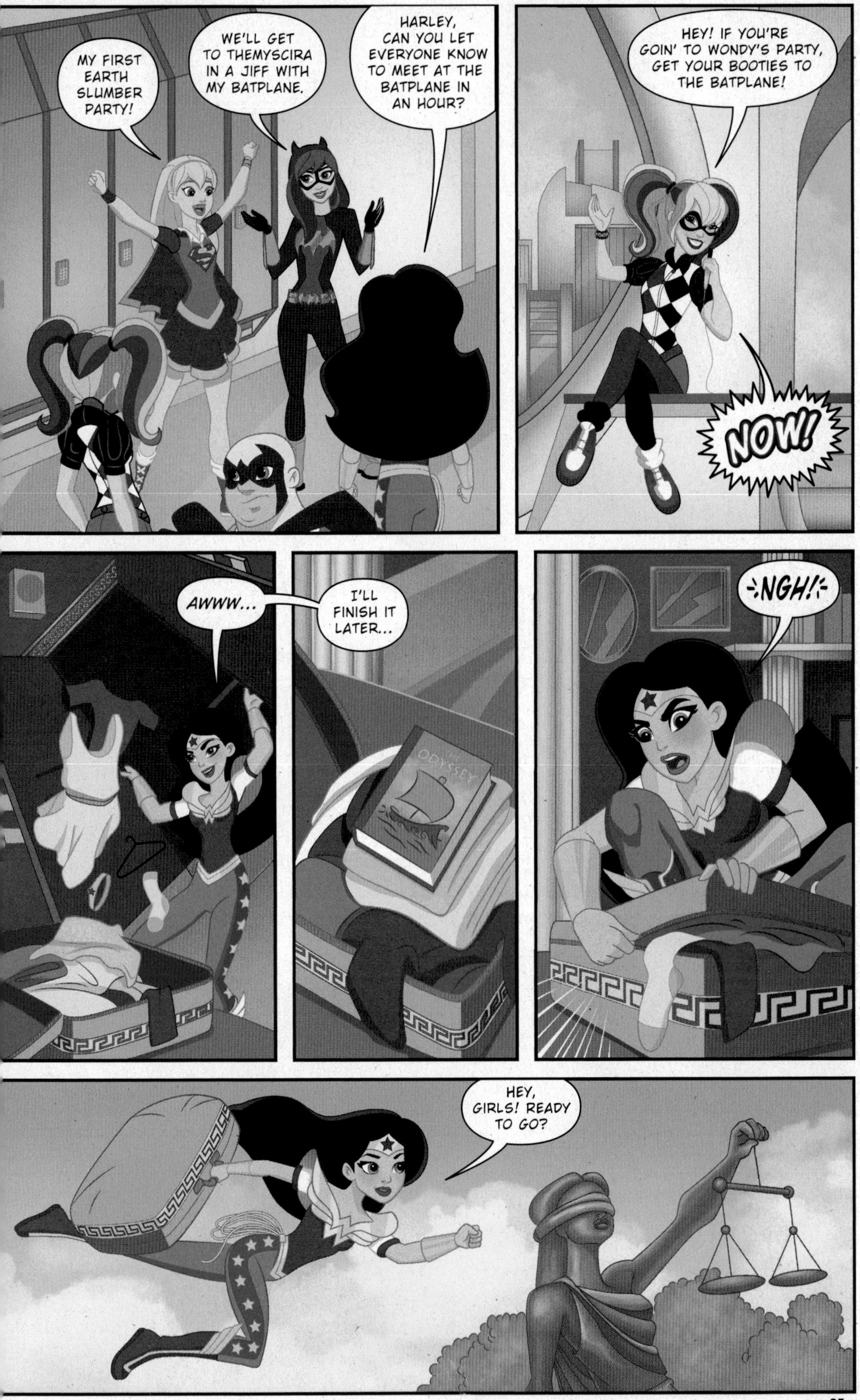
MY FIRST EARTH SLUMBER PARTY!
WE'LL GET TO THEMYSCIRA IN A JIFF WITH MY BATPLANE.
HARLEY, CAN YOU LET EVERYONE KNOW TO MEET AT THE BATPLANE IN AN HOUR?
HEY! IF YOU'RE GOIN' TO WONDY'S PARTY, GET YOUR BOOTIES TO THE BATPLANE!
NOW!
AWWW...
I'LL FINISH IT LATER...
THE ODYSSEY
-NGH!-
HEY, GIRLS! READY TO GO?

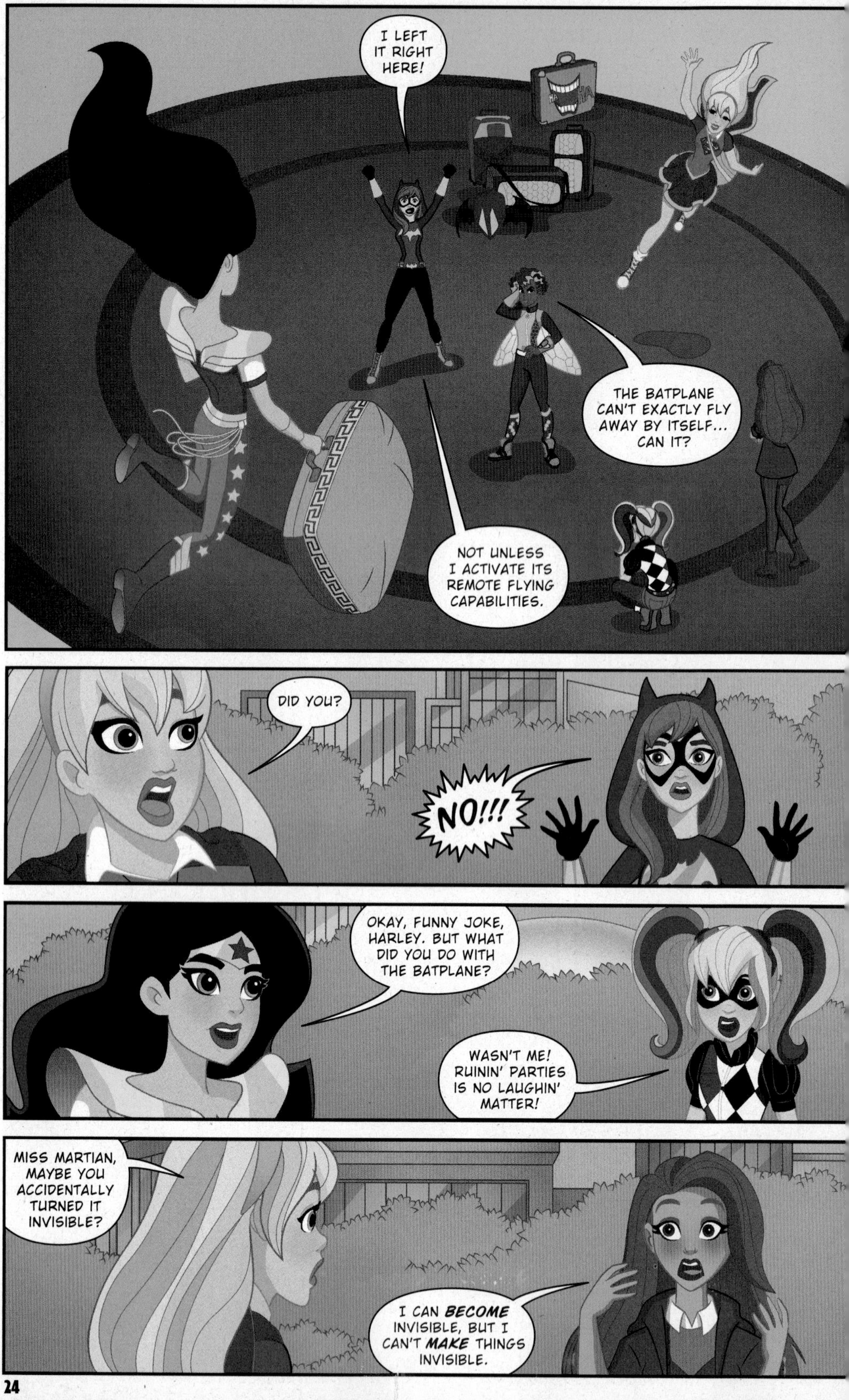
I LEFT IT RIGHT HERE!
THE BATPLANE CAN'T EXACTLY FLY AWAY BY ITSELF... CAN IT?
NOT UNLESS I ACTIVATE ITS REMOTE FLYING CAPABILITIES.
DID YOU?
NO!!!
OKAY, FUNNY JOKE, HARLEY. BUT WHAT DID YOU DO WITH THE BATPLANE?
WASN'T ME! RUININ' PARTIES IS NO LAUGHIN' MATTER!
MISS MARTIAN, MAYBE YOU ACCIDENTALLY TURNED IT INVISIBLE?
I CAN *BECOME* INVISIBLE, BUT I CAN'T *MAKE* THINGS INVISIBLE.

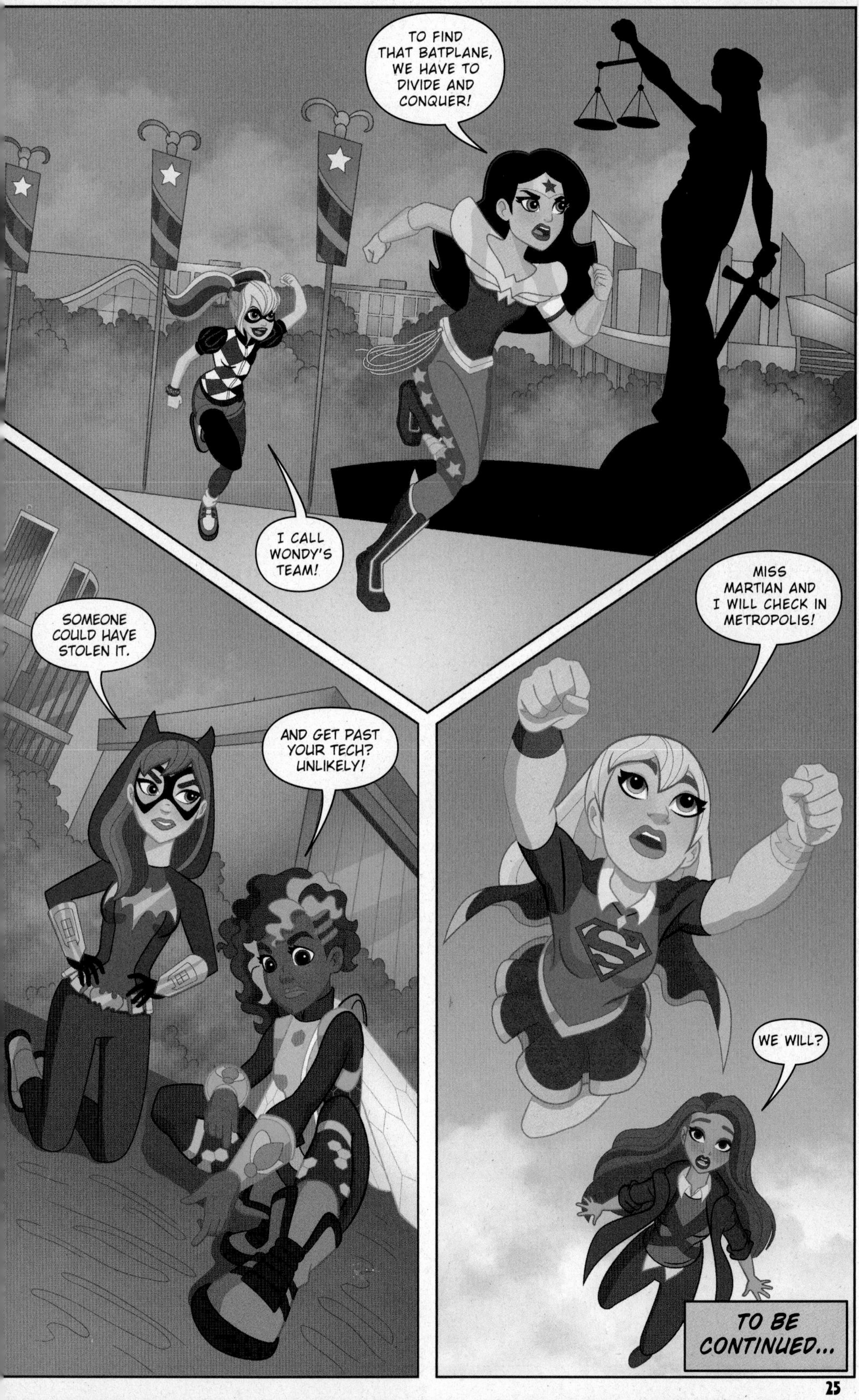
TO FIND THAT BATPLANE, WE HAVE TO DIVIDE AND CONQUER!
I CALL WONDY'S TEAM!
SOMEONE COULD HAVE STOLEN IT.
AND GET PAST YOUR TECH? UNLIKELY!
MISS MARTIAN AND I WILL CHECK IN METROPOLIS!
WE WILL?
TO BE CONTINUED...

CHAPTER TWO
THE CYCLOPS

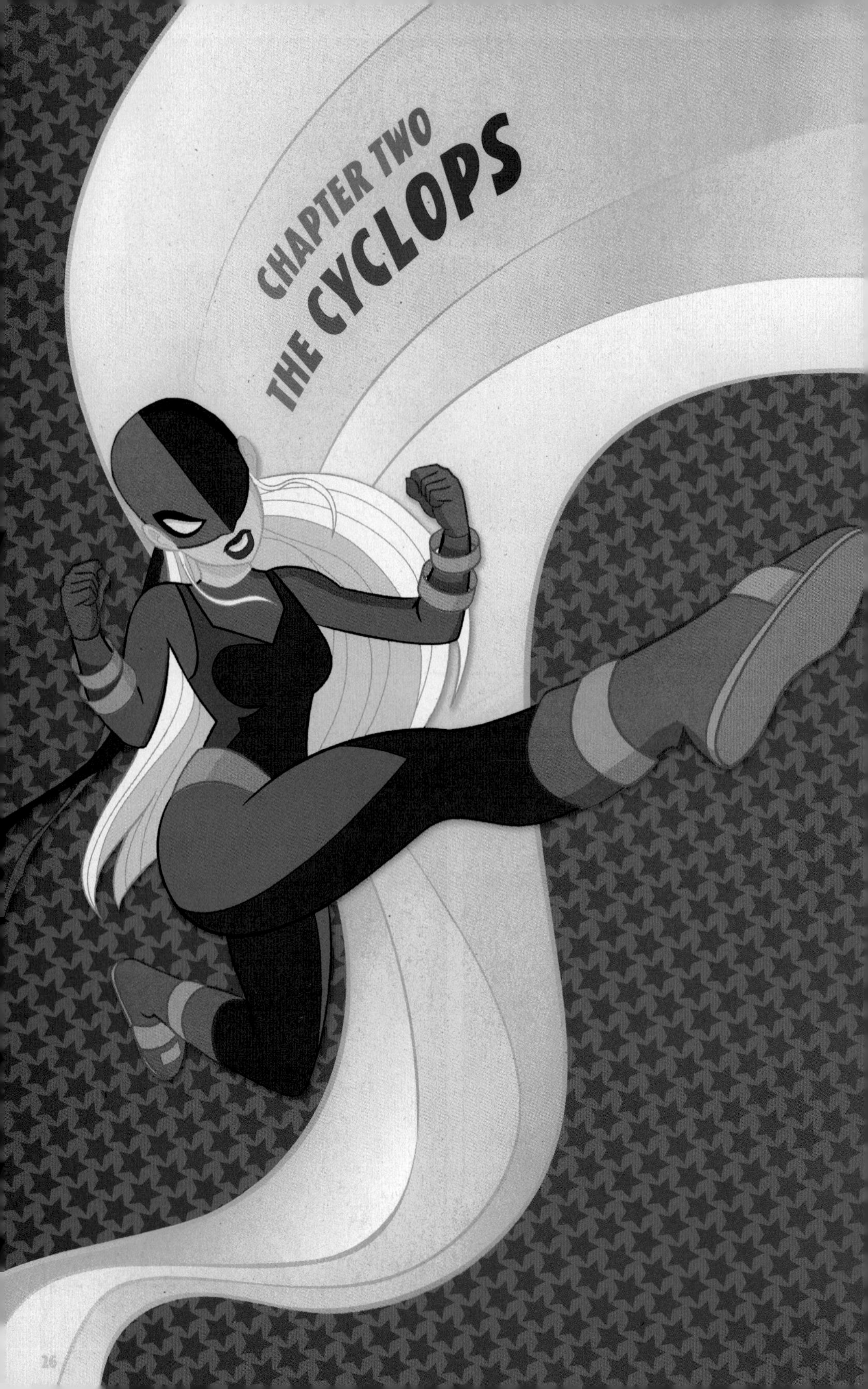

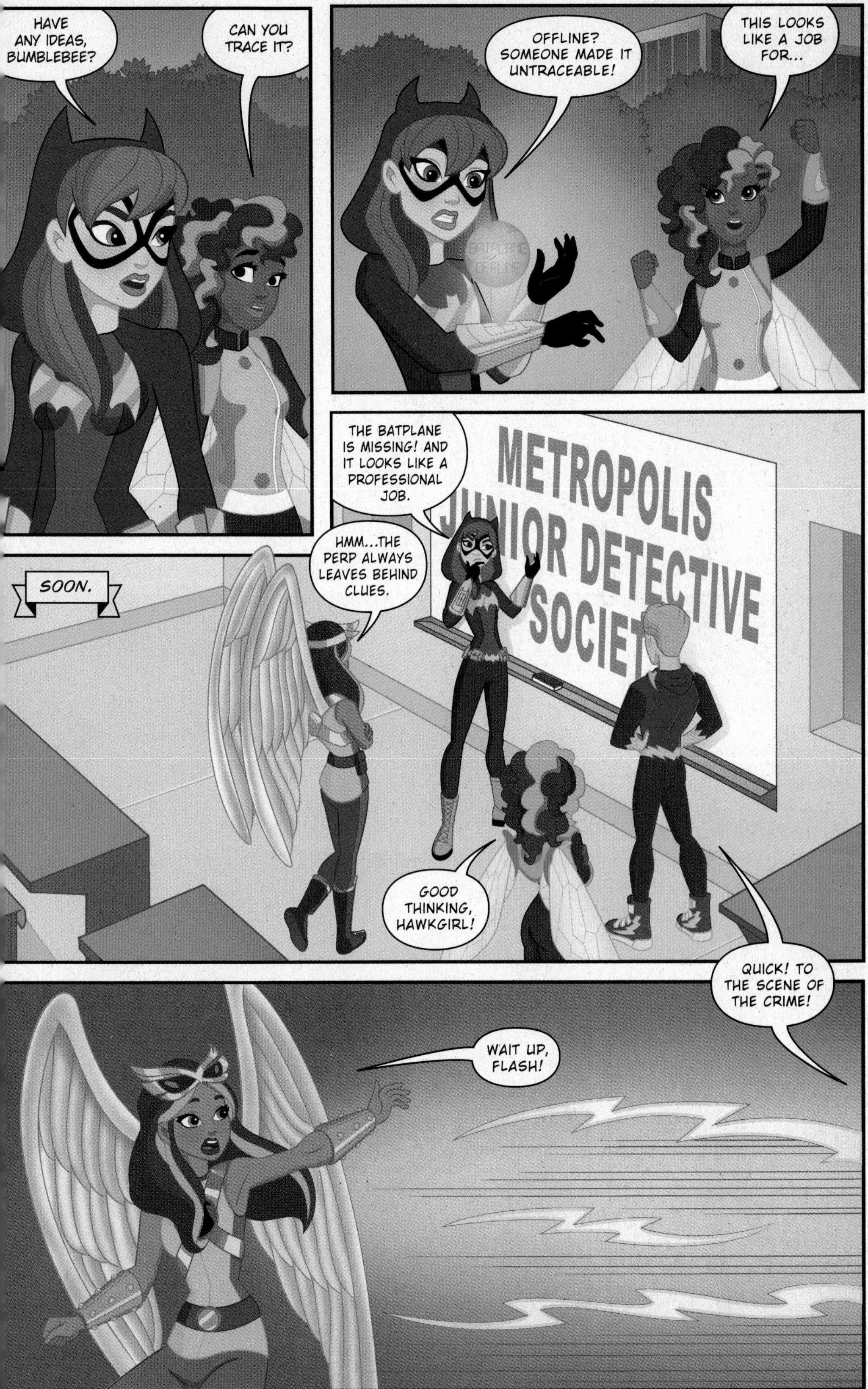
HAVE ANY IDEAS, BUMBLEBEE?
CAN YOU TRACE IT?
OFFLINE? SOMEONE MADE IT UNTRACEABLE!
BATPLANE OFFLINE
THIS LOOKS LIKE A JOB FOR...
SOON.
THE BATPLANE IS MISSING! AND IT LOOKS LIKE A PROFESSIONAL JOB.
METROPOLIS JUNIOR DETECTIVE SOCIET
HMM...THE PERP ALWAYS LEAVES BEHIND CLUES.
GOOD THINKING, HAWKGIRL!
QUICK! TO THE SCENE OF THE CRIME!
WAIT UP, FLASH!

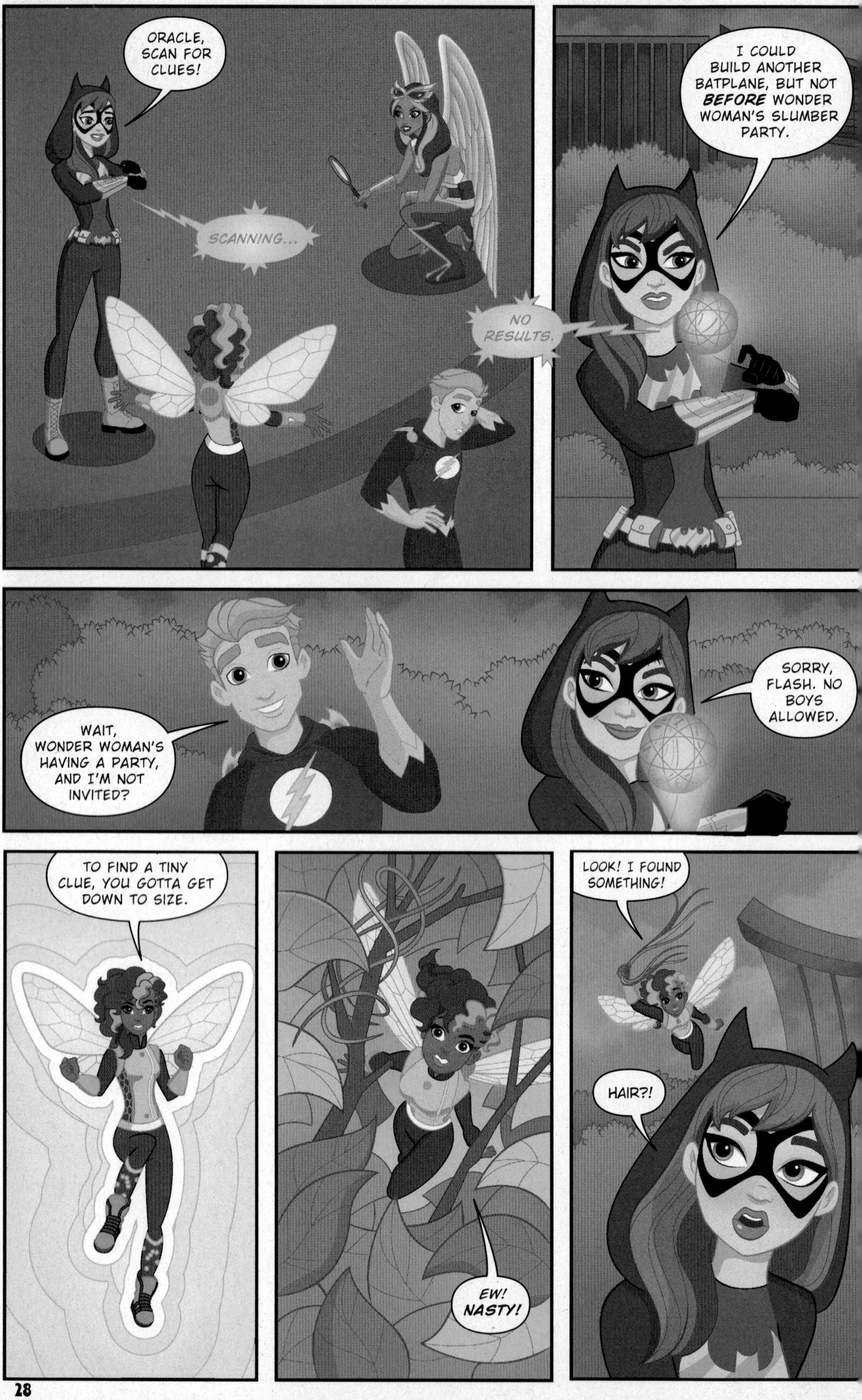
ORACLE, SCAN FOR CLUES!
SCANNING...
NO RESULTS.
I COULD BUILD ANOTHER BATPLANE, BUT NOT BEFORE WONDER WOMAN'S SLUMBER PARTY.
WAIT, WONDER WOMAN'S HAVING A PARTY, AND I'M NOT INVITED?
SORRY, FLASH. NO BOYS ALLOWED.
TO FIND A TINY CLUE, YOU GOTTA GET DOWN TO SIZE.
EW! NASTY!
LOOK! I FOUND SOMETHING!
HAIR?!

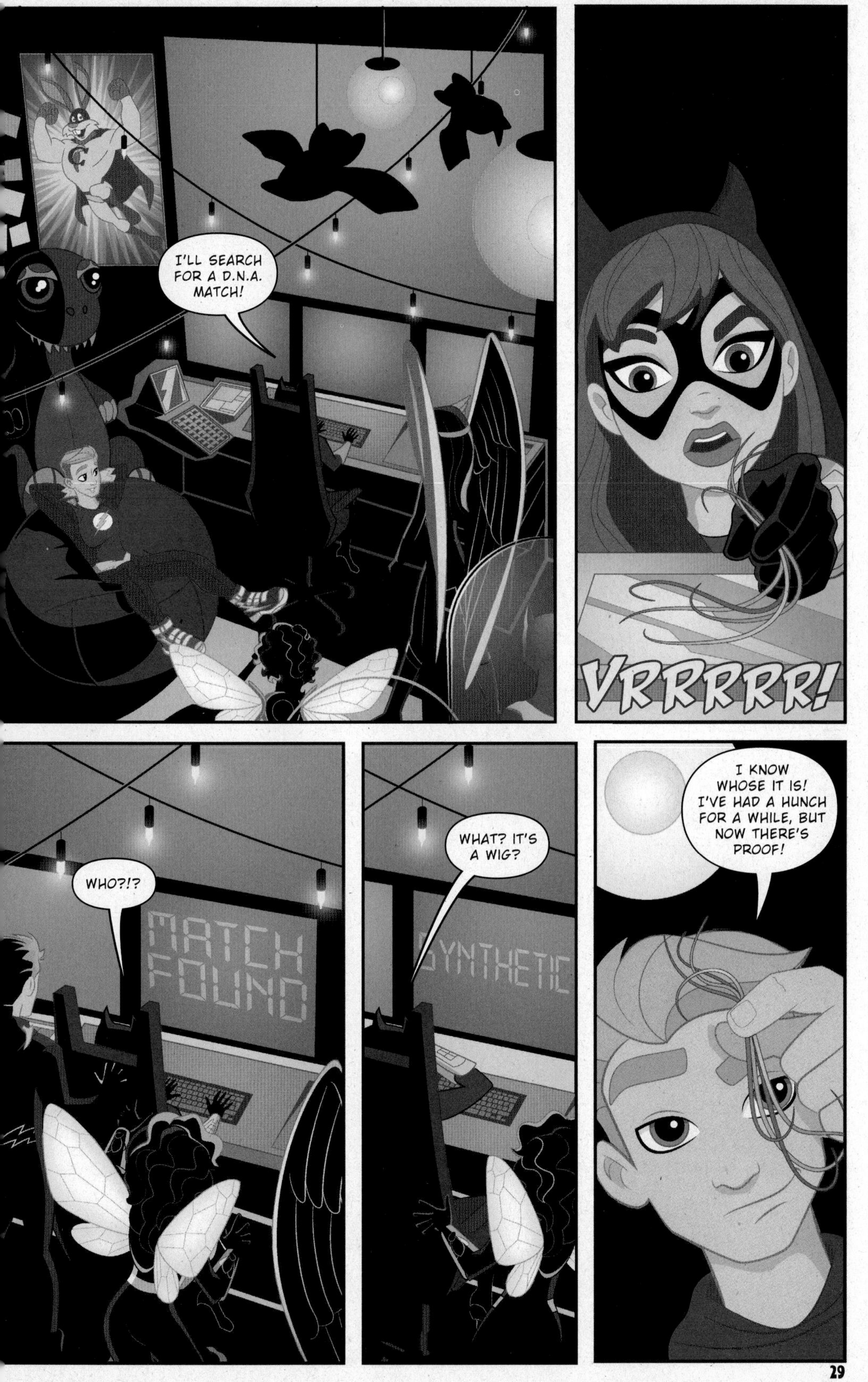
I'LL SEARCH FOR A D.N.A. MATCH!
VRRRRR!
WHO?!?
MATCH FOUND
WHAT? IT'S A WIG?
SYNTHETIC
I KNOW WHOSE IT IS! I'VE HAD A HUNCH FOR A WHILE, BUT NOW THERE'S PROOF!

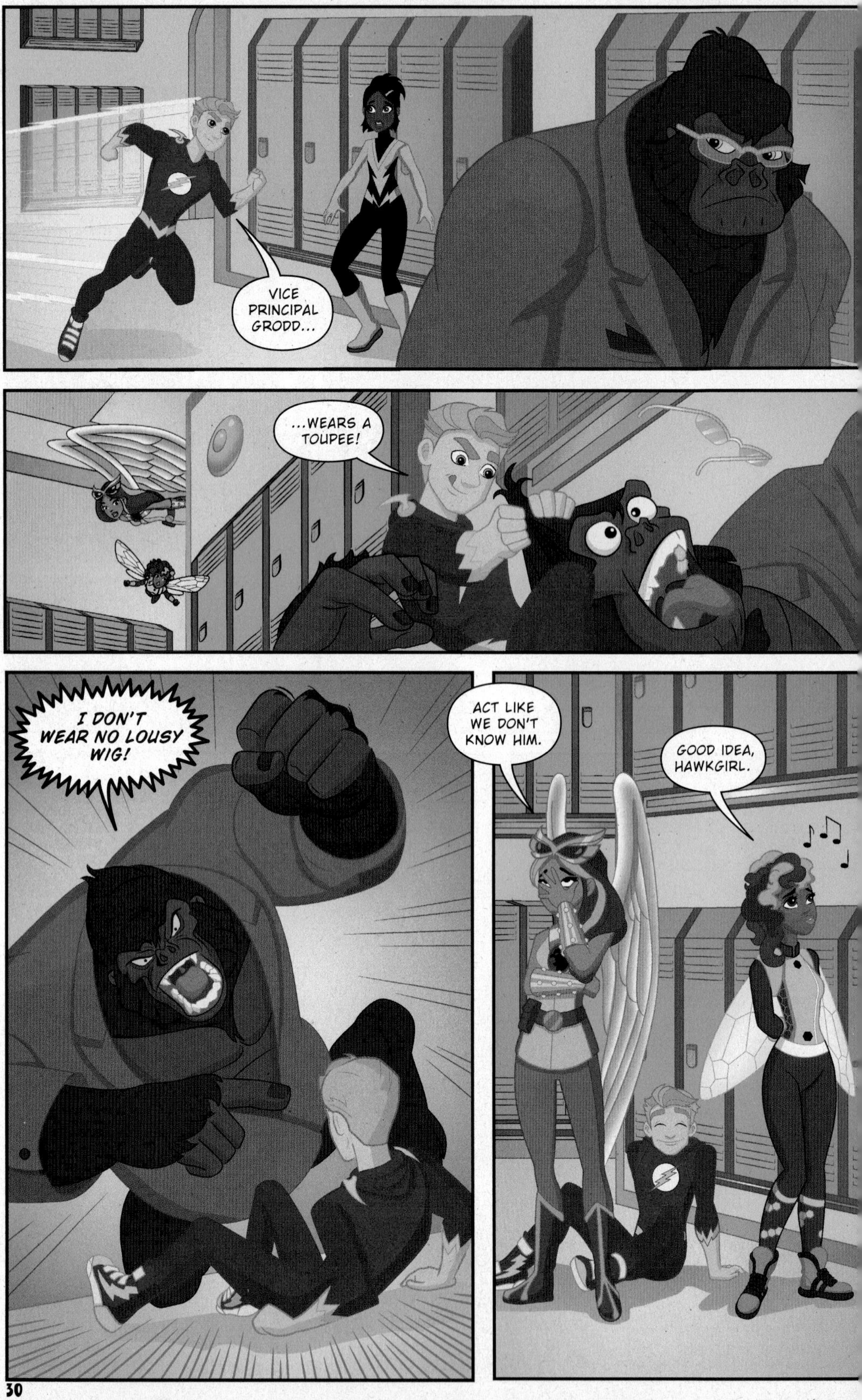
VICE PRINCIPAL GRODD...
...WEARS A TOUPEE!
I DON'T WEAR NO LOUSY WIG!
ACT LIKE WE DON'T KNOW HIM.
GOOD IDEA, HAWKGIRL.

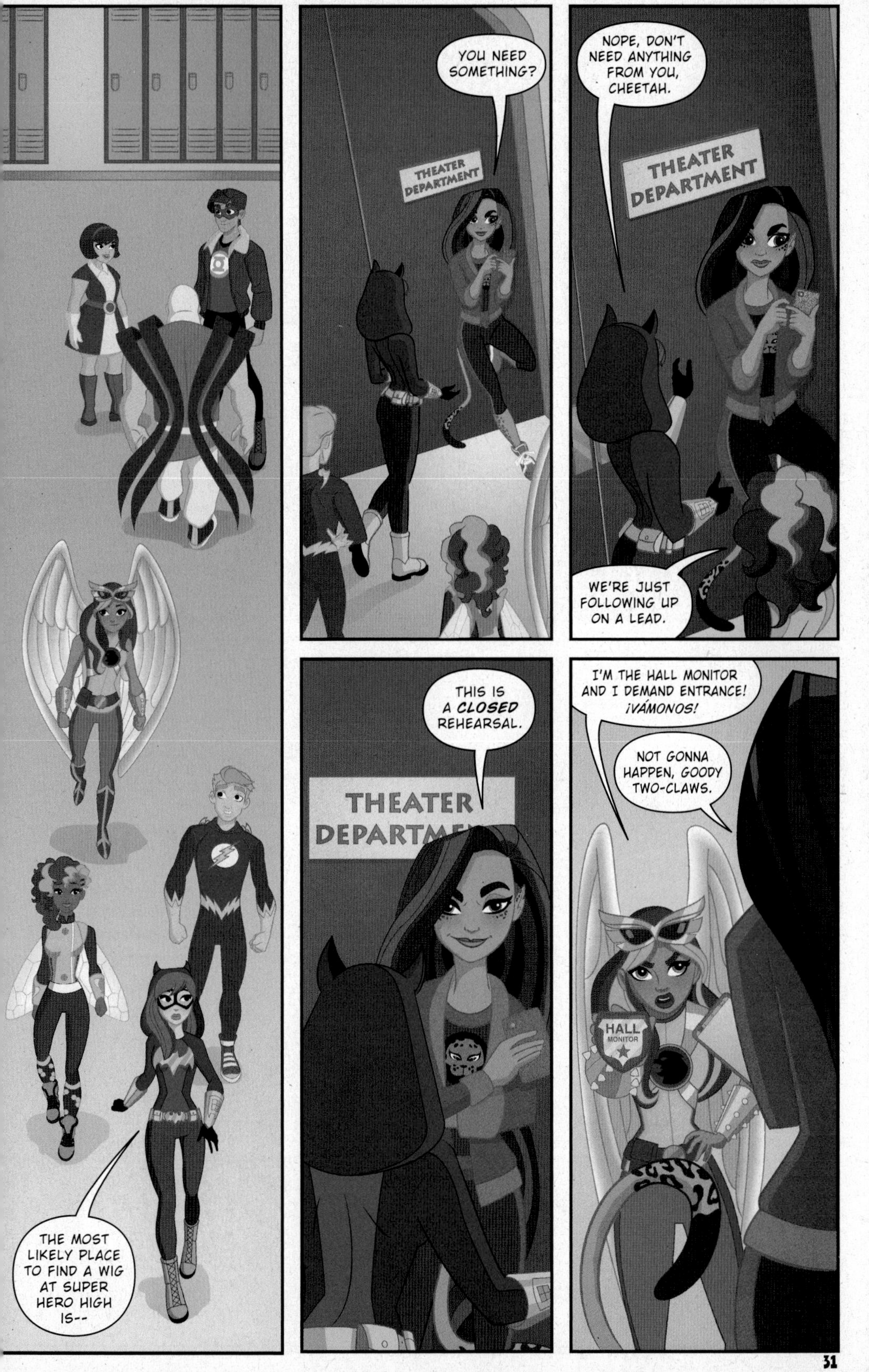
THE MOST LIKELY PLACE TO FIND A WIG AT SUPER HERO HIGH IS--
THEATER DEPARTMENT
YOU NEED SOMETHING?
THEATER DEPARTMENT
NOPE, DON'T NEED ANYTHING FROM YOU, CHEETAH.
WE'RE JUST FOLLOWING UP ON A LEAD.
THIS IS A ***CLOSED*** REHEARSAL.
I'M THE HALL MONITOR AND I DEMAND ENTRANCE! *¡VÁMONOS!*
NOT GONNA HAPPEN, GOODY TWO-CLAWS.
HALL MONITOR

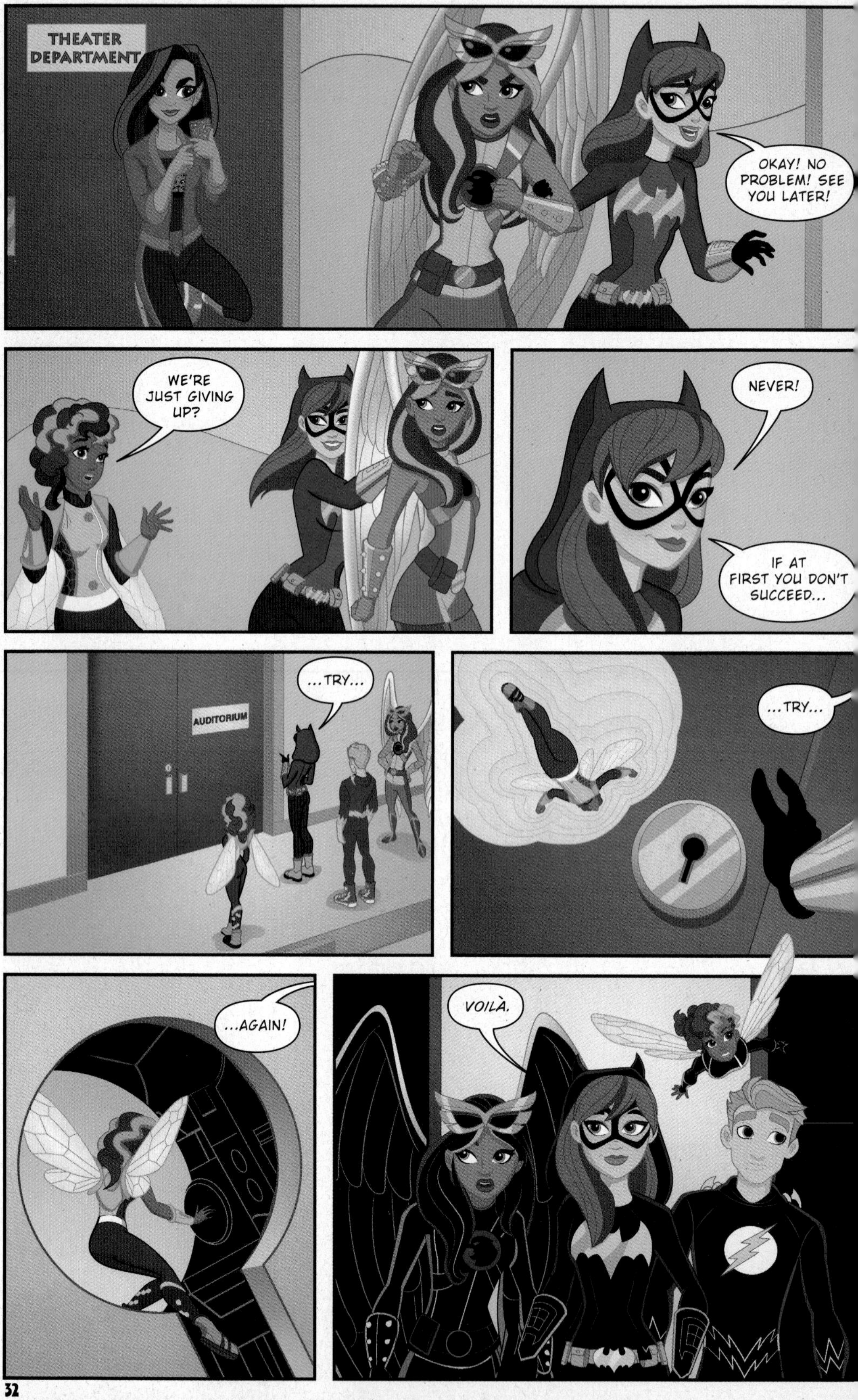
THEATER DEPARTMENT
OKAY! NO PROBLEM! SEE YOU LATER!
WE'RE JUST GIVING UP?
NEVER!
IF AT FIRST YOU DON'T SUCCEED...
AUDITORIUM
...TRY...
...TRY...
...AGAIN!
VOILÀ.

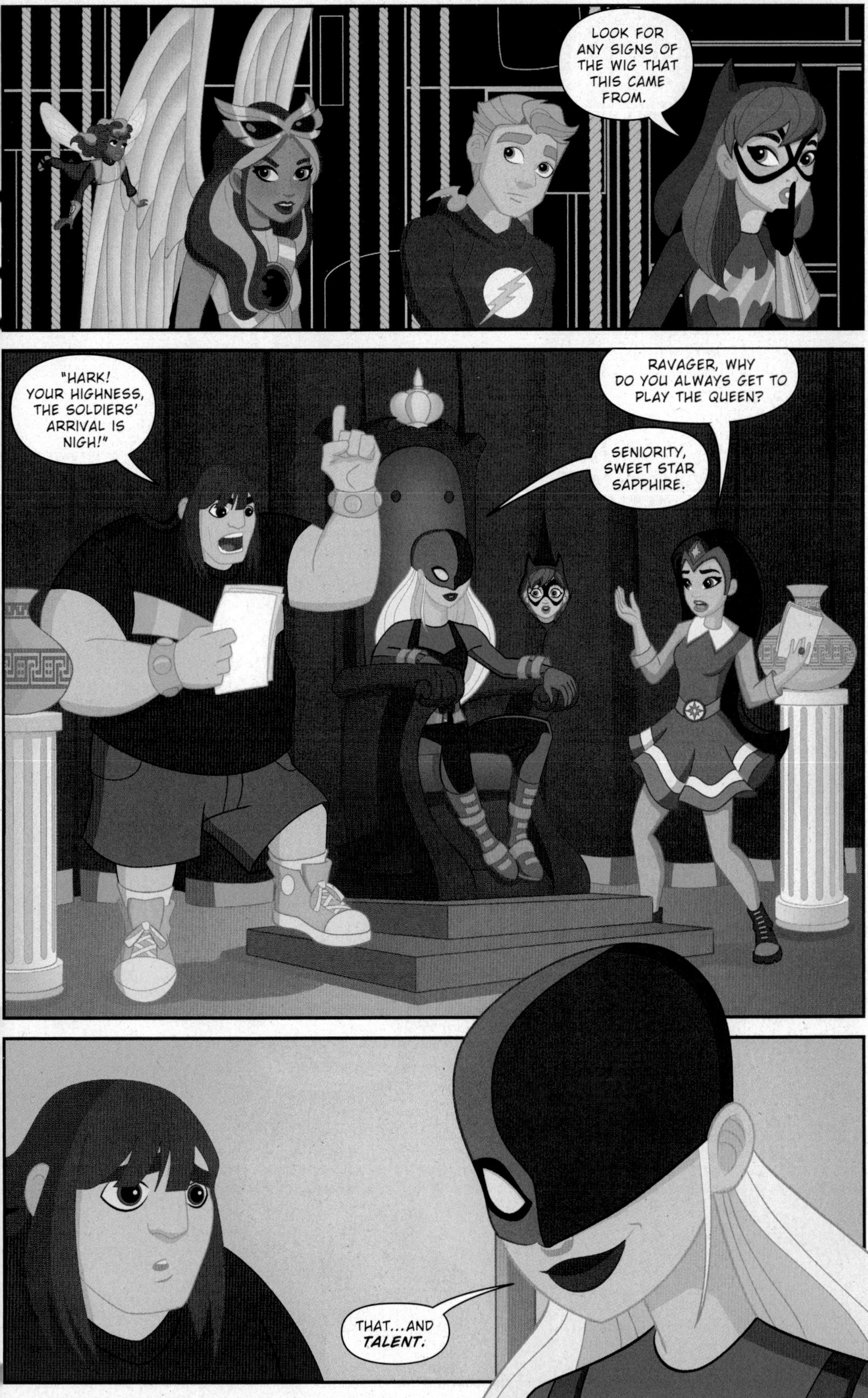
LOOK FOR ANY SIGNS OF THE WIG THAT THIS CAME FROM.
"HARK! YOUR HIGHNESS, THE SOLDIERS' ARRIVAL IS NIGH!"
RAVAGER, WHY DO YOU ALWAYS GET TO PLAY THE QUEEN?
SENIORITY, SWEET STAR SAPPHIRE.
THAT...AND ***TALENT.***

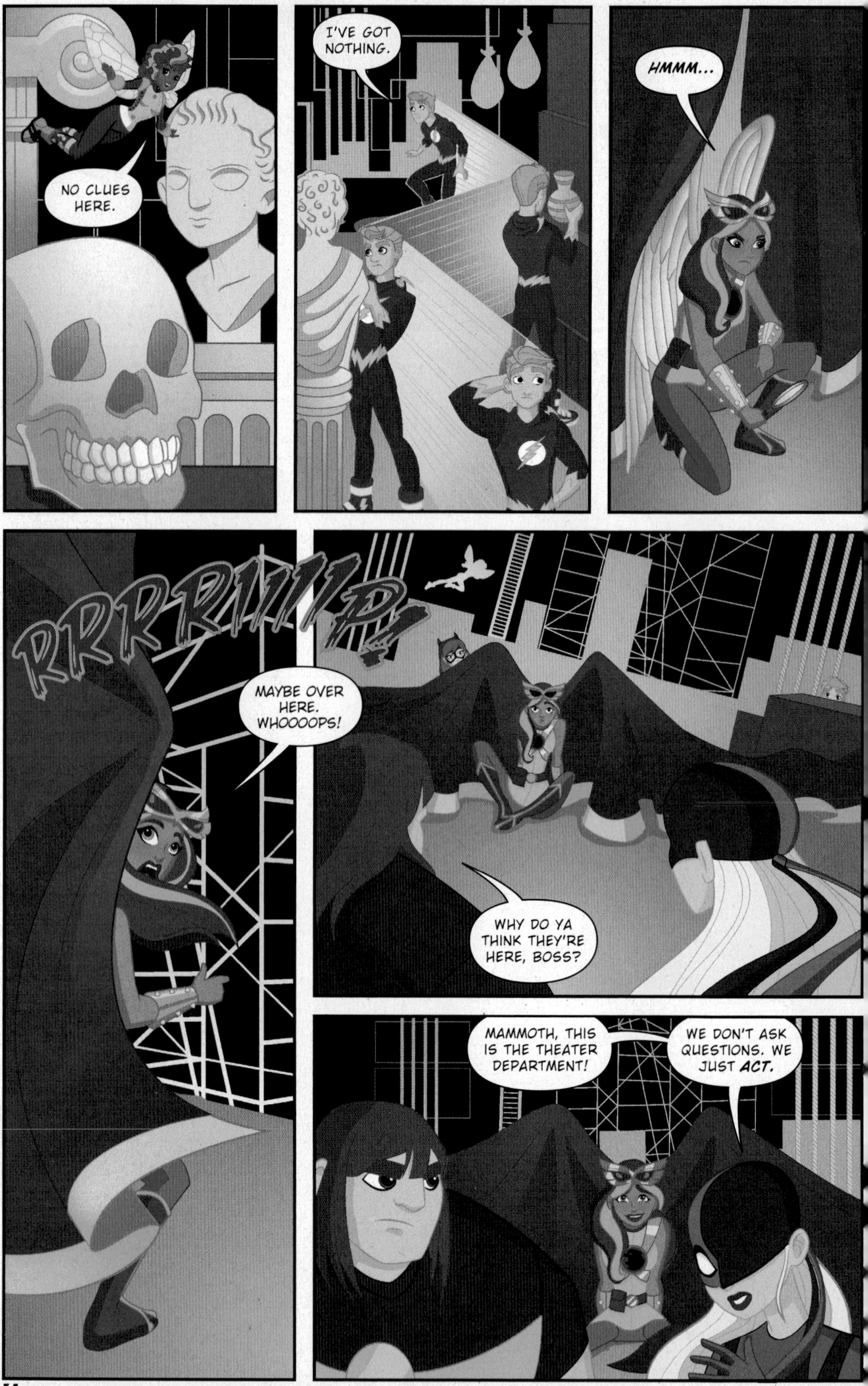
NO CLUES HERE.
I'VE GOT NOTHING.
HMMM...
RRRRIIIIP!
MAYBE OVER HERE. WHOOOOPS!
WHY DO YA THINK THEY'RE HERE, BOSS?
MAMMOTH, THIS IS THE THEATER DEPARTMENT!
WE DON'T ASK QUESTIONS. WE JUST ACT.

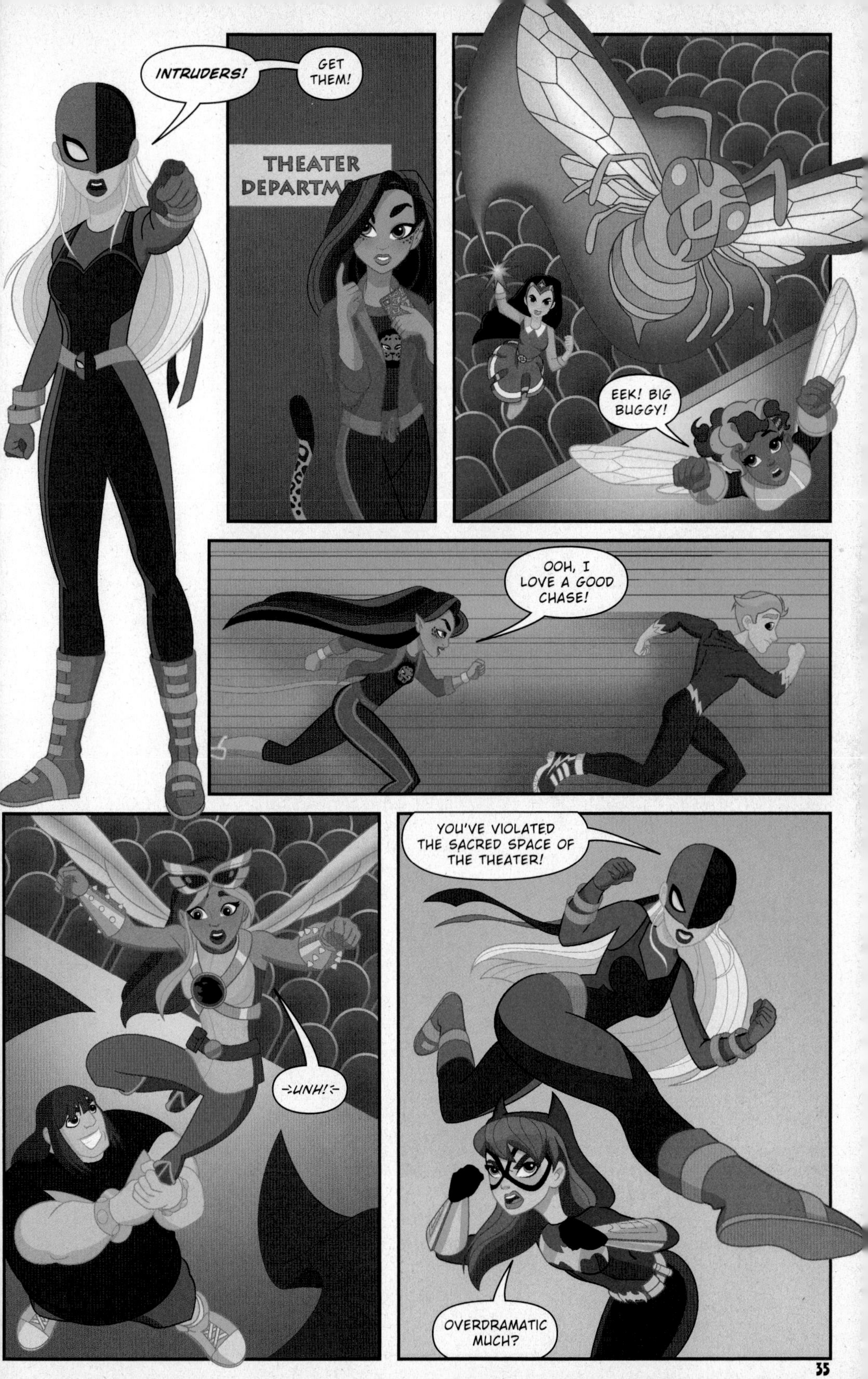
INTRUDERS!
GET THEM!
THEATER DEPARTM
EEK! BIG BUGGY!
OOH, I LOVE A GOOD CHASE!
UNH!
YOU'VE VIOLATED THE SACRED SPACE OF THE THEATER!
OVERDRAMATIC MUCH?

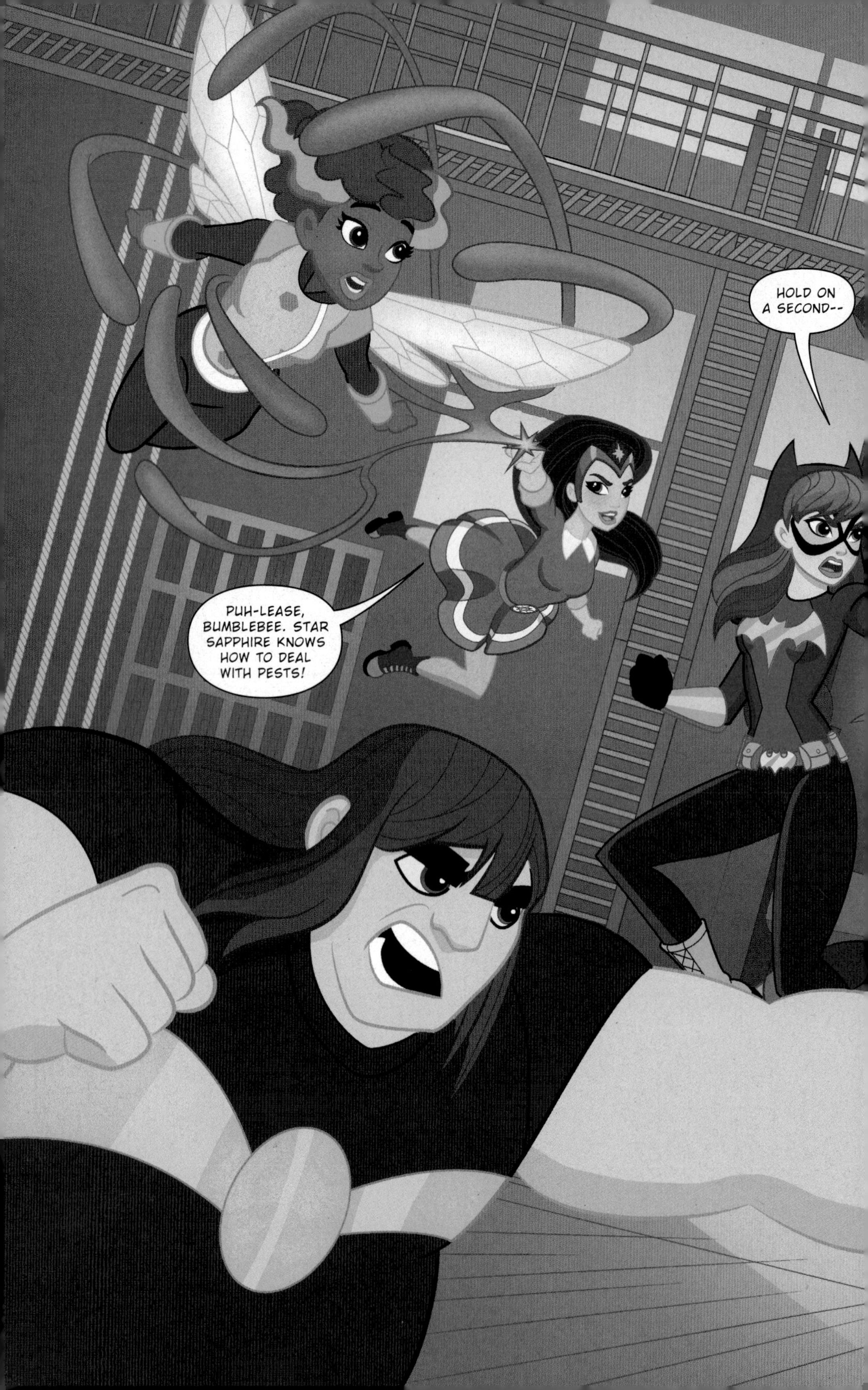
HOLD ON A SECOND--
PUH-LEASE, BUMBLEBEE. STAR SAPPHIRE KNOWS HOW TO DEAL WITH PESTS!

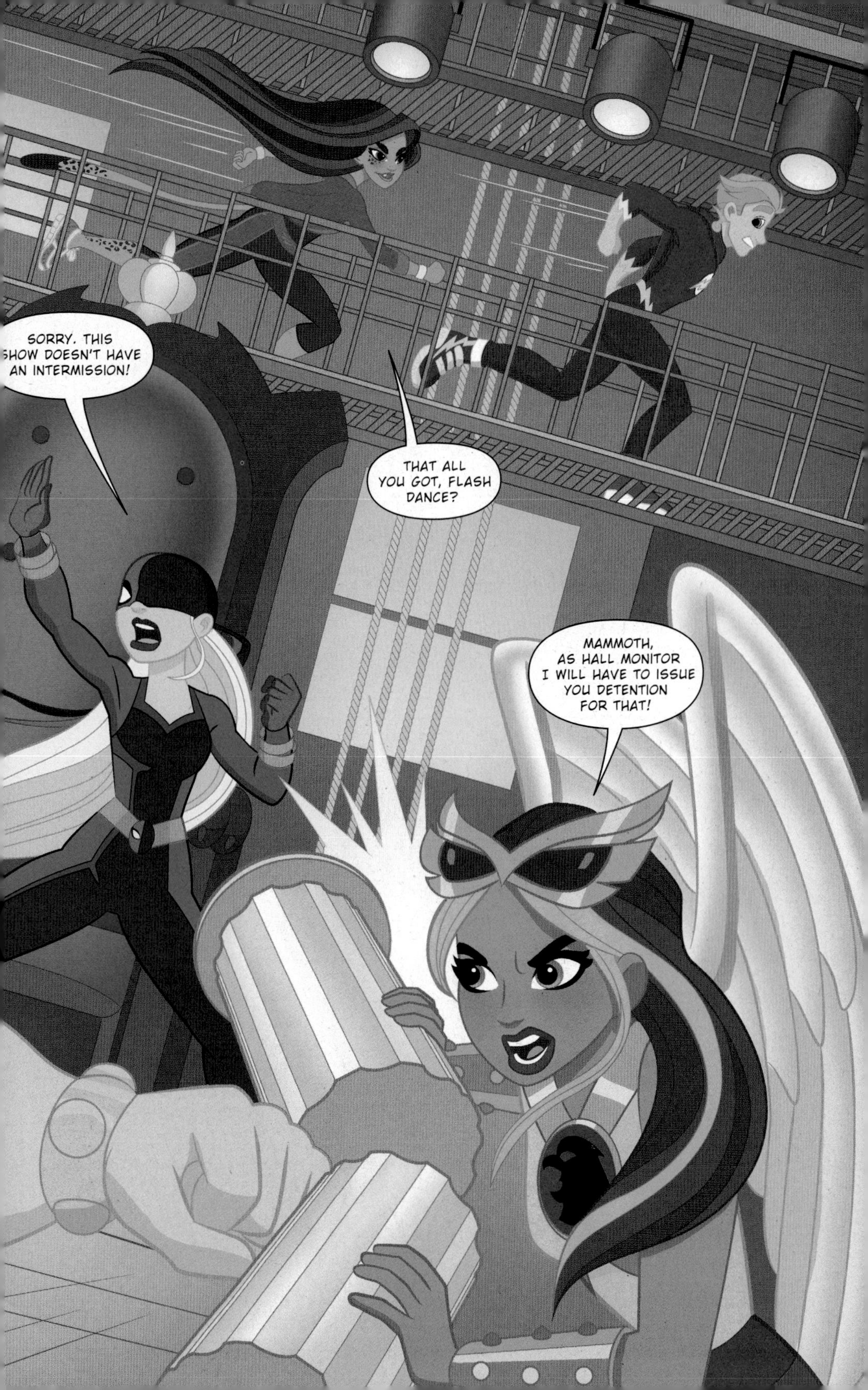
SORRY. THIS SHOW DOESN'T HAVE AN INTERMISSION!
THAT ALL YOU GOT, FLASH DANCE?
MAMMOTH, AS HALL MONITOR I WILL HAVE TO ISSUE YOU DETENTION FOR THAT!

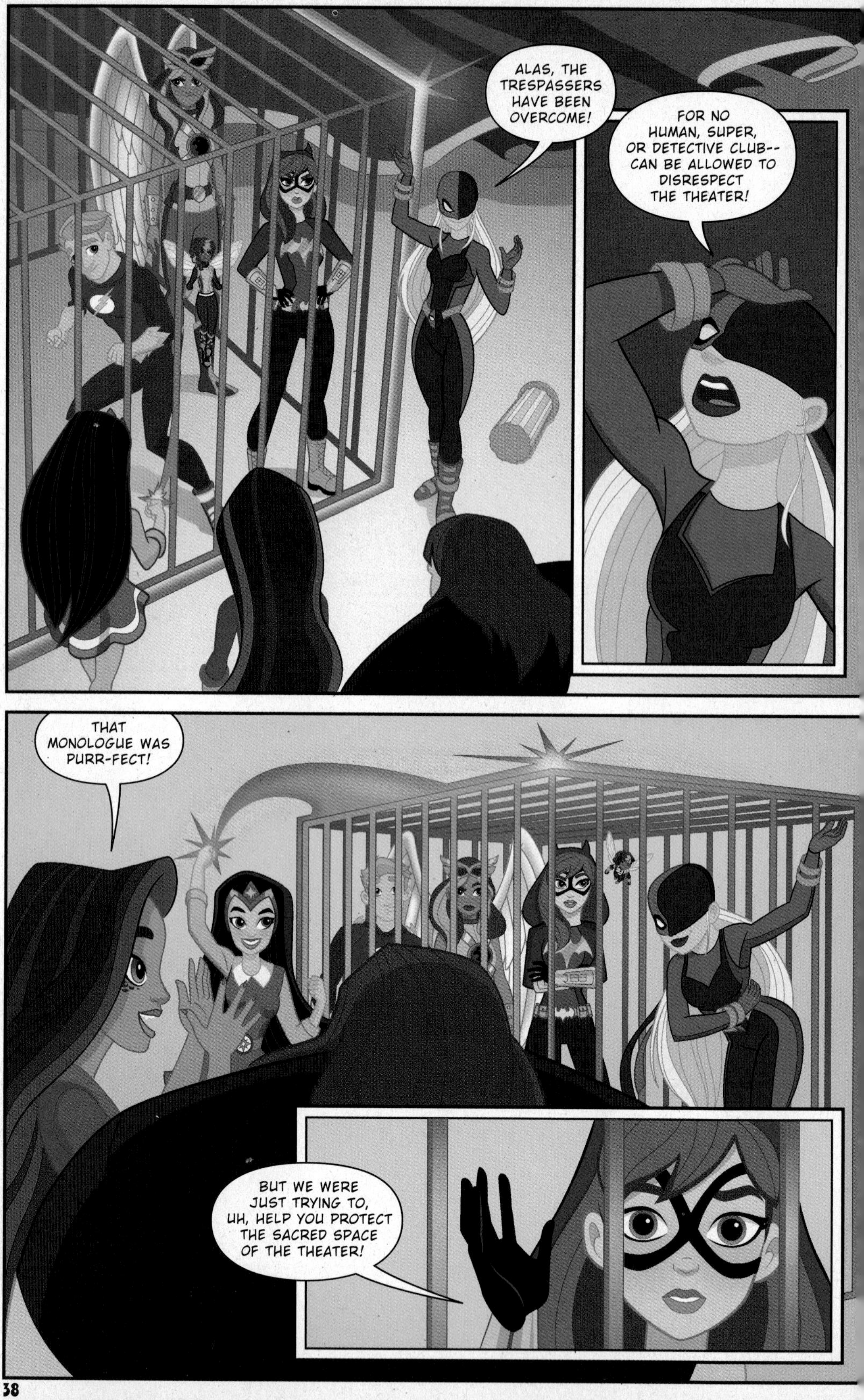
ALAS, THE TRESPASSERS HAVE BEEN OVERCOME!
FOR NO HUMAN, SUPER, OR DETECTIVE CLUB-- CAN BE ALLOWED TO DISRESPECT THE THEATER!
THAT MONOLOGUE WAS PURR-FECT!
BUT WE WERE JUST TRYING TO, UH, HELP YOU PROTECT THE SACRED SPACE OF THE THEATER!

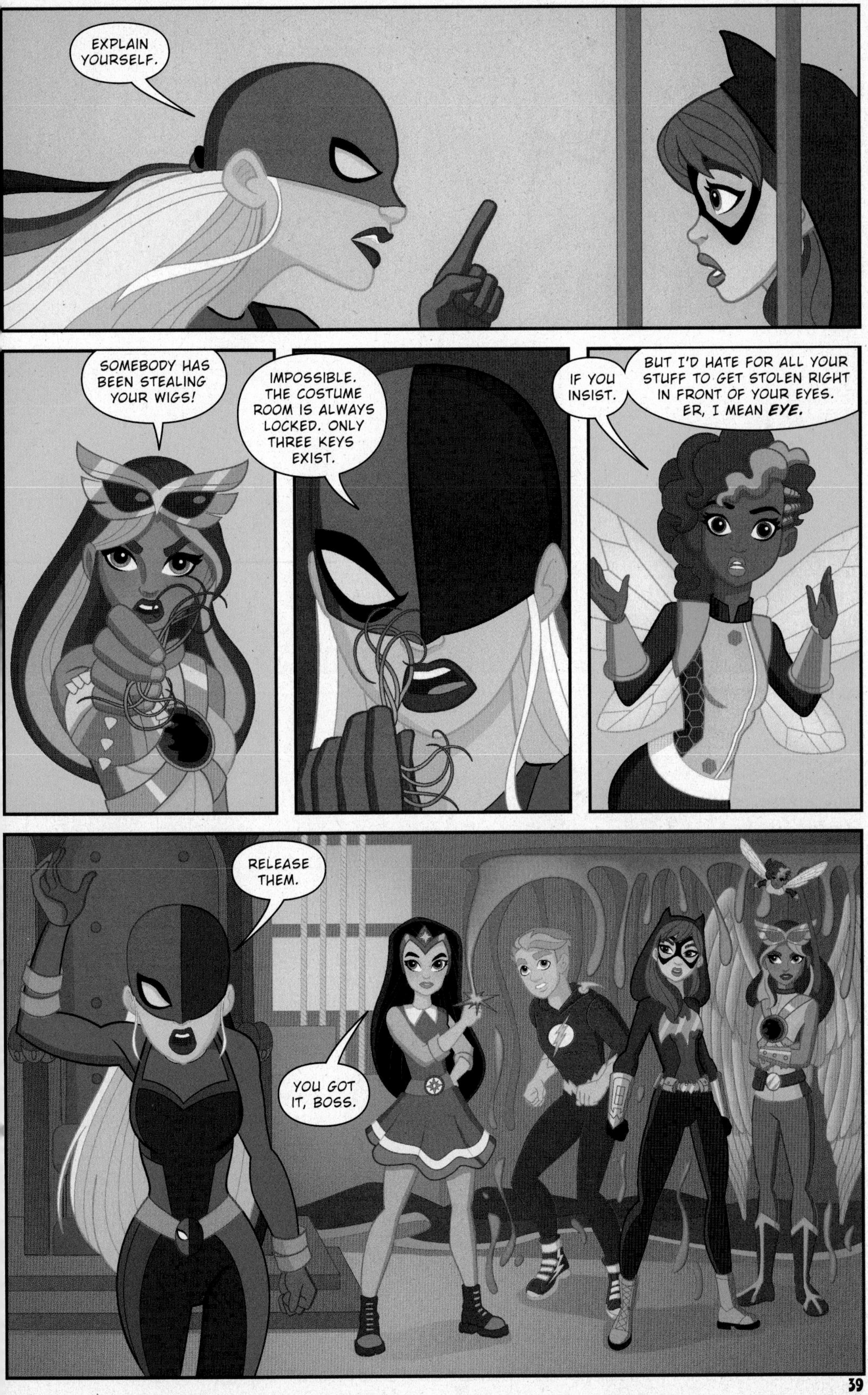
EXPLAIN YOURSELF.
SOMEBODY HAS BEEN STEALING YOUR WIGS!
IMPOSSIBLE. THE COSTUME ROOM IS ALWAYS LOCKED. ONLY THREE KEYS EXIST.
IF YOU INSIST.
BUT I'D HATE FOR ALL YOUR STUFF TO GET STOLEN RIGHT IN FRONT OF YOUR EYES. ER, I MEAN ***EYE.***
RELEASE THEM.
YOU GOT IT, BOSS.

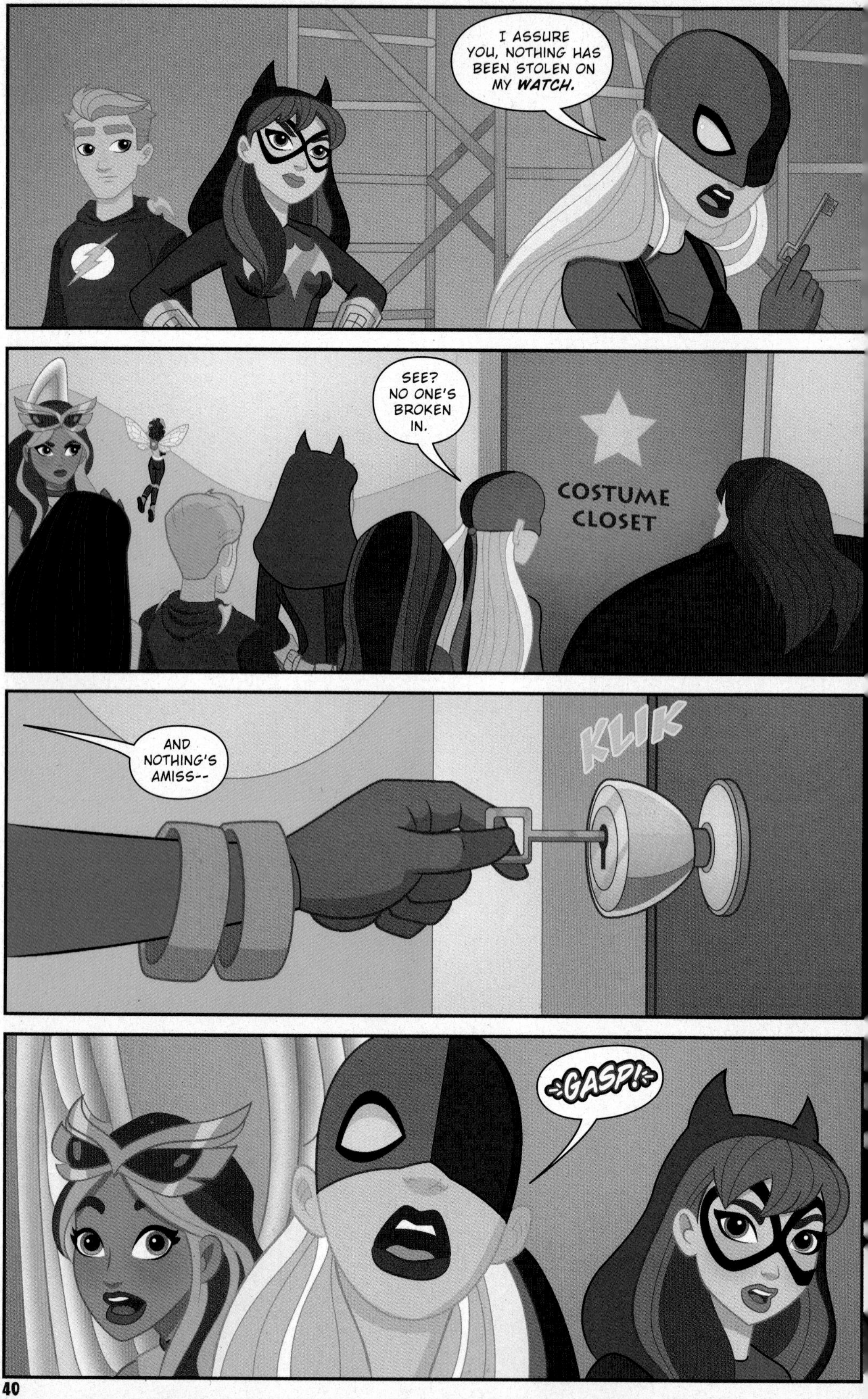
I ASSURE YOU, NOTHING HAS BEEN STOLEN ON MY WATCH.
SEE? NO ONE'S BROKEN IN.
COSTUME CLOSET
AND NOTHING'S AMISS--
KLIK
GASP!

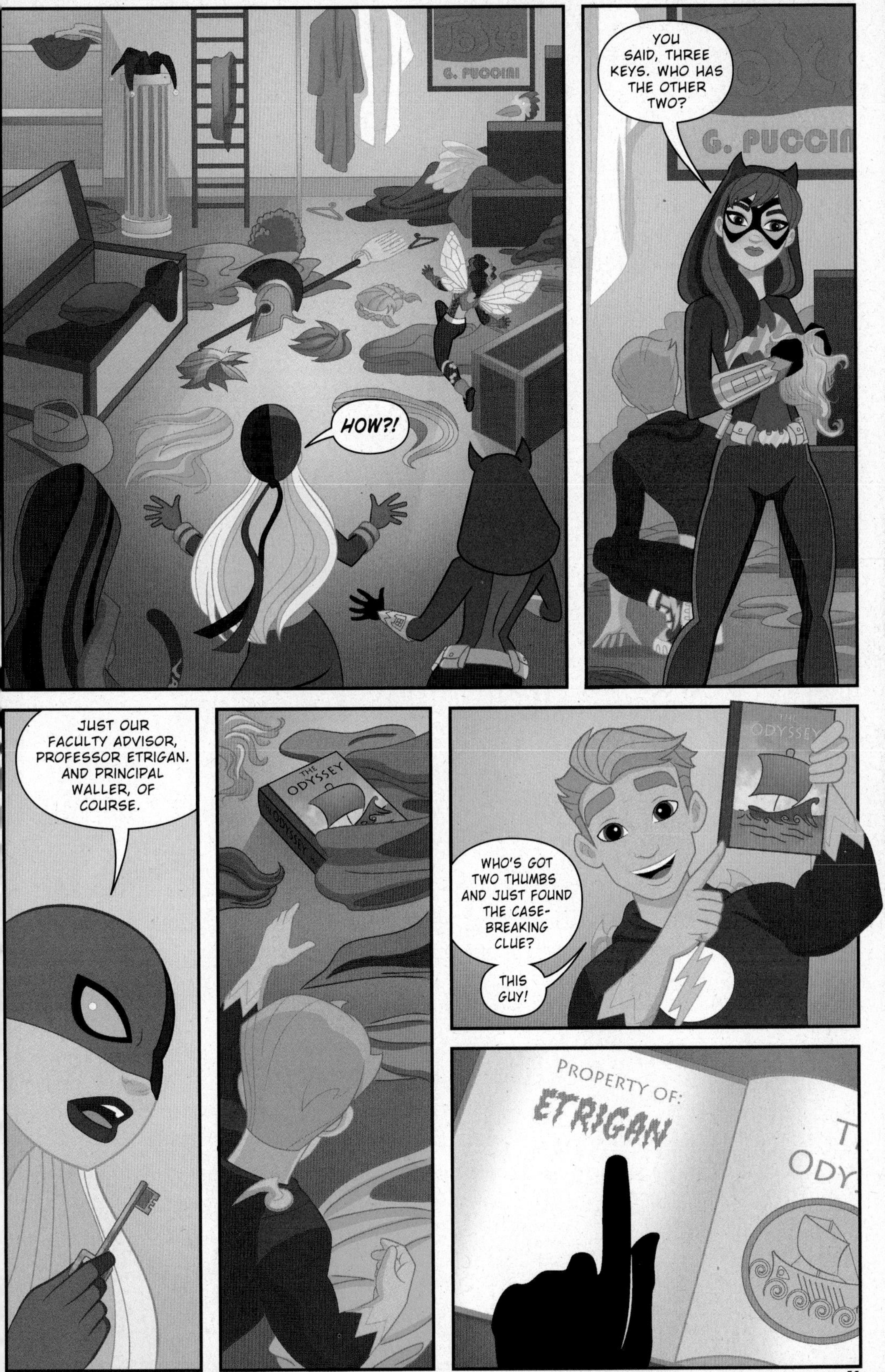
G. PUCCINI
HOW?!
YOU SAID, THREE KEYS. WHO HAS THE OTHER TWO?
G. PUCCINI
JUST OUR FACULTY ADVISOR, PROFESSOR ETRIGAN. AND PRINCIPAL WALLER, OF COURSE.
THE ODYSSEY
THE ODYSSEY
WHO'S GOT TWO THUMBS AND JUST FOUND THE CASE-BREAKING CLUE?
THIS GUY!
PROPERTY OF:
ETRIGAN

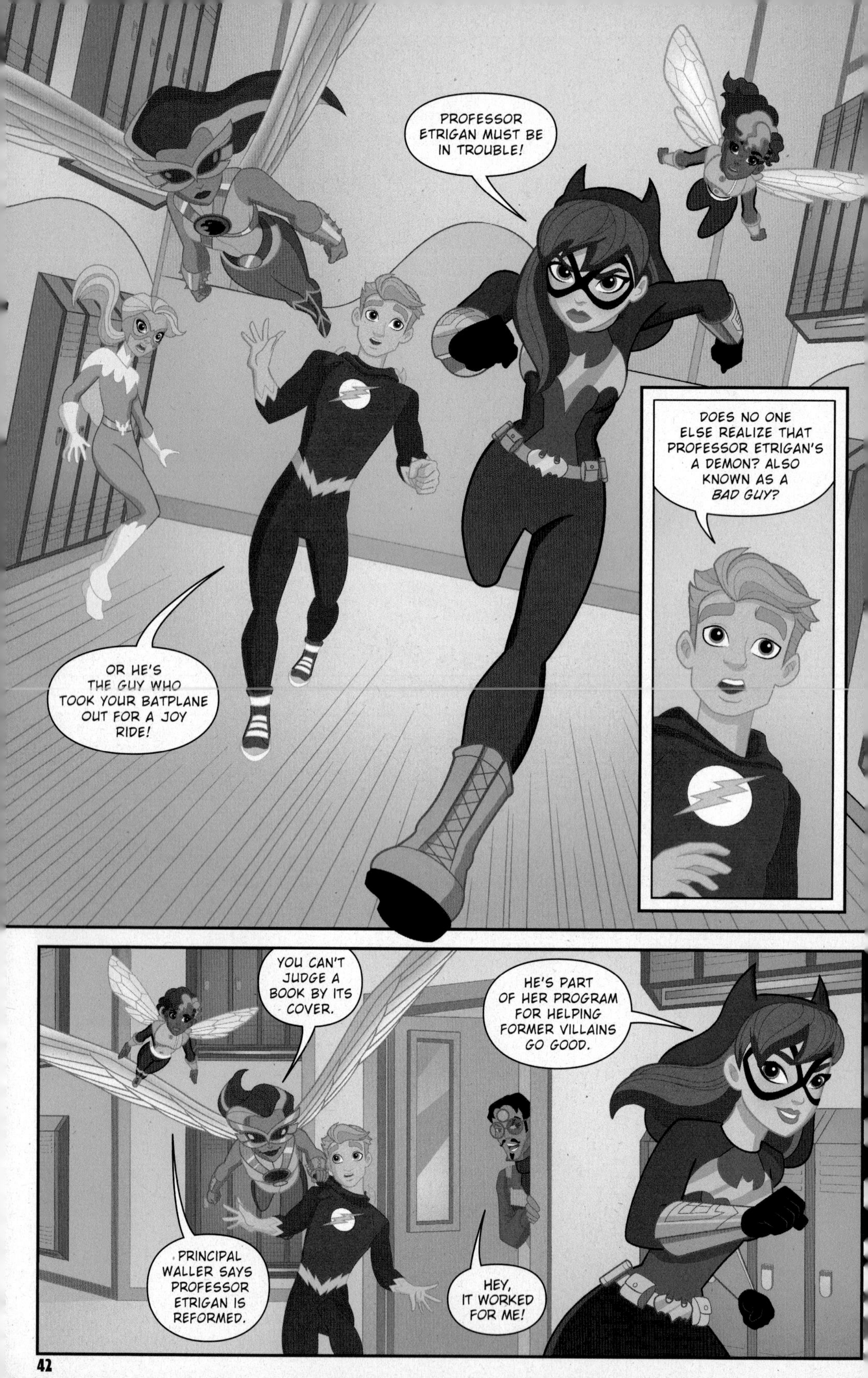
PROFESSOR ETRIGAN MUST BE IN TROUBLE!
OR HE'S THE GUY WHO TOOK YOUR BATPLANE OUT FOR A JOY RIDE!
DOES NO ONE ELSE REALIZE THAT PROFESSOR ETRIGAN'S A DEMON? ALSO KNOWN AS A *BAD GUY?*
YOU CAN'T JUDGE A BOOK BY ITS COVER.
PRINCIPAL WALLER SAYS PROFESSOR ETRIGAN IS REFORMED.
HE'S PART OF HER PROGRAM FOR HELPING FORMER VILLAINS GO GOOD.
HEY, IT WORKED FOR ME!

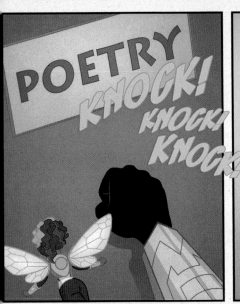

POETRY

KNOCK!
KNOCK!
KNOCK!

HELLO? PROFESSOR ETRIGAN?

WHOA! PROFESSOR ETRIGAN EVEN WRECKED HIS OWN CLASSROOM SO WE WOULDN'T SUSPECT HIM.

FLASH, DON'T YOU REMEMBER LEARNING ABOUT OCCAM'S RAZOR IN FORENSICS CLASS?

YEAH, YEAH. THE SIMPLEST EXPLANATION IS USUALLY CORRECT.

SIMPLEST EXPLANATION HERE IS THAT SOMEONE WAS AFTER PROFESSOR ETRIGAN.

AND THEY GOT HIM.

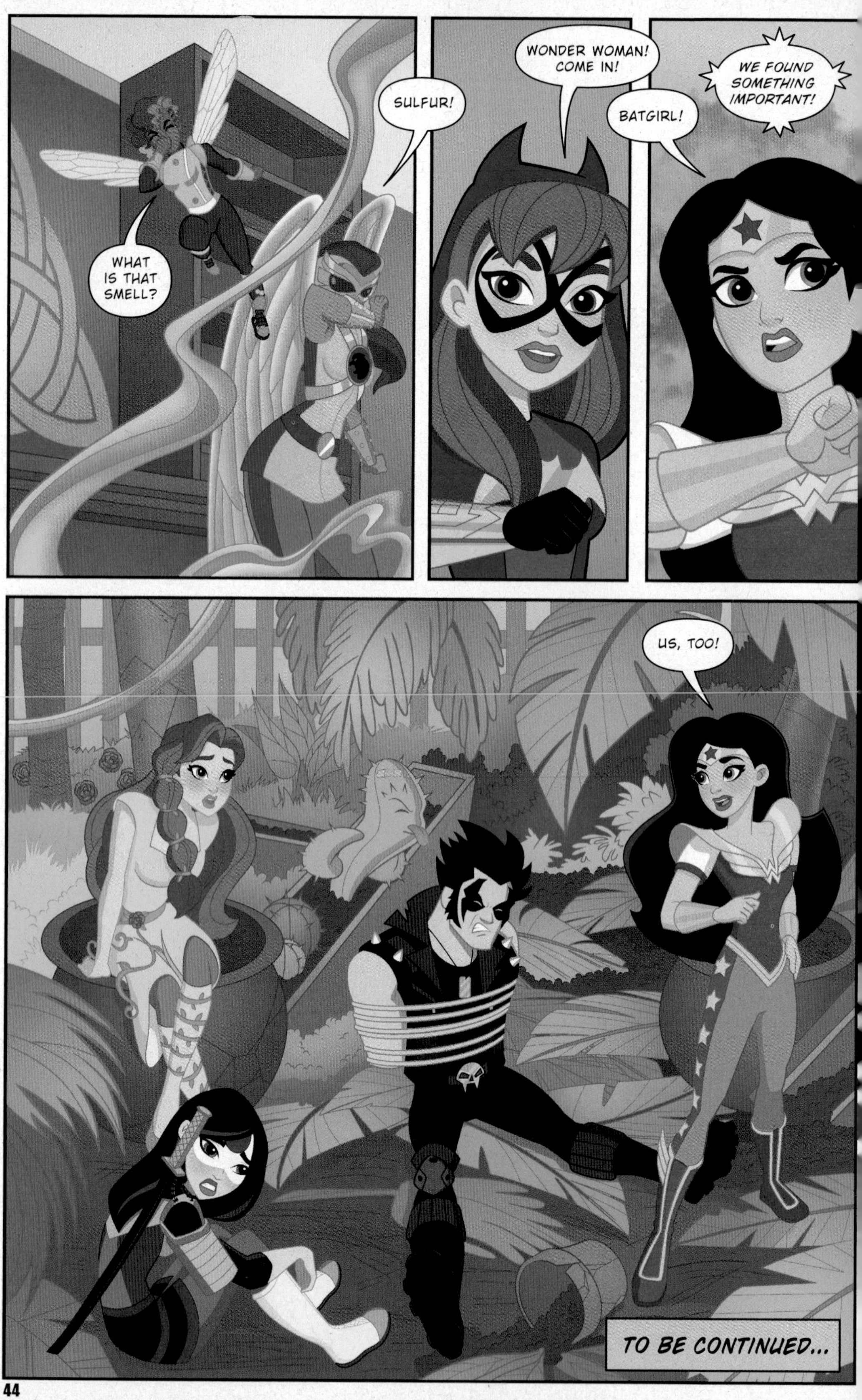

WHAT IS THAT SMELL?
SULFUR!
WONDER WOMAN! COME IN!
BATGIRL!
WE FOUND SOMETHING IMPORTANT!
US, TOO!
TO BE CONTINUED...

CHAPTER THREE
THE WITCH

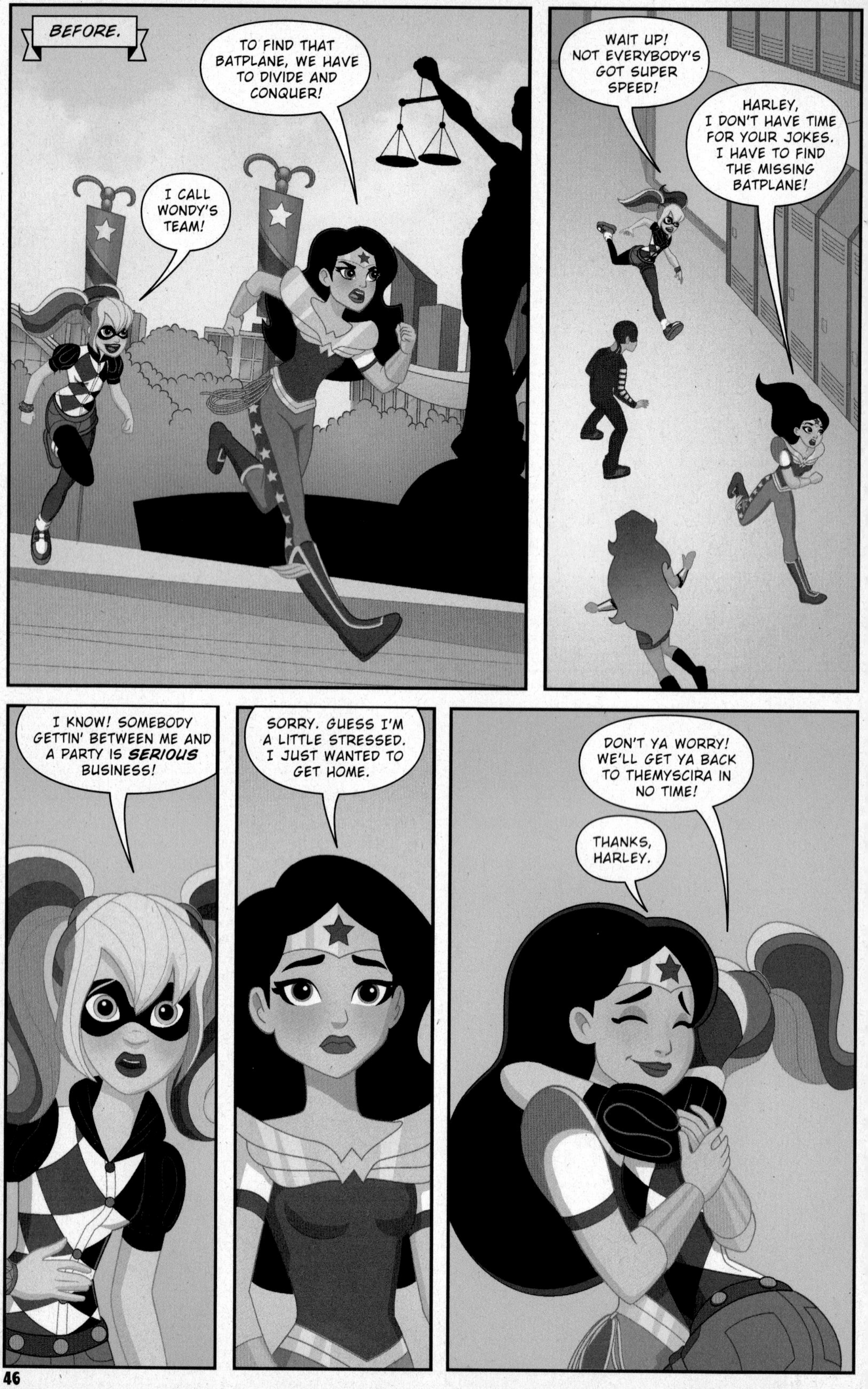
BEFORE.
TO FIND THAT BATPLANE, WE HAVE TO DIVIDE AND CONQUER!
I CALL WONDY'S TEAM!
WAIT UP! NOT EVERYBODY'S GOT SUPER SPEED!
HARLEY, I DON'T HAVE TIME FOR YOUR JOKES. I HAVE TO FIND THE MISSING BATPLANE!
I KNOW! SOMEBODY GETTIN' BETWEEN ME AND A PARTY IS SERIOUS BUSINESS!
SORRY. GUESS I'M A LITTLE STRESSED. I JUST WANTED TO GET HOME.
DON'T YA WORRY! WE'LL GET YA BACK TO THEMYSCIRA IN NO TIME!
THANKS, HARLEY.

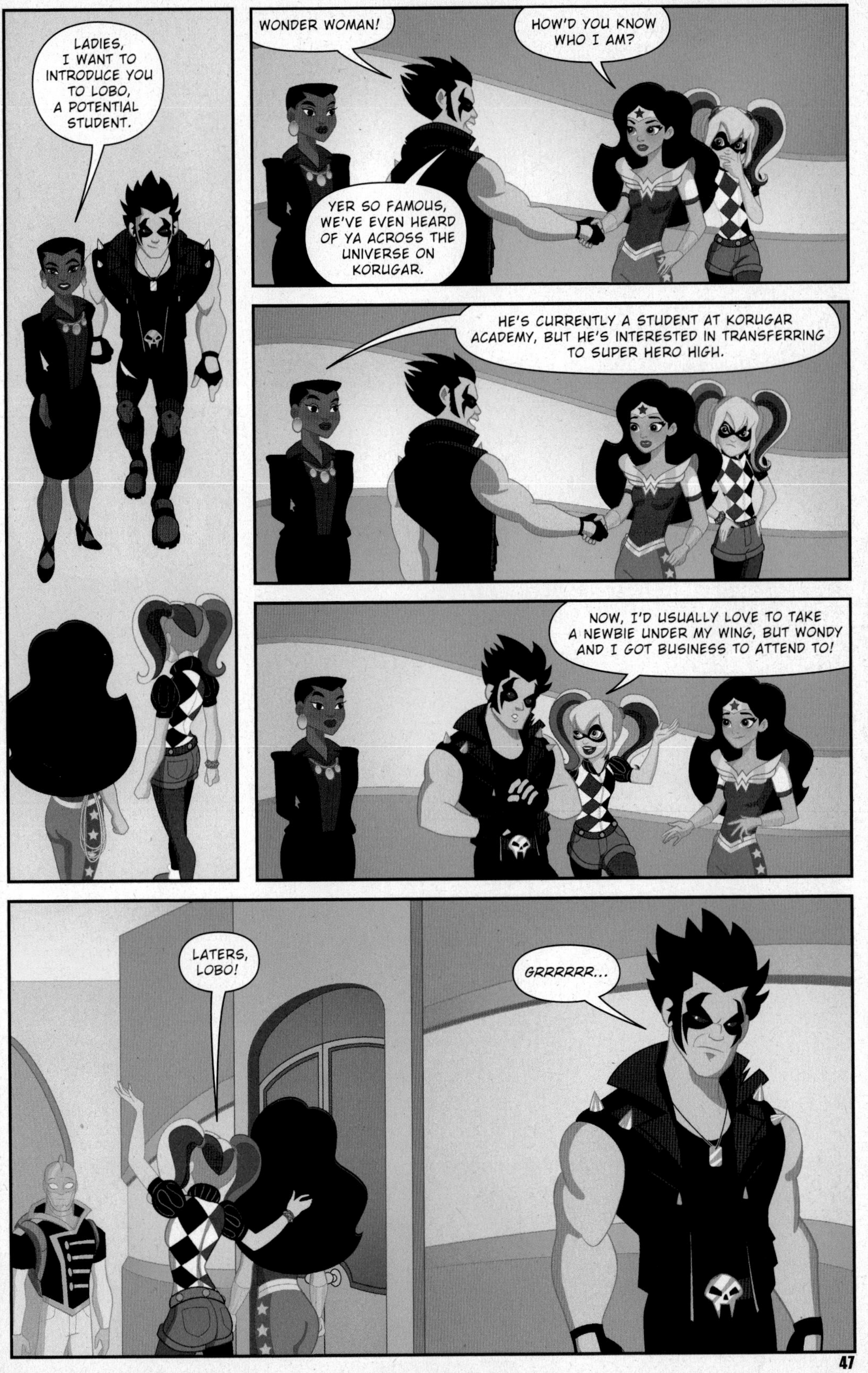
LADIES, I WANT TO INTRODUCE YOU TO LOBO, A POTENTIAL STUDENT.
WONDER WOMAN!
HOW'D YOU KNOW WHO I AM?
YER SO FAMOUS, WE'VE EVEN HEARD OF YA ACROSS THE UNIVERSE ON KORUGAR.
HE'S CURRENTLY A STUDENT AT KORUGAR ACADEMY, BUT HE'S INTERESTED IN TRANSFERRING TO SUPER HERO HIGH.
NOW, I'D USUALLY LOVE TO TAKE A NEWBIE UNDER MY WING, BUT WONDY AND I GOT BUSINESS TO ATTEND TO!
LATERS, LOBO!
GRRRRRR...

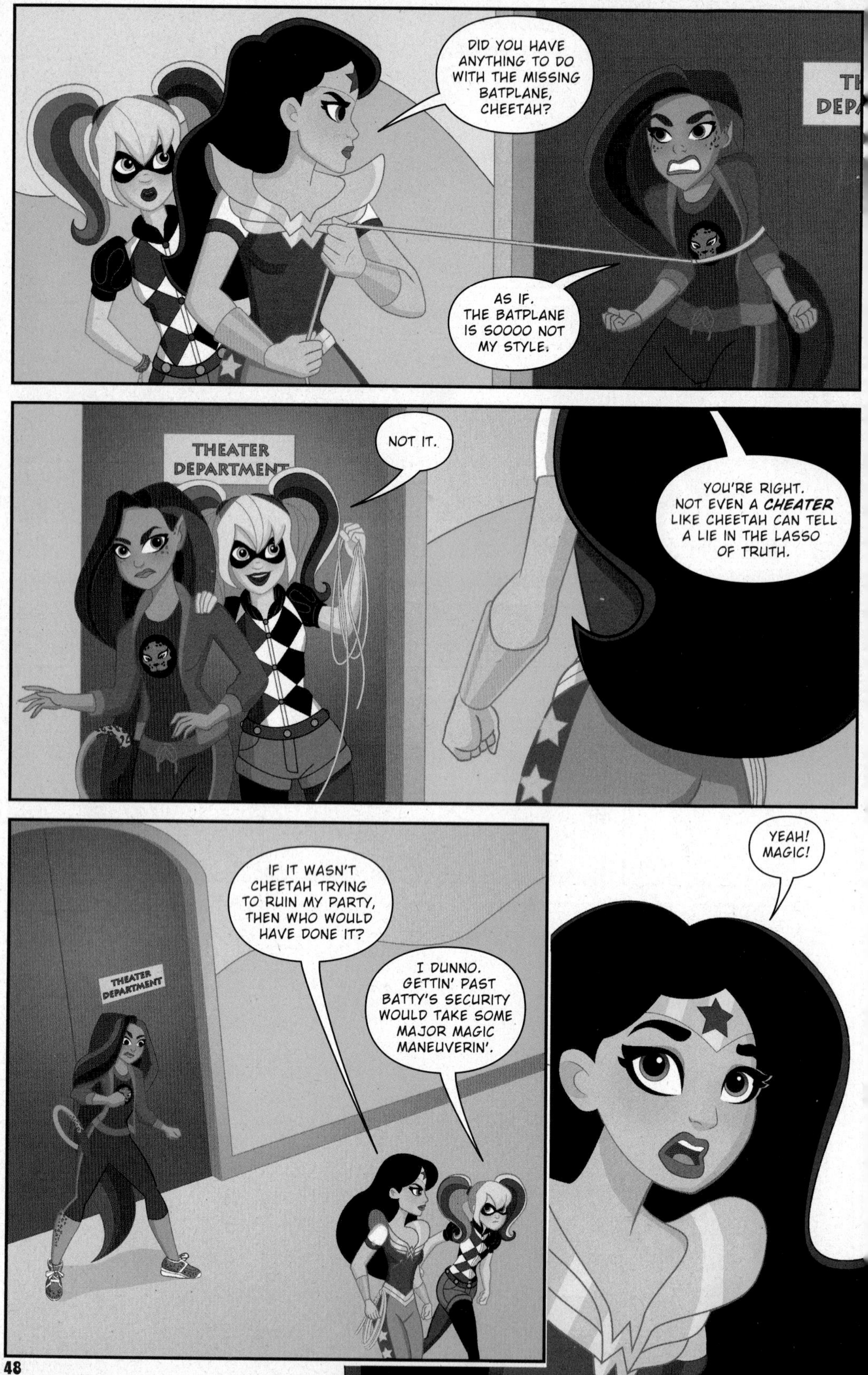
DID YOU HAVE ANYTHING TO DO WITH THE MISSING BATPLANE, CHEETAH?
AS IF. THE BATPLANE IS SOOOO NOT MY STYLE.
THEATER DEPARTMENT
NOT IT.
YOU'RE RIGHT. NOT EVEN A *CHEATER* LIKE CHEETAH CAN TELL A LIE IN THE LASSO OF TRUTH.
THEATER DEPARTMENT
IF IT WASN'T CHEETAH TRYING TO RUIN MY PARTY, THEN WHO WOULD HAVE DONE IT?
I DUNNO. GETTIN' PAST BATTY'S SECURITY WOULD TAKE SOME MAJOR MAGIC MANEUVERIN'.
YEAH! MAGIC!

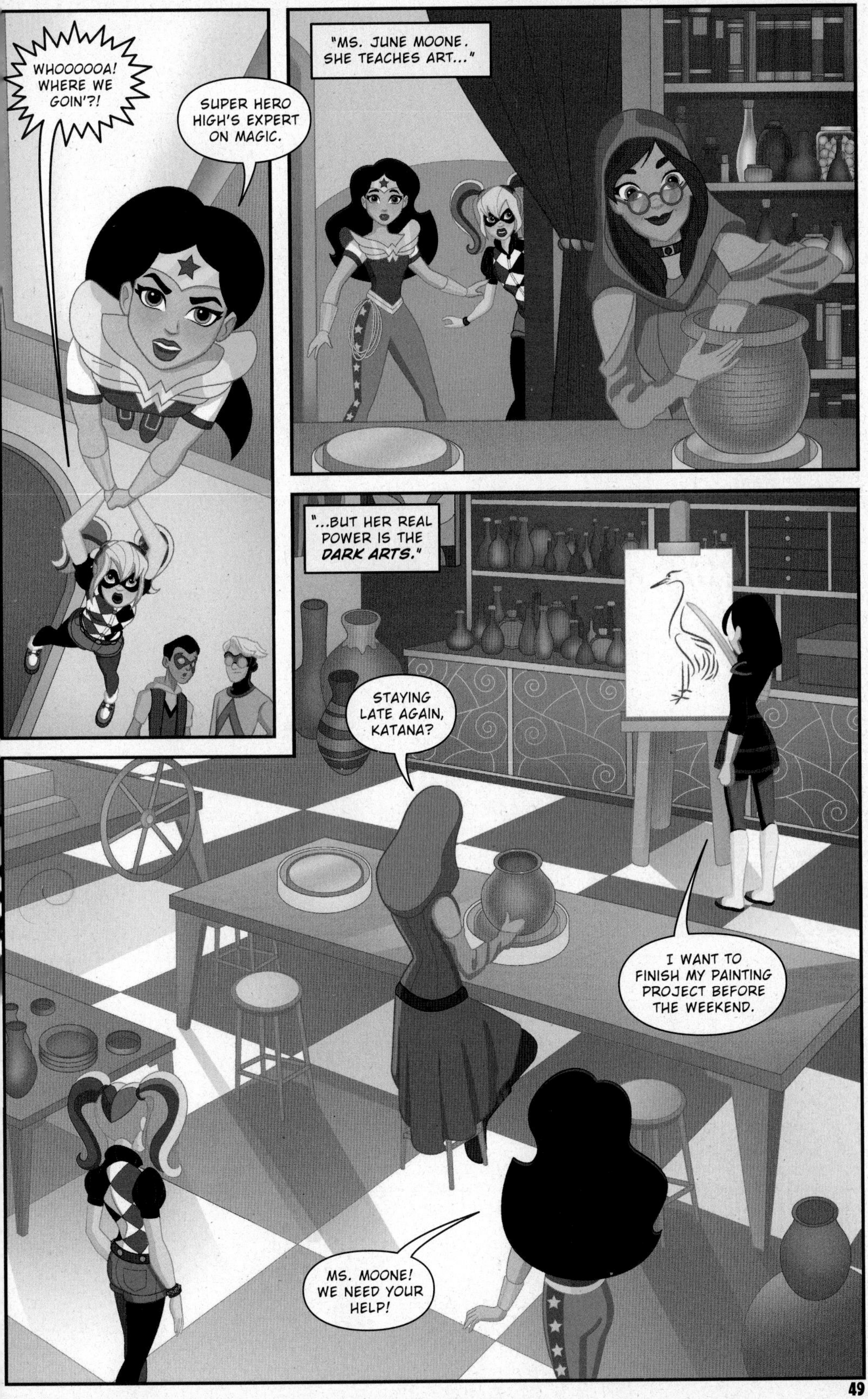
WHOOOOOA! WHERE WE GOIN'?!
SUPER HERO HIGH'S EXPERT ON MAGIC.
"MS. JUNE MOONE. SHE TEACHES ART..."
"...BUT HER REAL POWER IS THE *DARK ARTS.*"
STAYING LATE AGAIN, KATANA?
I WANT TO FINISH MY PAINTING PROJECT BEFORE THE WEEKEND.
MS. MOONE! WE NEED YOUR HELP!

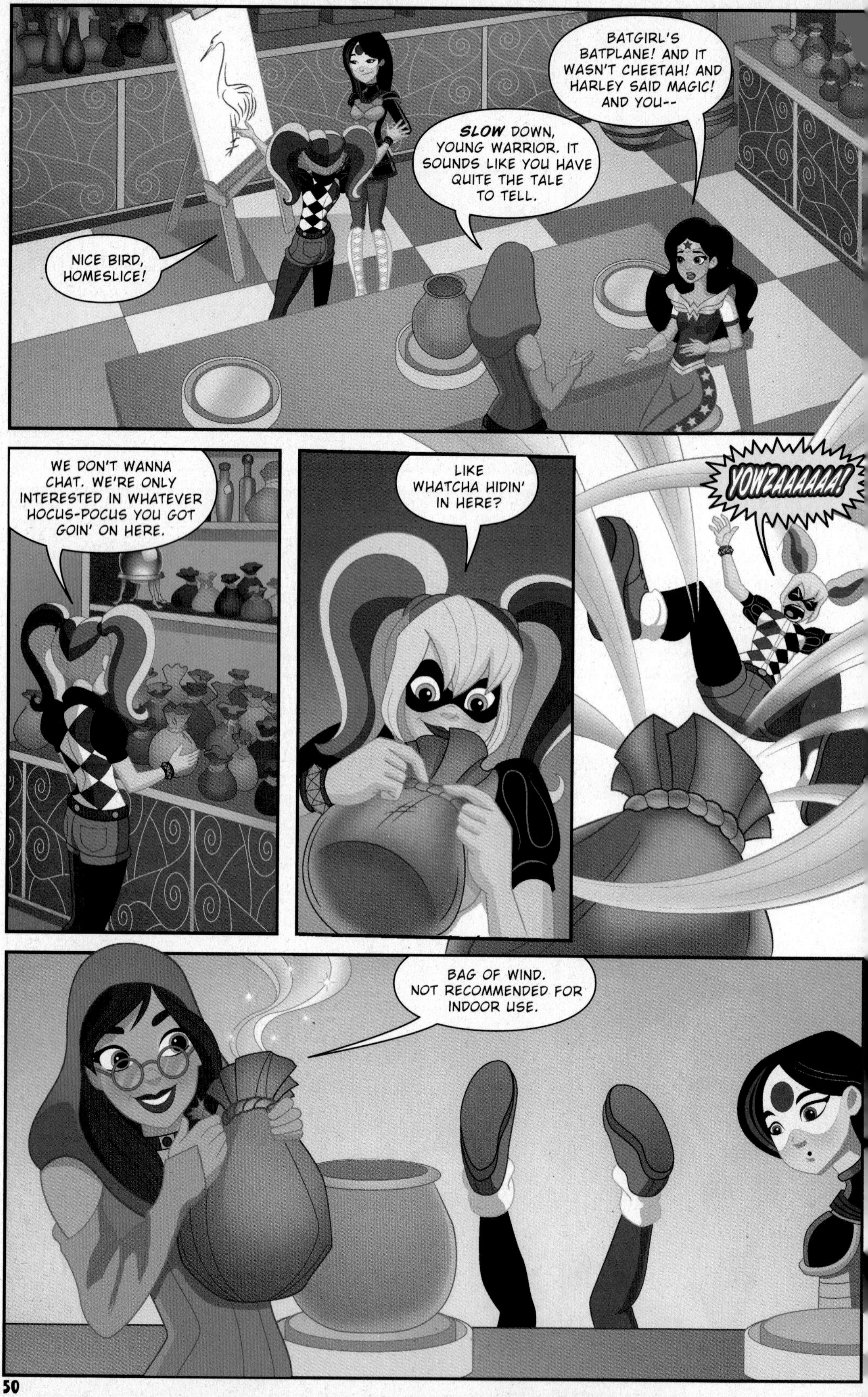
BATGIRL'S BATPLANE! AND IT WASN'T CHEETAH! AND HARLEY SAID MAGIC! AND YOU--
SLOW DOWN, YOUNG WARRIOR. IT SOUNDS LIKE YOU HAVE QUITE THE TALE TO TELL.
NICE BIRD, HOMESLICE!
WE DON'T WANNA CHAT. WE'RE ONLY INTERESTED IN WHATEVER HOCUS-POCUS YOU GOT GOIN' ON HERE.
LIKE WHATCHA HIDIN' IN HERE?
YOWZAAAAAA!
BAG OF WIND. NOT RECOMMENDED FOR INDOOR USE.

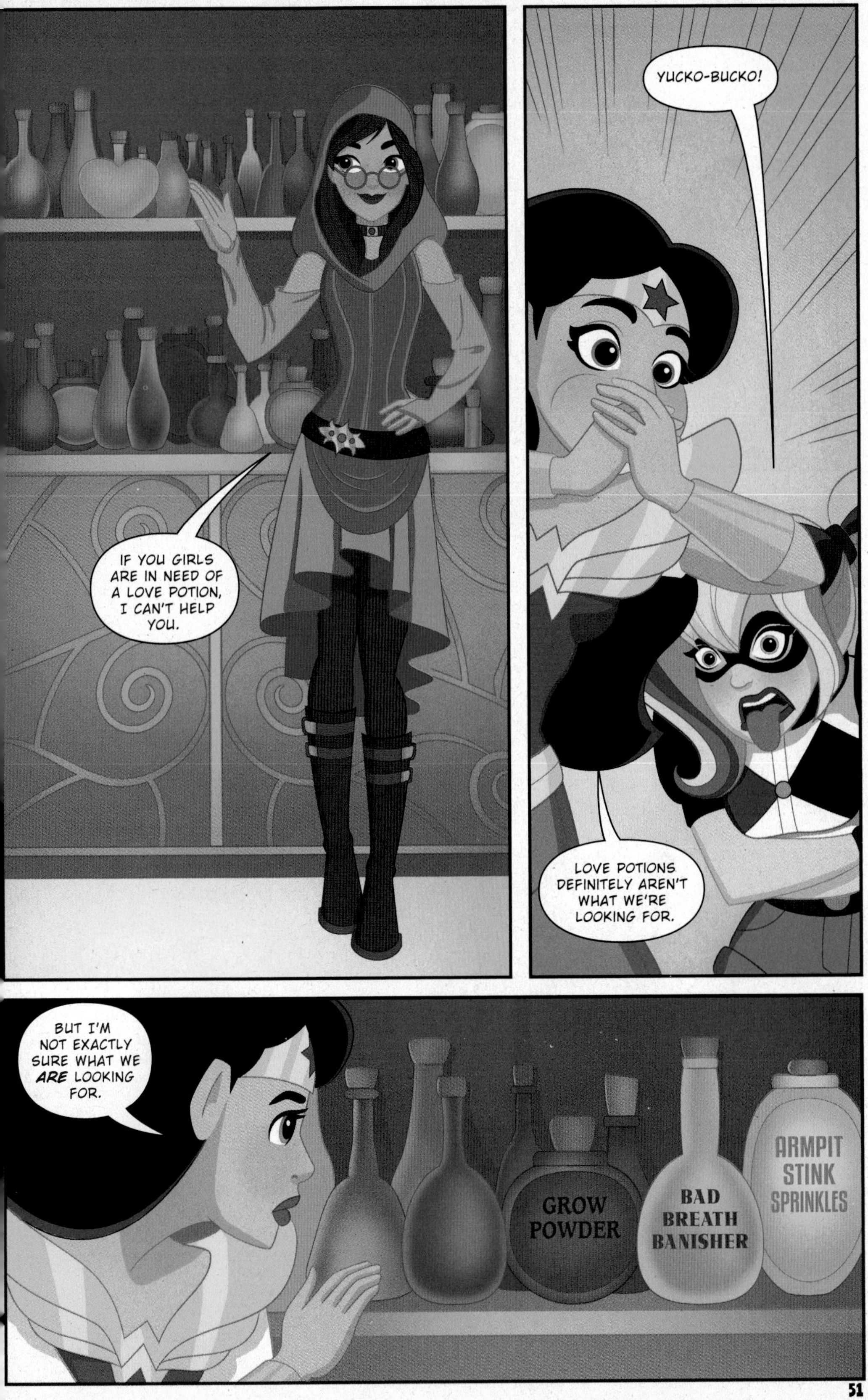
IF YOU GIRLS ARE IN NEED OF A LOVE POTION, I CAN'T HELP YOU.
YUCKO-BUCKO!
LOVE POTIONS DEFINITELY AREN'T WHAT WE'RE LOOKING FOR.
BUT I'M NOT EXACTLY SURE WHAT WE *ARE* LOOKING FOR.
GROW POWDER
BAD BREATH BANISHER
ARMPIT STINK SPRINKLES

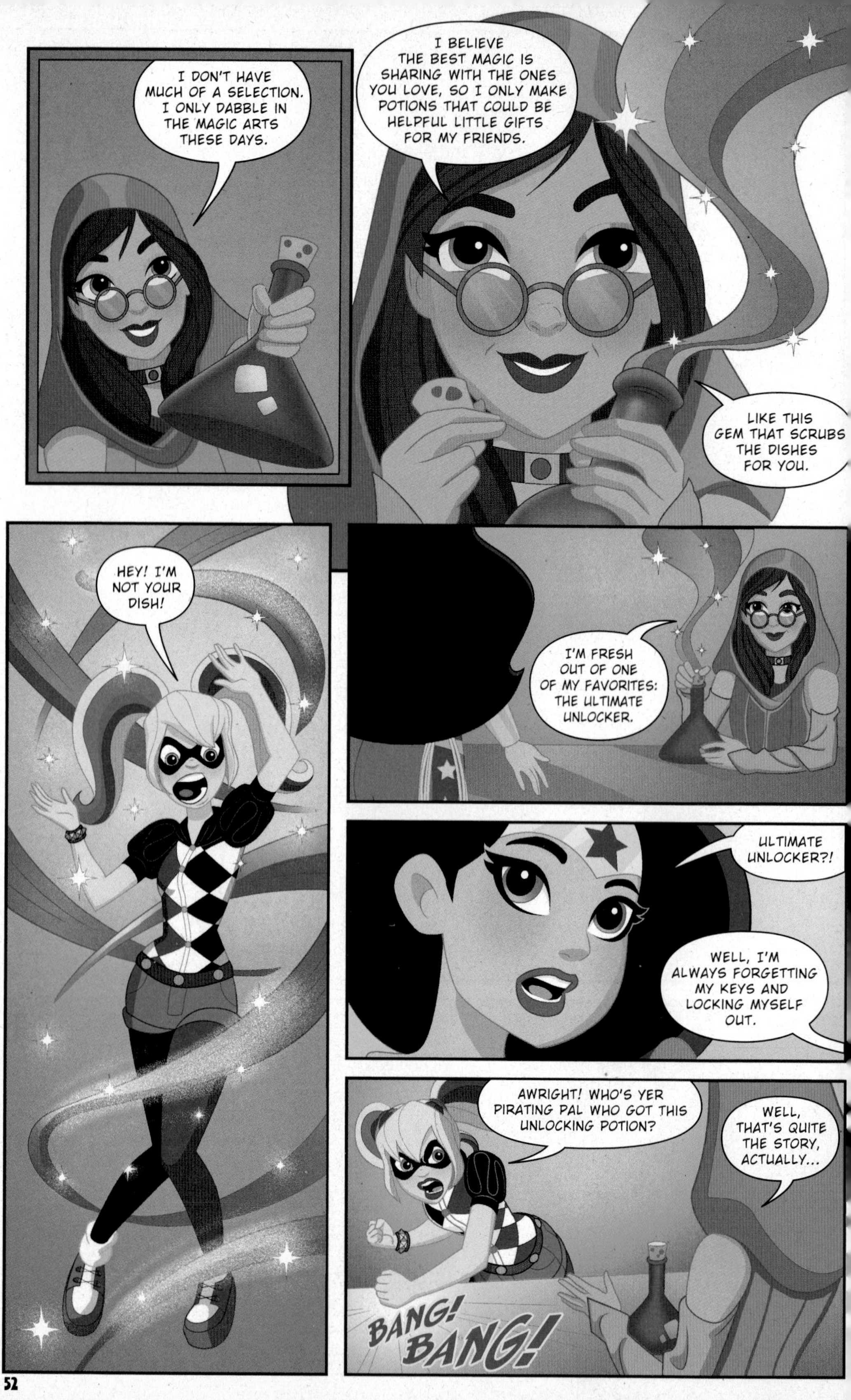
I DON'T HAVE MUCH OF A SELECTION. I ONLY DABBLE IN THE MAGIC ARTS THESE DAYS.
I BELIEVE THE BEST MAGIC IS SHARING WITH THE ONES YOU LOVE, SO I ONLY MAKE POTIONS THAT COULD BE HELPFUL LITTLE GIFTS FOR MY FRIENDS.
LIKE THIS GEM THAT SCRUBS THE DISHES FOR YOU.
HEY! I'M NOT YOUR DISH!
I'M FRESH OUT OF ONE OF MY FAVORITES: THE ULTIMATE UNLOCKER.
ULTIMATE UNLOCKER?!
WELL, I'M ALWAYS FORGETTING MY KEYS AND LOCKING MYSELF OUT.
AWRIGHT! WHO'S YER PIRATING PAL WHO GOT THIS UNLOCKING POTION?
WELL, THAT'S QUITE THE STORY, ACTUALLY...
BANG! BANG!

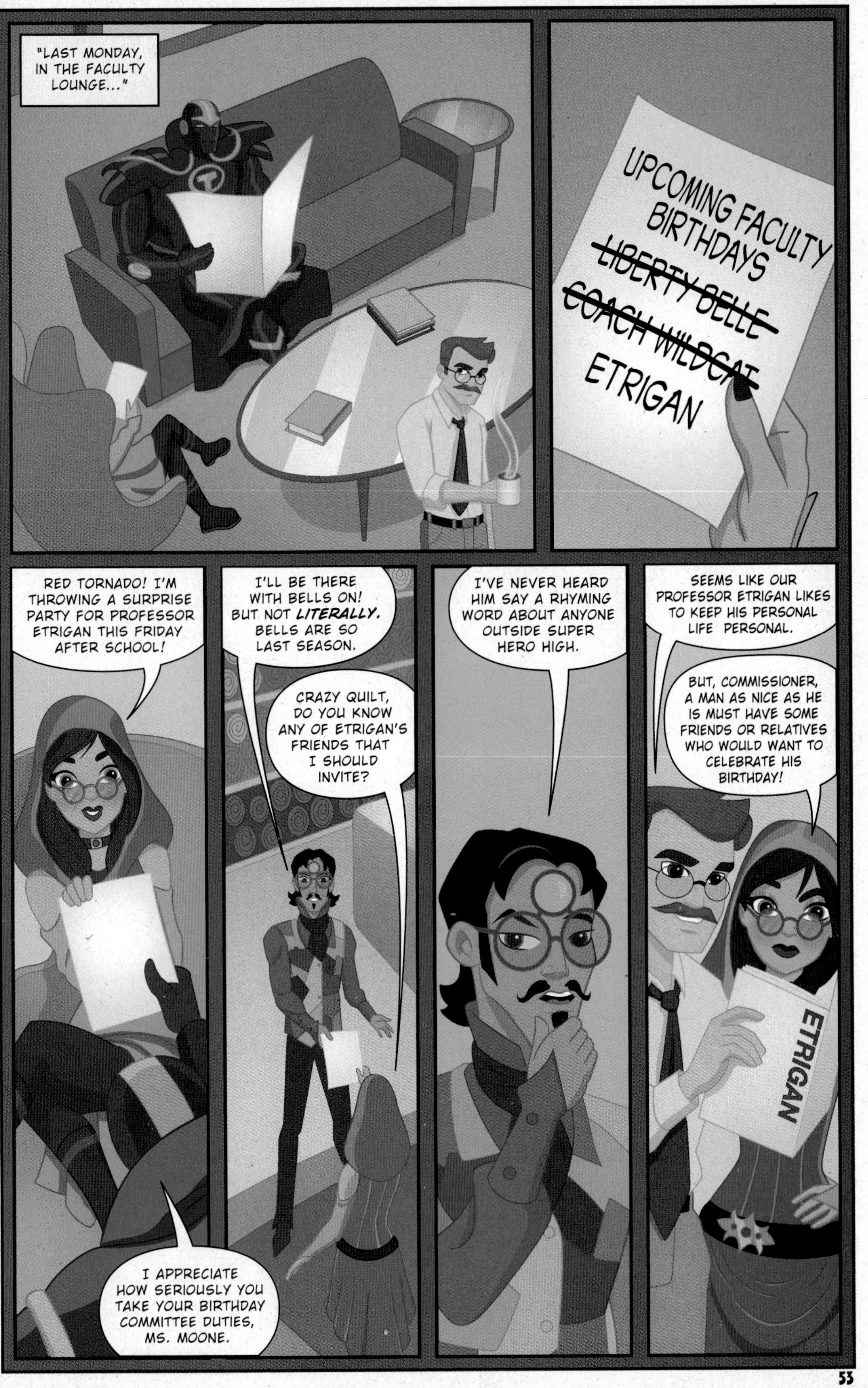
"LAST MONDAY, IN THE FACULTY LOUNGE..."
UPCOMING FACULTY BIRTHDAYS
LIBERTY BELLE
COACH WILDCAT
ETRIGAN
RED TORNADO! I'M THROWING A SURPRISE PARTY FOR PROFESSOR ETRIGAN THIS FRIDAY AFTER SCHOOL!
I APPRECIATE HOW SERIOUSLY YOU TAKE YOUR BIRTHDAY COMMITTEE DUTIES, MS. MOONE.
I'LL BE THERE WITH BELLS ON! BUT NOT *LITERALLY.* BELLS ARE SO LAST SEASON.
CRAZY QUILT, DO YOU KNOW ANY OF ETRIGAN'S FRIENDS THAT I SHOULD INVITE?
I'VE NEVER HEARD HIM SAY A RHYMING WORD ABOUT ANYONE OUTSIDE SUPER HERO HIGH.
SEEMS LIKE OUR PROFESSOR ETRIGAN LIKES TO KEEP HIS PERSONAL LIFE PERSONAL.
BUT, COMMISSIONER, A MAN AS NICE AS HE IS MUST HAVE SOME FRIENDS OR RELATIVES WHO WOULD WANT TO CELEBRATE HIS BIRTHDAY!
ETRIGAN

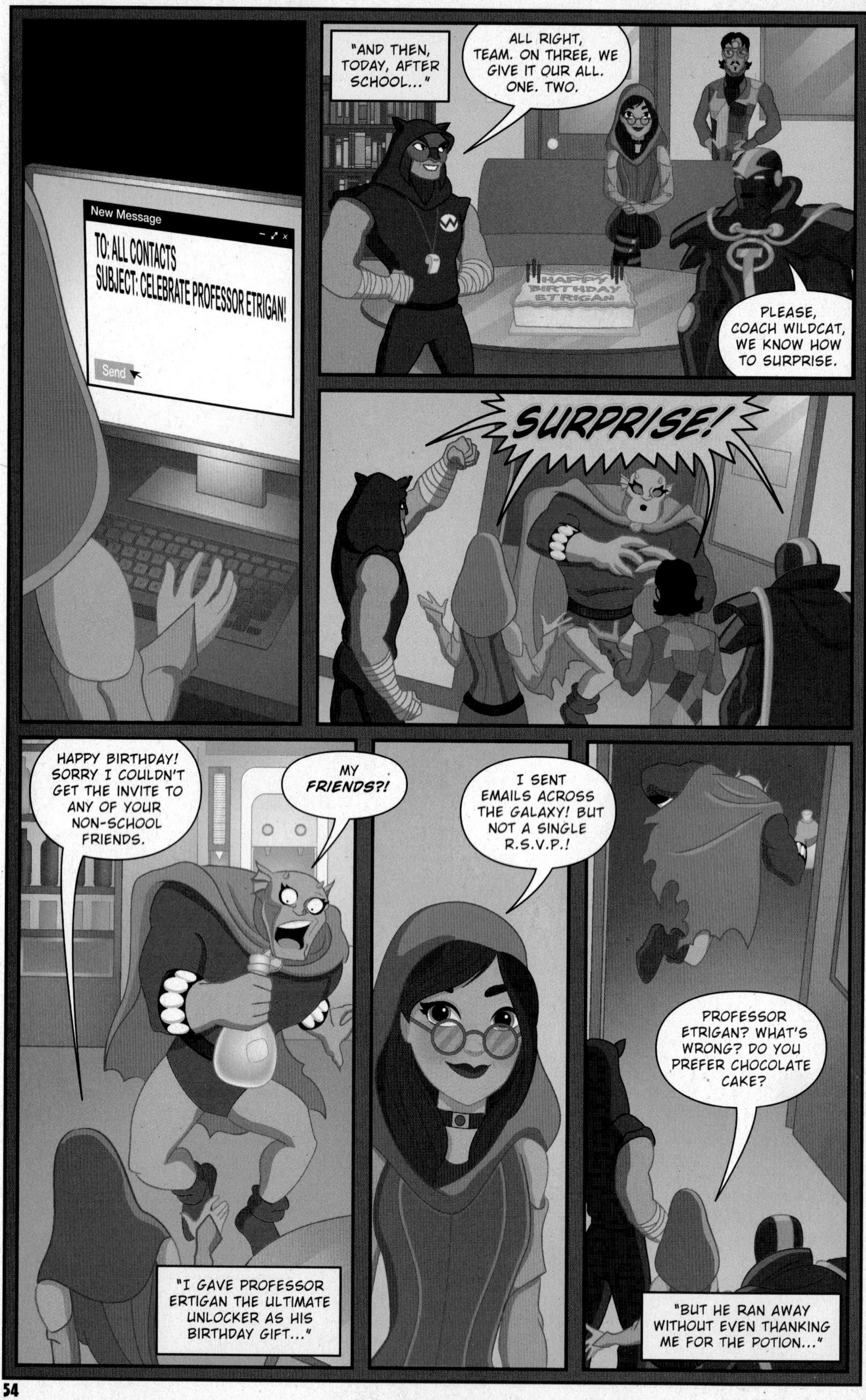
New Message
TO: ALL CONTACTS
SUBJECT: CELEBRATE PROFESSOR ETRIGAN!
Send
"AND THEN, TODAY, AFTER SCHOOL..."
ALL RIGHT, TEAM. ON THREE, WE GIVE IT OUR ALL. ONE. TWO.
HAPPY BIRTHDAY ETRIGAN
PLEASE, COACH WILDCAT, WE KNOW HOW TO SURPRISE.
SURPRISE!
HAPPY BIRTHDAY! SORRY I COULDN'T GET THE INVITE TO ANY OF YOUR NON-SCHOOL FRIENDS.
MY FRIENDS?!
"I GAVE PROFESSOR ERTIGAN THE ULTIMATE UNLOCKER AS HIS BIRTHDAY GIFT..."
I SENT EMAILS ACROSS THE GALAXY! BUT NOT A SINGLE R.S.V.P.!
PROFESSOR ETRIGAN? WHAT'S WRONG? DO YOU PREFER CHOCOLATE CAKE?
"BUT HE RAN AWAY WITHOUT EVEN THANKING ME FOR THE POTION..."

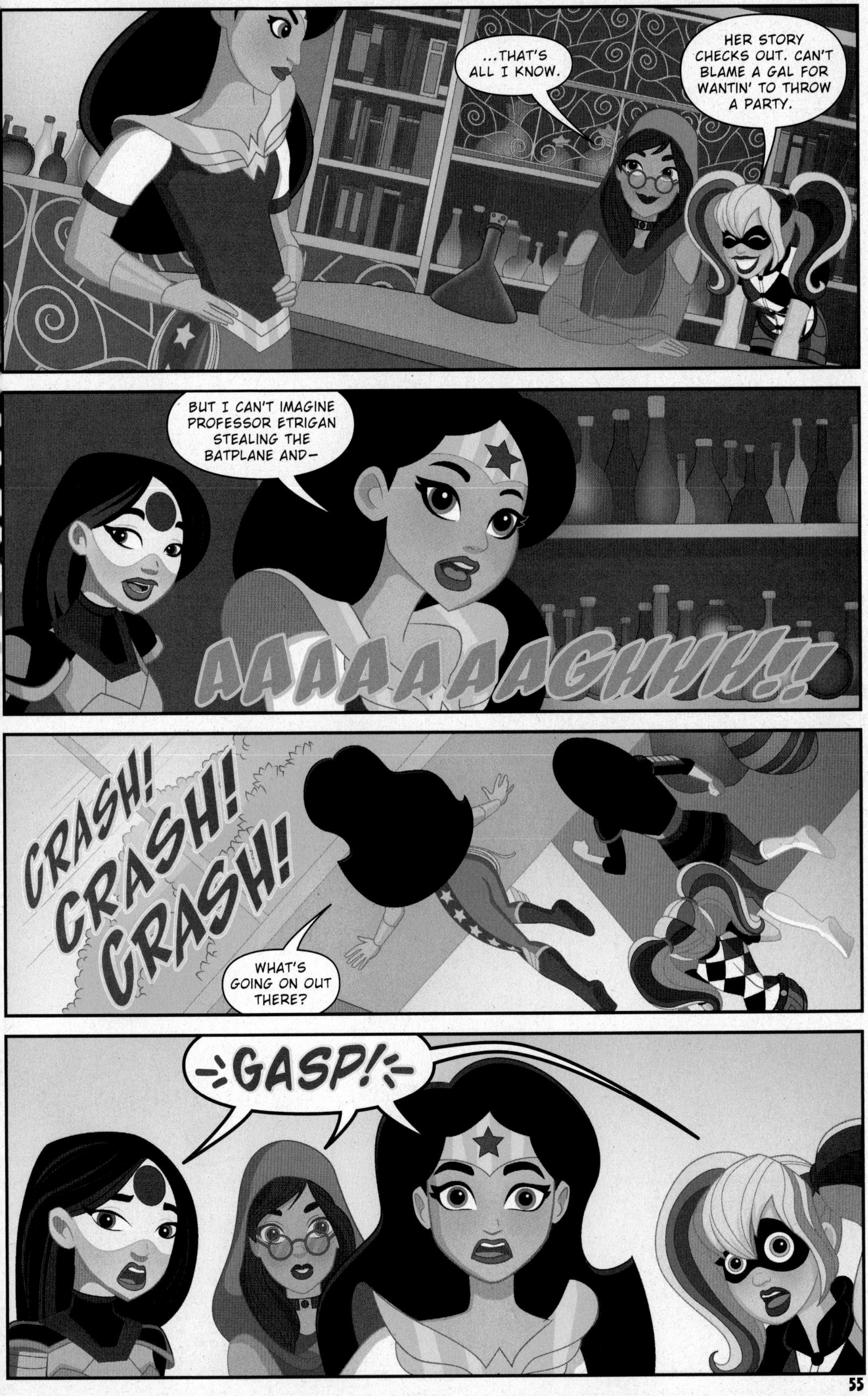
...THAT'S ALL I KNOW.
HER STORY CHECKS OUT. CAN'T BLAME A GAL FOR WANTIN' TO THROW A PARTY.
BUT I CAN'T IMAGINE PROFESSOR ETRIGAN STEALING THE BATPLANE AND—
AAAAAAAAGHHH!!
CRASH! CRASH! CRASH!
WHAT'S GOING ON OUT THERE?
GASP!

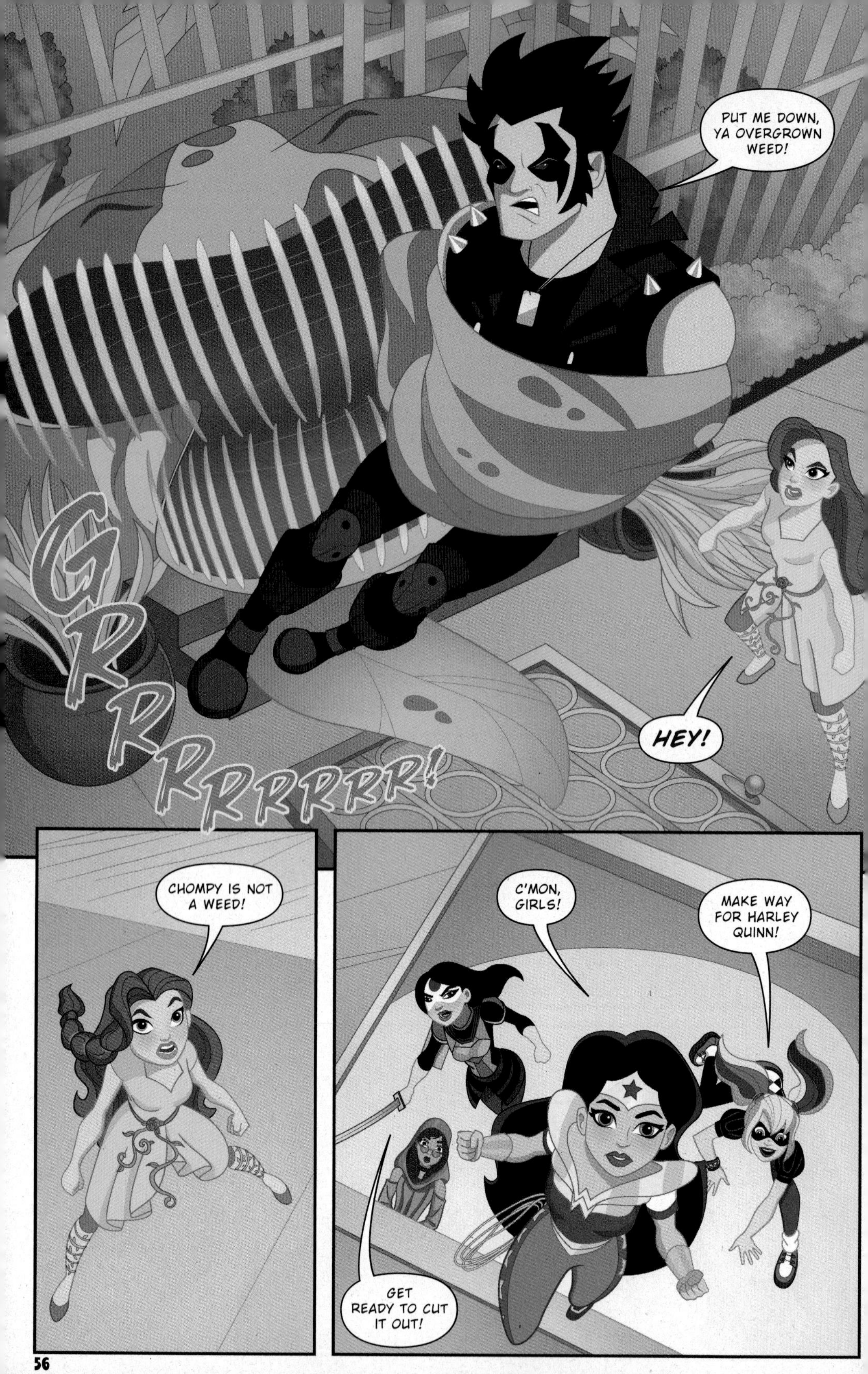
PUT ME DOWN, YA OVERGROWN WEED!
GRRRRRRRRR!
HEY!
CHOMPY IS NOT A WEED!
C'MON, GIRLS!
MAKE WAY FOR HARLEY QUINN!
GET READY TO CUT IT OUT!

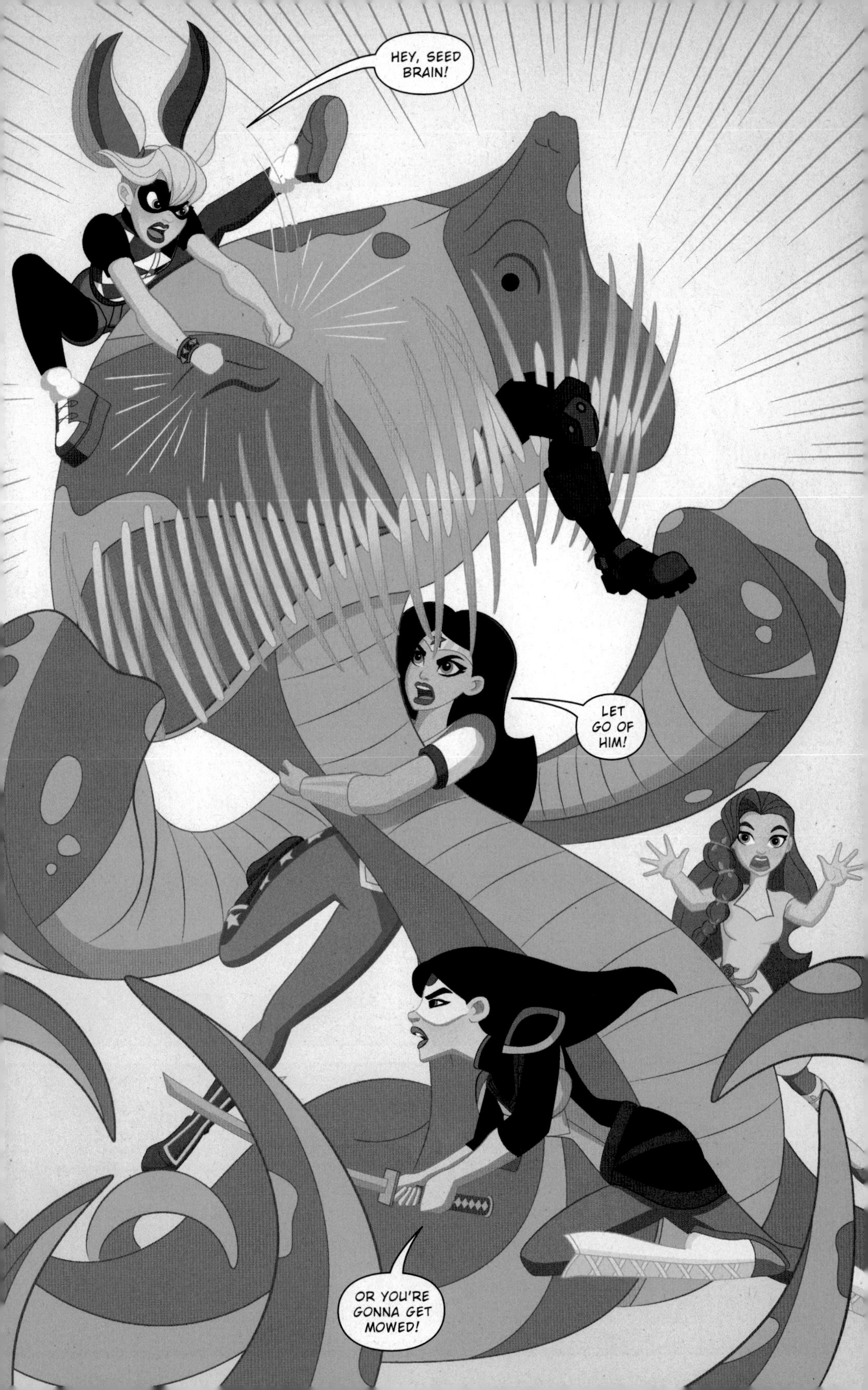
HEY, SEED BRAIN!
LET GO OF HIM!
OR YOU'RE GONNA GET MOWED!

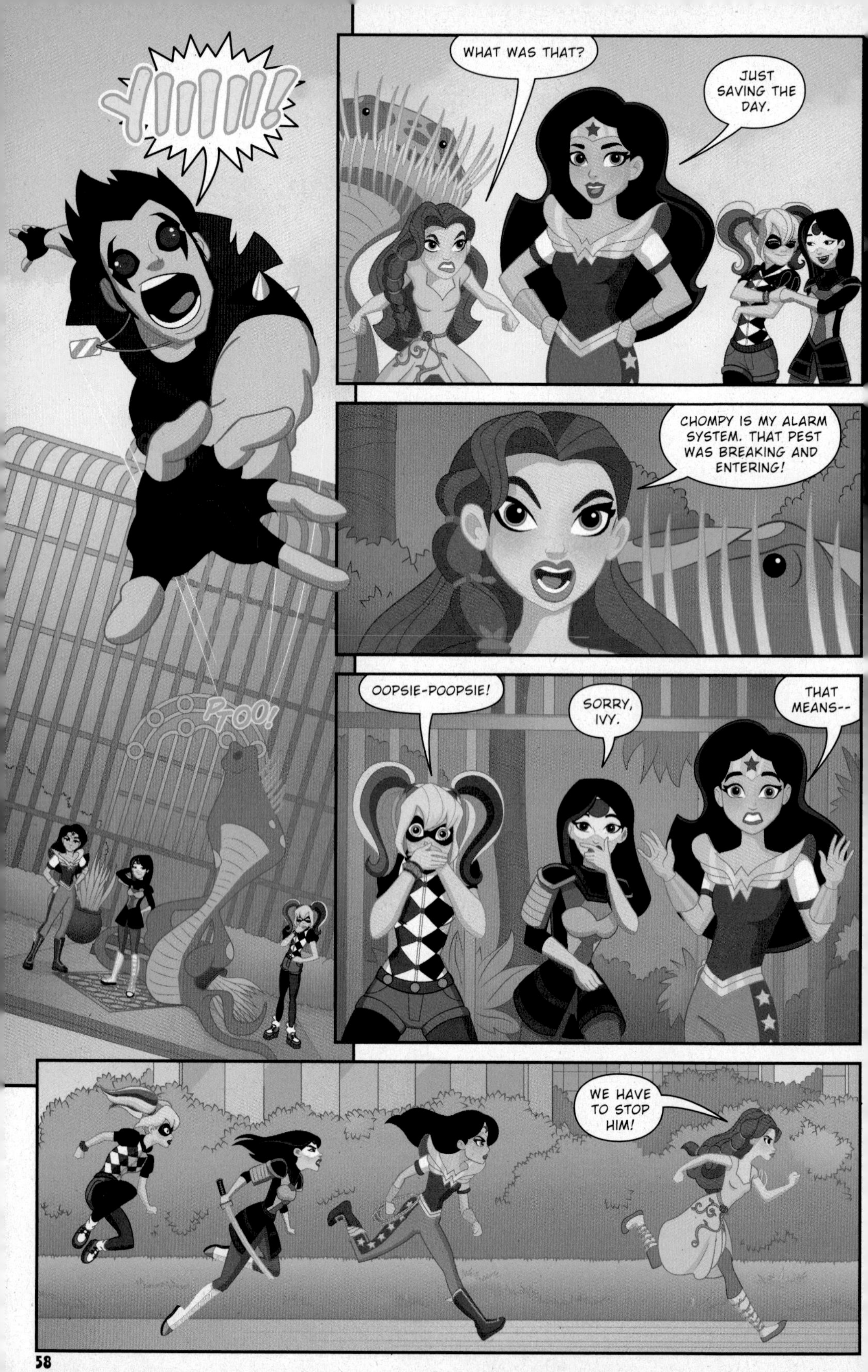
YIIIIII!
PTOO!
WHAT WAS THAT?
JUST SAVING THE DAY.
CHOMPY IS MY ALARM SYSTEM. THAT PEST WAS BREAKING AND ENTERING!
OOPSIE-POOPSIE!
SORRY, IVY.
THAT MEANS--
WE HAVE TO STOP HIM!

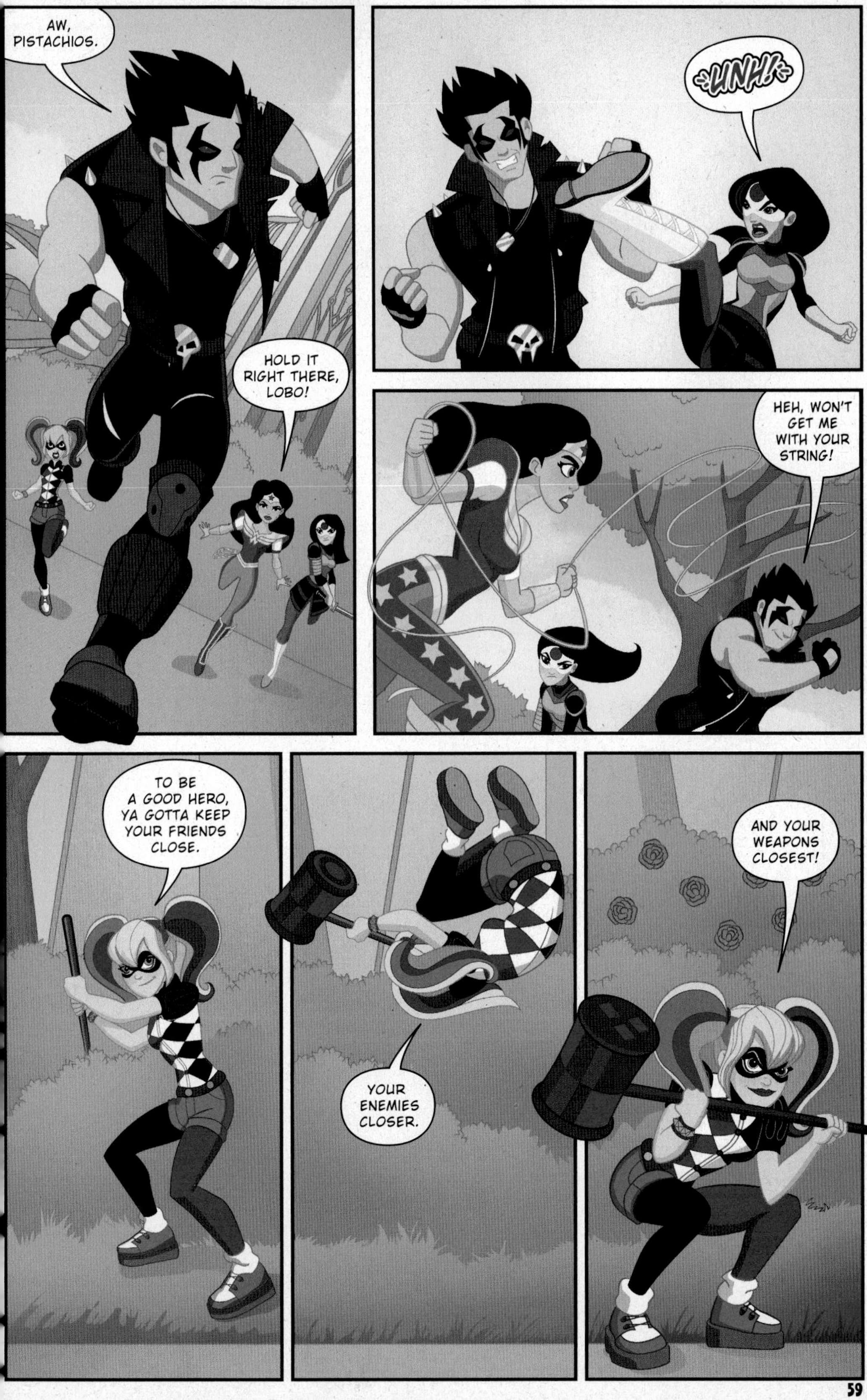
AW, PISTACHIOS.
HOLD IT RIGHT THERE, LOBO!
UNH!
HEH, WON'T GET ME WITH YOUR STRING!
TO BE A GOOD HERO, YA GOTTA KEEP YOUR FRIENDS CLOSE.
YOUR ENEMIES CLOSER.
AND YOUR WEAPONS CLOSEST!

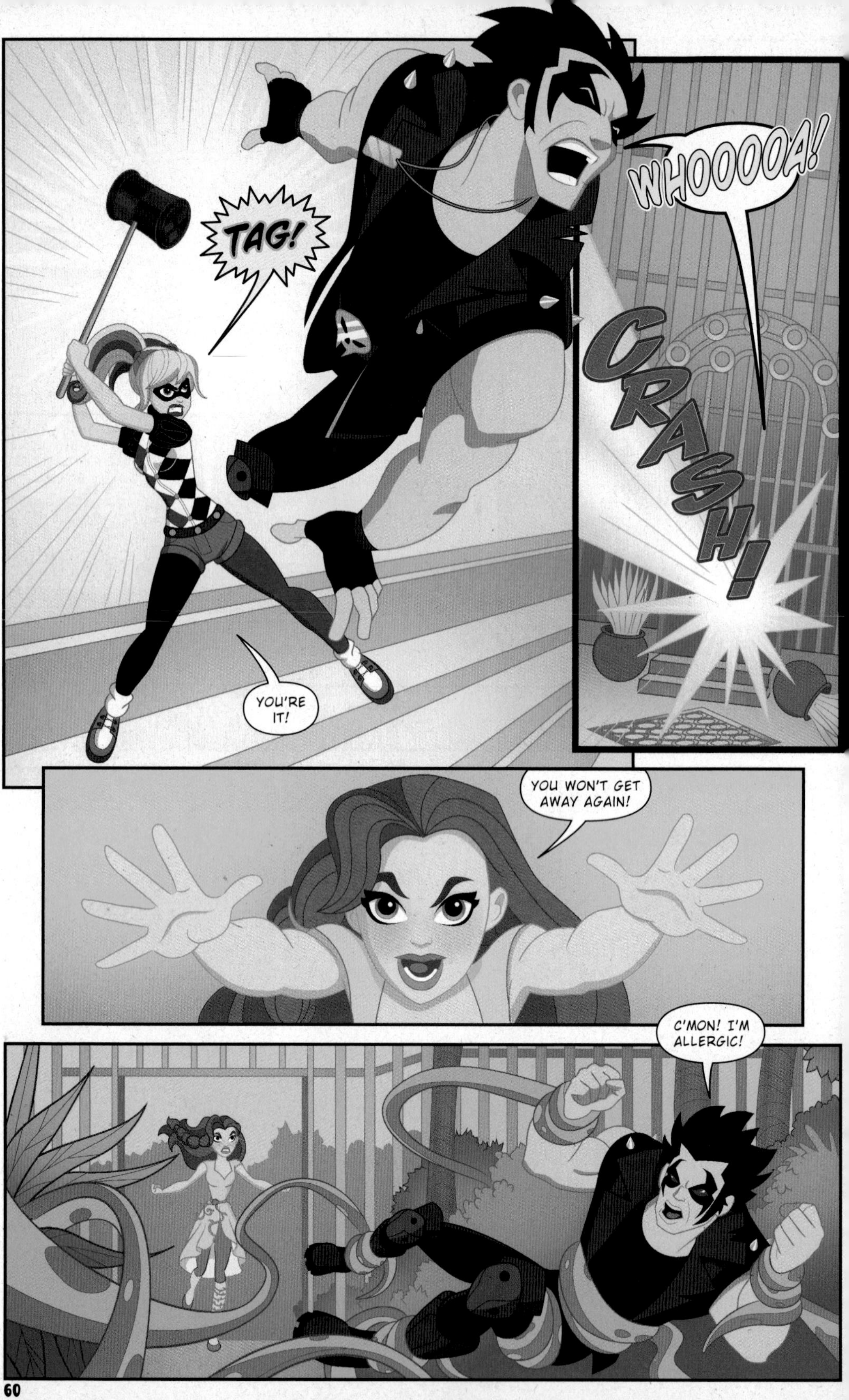
TAG!
YOU'RE IT!
WHOOOOA!
CRASH!
YOU WON'T GET AWAY AGAIN!
C'MON! I'M ALLERGIC!

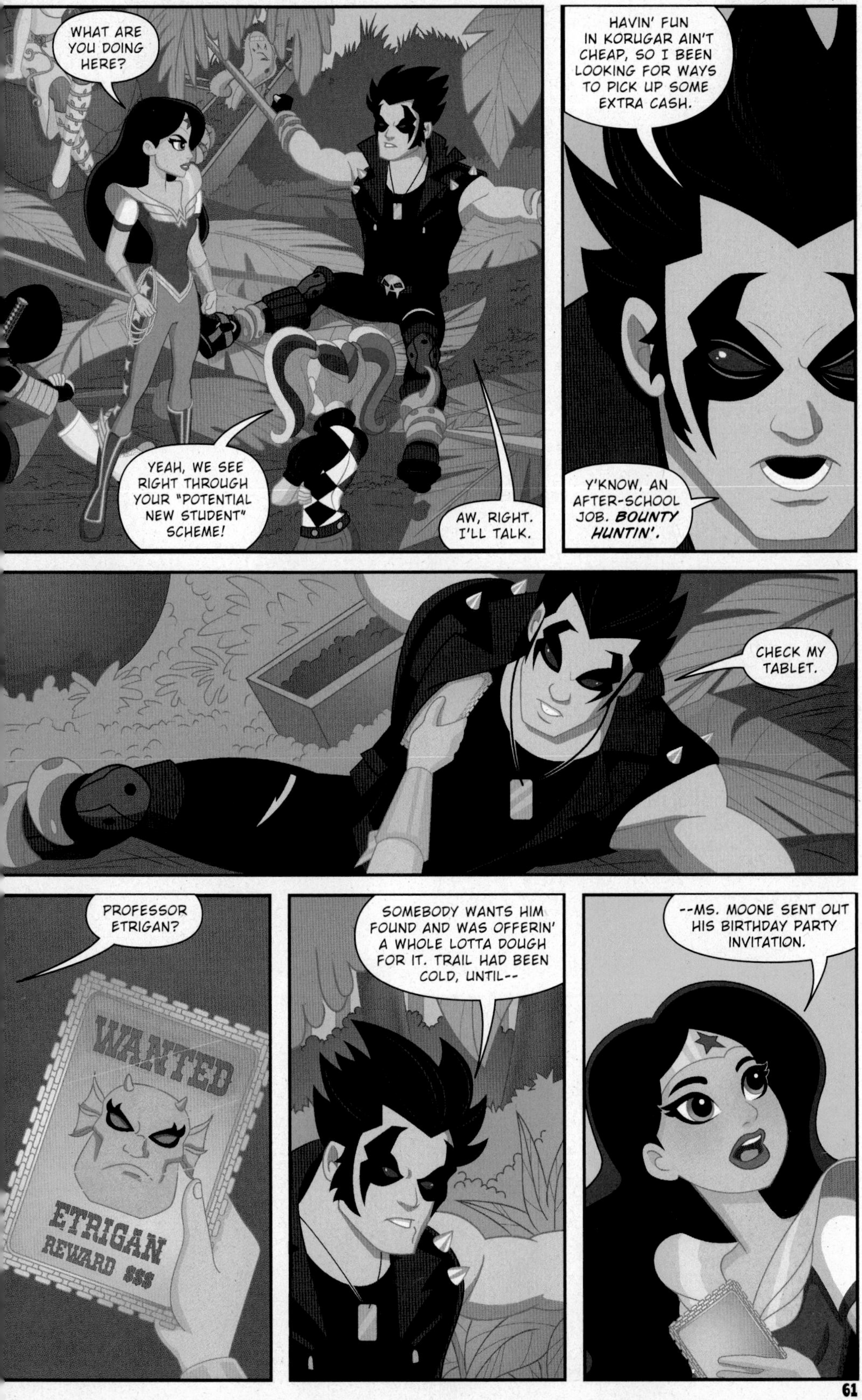
WHAT ARE YOU DOING HERE?
YEAH, WE SEE RIGHT THROUGH YOUR "POTENTIAL NEW STUDENT" SCHEME!
AW, RIGHT. I'LL TALK.
HAVIN' FUN IN KORUGAR AIN'T CHEAP, SO I BEEN LOOKING FOR WAYS TO PICK UP SOME EXTRA CASH.
Y'KNOW, AN AFTER-SCHOOL JOB. ***BOUNTY HUNTIN'.***
CHECK MY TABLET.
PROFESSOR ETRIGAN?
WANTED
ETRIGAN
REWARD $$$
SOMEBODY WANTS HIM FOUND AND WAS OFFERIN' A WHOLE LOTTA DOUGH FOR IT. TRAIL HAD BEEN COLD, UNTIL--
--MS. MOONE SENT OUT HIS BIRTHDAY PARTY INVITATION.

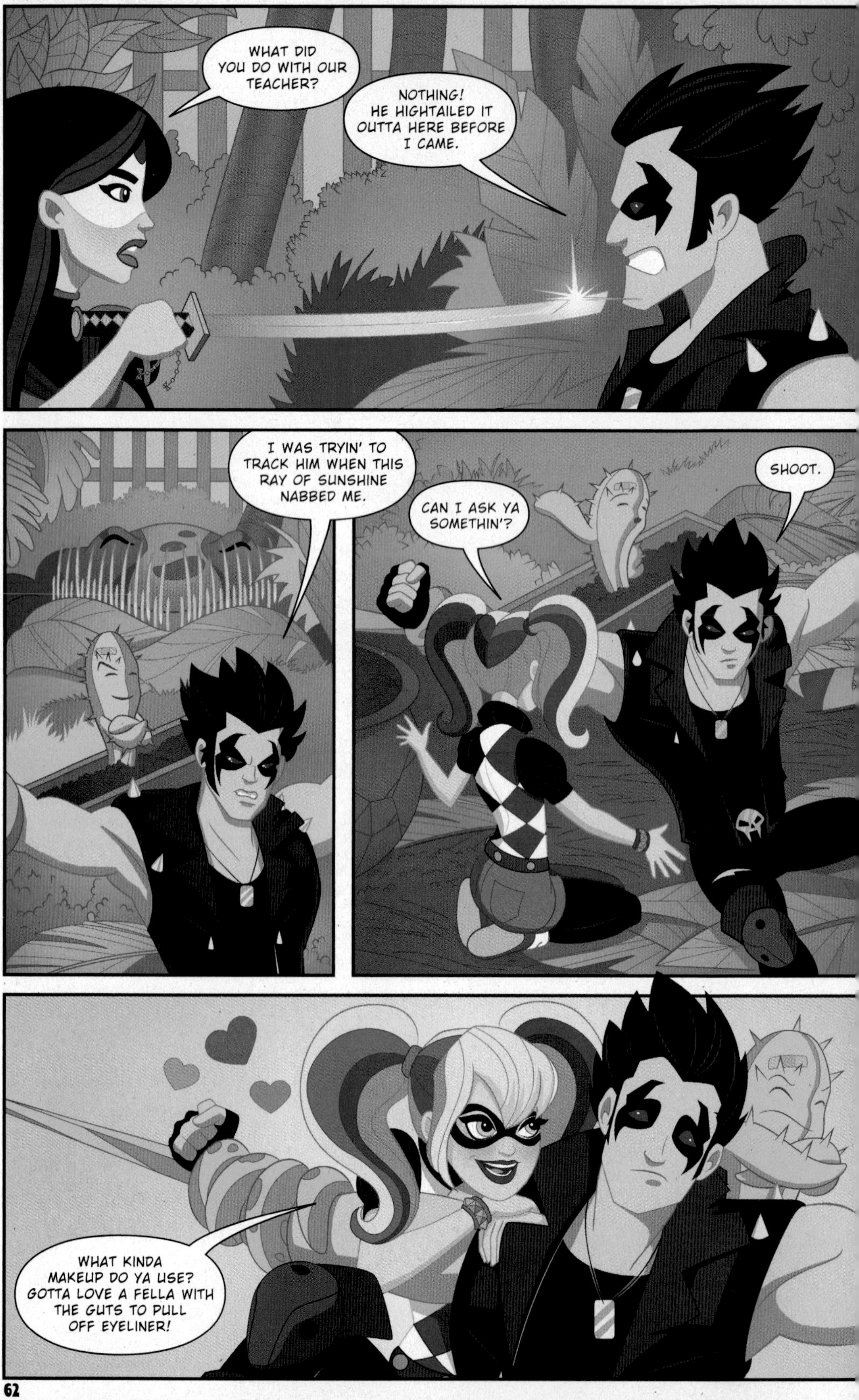
WHAT DID YOU DO WITH OUR TEACHER?
NOTHING! HE HIGHTAILED IT OUTTA HERE BEFORE I CAME.
I WAS TRYIN' TO TRACK HIM WHEN THIS RAY OF SUNSHINE NABBED ME.
CAN I ASK YA SOMETHIN'?
SHOOT.
WHAT KINDA MAKEUP DO YA USE? GOTTA LOVE A FELLA WITH THE GUTS TO PULL OFF EYELINER!

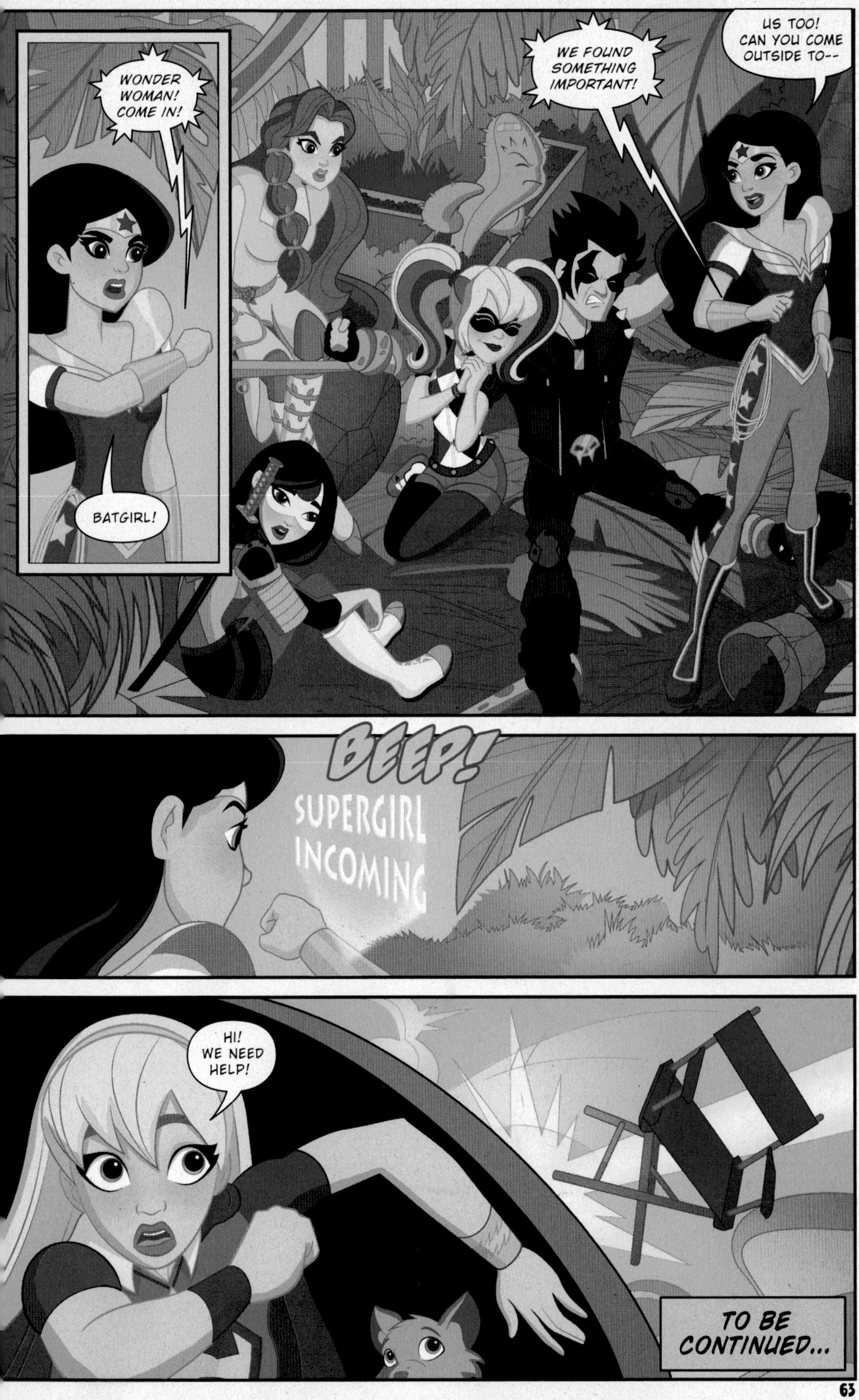
WONDER WOMAN! COME IN!
BATGIRL!
WE FOUND SOMETHING IMPORTANT!
US TOO! CAN YOU COME OUTSIDE TO--
BEEP!
SUPERGIRL INCOMING
HI! WE NEED HELP!
TO BE CONTINUED...

CHAPTER FOUR
THE SIRENS

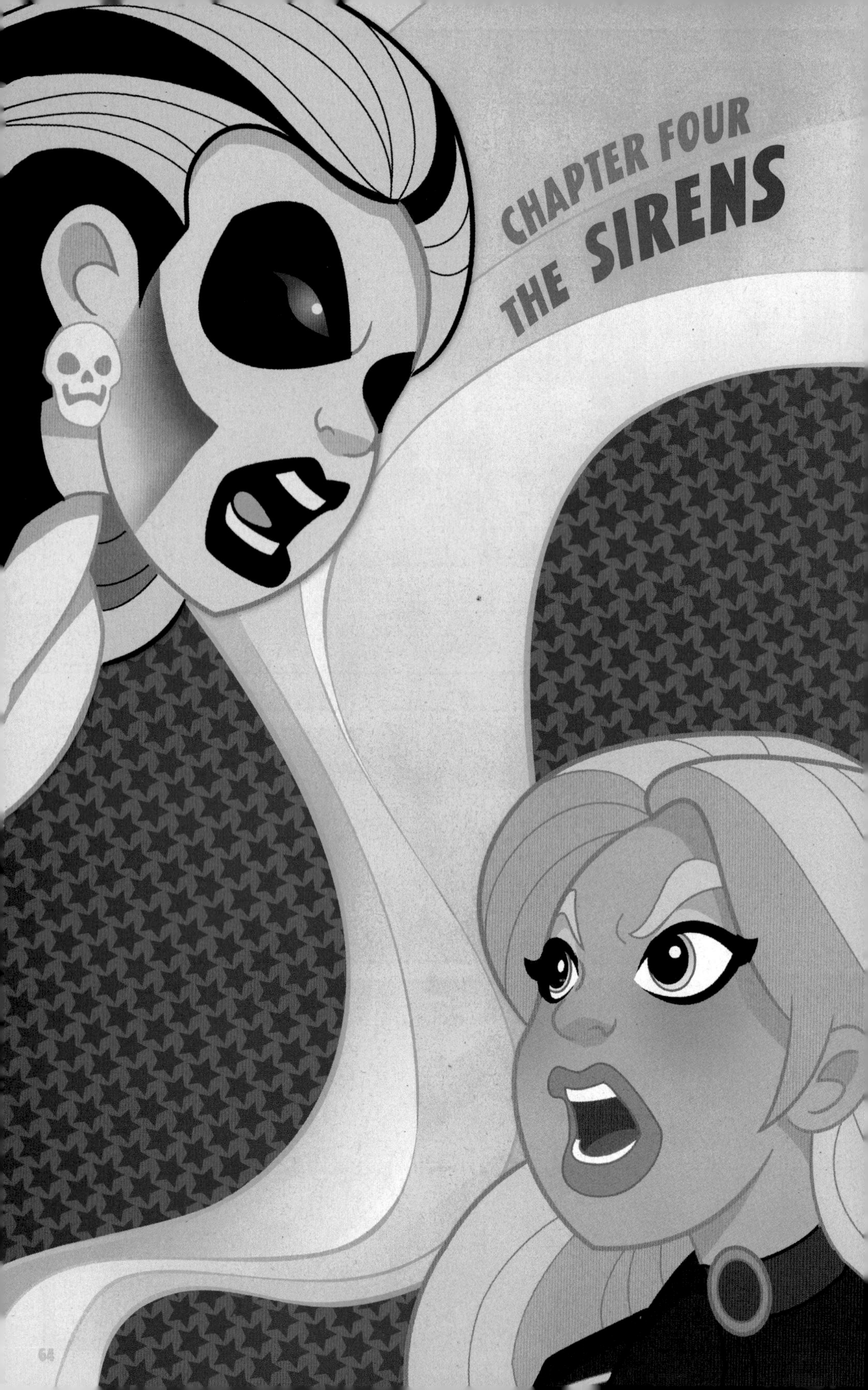

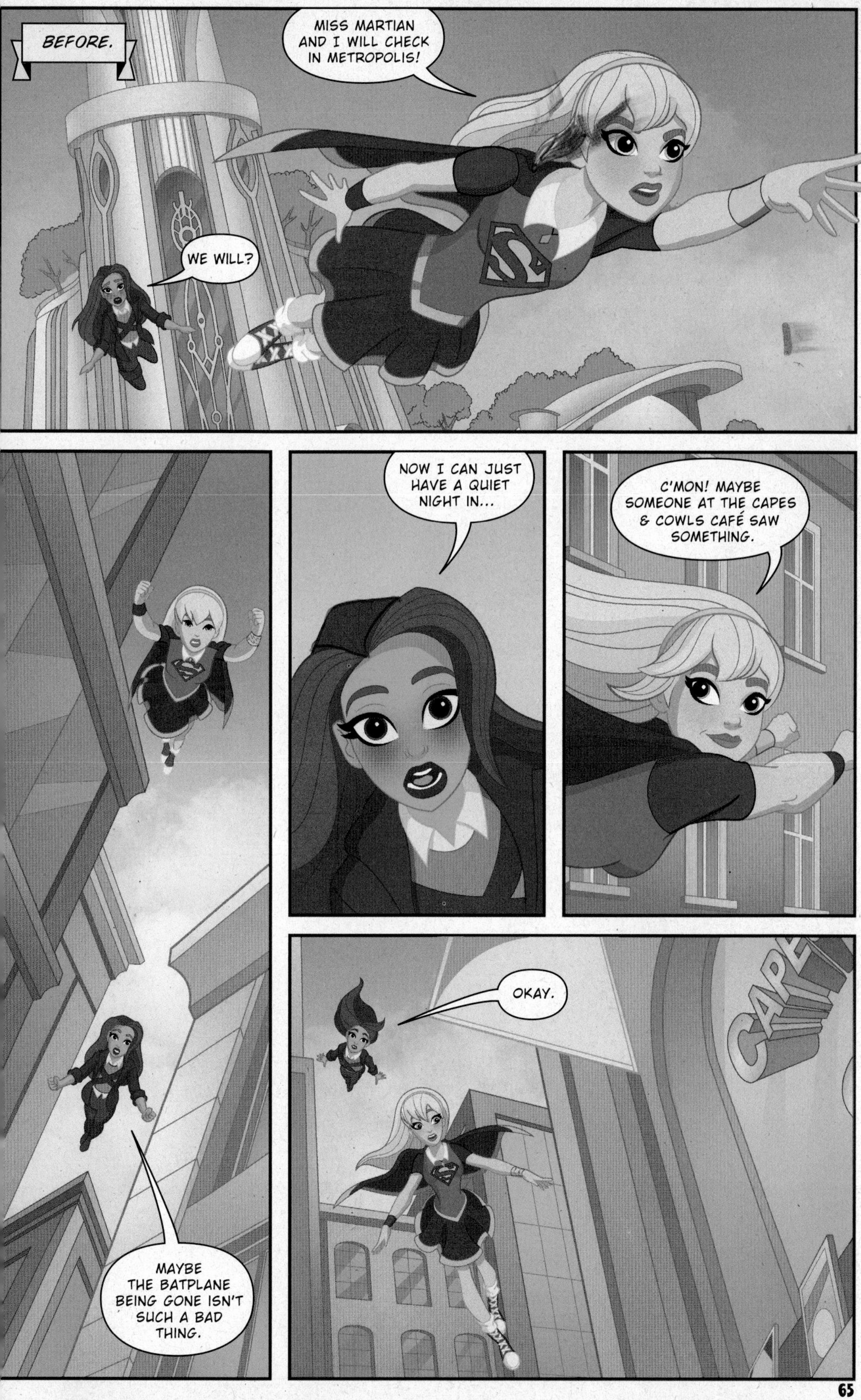
BEFORE.
MISS MARTIAN AND I WILL CHECK IN METROPOLIS!
WE WILL?
NOW I CAN JUST HAVE A QUIET NIGHT IN...
C'MON! MAYBE SOMEONE AT THE CAPES & COWLS CAFÉ SAW SOMETHING.
MAYBE THE BATPLANE BEING GONE ISN'T SUCH A BAD THING.
OKAY.

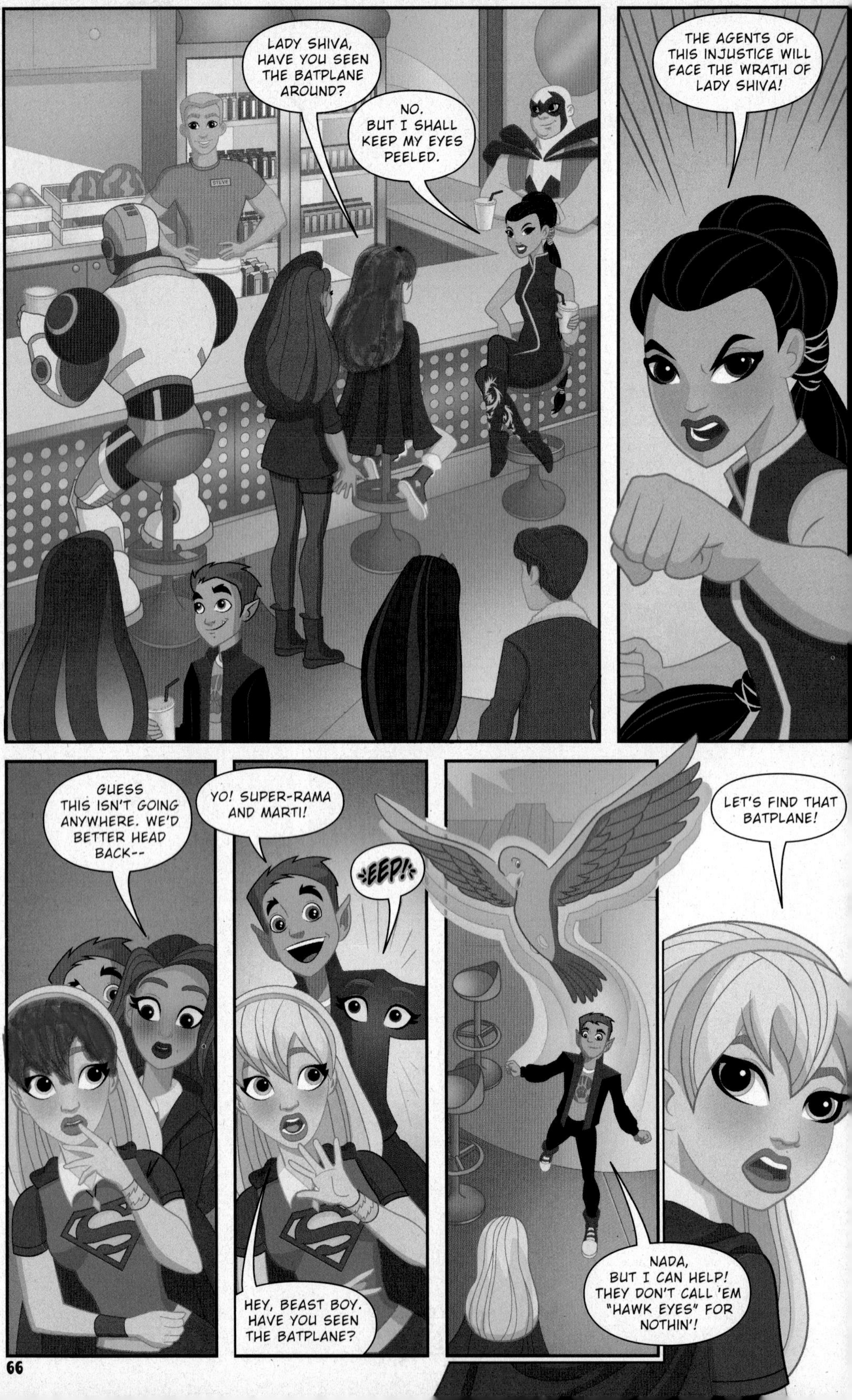
LADY SHIVA, HAVE YOU SEEN THE BATPLANE AROUND?
NO. BUT I SHALL KEEP MY EYES PEELED.
STEVE
THE AGENTS OF THIS INJUSTICE WILL FACE THE WRATH OF LADY SHIVA!
GUESS THIS ISN'T GOING ANYWHERE. WE'D BETTER HEAD BACK--
YO! SUPER-RAMA AND MARTI!
EEP!
HEY, BEAST BOY. HAVE YOU SEEN THE BATPLANE?
NADA, BUT I CAN HELP! THEY DON'T CALL 'EM "HAWK EYES" FOR NOTHIN'!
LET'S FIND THAT BATPLANE!

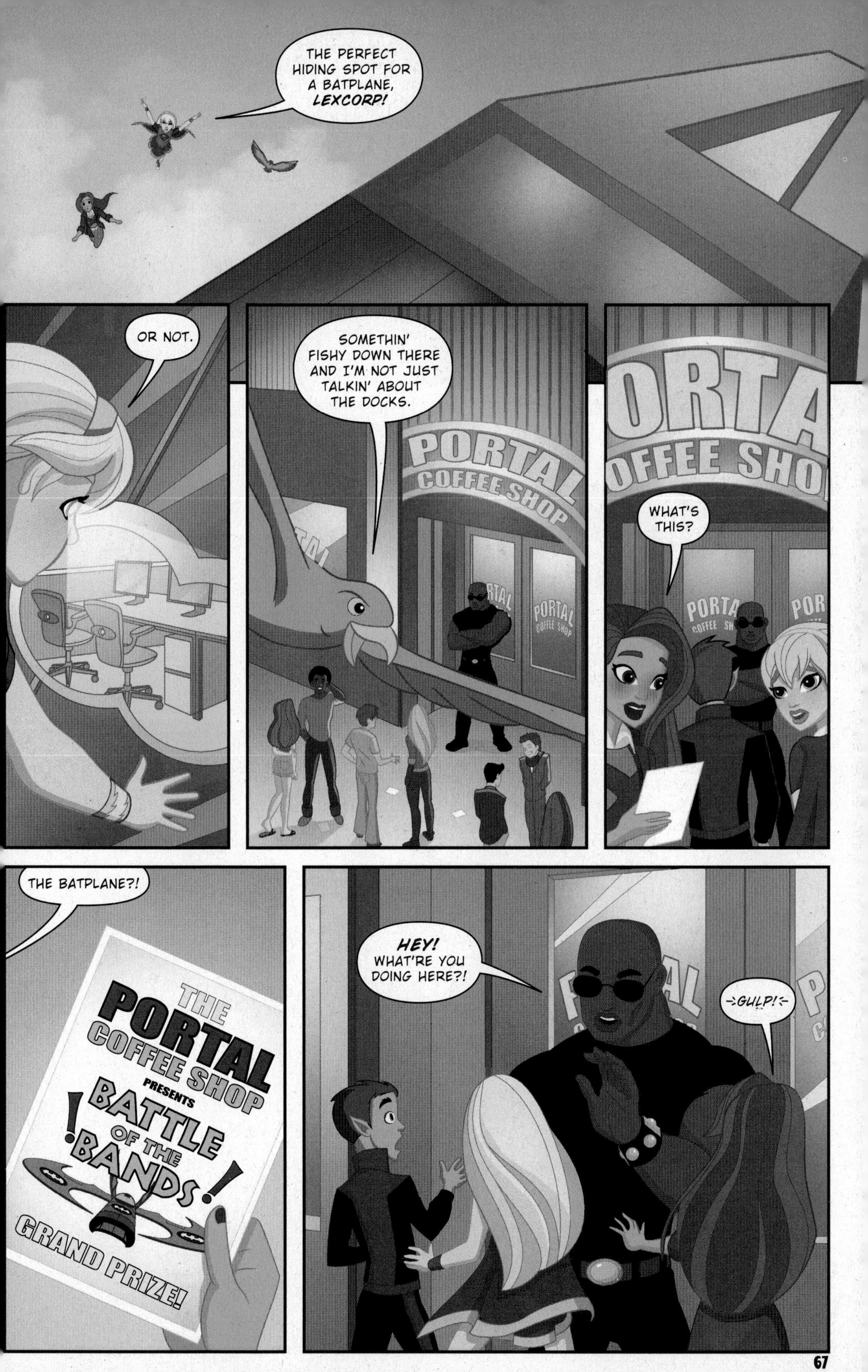
THE PERFECT HIDING SPOT FOR A BATPLANE, *LEXCORP!*
OR NOT.
SOMETHIN' FISHY DOWN THERE AND I'M NOT JUST TALKIN' ABOUT THE DOCKS.
PORTAL COFFEE SHOP
WHAT'S THIS?
THE BATPLANE?!
THE PORTAL COFFEE SHOP PRESENTS BATTLE OF THE BANDS! GRAND PRIZE!
HEY! WHAT'RE YOU DOING HERE?!
GULP!

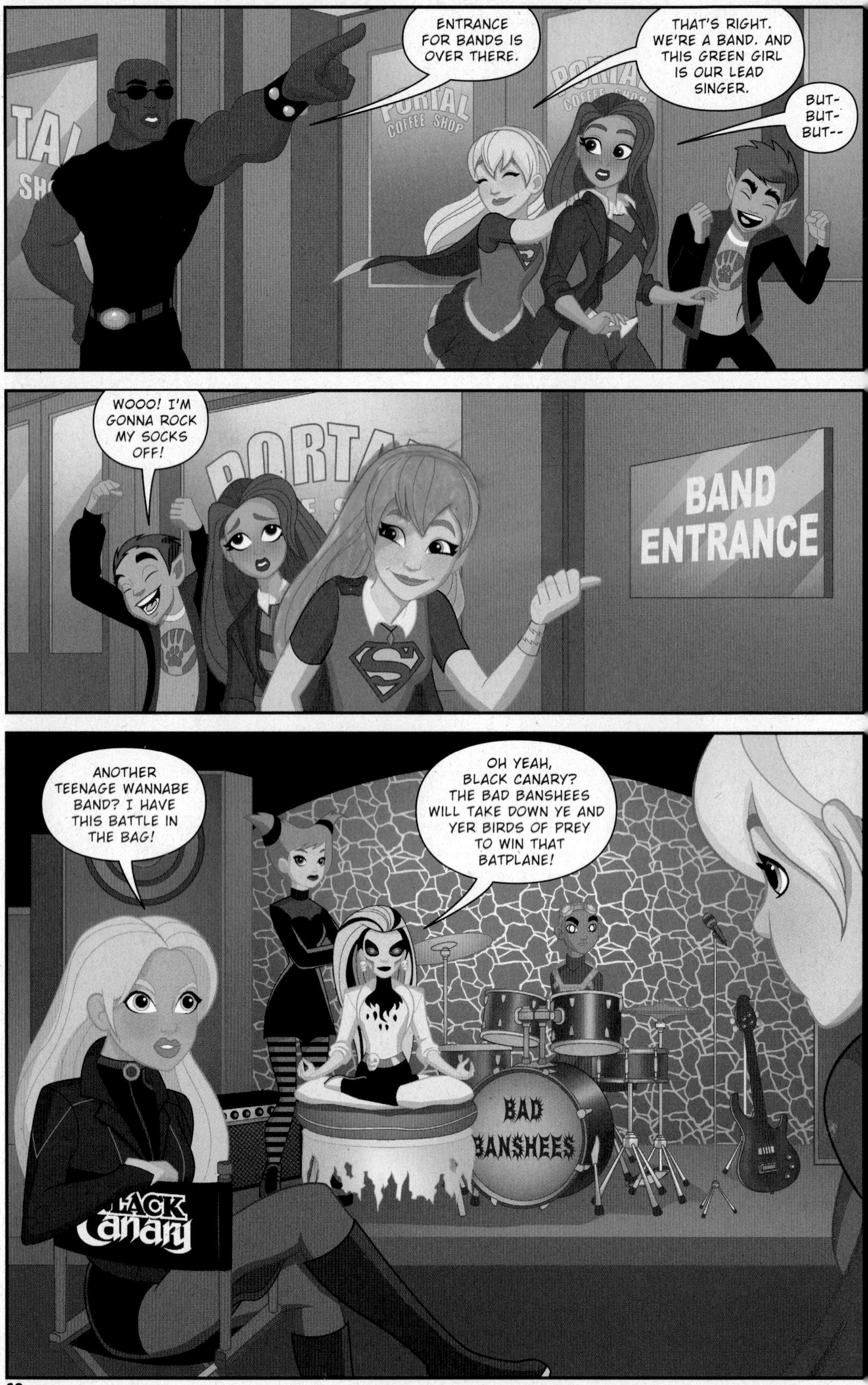
ENTRANCE FOR BANDS IS OVER THERE.
THAT'S RIGHT. WE'RE A BAND. AND THIS GREEN GIRL IS OUR LEAD SINGER.
BUT-BUT-BUT--
PORTAL COFFEE SHOP
WOOO! I'M GONNA ROCK MY SOCKS OFF!
BAND ENTRANCE
ANOTHER TEENAGE WANNABE BAND? I HAVE THIS BATTLE IN THE BAG!
OH YEAH, BLACK CANARY? THE BAD BANSHEES WILL TAKE DOWN YE AND YER BIRDS OF PREY TO WIN THAT BATPLANE!
BAD BANSHEES
Canary

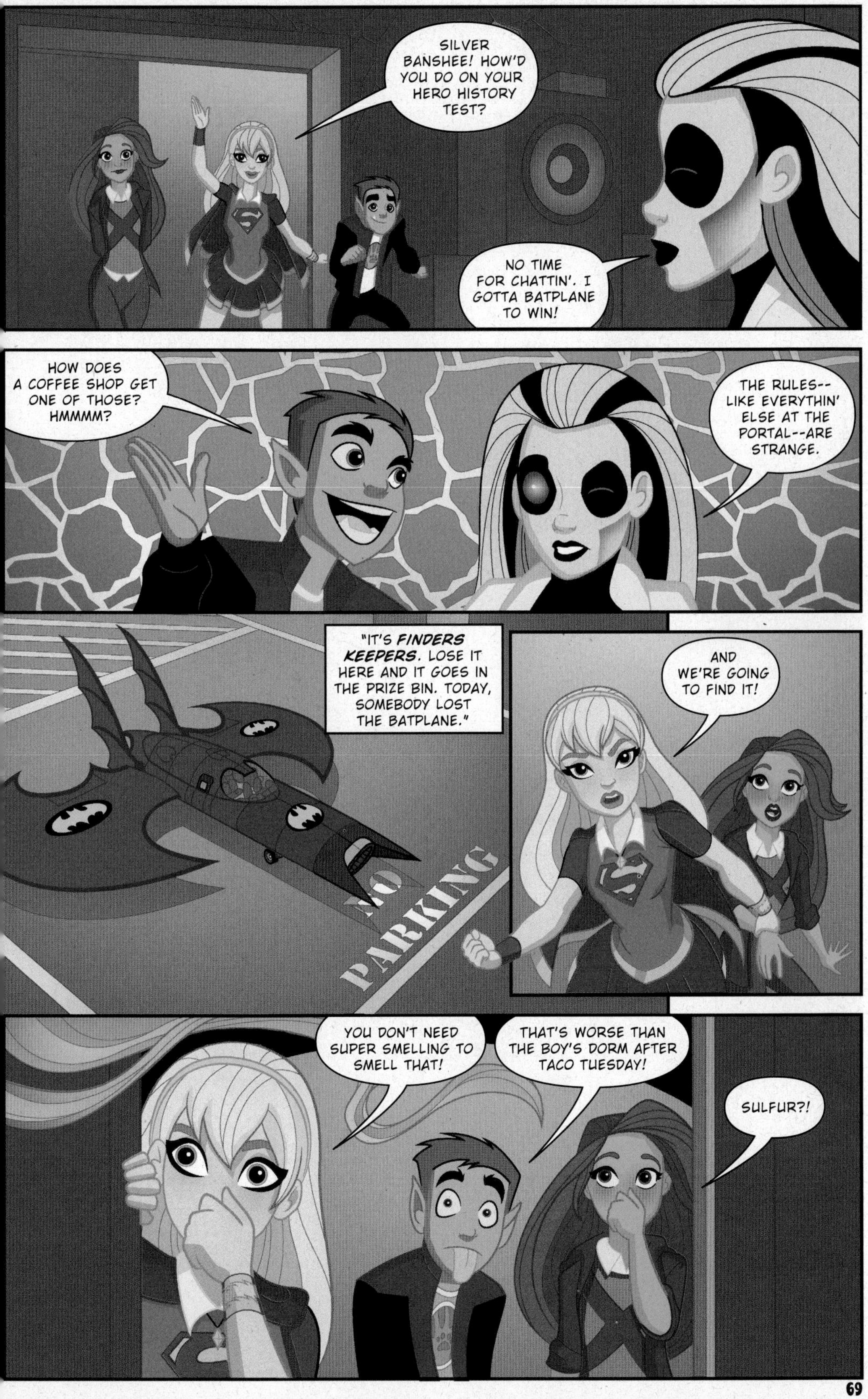
SILVER BANSHEE! HOW'D YOU DO ON YOUR HERO HISTORY TEST?
NO TIME FOR CHATTIN'. I GOTTA BATPLANE TO WIN!
HOW DOES A COFFEE SHOP GET ONE OF THOSE? HMMMM?
THE RULES-- LIKE EVERYTHIN' ELSE AT THE PORTAL--ARE STRANGE.
"IT'S FINDERS KEEPERS. LOSE IT HERE AND IT GOES IN THE PRIZE BIN. TODAY, SOMEBODY LOST THE BATPLANE."
NO PARKING
AND WE'RE GOING TO FIND IT!
YOU DON'T NEED SUPER SMELLING TO SMELL THAT!
THAT'S WORSE THAN THE BOY'S DORM AFTER TACO TUESDAY!
SULFUR?!

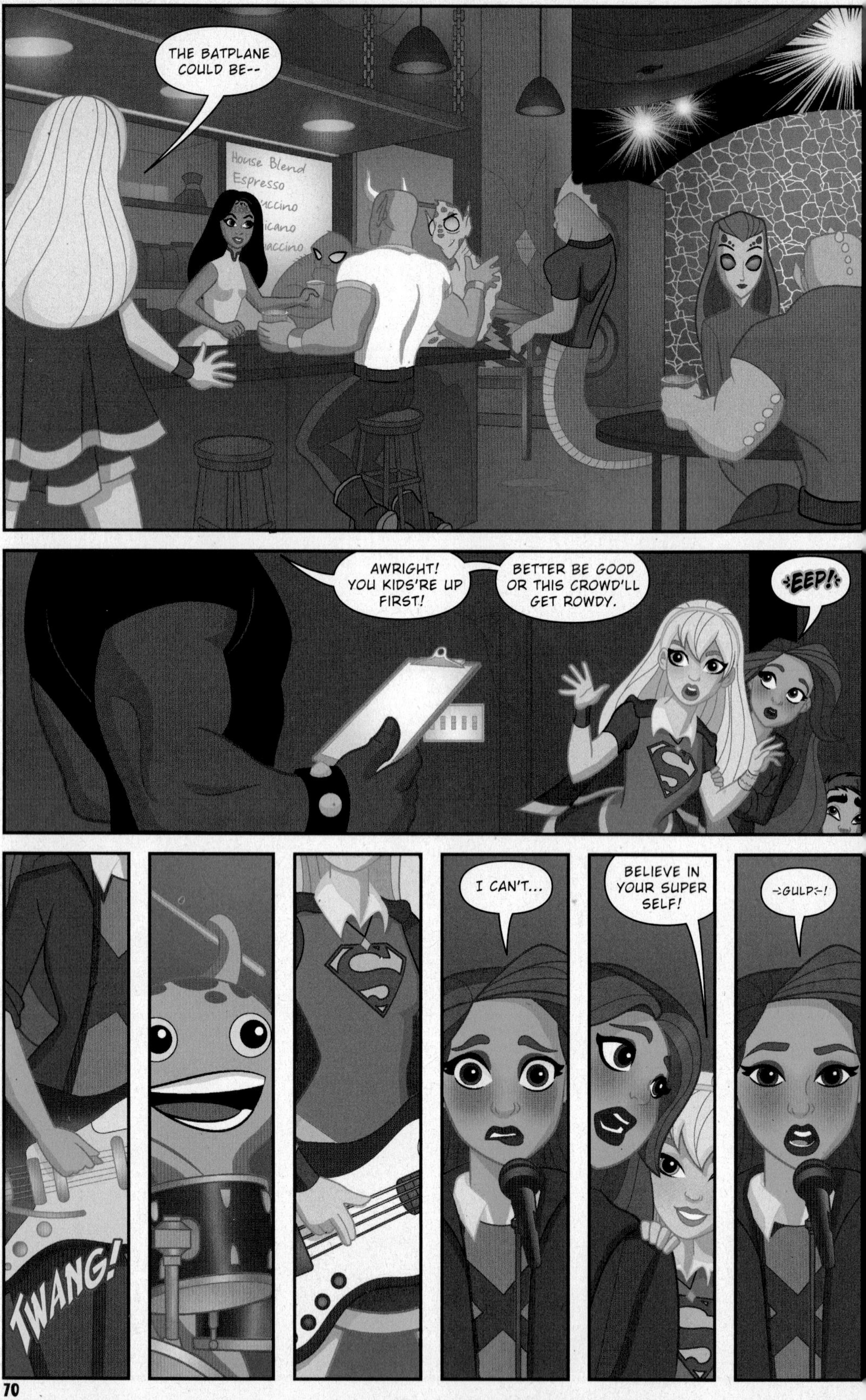
THE BATPLANE COULD BE--
House Blend
Espresso
AWRIGHT! YOU KIDS'RE UP FIRST!
BETTER BE GOOD OR THIS CROWD'LL GET ROWDY.
EEP!
TWANG!
I CAN'T...
BELIEVE IN YOUR SUPER SELF!
GULP!

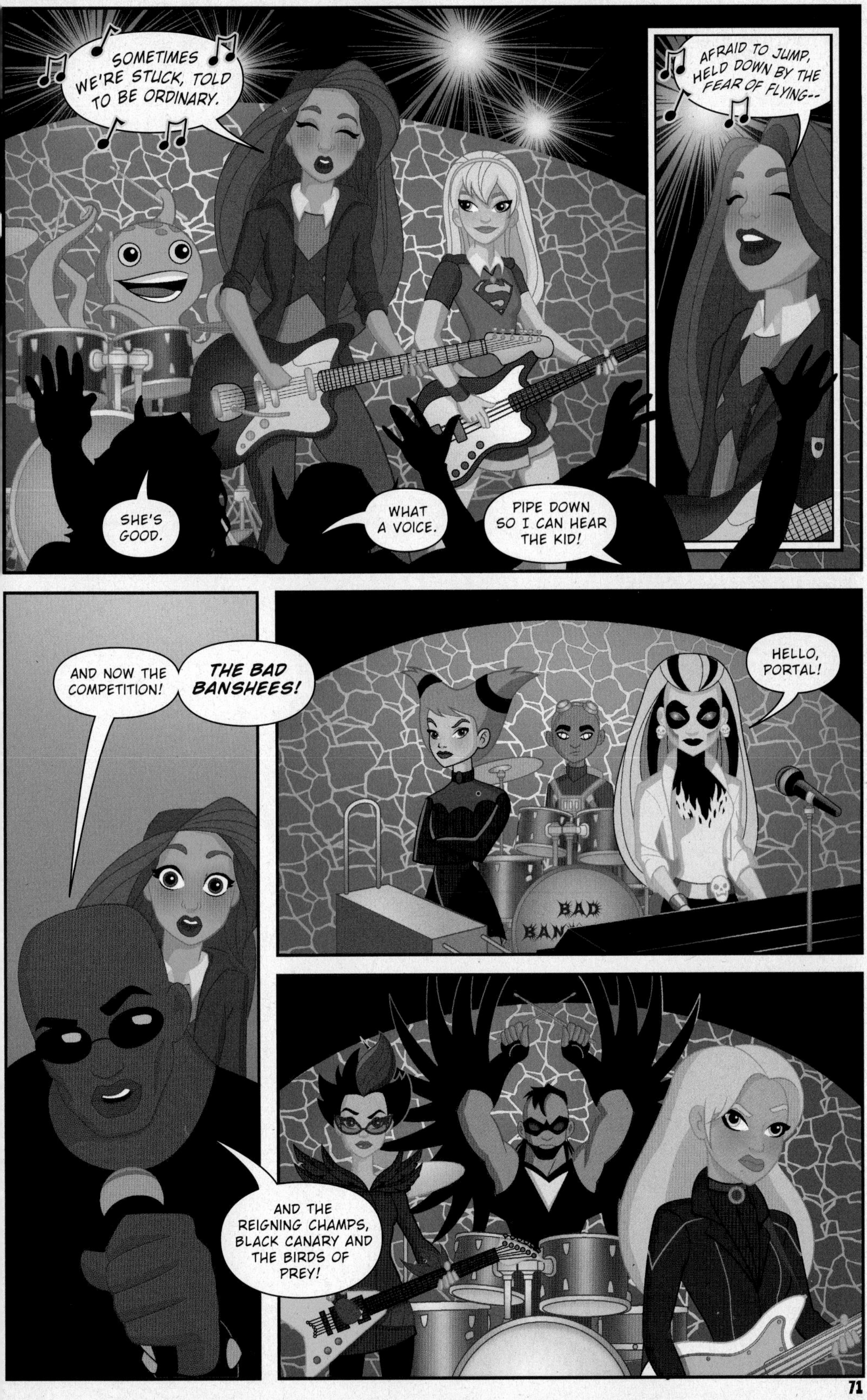
SOMETIMES WE'RE STUCK, TOLD TO BE ORDINARY.
AFRAID TO JUMP, HELD DOWN BY THE FEAR OF FLYING--
SHE'S GOOD.
WHAT A VOICE.
PIPE DOWN SO I CAN HEAR THE KID!
AND NOW THE COMPETITION!
THE BAD BANSHEES!
HELLO, PORTAL!
BAD
AND THE REIGNING CHAMPS, BLACK CANARY AND THE BIRDS OF PREY!

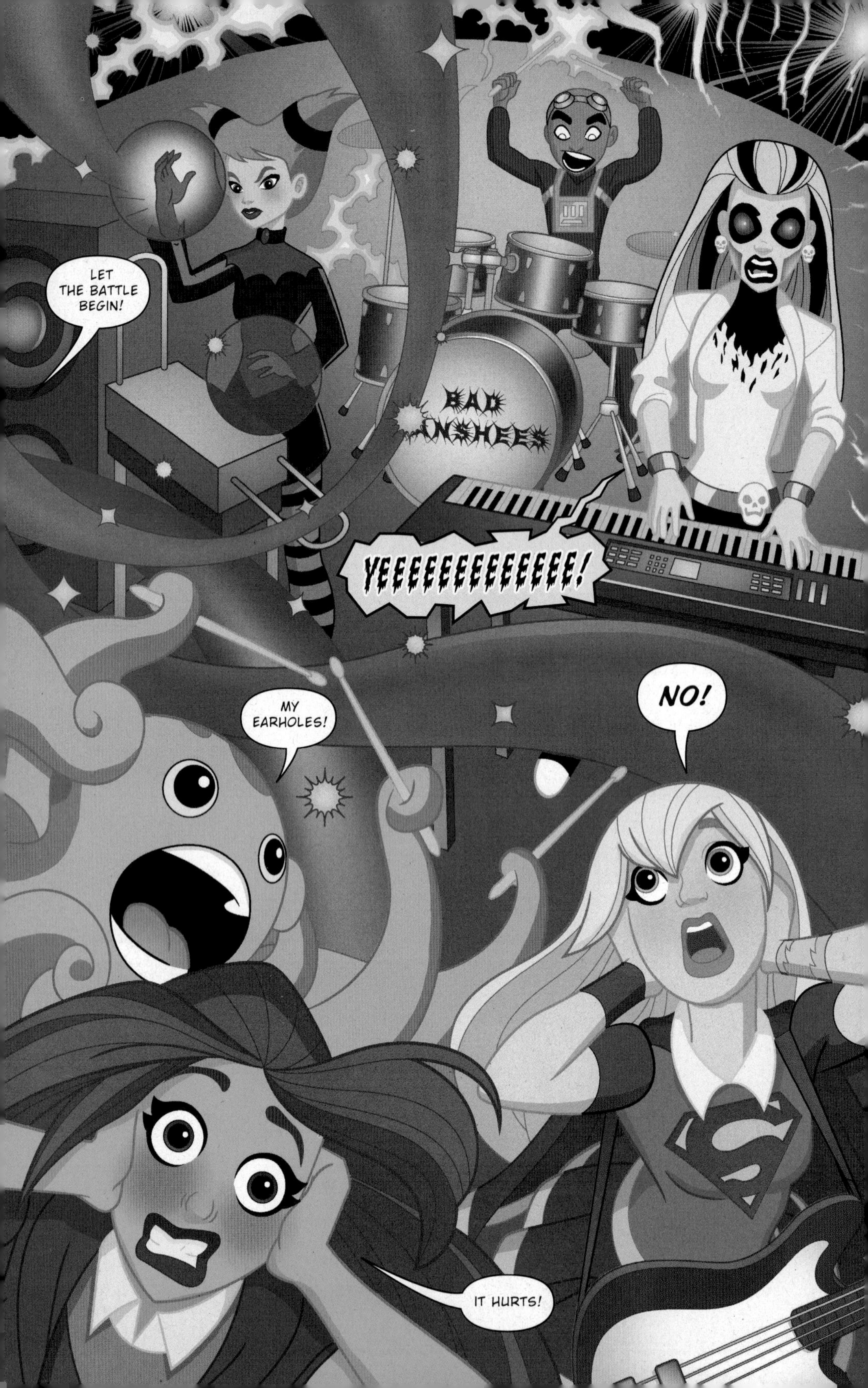
LET THE BATTLE BEGIN!
BAD BANSHEES
YEEEEEEEEEEEEEE!
MY EARHOLES!
NO!
IT HURTS!

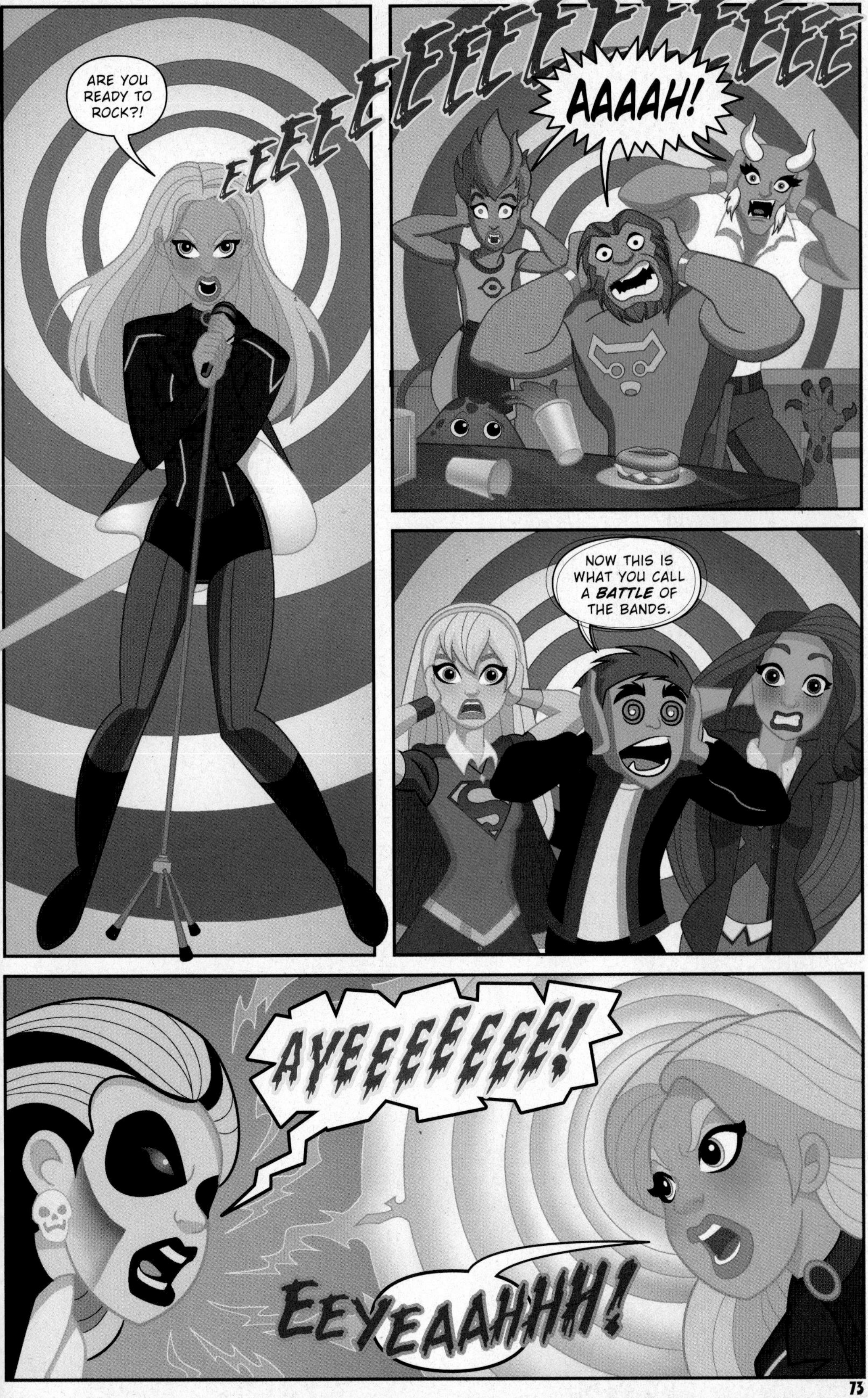
ARE YOU READY TO ROCK?!
EEEEEEEEEEEEEEEEEE
AAAAH!
NOW THIS IS WHAT YOU CALL A *BATTLE* OF THE BANDS.
AYEEEEEEEE!
EEYEAAHHH!

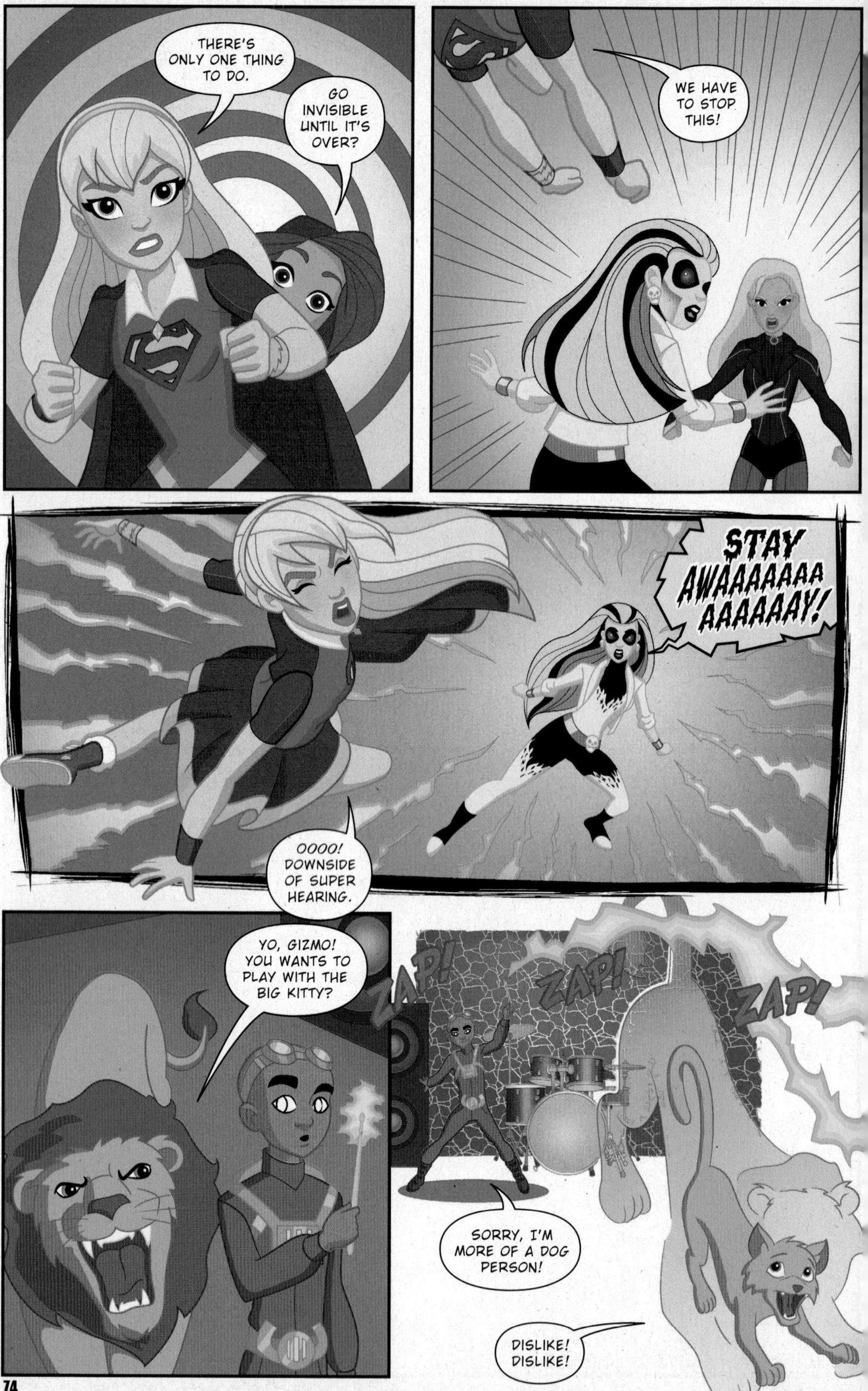
THERE'S ONLY ONE THING TO DO.
GO INVISIBLE UNTIL IT'S OVER?
WE HAVE TO STOP THIS!
STAY AWAAAAAAA AAAAAAY!
OOOO! DOWNSIDE OF SUPER HEARING.
YO, GIZMO! YOU WANTS TO PLAY WITH THE BIG KITTY?
ZAP!
ZAP!
ZAP!
SORRY, I'M MORE OF A DOG PERSON!
DISLIKE! DISLIKE!

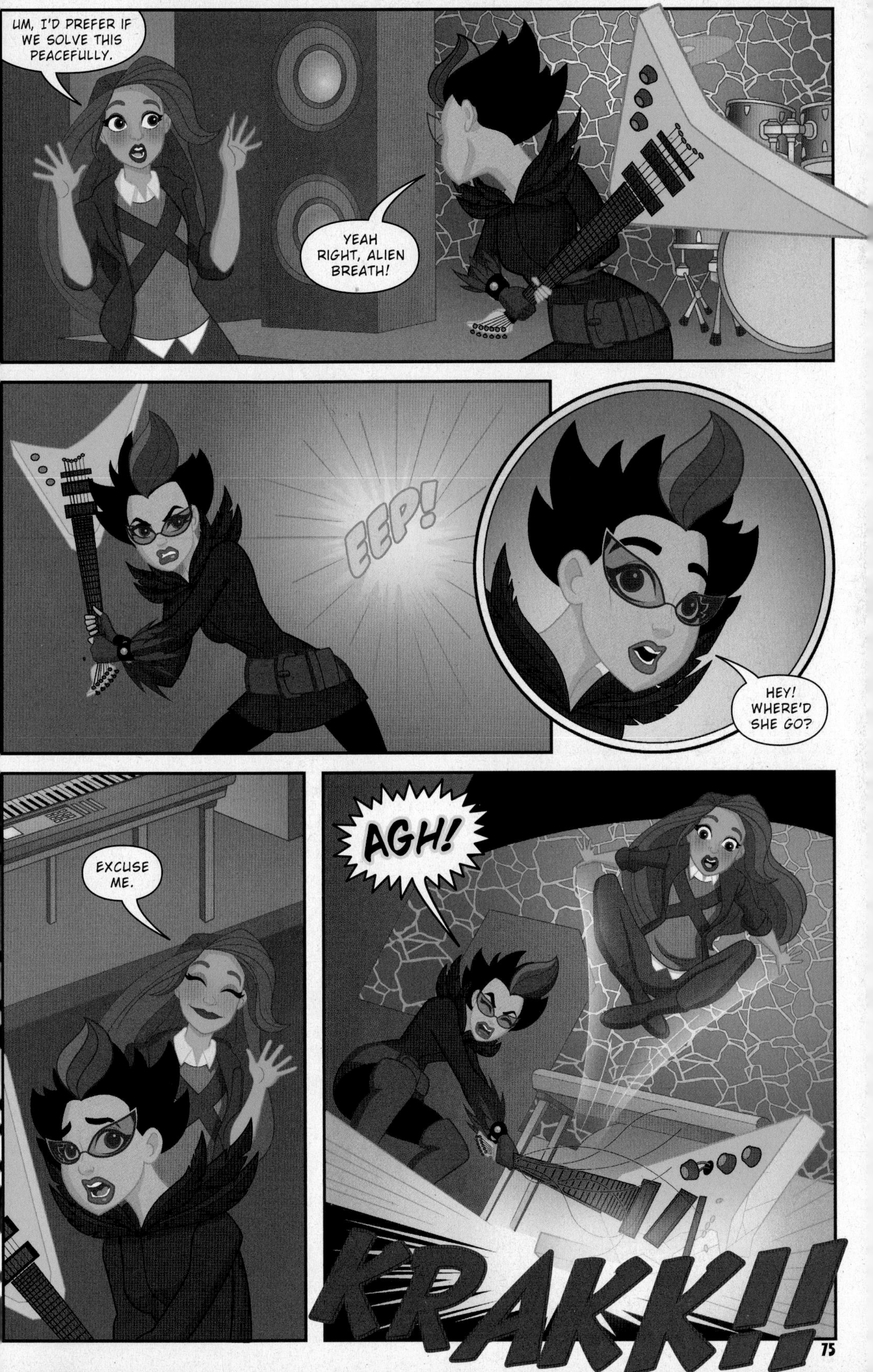
UM, I'D PREFER IF WE SOLVE THIS PEACEFULLY.
YEAH RIGHT, ALIEN BREATH!
EEP!
HEY! WHERE'D SHE GO?
EXCUSE ME.
AGH!
KRAKK!!

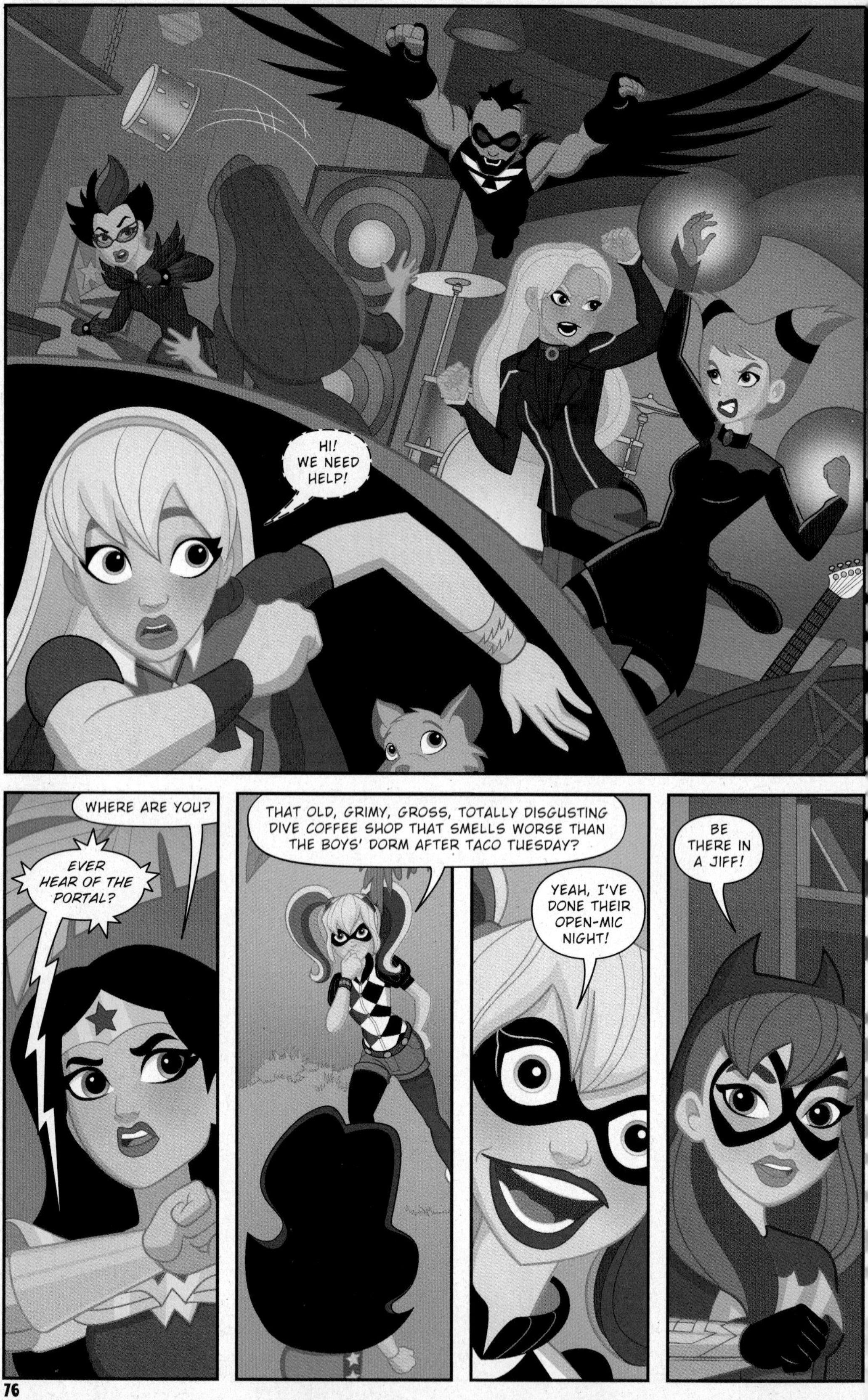
HI! WE NEED HELP!
WHERE ARE YOU?
EVER HEAR OF THE PORTAL?
THAT OLD, GRIMY, GROSS, TOTALLY DISGUSTING DIVE COFFEE SHOP THAT SMELLS WORSE THAN THE BOYS' DORM AFTER TACO TUESDAY?
YEAH, I'VE DONE THEIR OPEN-MIC NIGHT!
BE THERE IN A JIFF!

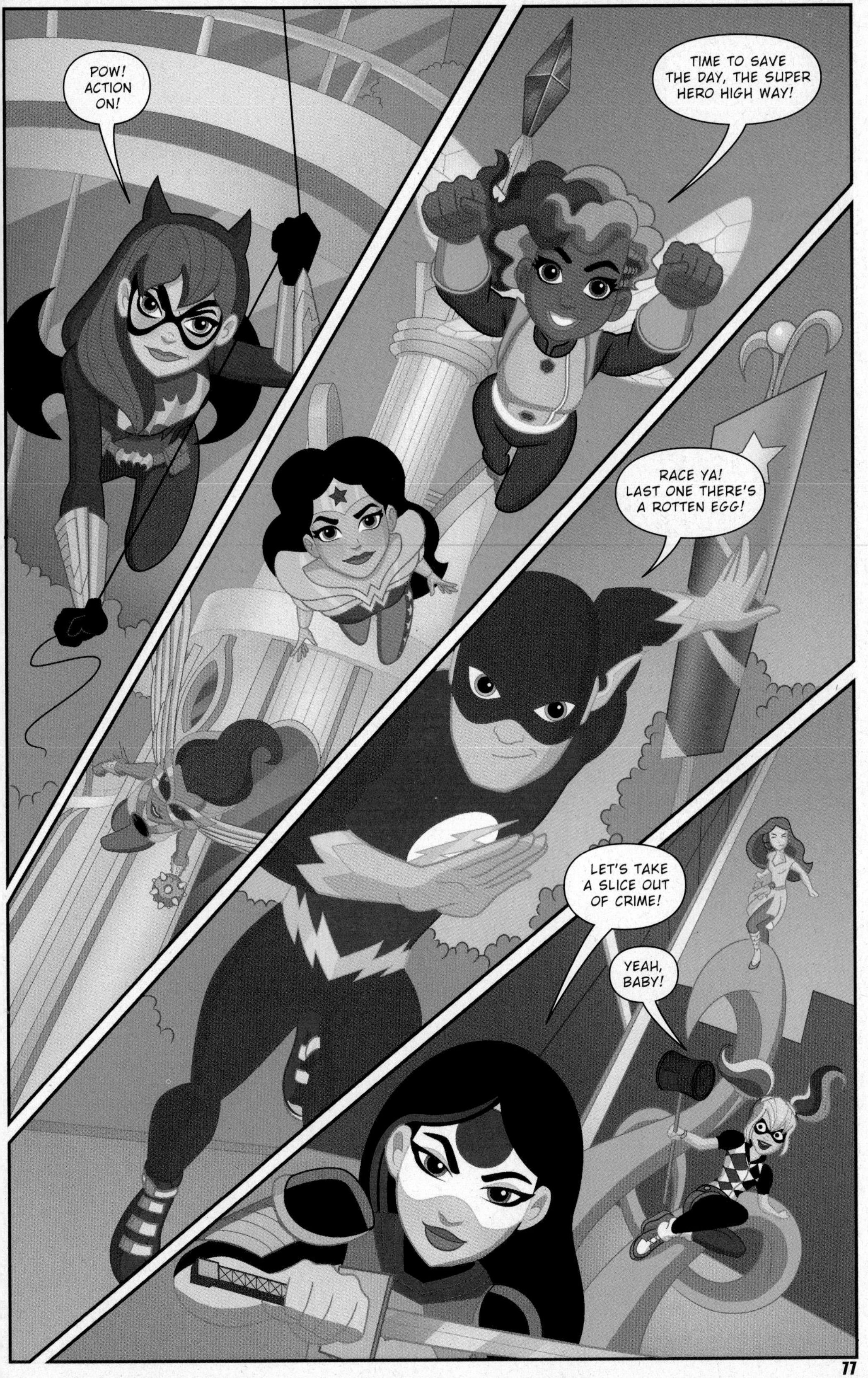
POW! ACTION ON!
TIME TO SAVE THE DAY, THE SUPER HERO HIGH WAY!
RACE YA! LAST ONE THERE'S A ROTTEN EGG!
LET'S TAKE A SLICE OUT OF CRIME!
YEAH, BABY!

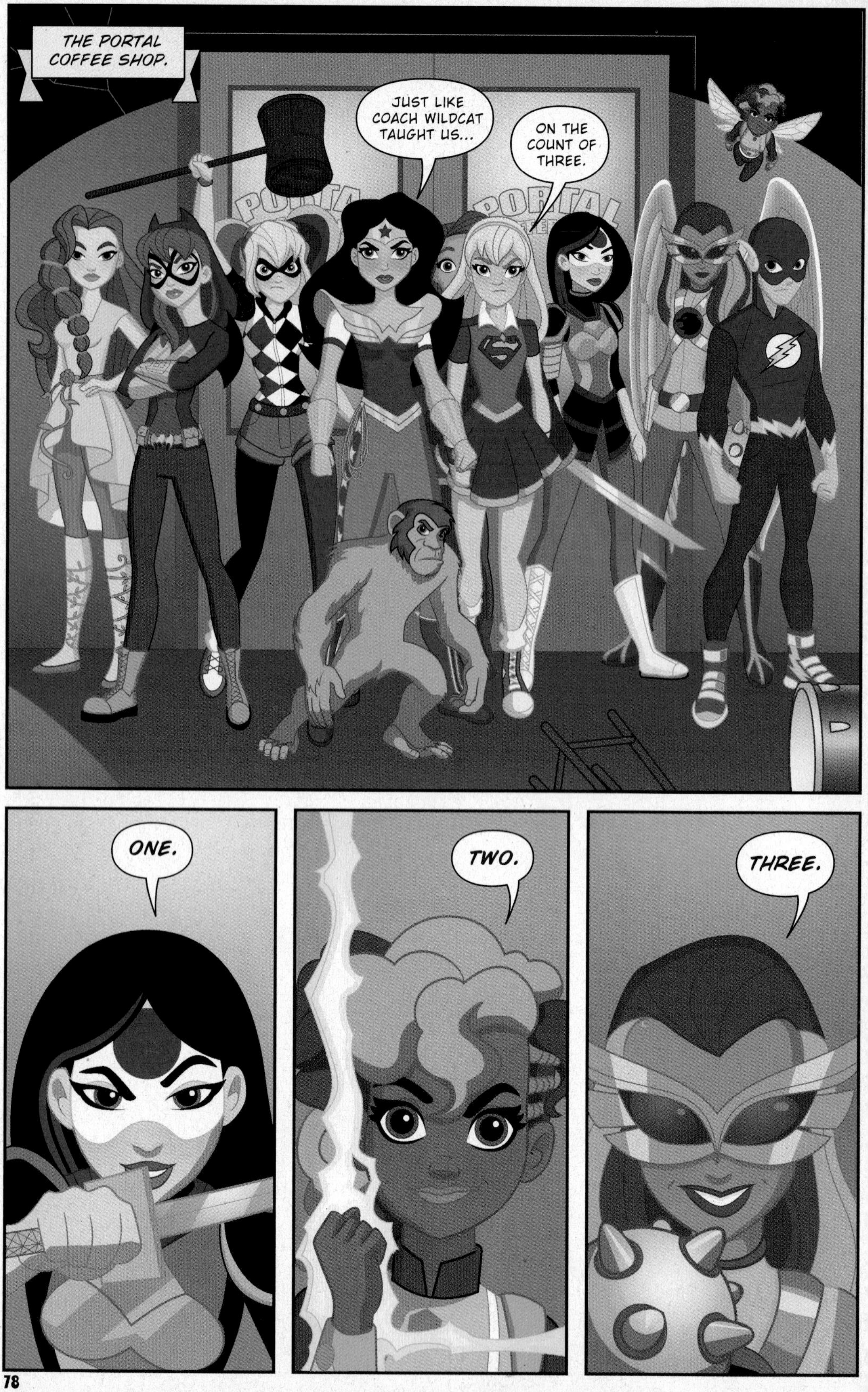
THE PORTAL COFFEE SHOP.
JUST LIKE COACH WILDCAT TAUGHT US...
ON THE COUNT OF THREE.
ONE.
TWO.
THREE.

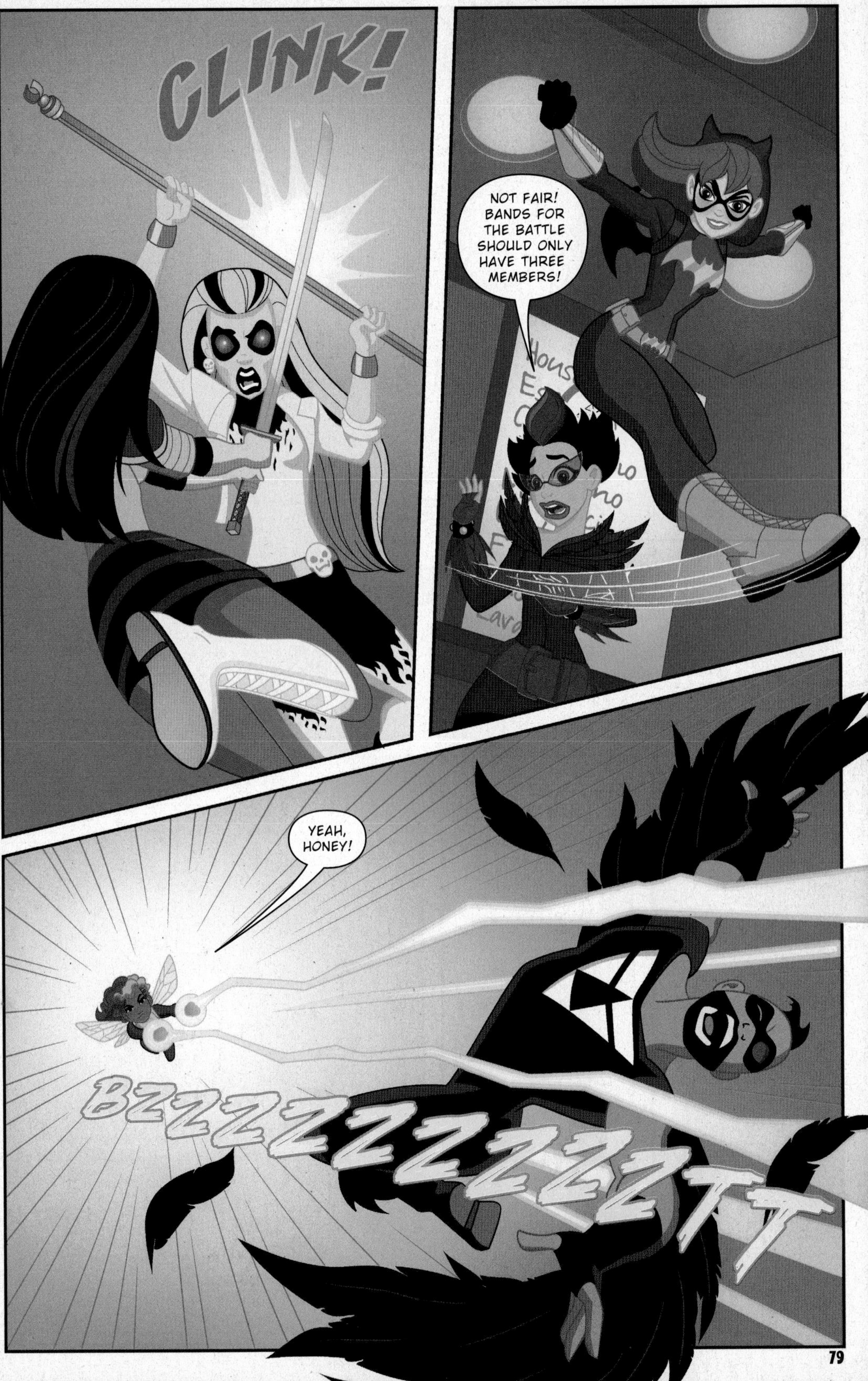
CLINK!
NOT FAIR! BANDS FOR THE BATTLE SHOULD ONLY HAVE THREE MEMBERS!
YEAH, HONEY!
BZZZZZZZZZZTT

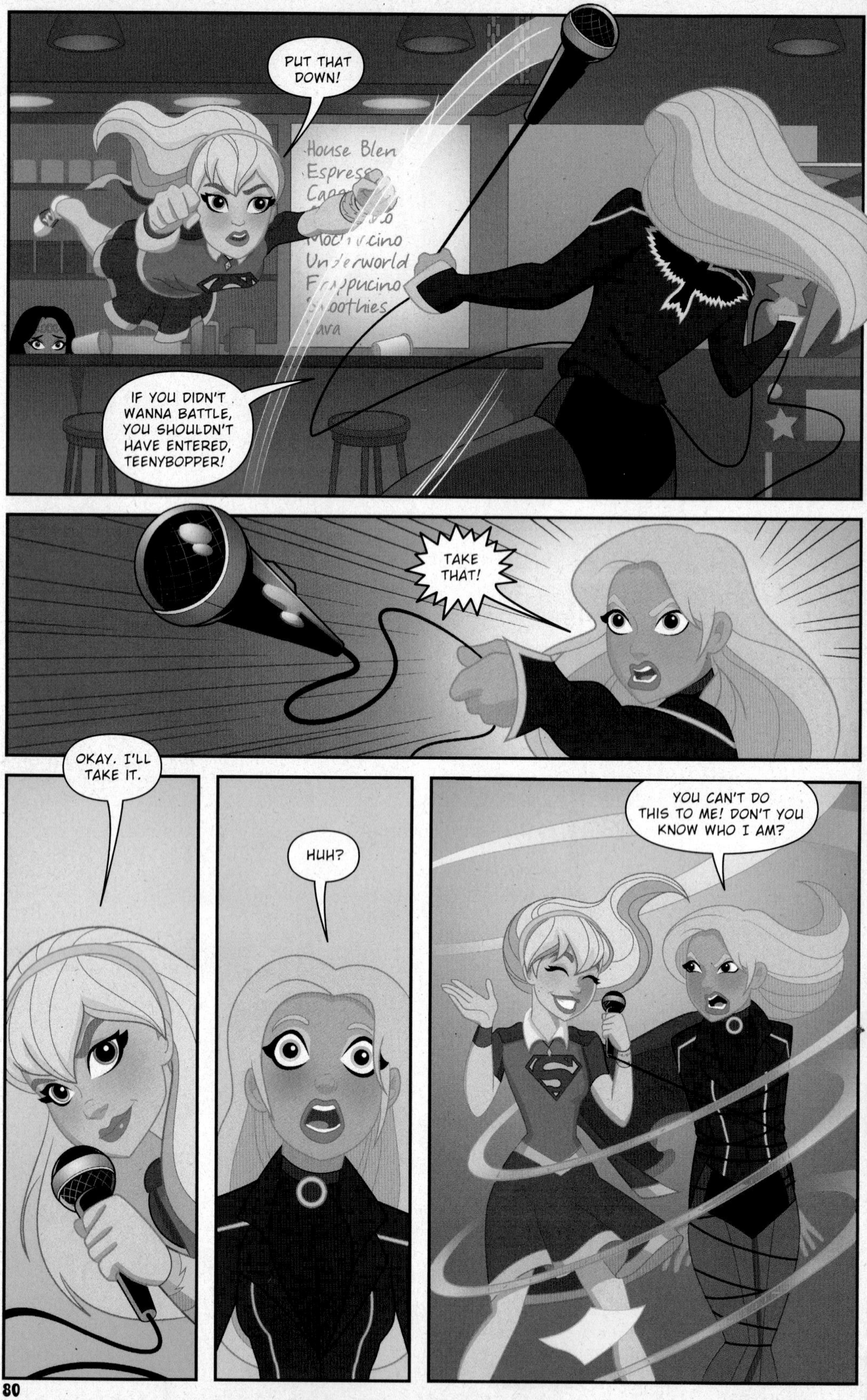
PUT THAT DOWN!
IF YOU DIDN'T WANNA BATTLE, YOU SHOULDN'T HAVE ENTERED, TEENYBOPPER!
TAKE THAT!
OKAY. I'LL TAKE IT.
HUH?
YOU CAN'T DO THIS TO ME! DON'T YOU KNOW WHO I AM?

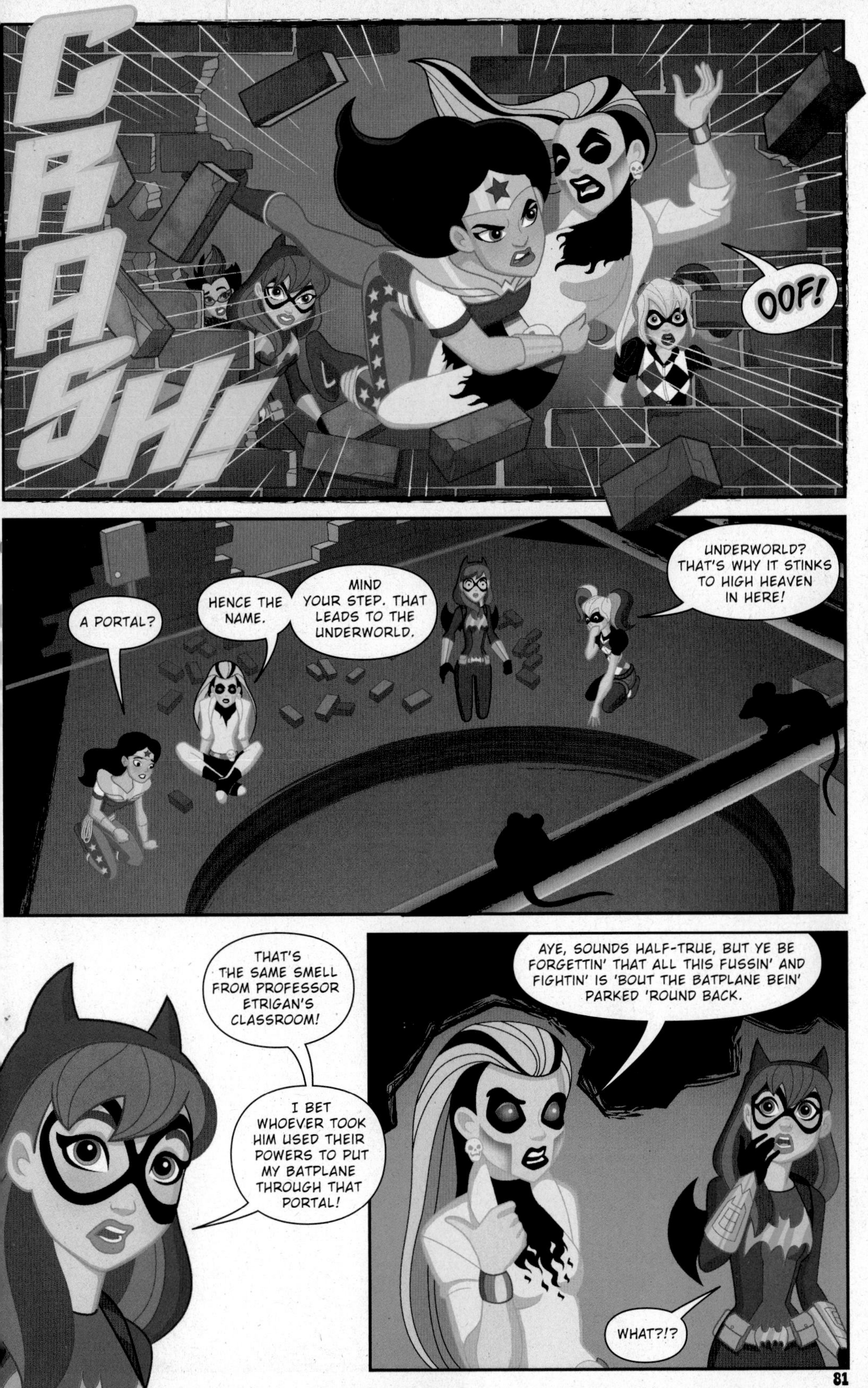
CRASH!
OOF!
A PORTAL?
HENCE THE NAME.
MIND YOUR STEP. THAT LEADS TO THE UNDERWORLD.
UNDERWORLD? THAT'S WHY IT STINKS TO HIGH HEAVEN IN HERE!
THAT'S THE SAME SMELL FROM PROFESSOR ETRIGAN'S CLASSROOM!
I BET WHOEVER TOOK HIM USED THEIR POWERS TO PUT MY BATPLANE THROUGH THAT PORTAL!
AYE, SOUNDS HALF-TRUE, BUT YE BE FORGETTIN' THAT ALL THIS FUSSIN' AND FIGHTIN' IS 'BOUT THE BATPLANE BEIN' PARKED 'ROUND BACK.
WHAT?!?

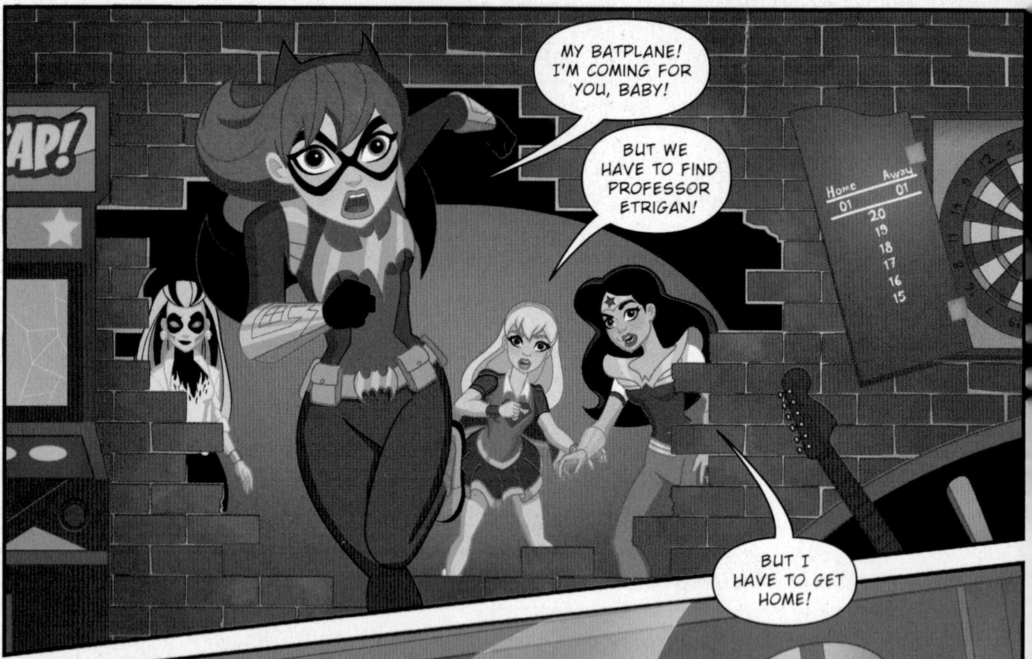

AP!
MY BATPLANE! I'M COMING FOR YOU, BABY!
BUT WE HAVE TO FIND PROFESSOR ETRIGAN!
Home Away
01 01
20
19
18
17
16
15
BUT I HAVE TO GET HOME!

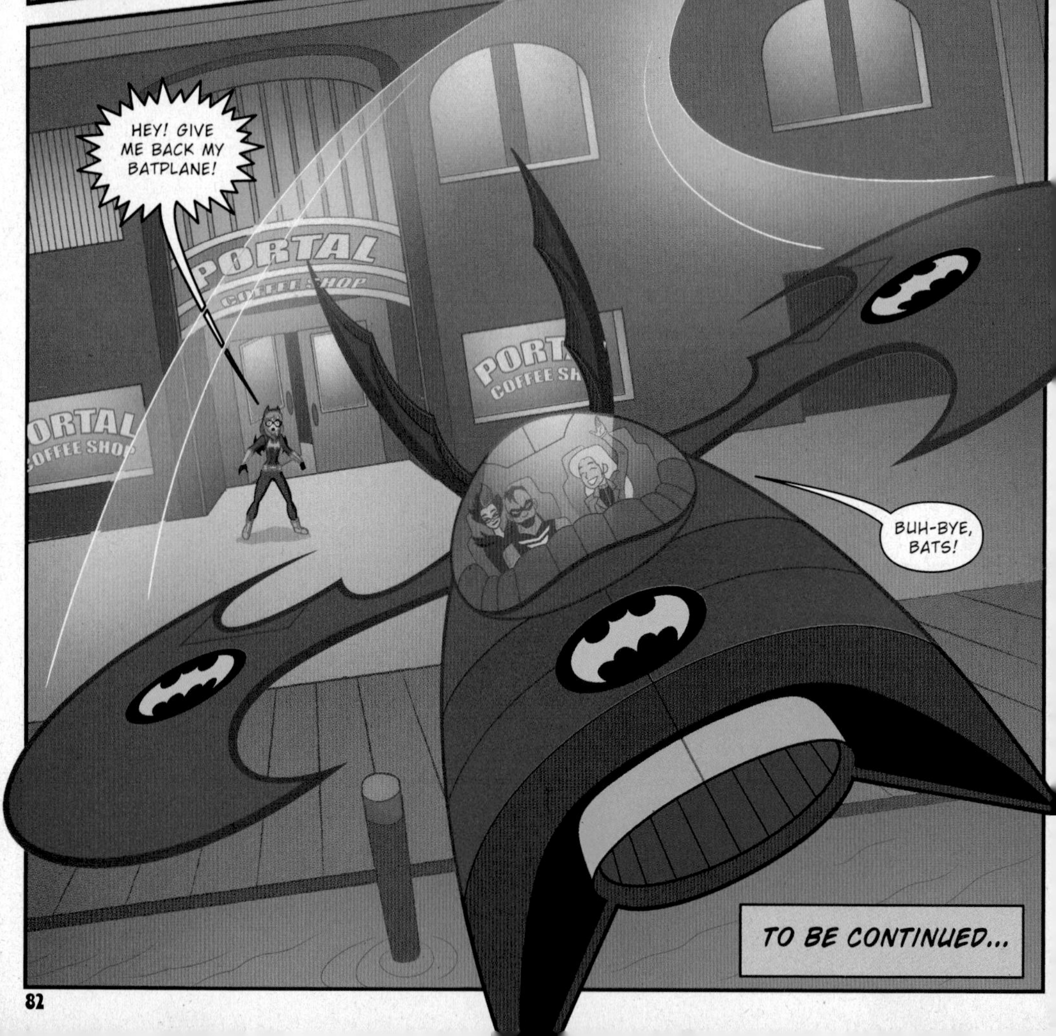

HEY! GIVE ME BACK MY BATPLANE!
PORTAL COFFEE SHOP
BUH-BYE, BATS!
TO BE CONTINUED...

CHAPTER FIVE
THE UNDERWORLD

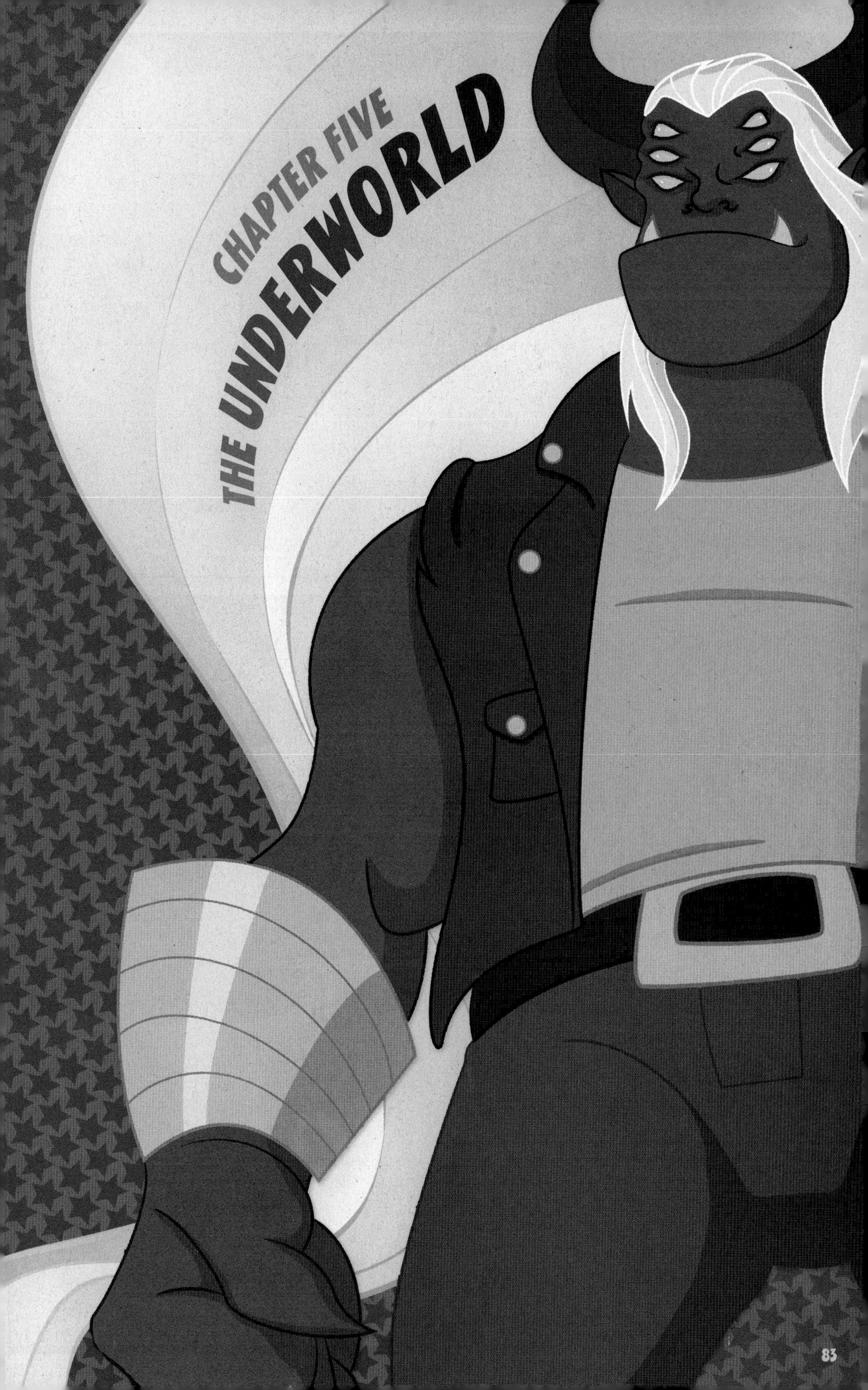

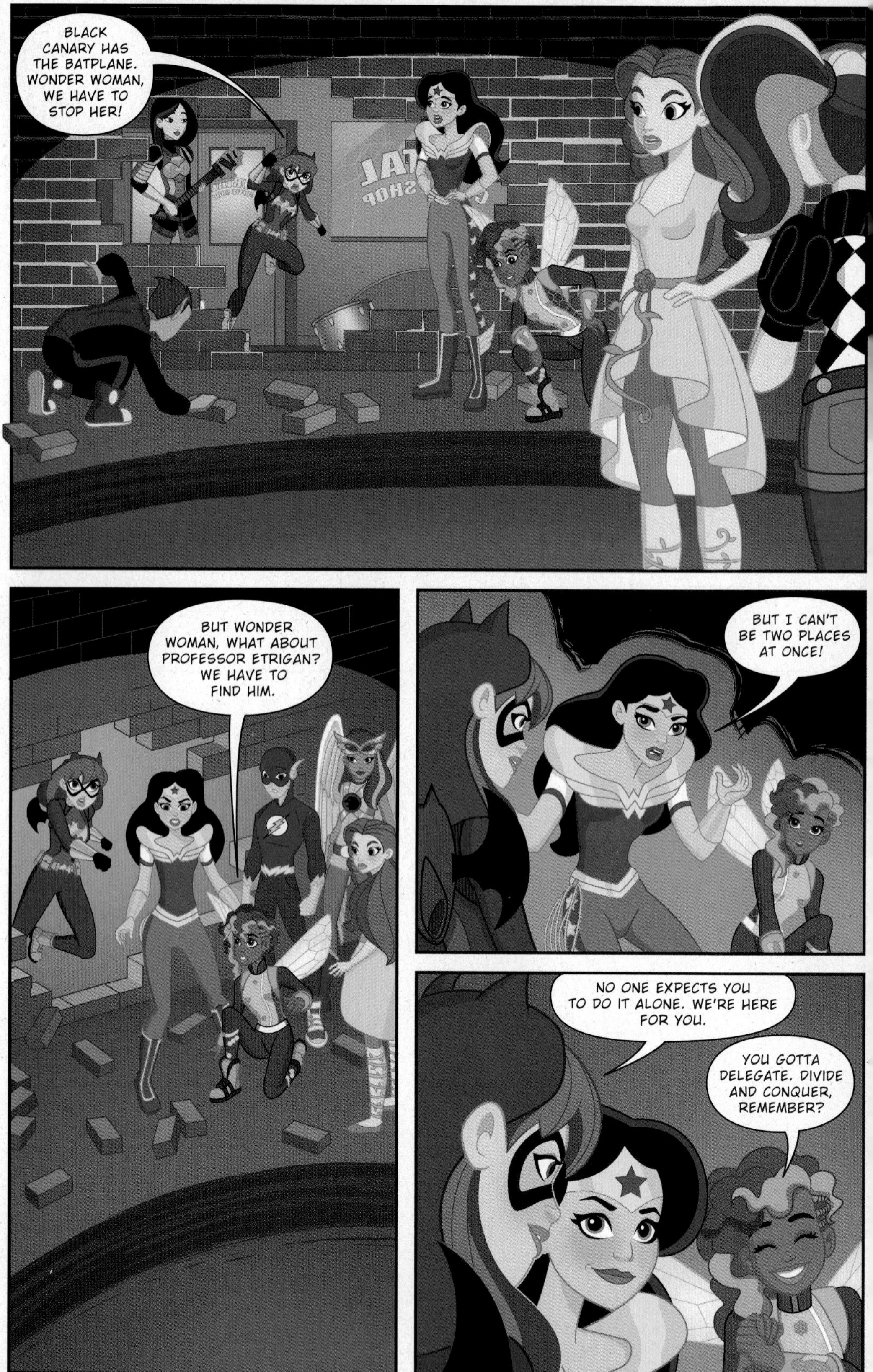
BLACK CANARY HAS THE BATPLANE. WONDER WOMAN, WE HAVE TO STOP HER!
BUT WONDER WOMAN, WHAT ABOUT PROFESSOR ETRIGAN? WE HAVE TO FIND HIM.
BUT I CAN'T BE TWO PLACES AT ONCE!
NO ONE EXPECTS YOU TO DO IT ALONE. WE'RE HERE FOR YOU.
YOU GOTTA DELEGATE. DIVIDE AND CONQUER, REMEMBER?

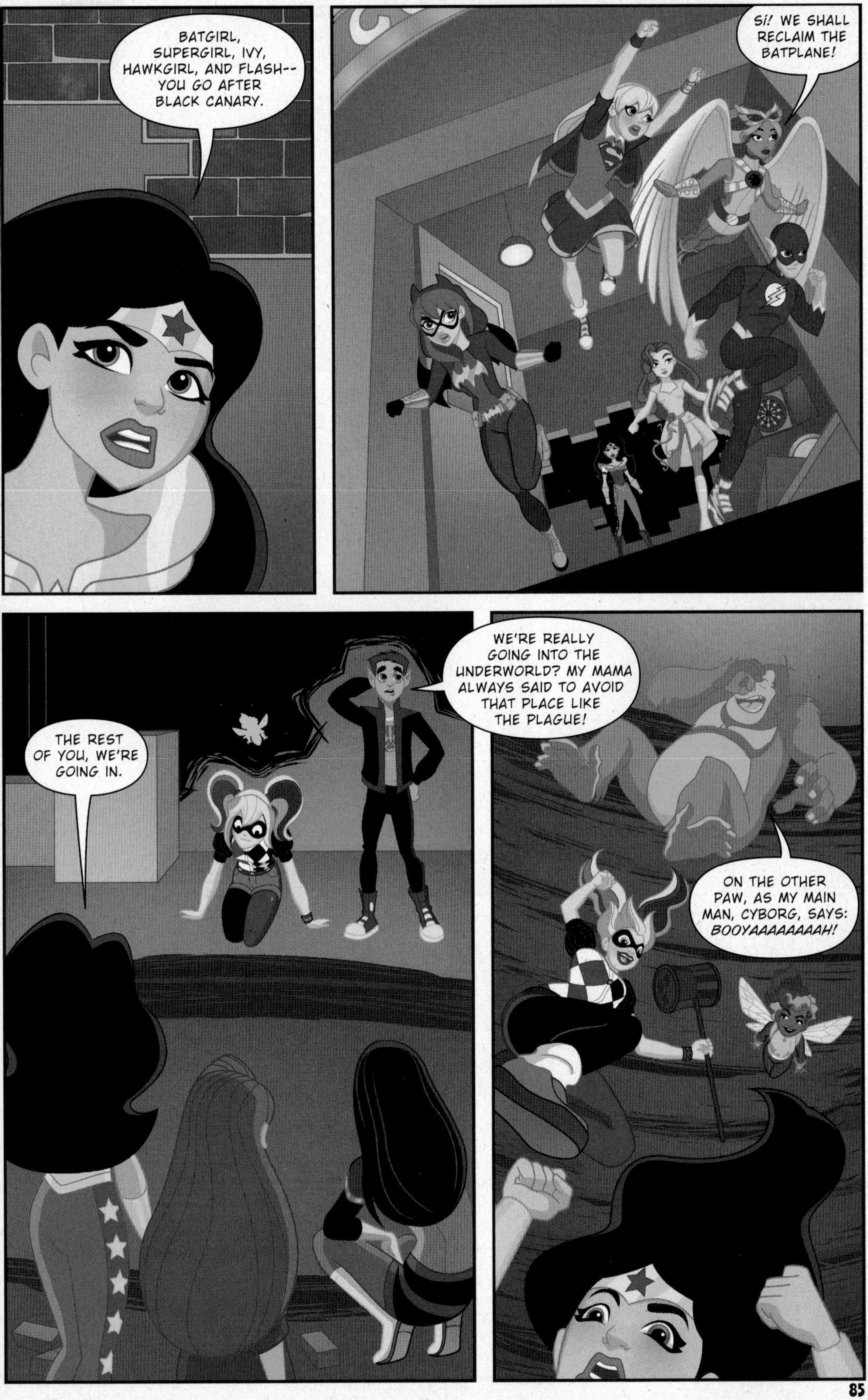
BATGIRL, SUPERGIRL, IVY, HAWKGIRL, AND FLASH-- YOU GO AFTER BLACK CANARY.
Sí! WE SHALL RECLAIM THE BATPLANE!
THE REST OF YOU, WE'RE GOING IN.
WE'RE REALLY GOING INTO THE UNDERWORLD? MY MAMA ALWAYS SAID TO AVOID THAT PLACE LIKE THE PLAGUE!
ON THE OTHER PAW, AS MY MAIN MAN, CYBORG, SAYS: *BOOYAAAAAAAAAH!*

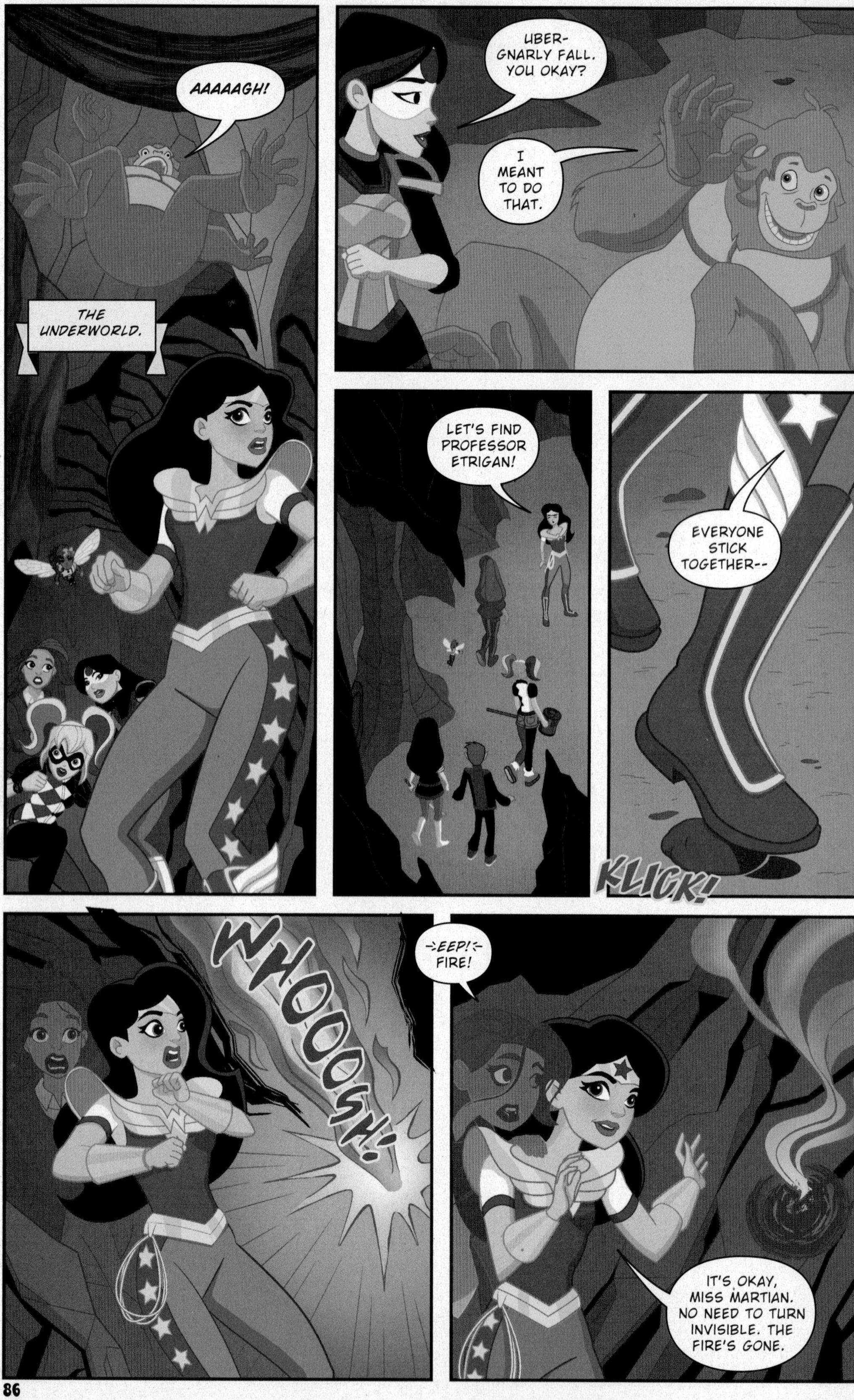
AAAAAGH!
THE UNDERWORLD.
UBER-GNARLY FALL. YOU OKAY?
I MEANT TO DO THAT.
LET'S FIND PROFESSOR ETRIGAN!
EVERYONE STICK TOGETHER--
KLICK!
WHOOOSH!
EEP! FIRE!
IT'S OKAY, MISS MARTIAN. NO NEED TO TURN INVISIBLE. THE FIRE'S GONE.

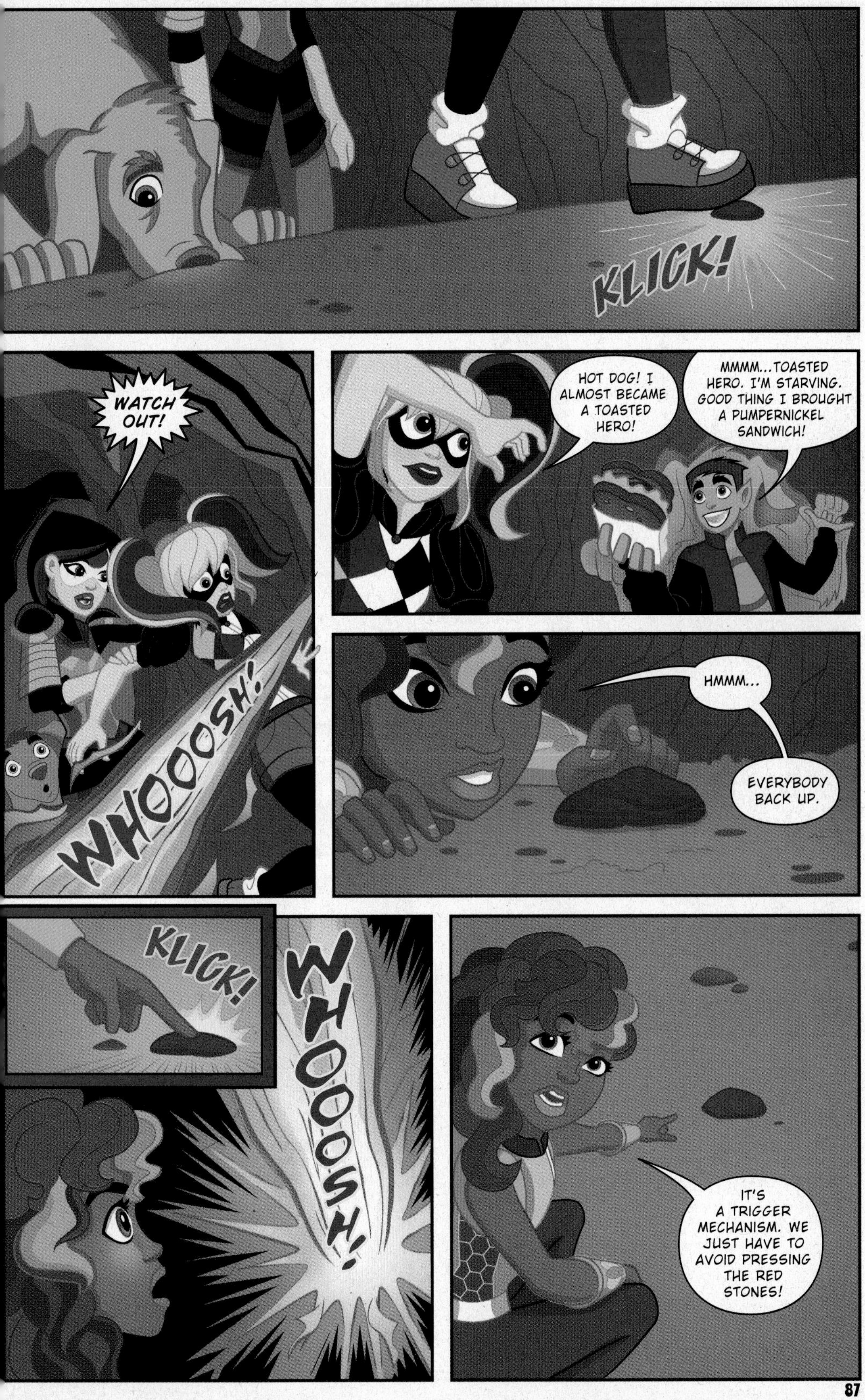
KLICK!
WATCH OUT!
WHOOOSH!
HOT DOG! I ALMOST BECAME A TOASTED HERO!
MMMM...TOASTED HERO. I'M STARVING. GOOD THING I BROUGHT A PUMPERNICKEL SANDWICH!
HMMM...
EVERYBODY BACK UP.
KLICK!
WHOOOOSH!
IT'S A TRIGGER MECHANISM. WE JUST HAVE TO AVOID PRESSING THE RED STONES!

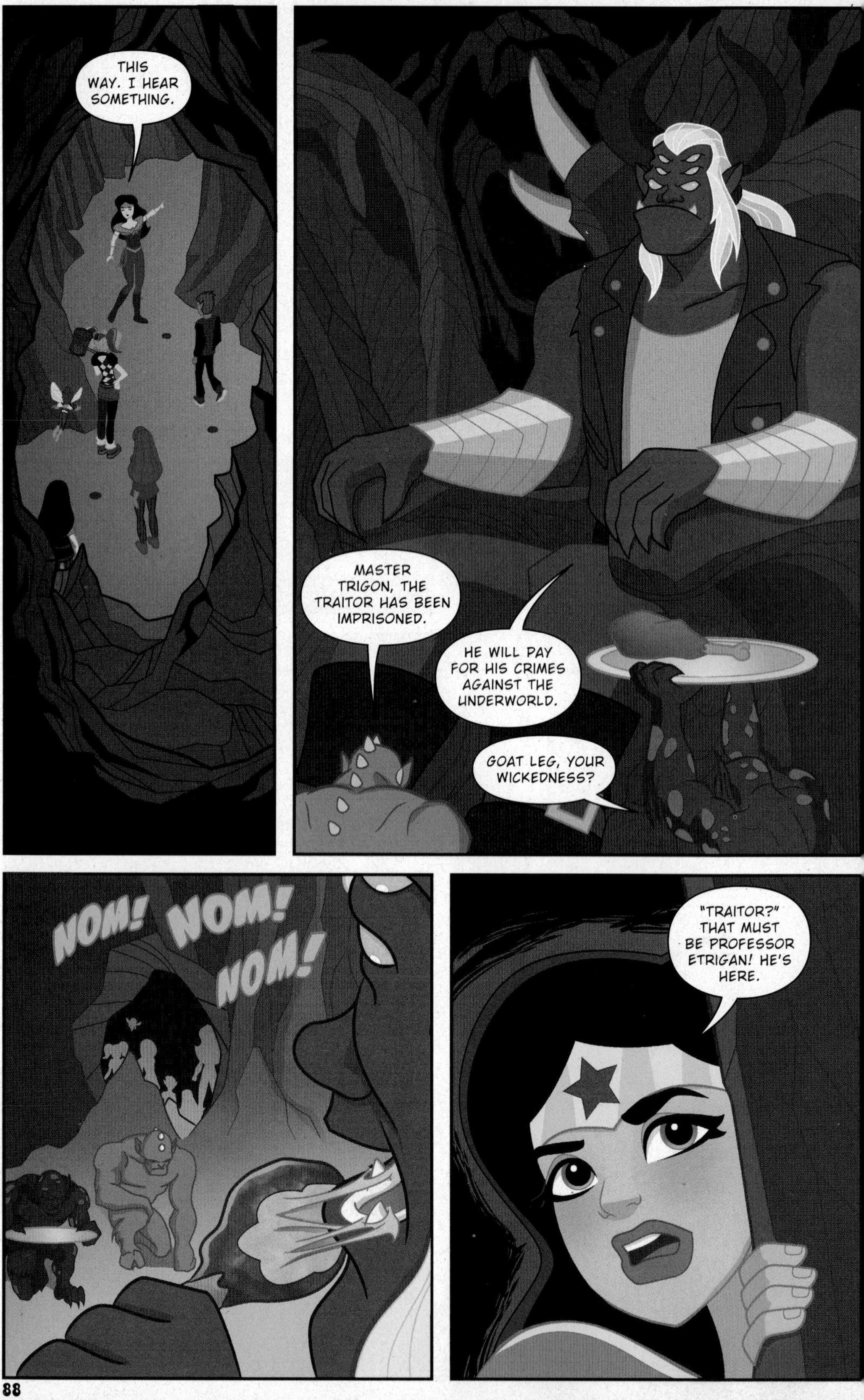
THIS WAY. I HEAR SOMETHING.
MASTER TRIGON, THE TRAITOR HAS BEEN IMPRISONED.
HE WILL PAY FOR HIS CRIMES AGAINST THE UNDERWORLD.
GOAT LEG, YOUR WICKEDNESS?
NOM! NOM! NOM!
"TRAITOR?" THAT MUST BE PROFESSOR ETRIGAN! HE'S HERE.

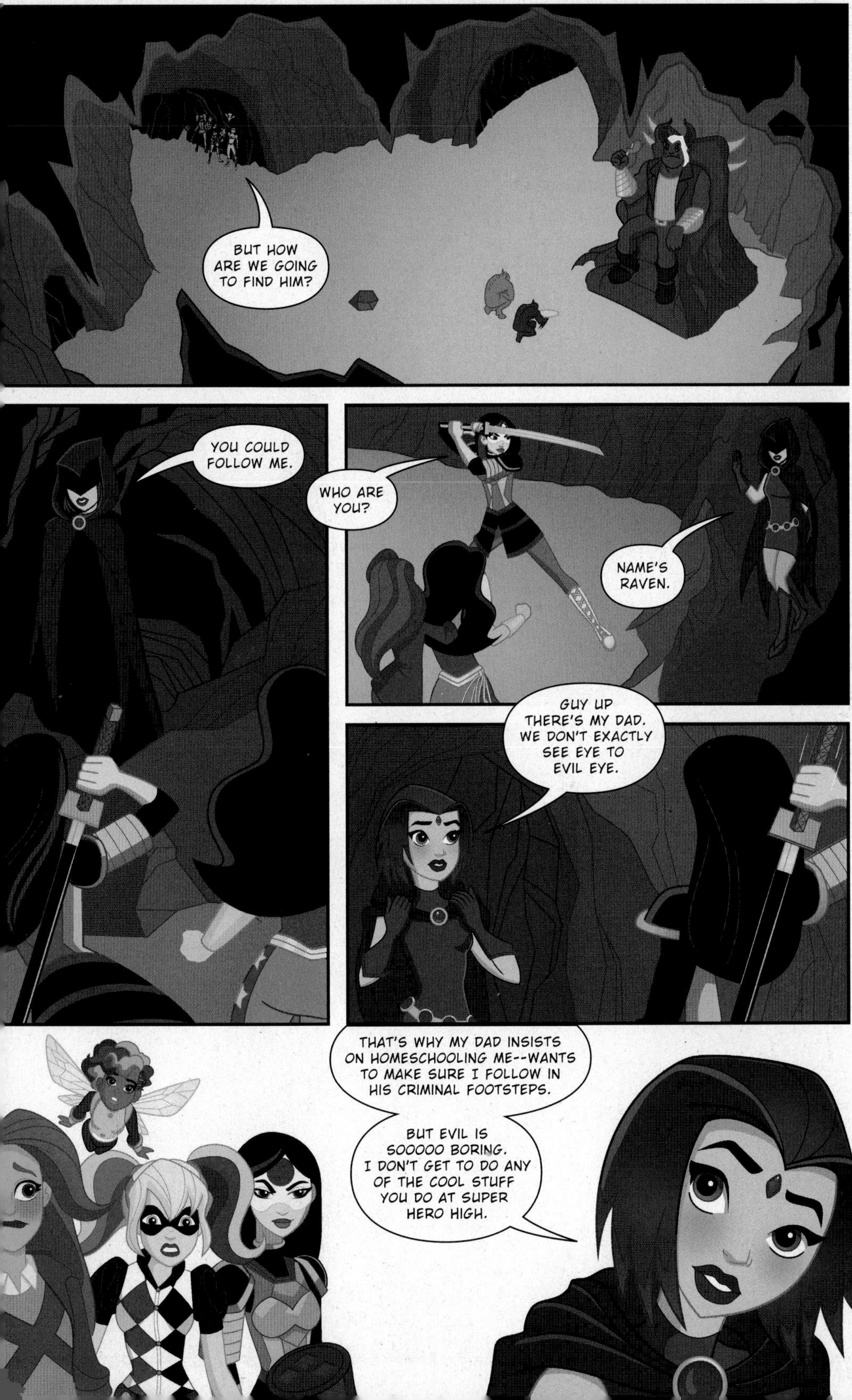
BUT HOW ARE WE GOING TO FIND HIM?
YOU COULD FOLLOW ME.
WHO ARE YOU?
NAME'S RAVEN.
GUY UP THERE'S MY DAD. WE DON'T EXACTLY SEE EYE TO EVIL EYE.
THAT'S WHY MY DAD INSISTS ON HOMESCHOOLING ME--WANTS TO MAKE SURE I FOLLOW IN HIS CRIMINAL FOOTSTEPS.
BUT EVIL IS SOOOOO BORING. I DON'T GET TO DO ANY OF THE COOL STUFF YOU DO AT SUPER HERO HIGH.

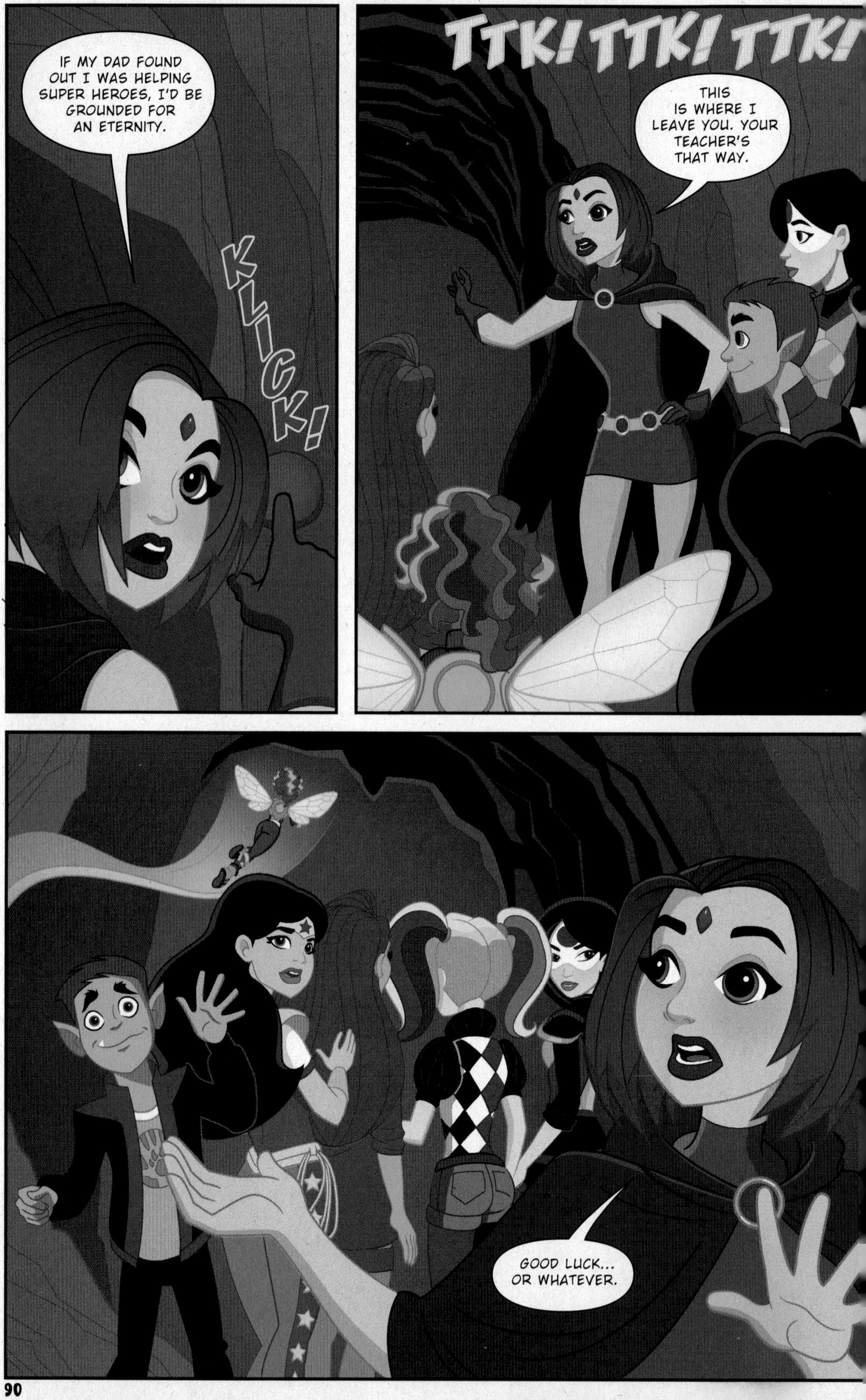
IF MY DAD FOUND OUT I WAS HELPING SUPER HEROES, I'D BE GROUNDED FOR AN ETERNITY.
KLICK!
TTK! TTK! TTK!
THIS IS WHERE I LEAVE YOU. YOUR TEACHER'S THAT WAY.
GOOD LUCK... OR WHATEVER.

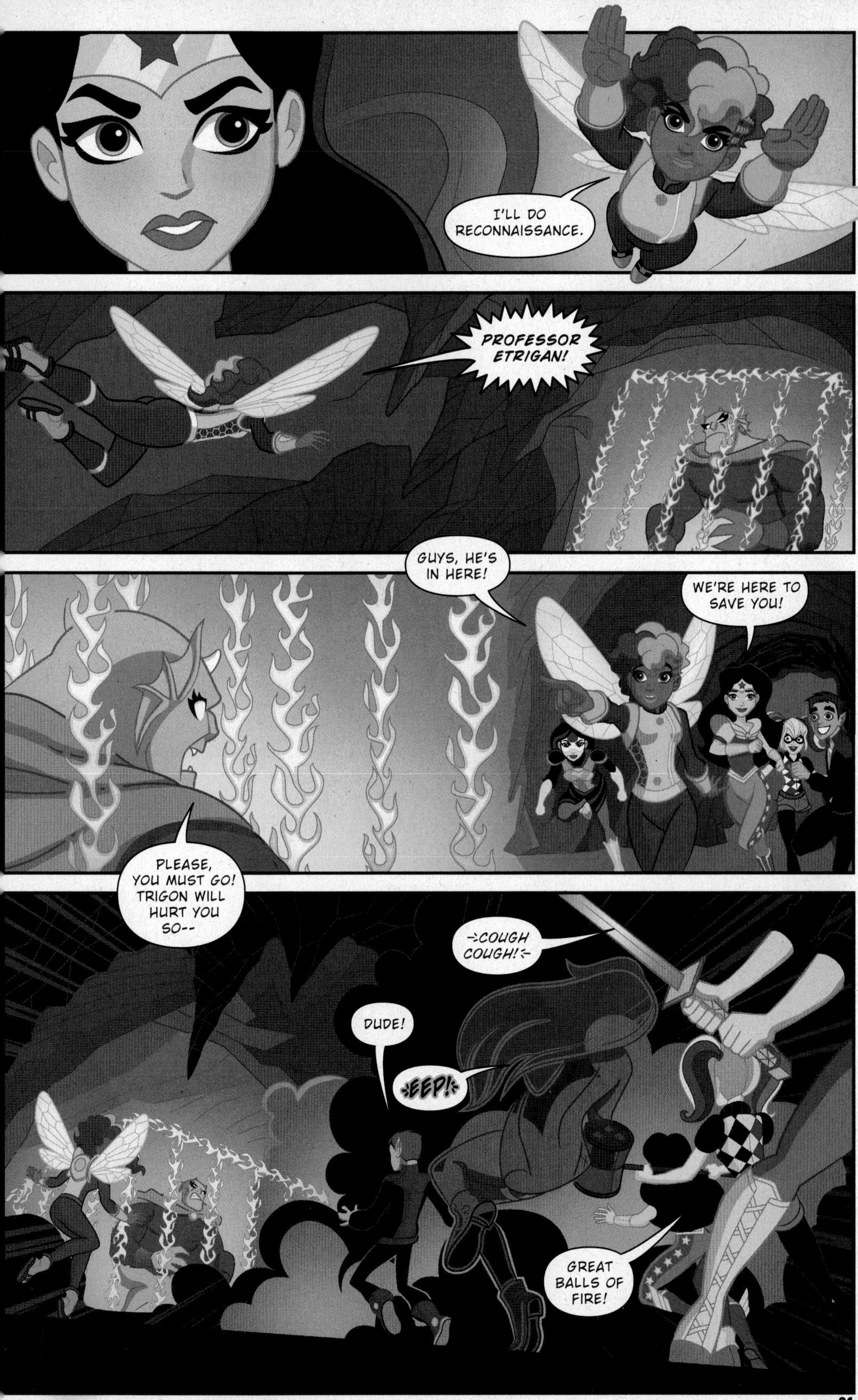
I'LL DO RECONNAISSANCE.
PROFESSOR ETRIGAN!
GUYS, HE'S IN HERE!
WE'RE HERE TO SAVE YOU!
PLEASE, YOU MUST GO! TRIGON WILL HURT YOU SO--
-COUGH COUGH!-
DUDE!
EEP!
GREAT BALLS OF FIRE!

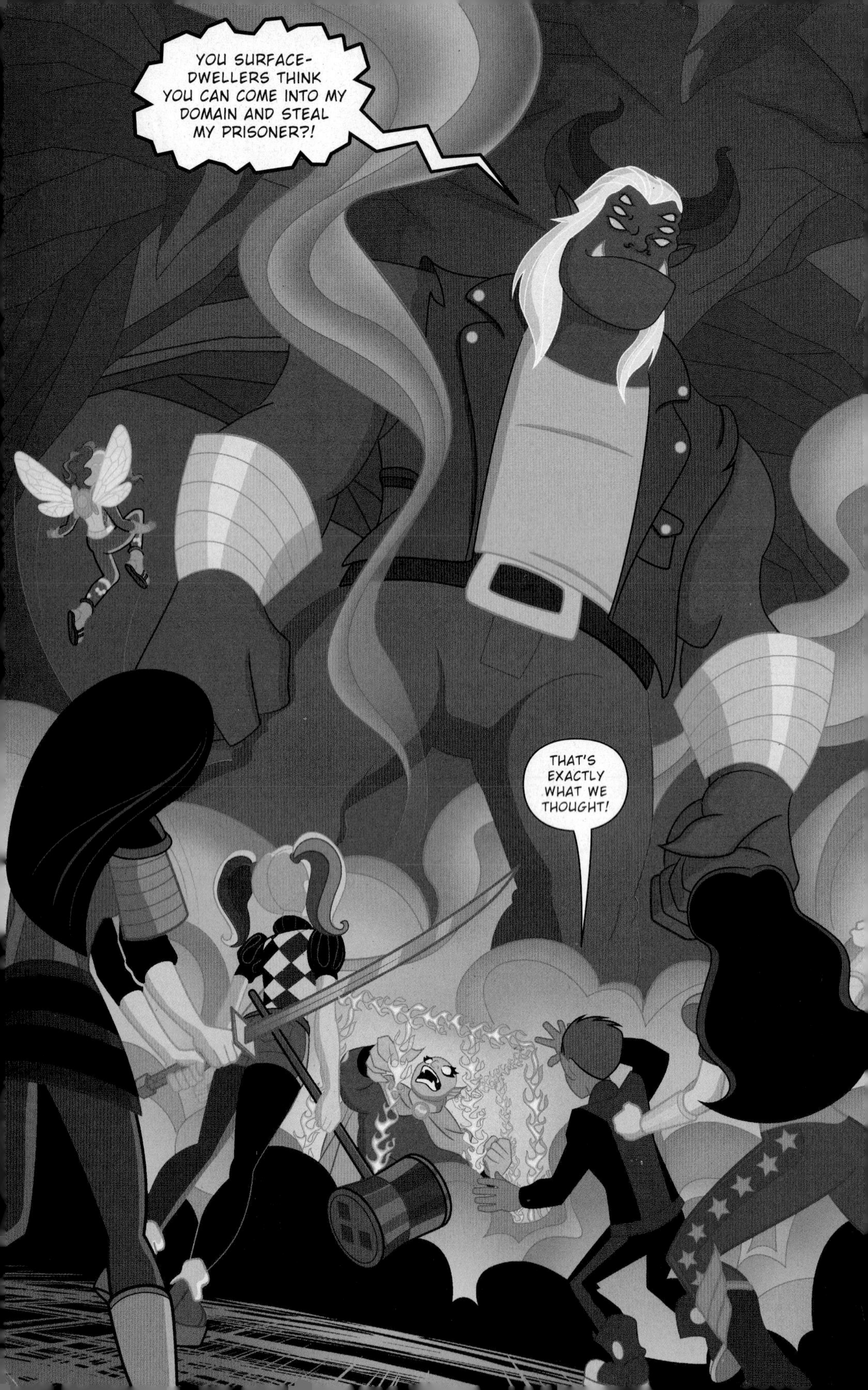
YOU SURFACE-DWELLERS THINK YOU CAN COME INTO MY DOMAIN AND STEAL MY PRISONER?!
THAT'S EXACTLY WHAT WE THOUGHT!

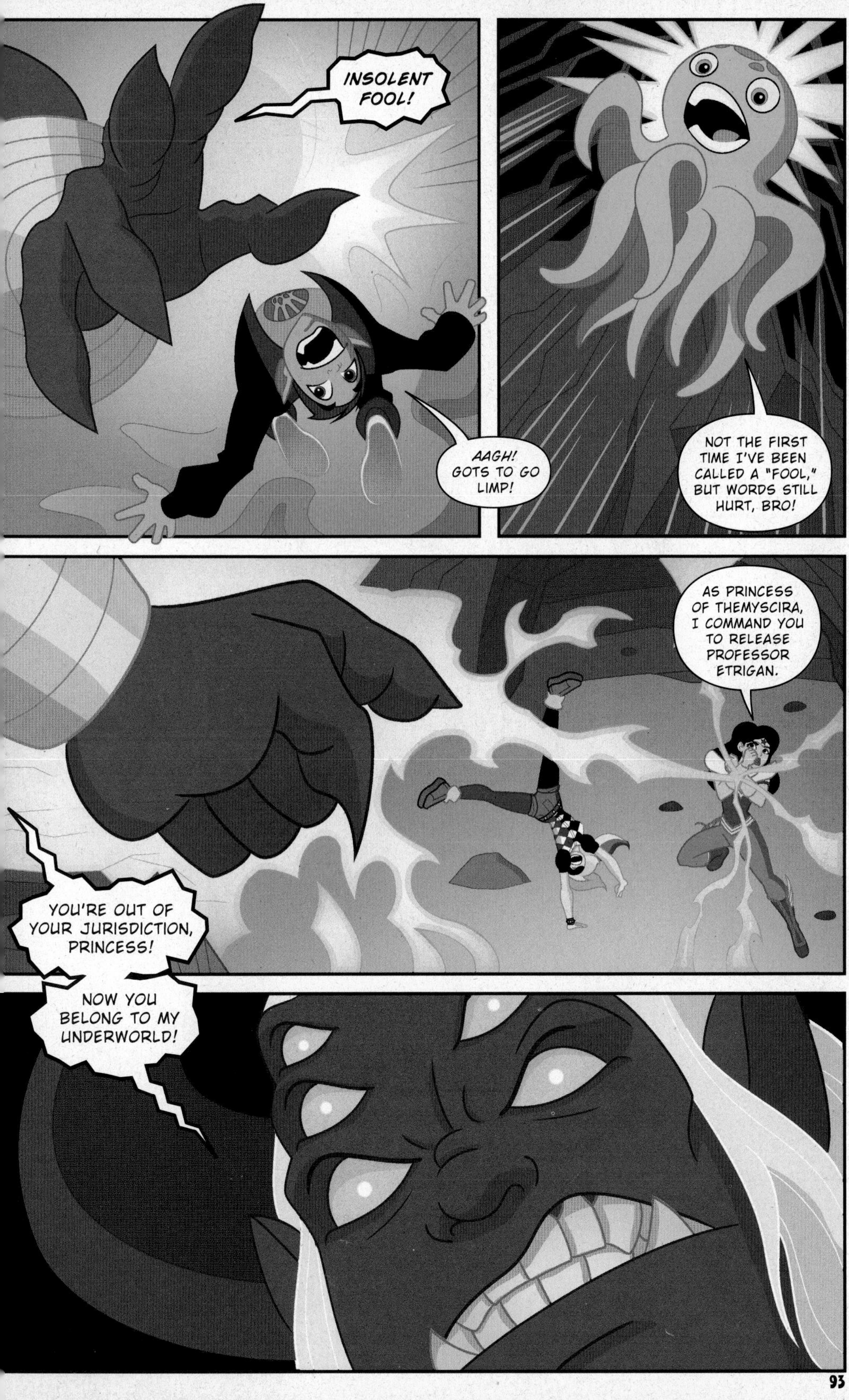
INSOLENT FOOL!
AAGH! GOTS TO GO LIMP!
NOT THE FIRST TIME I'VE BEEN CALLED A "FOOL," BUT WORDS STILL HURT, BRO!
AS PRINCESS OF THEMYSCIRA, I COMMAND YOU TO RELEASE PROFESSOR ETRIGAN.
YOU'RE OUT OF YOUR JURISDICTION, PRINCESS!
NOW YOU BELONG TO MY UNDERWORLD!

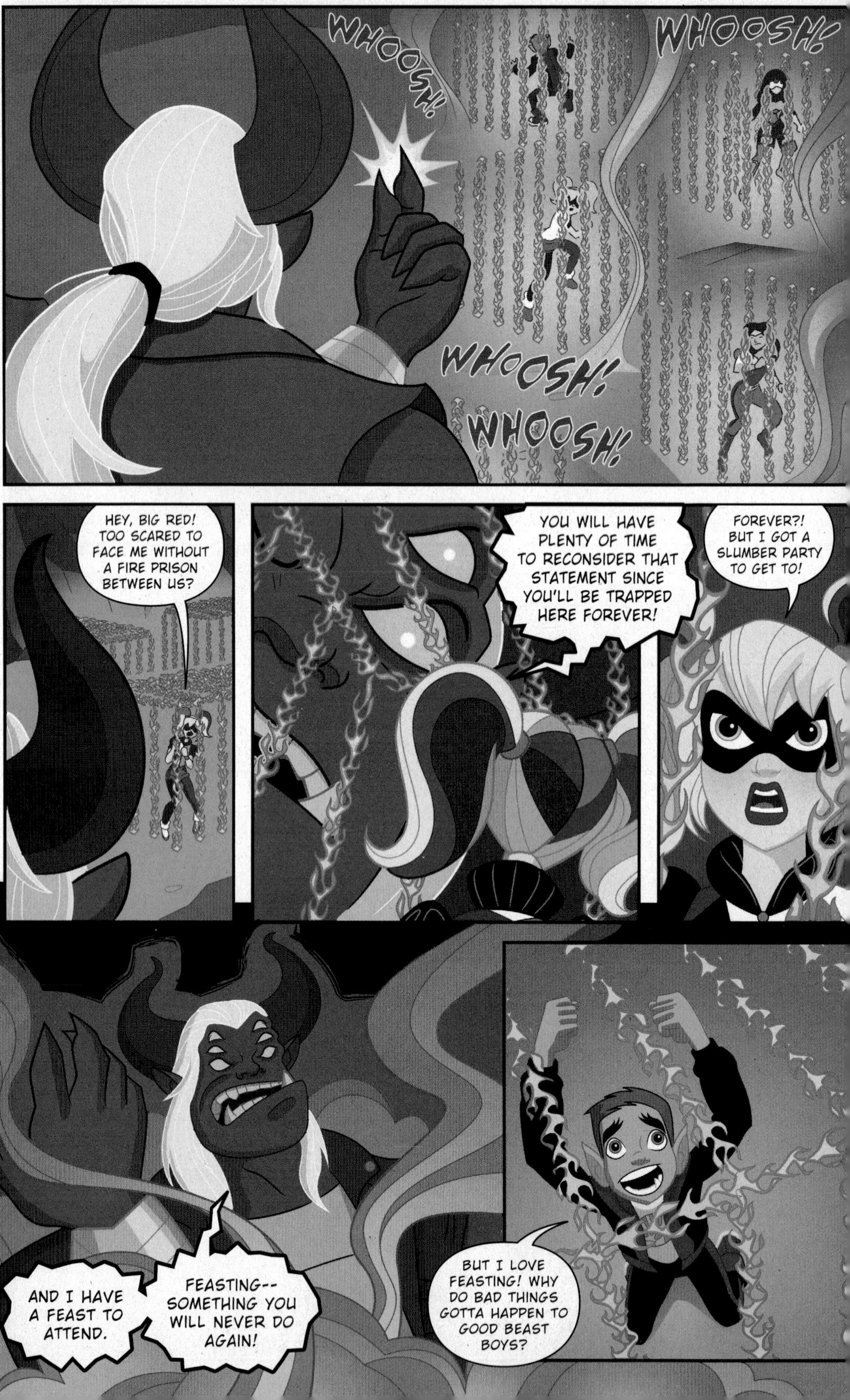
WHOOSH!
WHOOSH!
WHOOSH!
WHOOSH!
HEY, BIG RED! TOO SCARED TO FACE ME WITHOUT A FIRE PRISON BETWEEN US?
YOU WILL HAVE PLENTY OF TIME TO RECONSIDER THAT STATEMENT SINCE YOU'LL BE TRAPPED HERE FOREVER!
FOREVER?! BUT I GOT A SLUMBER PARTY TO GET TO!
AND I HAVE A FEAST TO ATTEND.
FEASTING-- SOMETHING YOU WILL NEVER DO AGAIN!
BUT I LOVE FEASTING! WHY DO BAD THINGS GOTTA HAPPEN TO GOOD BEAST BOYS?

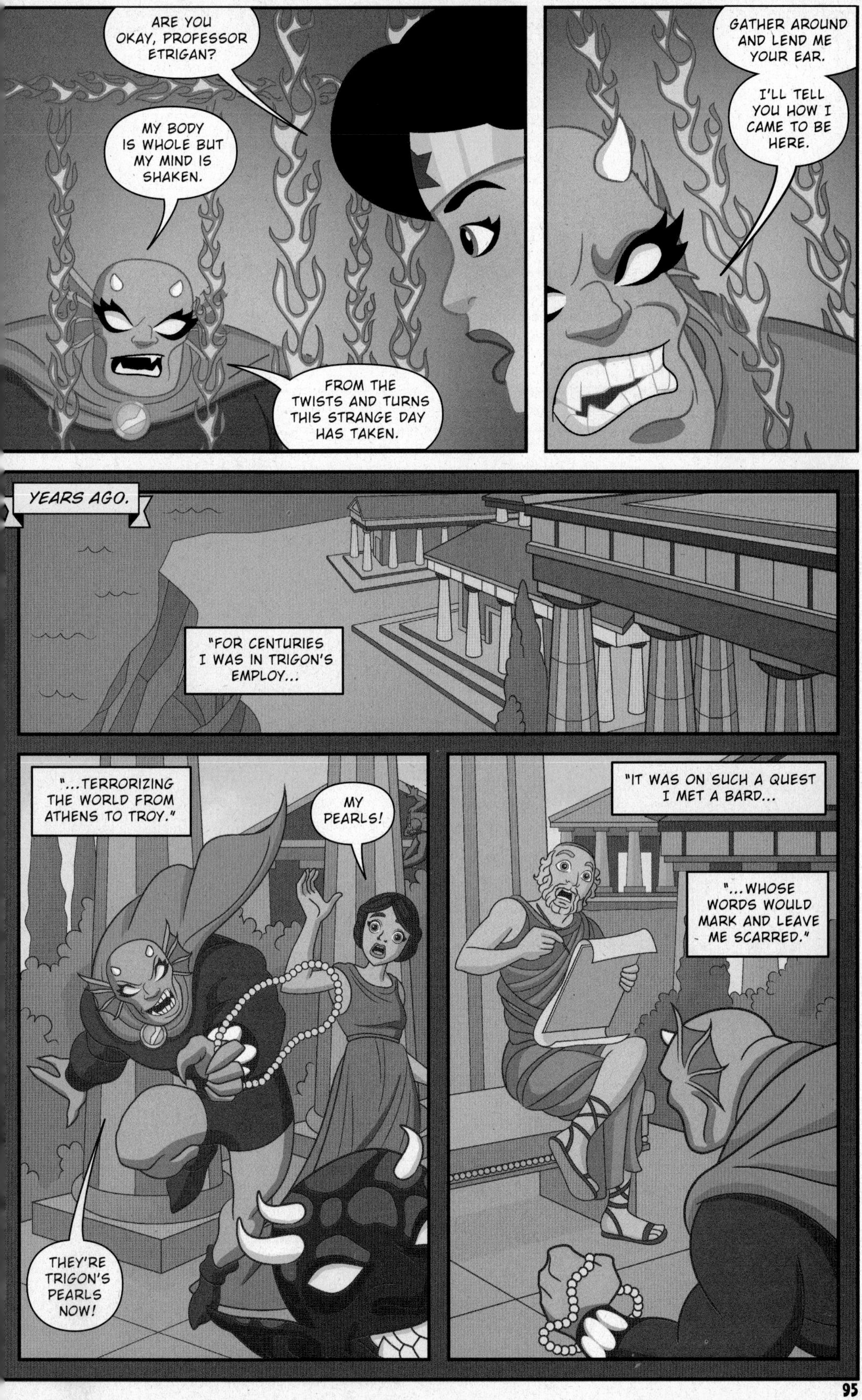
ARE YOU OKAY, PROFESSOR ETRIGAN?
MY BODY IS WHOLE BUT MY MIND IS SHAKEN.
FROM THE TWISTS AND TURNS THIS STRANGE DAY HAS TAKEN.
GATHER AROUND AND LEND ME YOUR EAR.
I'LL TELL YOU HOW I CAME TO BE HERE.
YEARS AGO.
"FOR CENTURIES I WAS IN TRIGON'S EMPLOY...
"...TERRORIZING THE WORLD FROM ATHENS TO TROY."
MY PEARLS!
THEY'RE TRIGON'S PEARLS NOW!
"IT WAS ON SUCH A QUEST I MET A BARD...
"...WHOSE WORDS WOULD MARK AND LEAVE ME SCARRED."

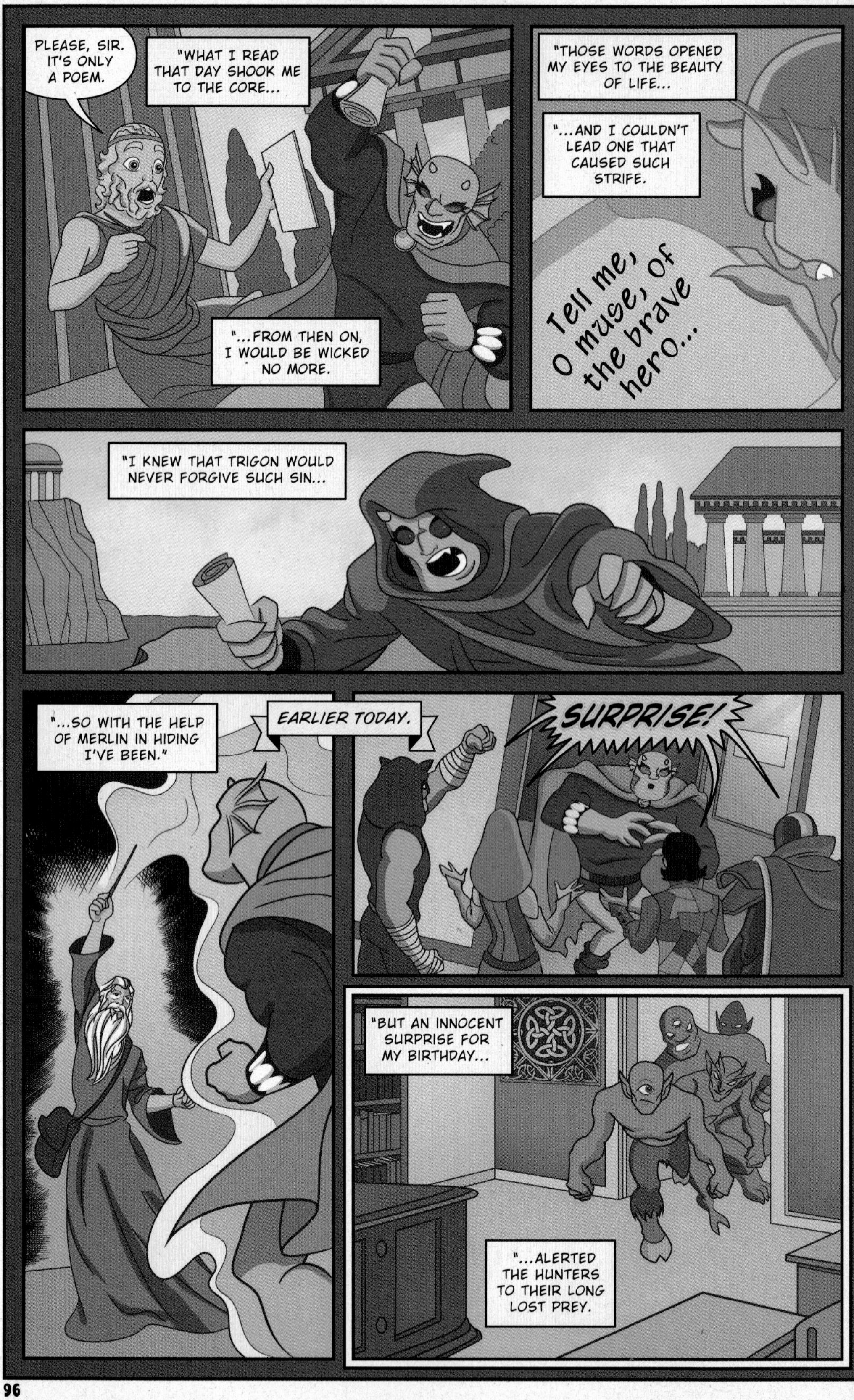
PLEASE, SIR. IT'S ONLY A POEM.
"WHAT I READ THAT DAY SHOOK ME TO THE CORE...
"...FROM THEN ON, I WOULD BE WICKED NO MORE.
"THOSE WORDS OPENED MY EYES TO THE BEAUTY OF LIFE...
"...AND I COULDN'T LEAD ONE THAT CAUSED SUCH STRIFE.
Tell me, O muse, of the brave hero...
"I KNEW THAT TRIGON WOULD NEVER FORGIVE SUCH SIN...
"...SO WITH THE HELP OF MERLIN IN HIDING I'VE BEEN."
EARLIER TODAY.
SURPRISE!
"BUT AN INNOCENT SURPRISE FOR MY BIRTHDAY...
"...ALERTED THE HUNTERS TO THEIR LONG LOST PREY.

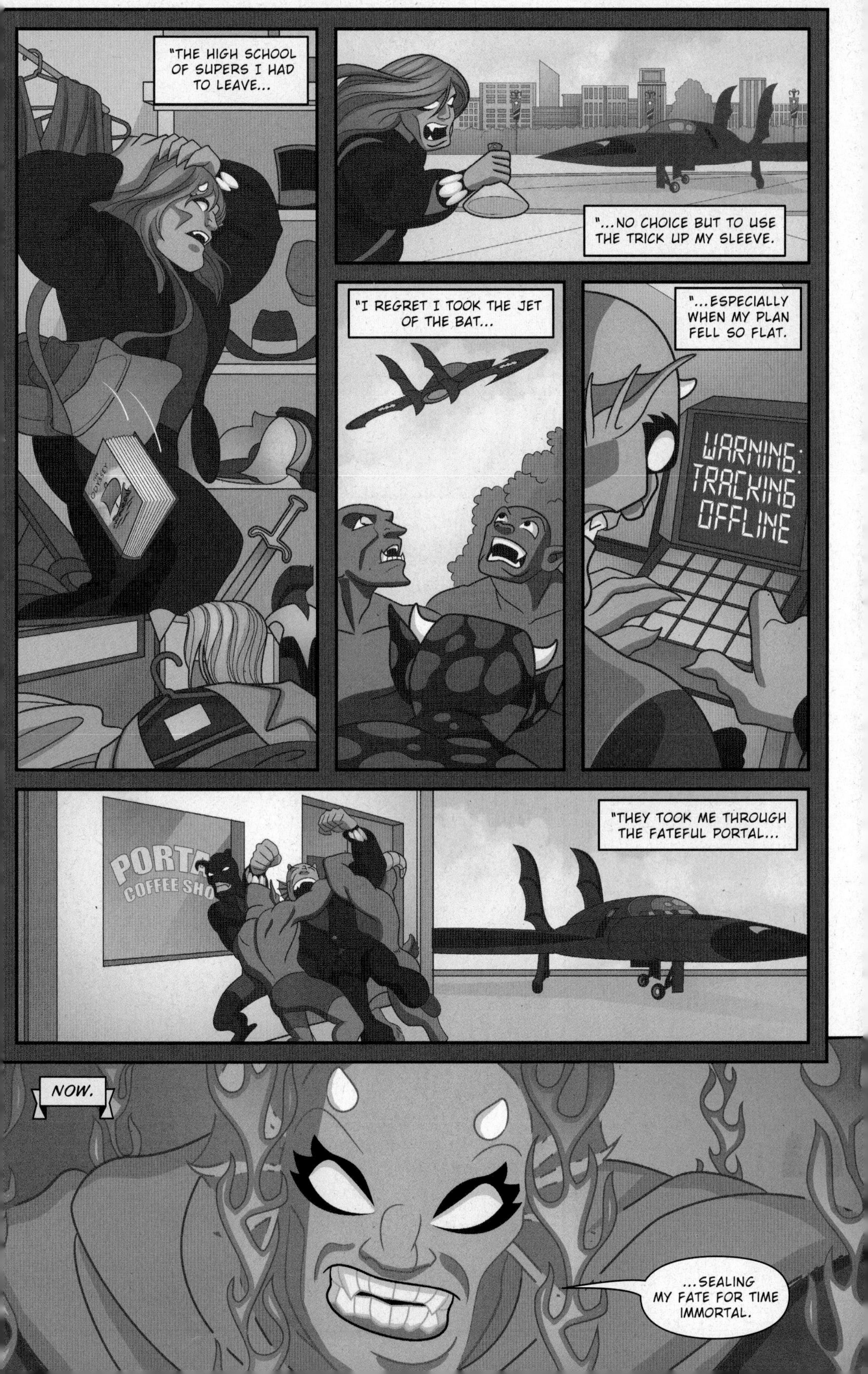
"THE HIGH SCHOOL OF SUPERS I HAD TO LEAVE...
"...NO CHOICE BUT TO USE THE TRICK UP MY SLEEVE.
"I REGRET I TOOK THE JET OF THE BAT...
"...ESPECIALLY WHEN MY PLAN FELL SO FLAT.
WARNING: TRACKING OFFLINE
THE ODYSSEY
PORTA
COFFEE SHO
"THEY TOOK ME THROUGH THE FATEFUL PORTAL...
NOW.
...SEALING MY FATE FOR TIME IMMORTAL.

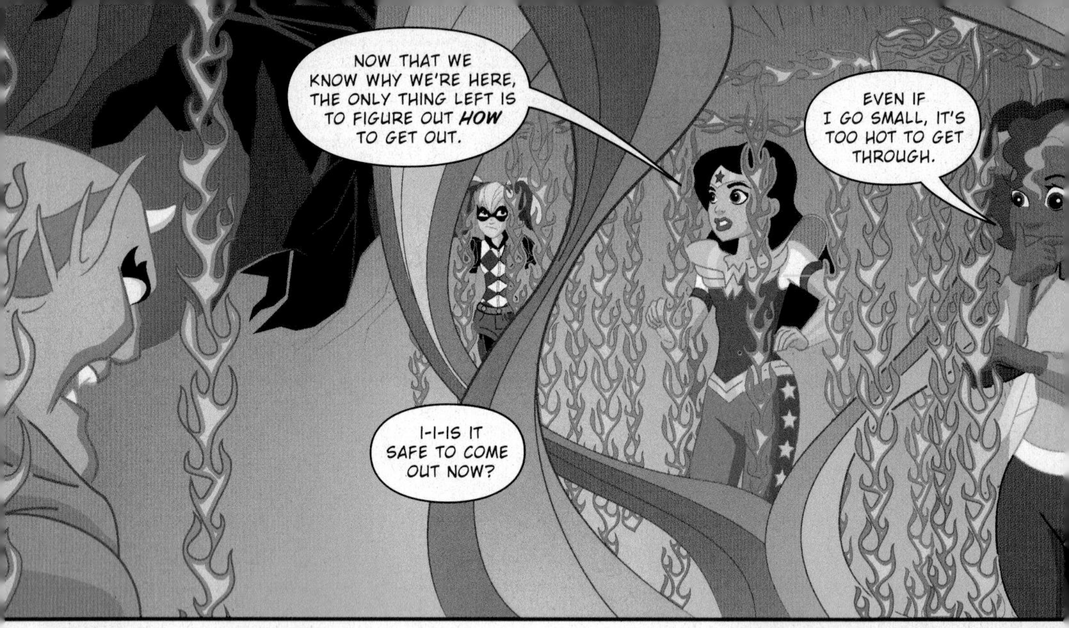
NOW THAT WE KNOW WHY WE'RE HERE, THE ONLY THING LEFT IS TO FIGURE OUT *HOW* TO GET OUT.
EVEN IF I GO SMALL, IT'S TOO HOT TO GET THROUGH.
I-I-IS IT SAFE TO COME OUT NOW?

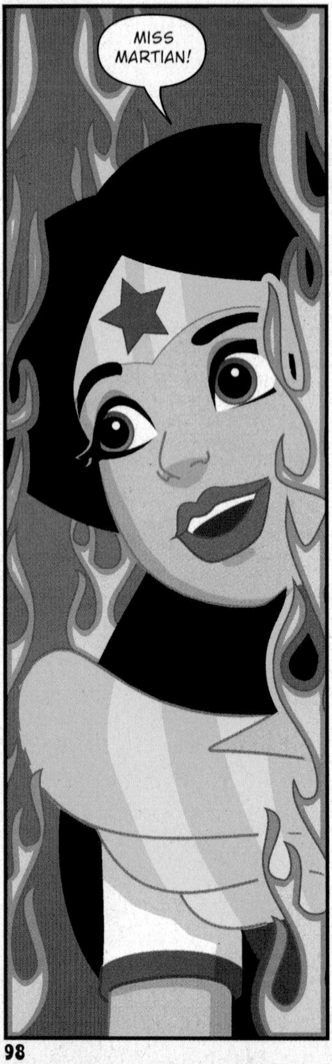
MISS MARTIAN!

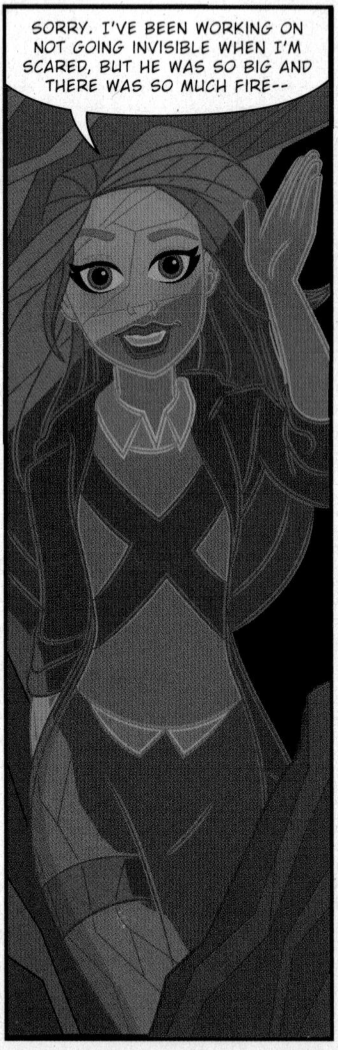
SORRY. I'VE BEEN WORKING ON NOT GOING INVISIBLE WHEN I'M SCARED, BUT HE WAS SO BIG AND THERE WAS SO MUCH FIRE--

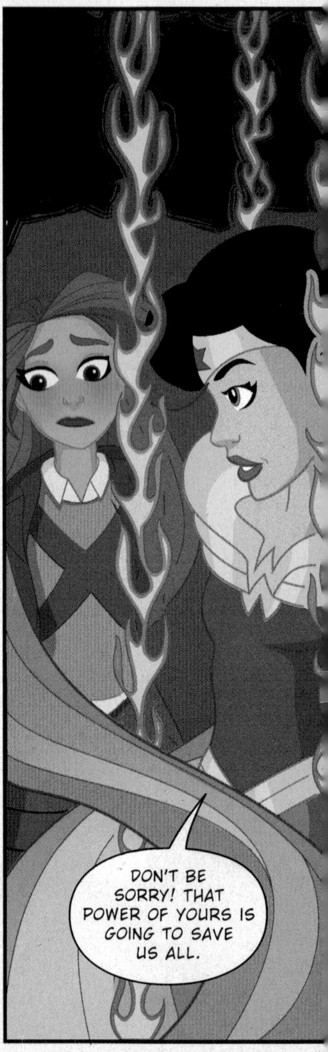
DON'T BE SORRY! THAT POWER OF YOURS IS GOING TO SAVE US ALL.

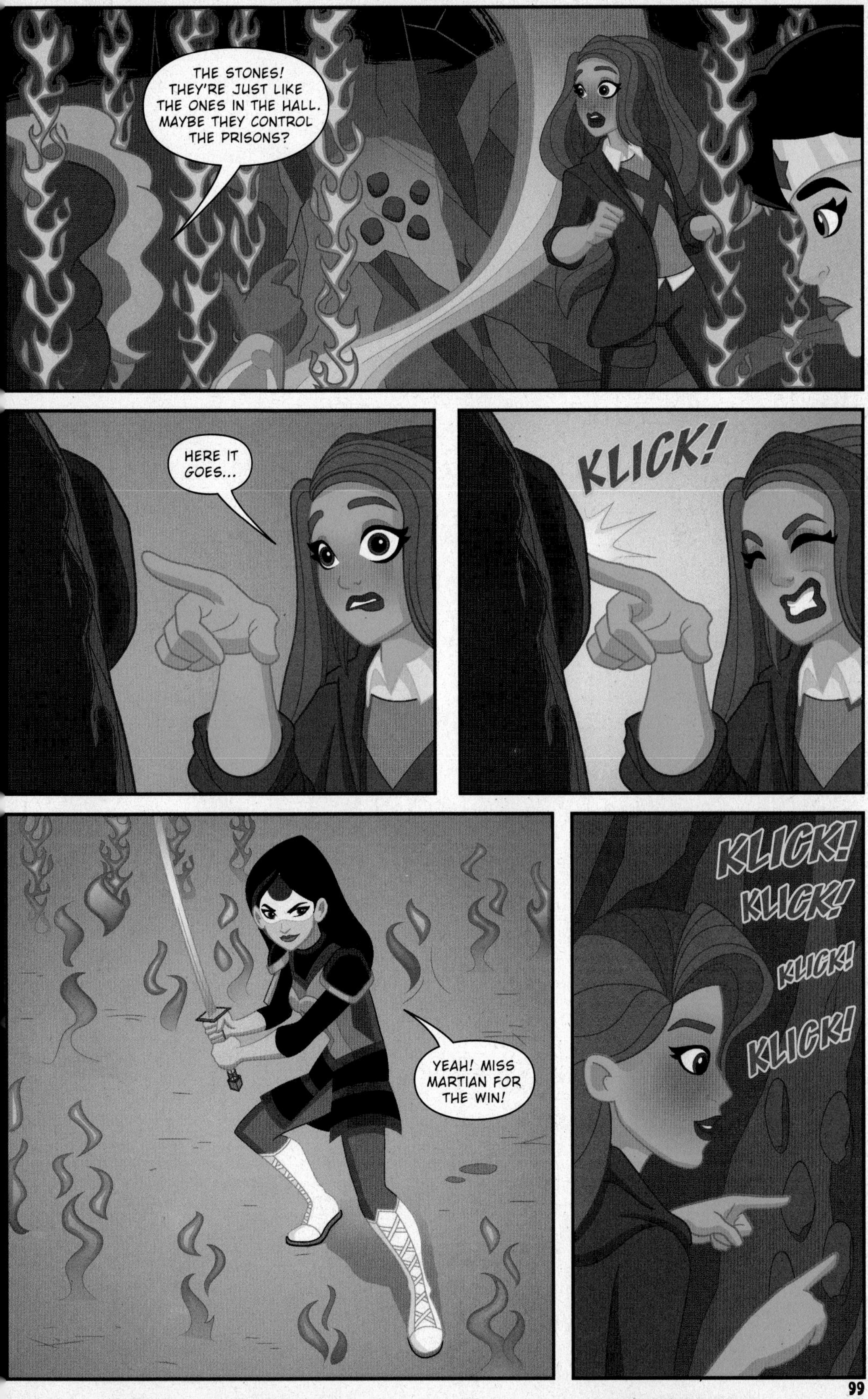
THE STONES! THEY'RE JUST LIKE THE ONES IN THE HALL. MAYBE THEY CONTROL THE PRISONS?
HERE IT GOES...
KLICK!
YEAH! MISS MARTIAN FOR THE WIN!
KLICK!
KLICK!
KLICK!
KLICK!

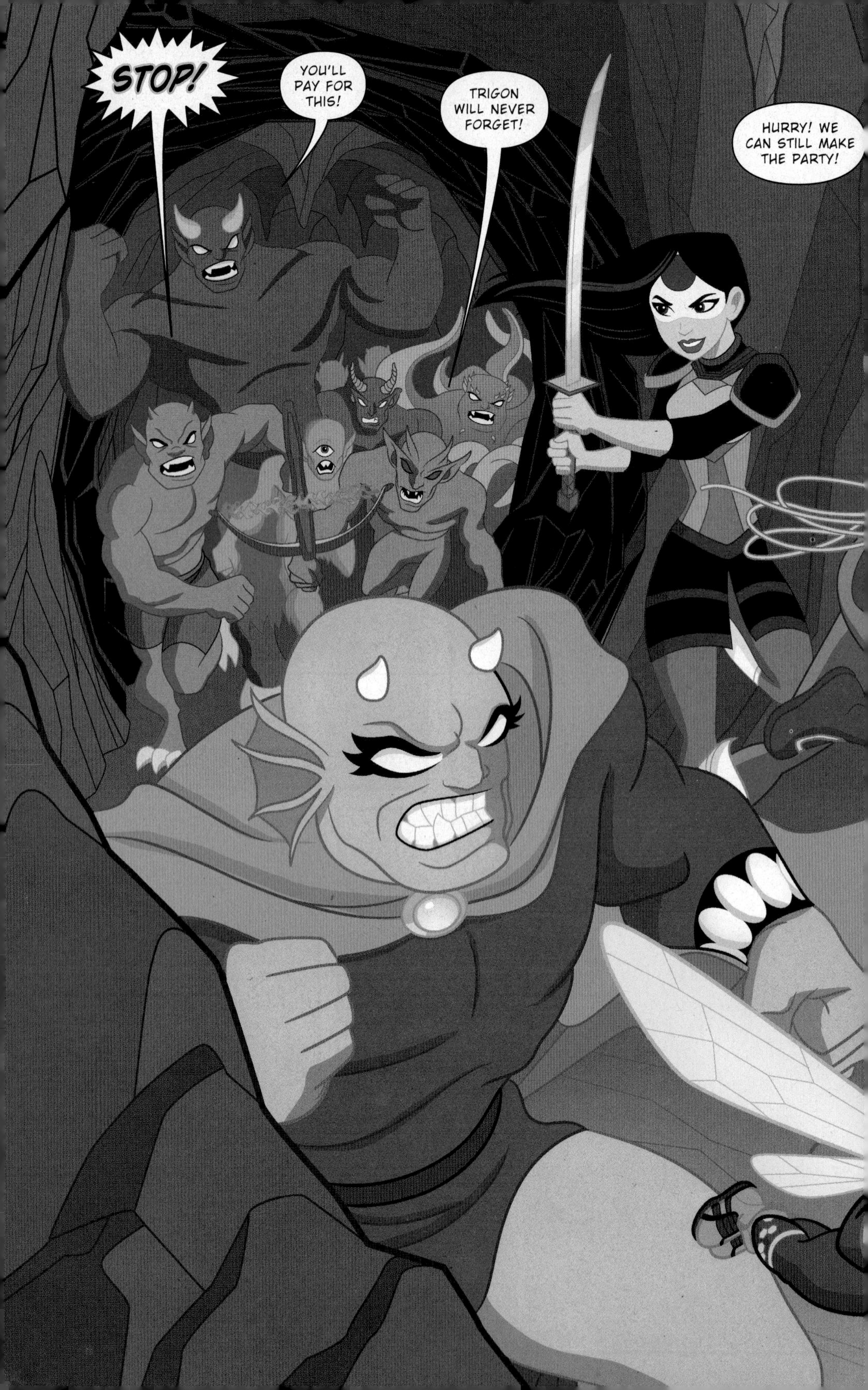
STOP!
YOU'LL PAY FOR THIS!
TRIGON WILL NEVER FORGET!
HURRY! WE CAN STILL MAKE THE PARTY!

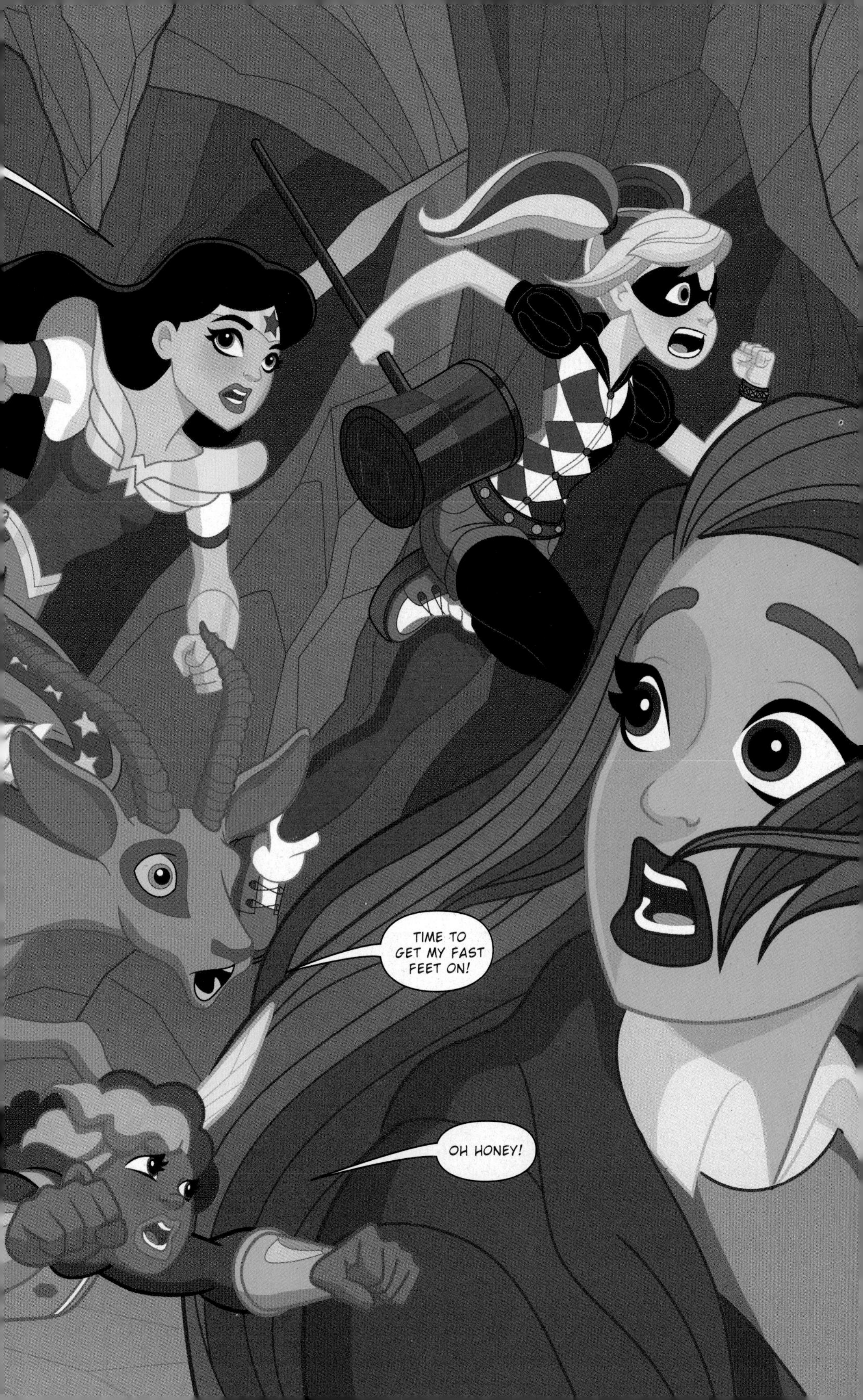
TIME TO GET MY FAST FEET ON!
OH HONEY!

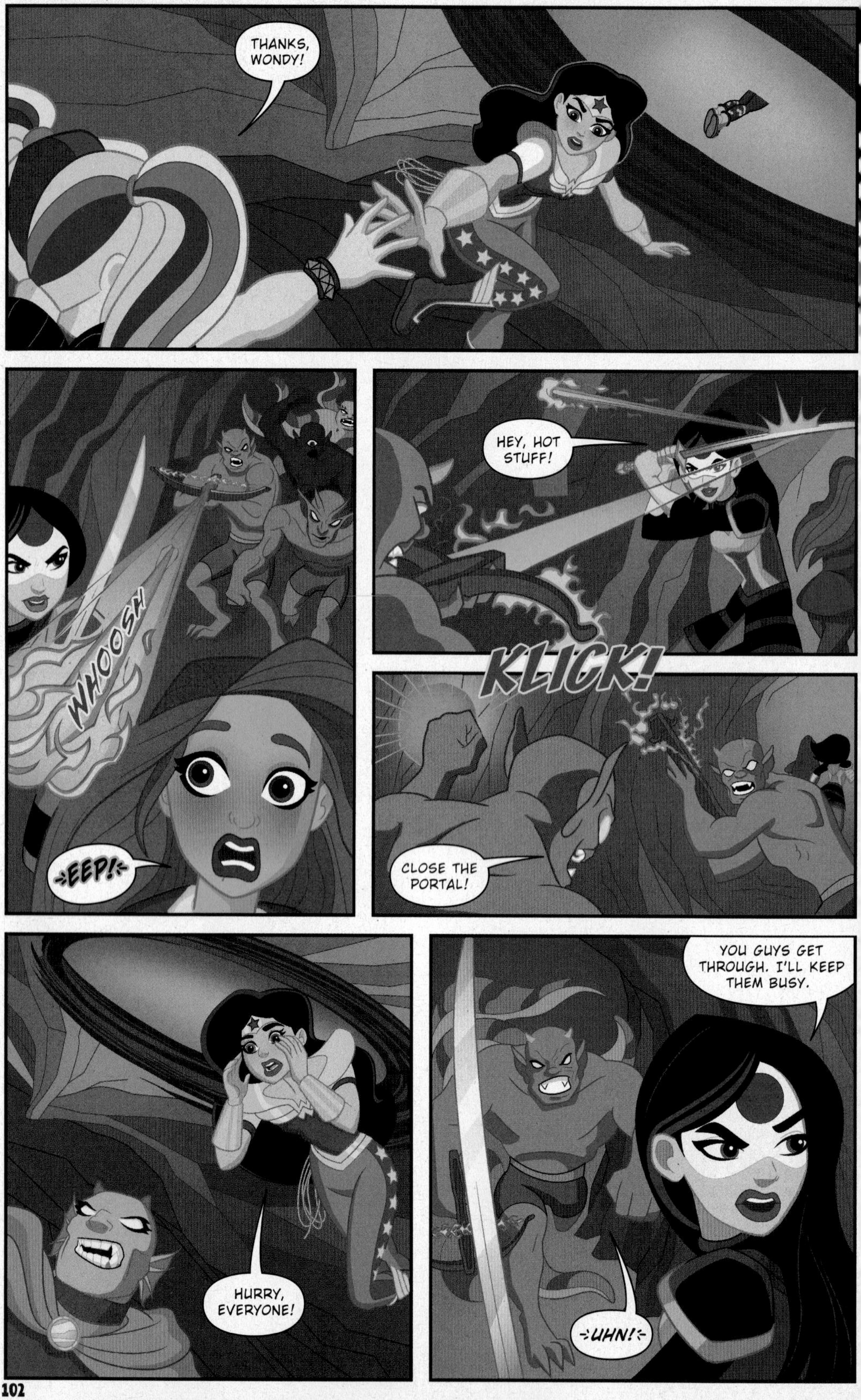
THANKS, WONDY!
WHOOSH
-EEP!-
HEY, HOT STUFF!
KLICK!
CLOSE THE PORTAL!
HURRY, EVERYONE!
YOU GUYS GET THROUGH. I'LL KEEP THEM BUSY.
-UHN!-

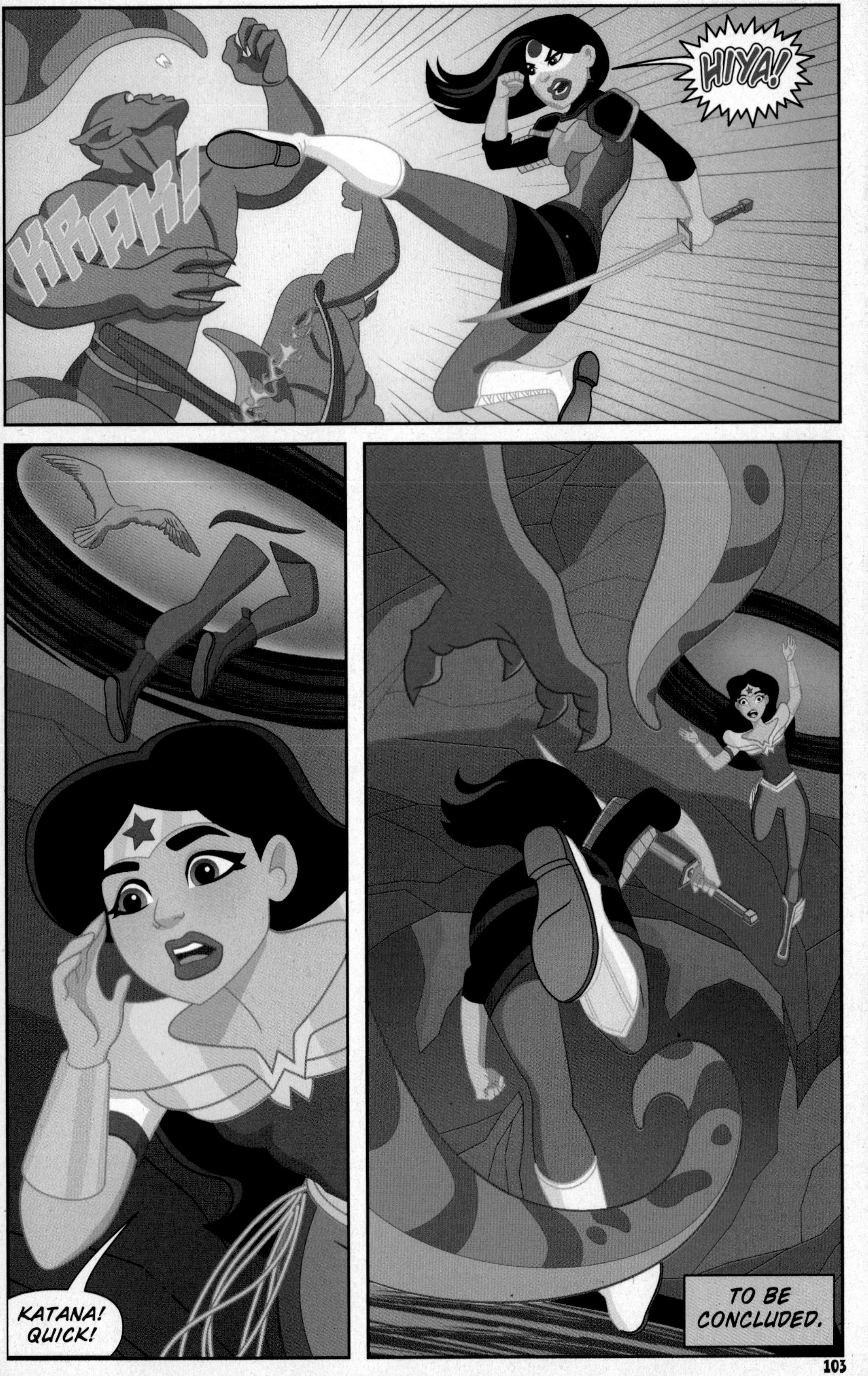
HIYA!
KRAK!
KATANA! QUICK!
TO BE CONCLUDED.

CHAPTER SIX
THE RETURN HOME

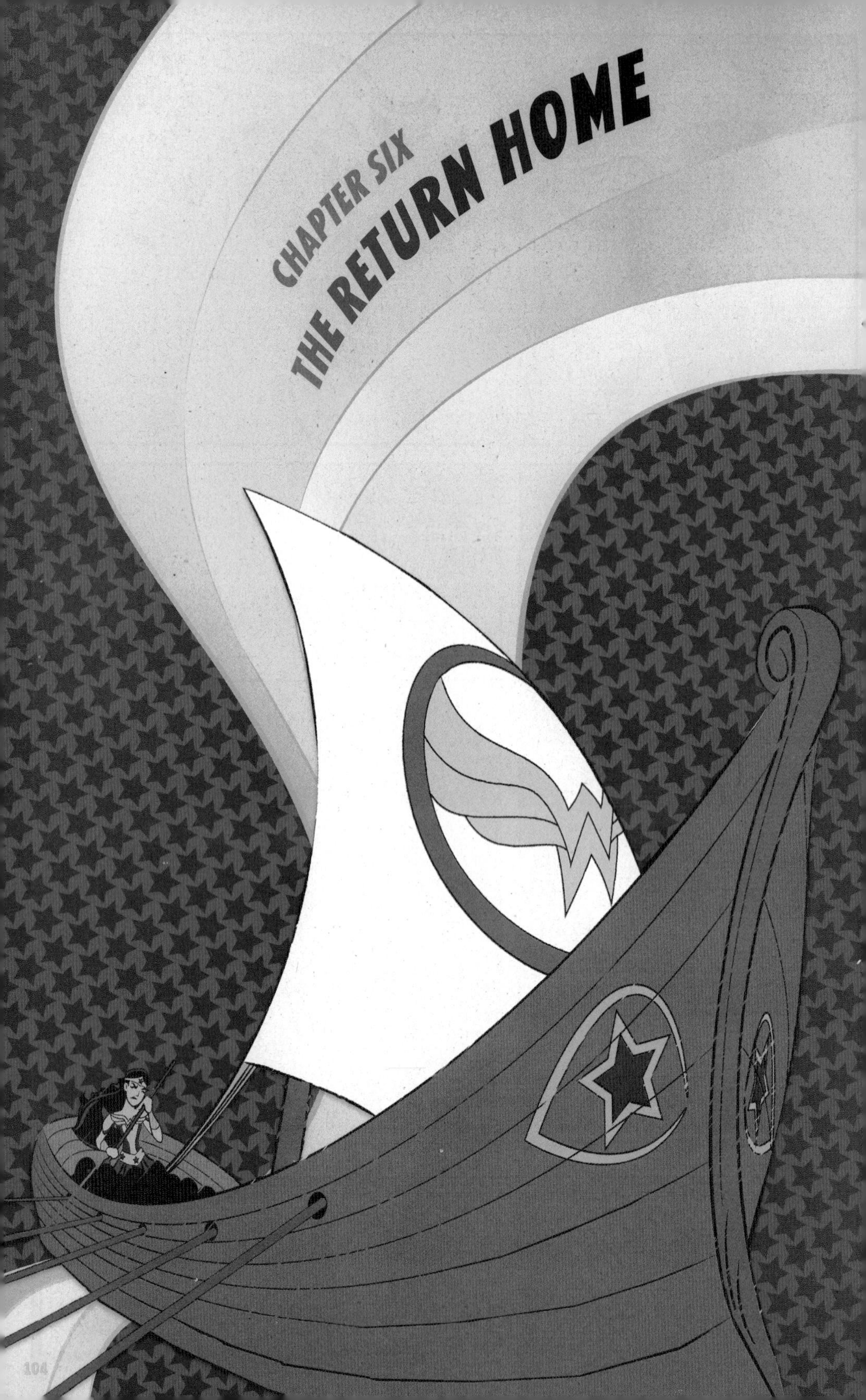

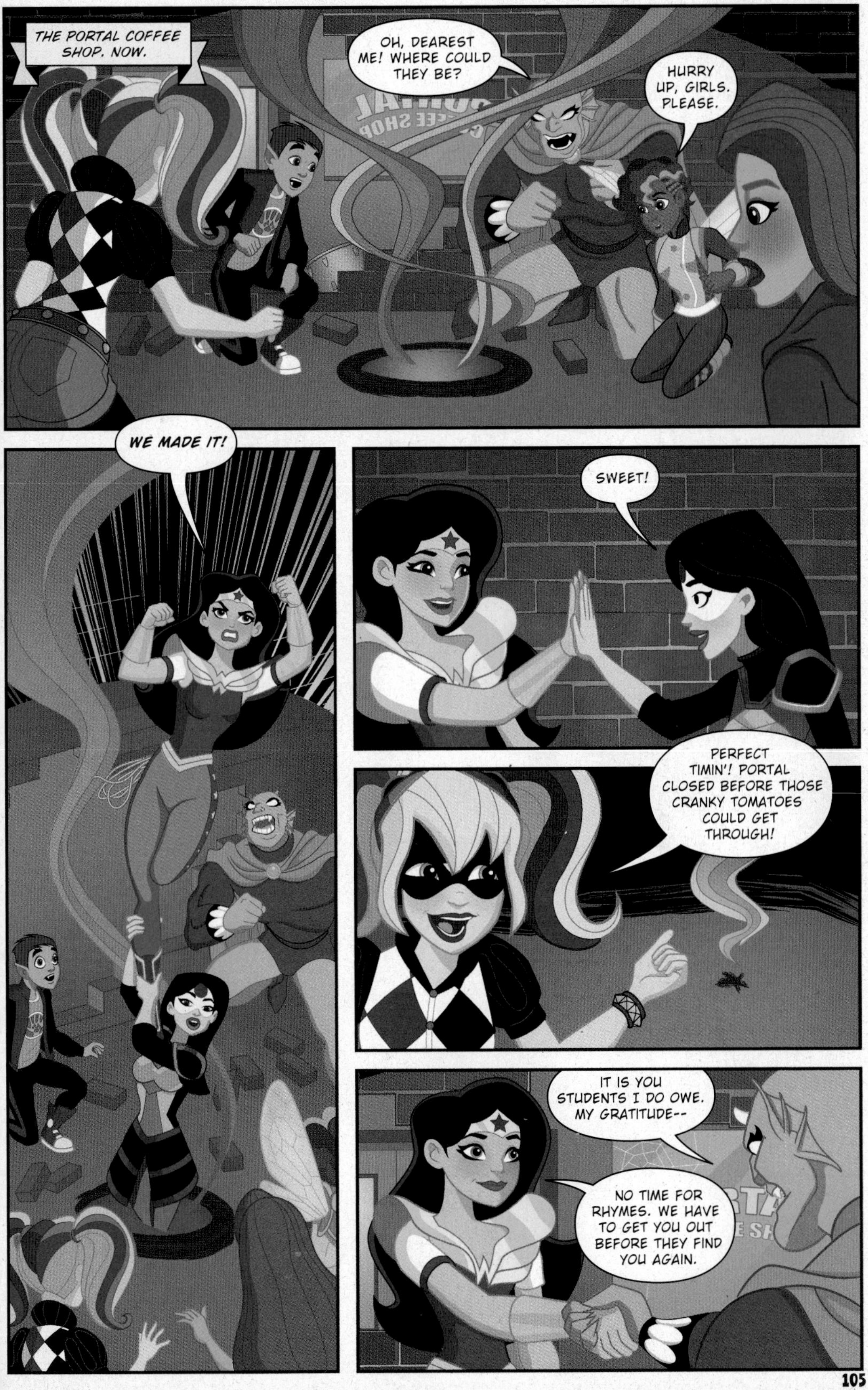
THE PORTAL COFFEE SHOP. NOW.
OH, DEAREST ME! WHERE COULD THEY BE?
HURRY UP, GIRLS. PLEASE.
WE MADE IT!
SWEET!
PERFECT TIMIN'! PORTAL CLOSED BEFORE THOSE CRANKY TOMATOES COULD GET THROUGH!
IT IS YOU STUDENTS I DO OWE. MY GRATITUDE--
NO TIME FOR RHYMES. WE HAVE TO GET YOU OUT BEFORE THEY FIND YOU AGAIN.

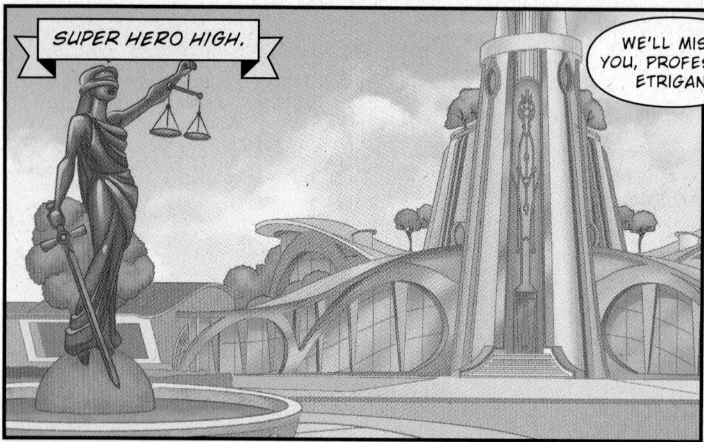
SUPER HERO HIGH.

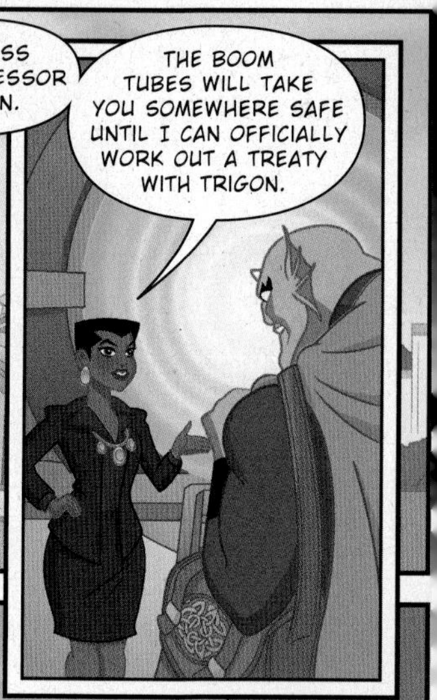
WE'LL MISS YOU, PROFESSOR ETRIGAN.
THE BOOM TUBES WILL TAKE YOU SOMEWHERE SAFE UNTIL I CAN OFFICIALLY WORK OUT A TREATY WITH TRIGON.

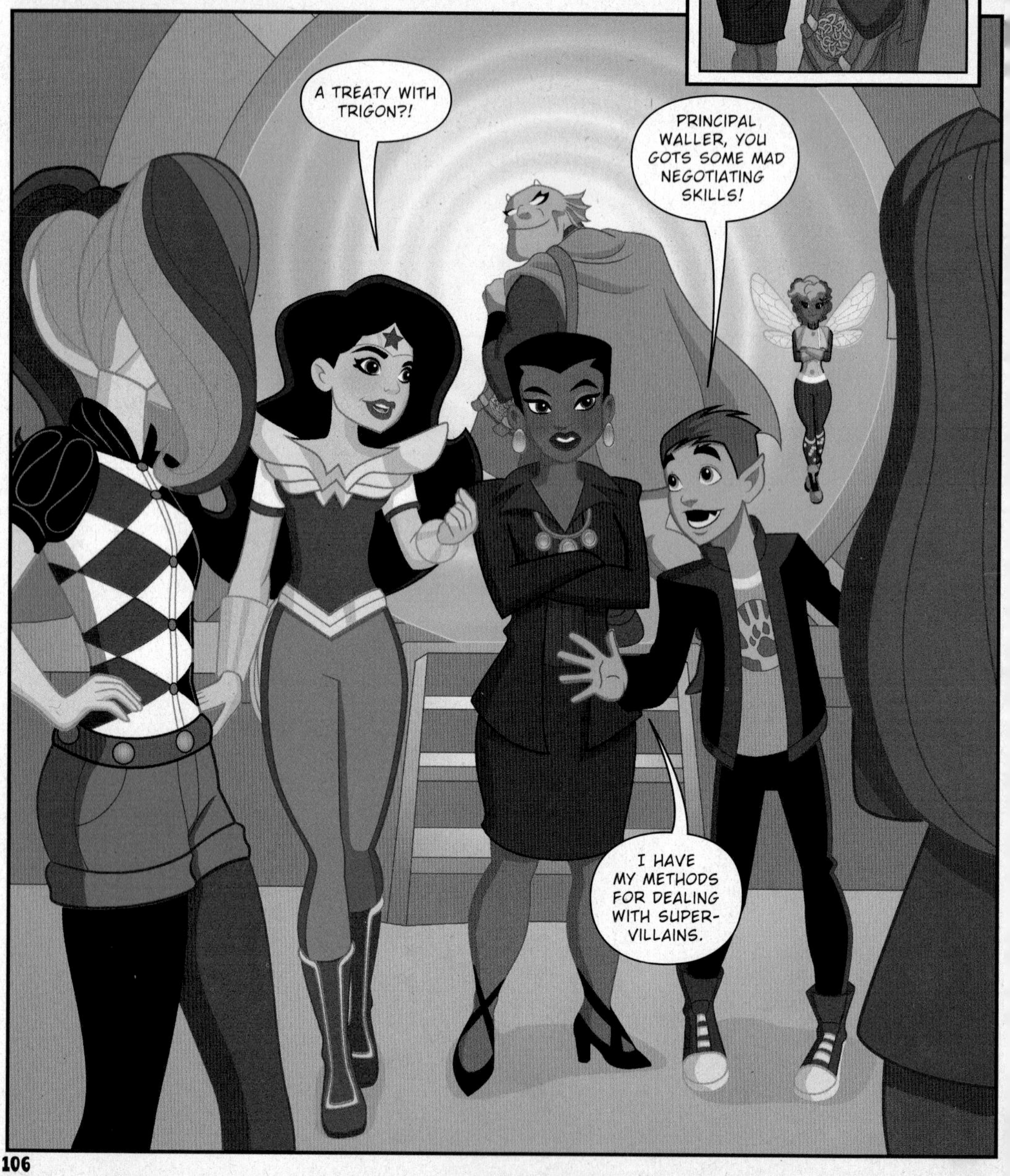
A TREATY WITH TRIGON?!
PRINCIPAL WALLER, YOU GOTS SOME MAD NEGOTIATING SKILLS!
I HAVE MY METHODS FOR DEALING WITH SUPER-VILLAINS.

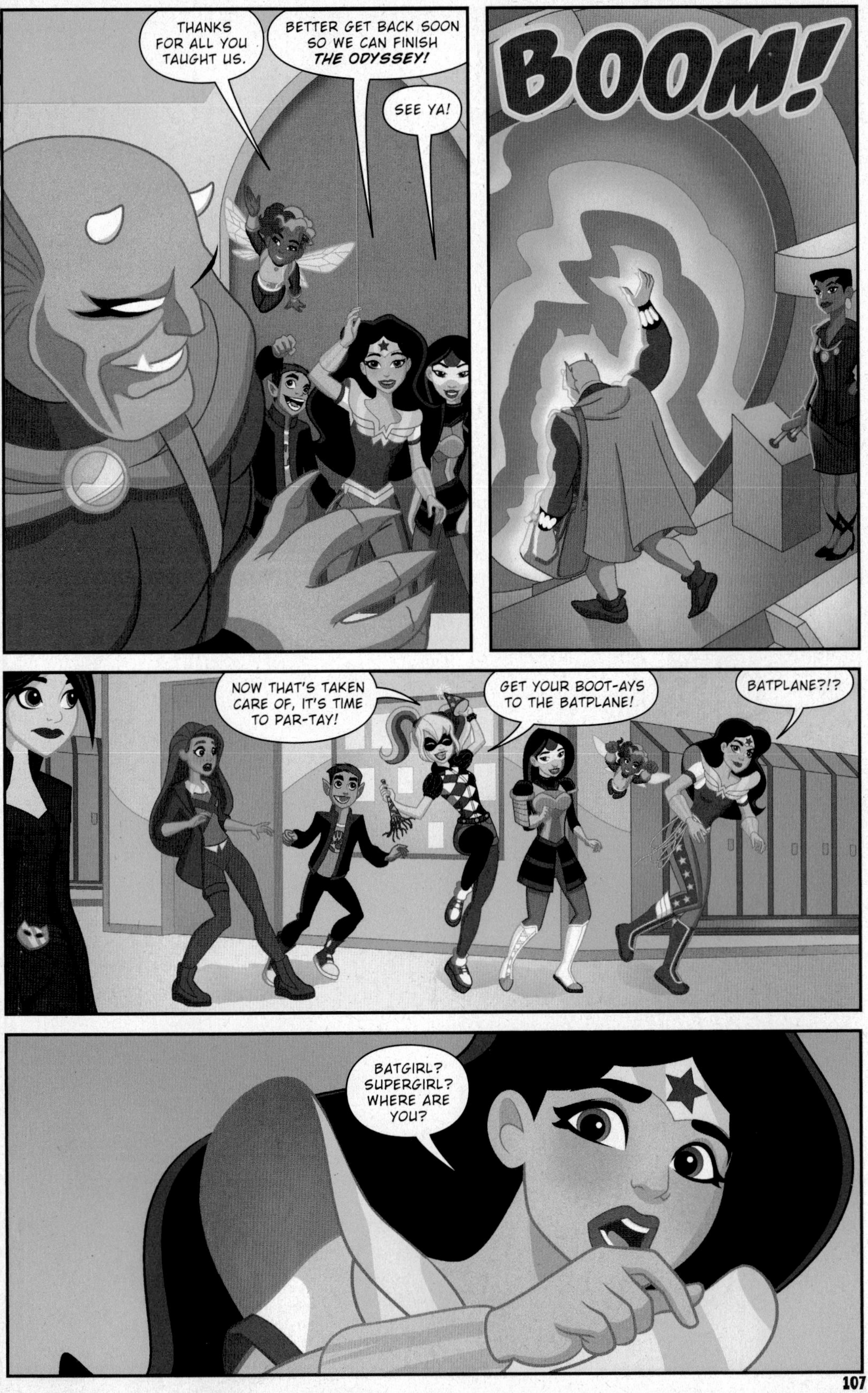
THANKS FOR ALL YOU TAUGHT US.
BETTER GET BACK SOON SO WE CAN FINISH *THE ODYSSEY!*
SEE YA!
BOOM!
NOW THAT'S TAKEN CARE OF, IT'S TIME TO PAR-TAY!
GET YOUR BOOT-AYS TO THE BATPLANE!
BATPLANE?!?
BATGIRL? SUPERGIRL? WHERE ARE YOU?

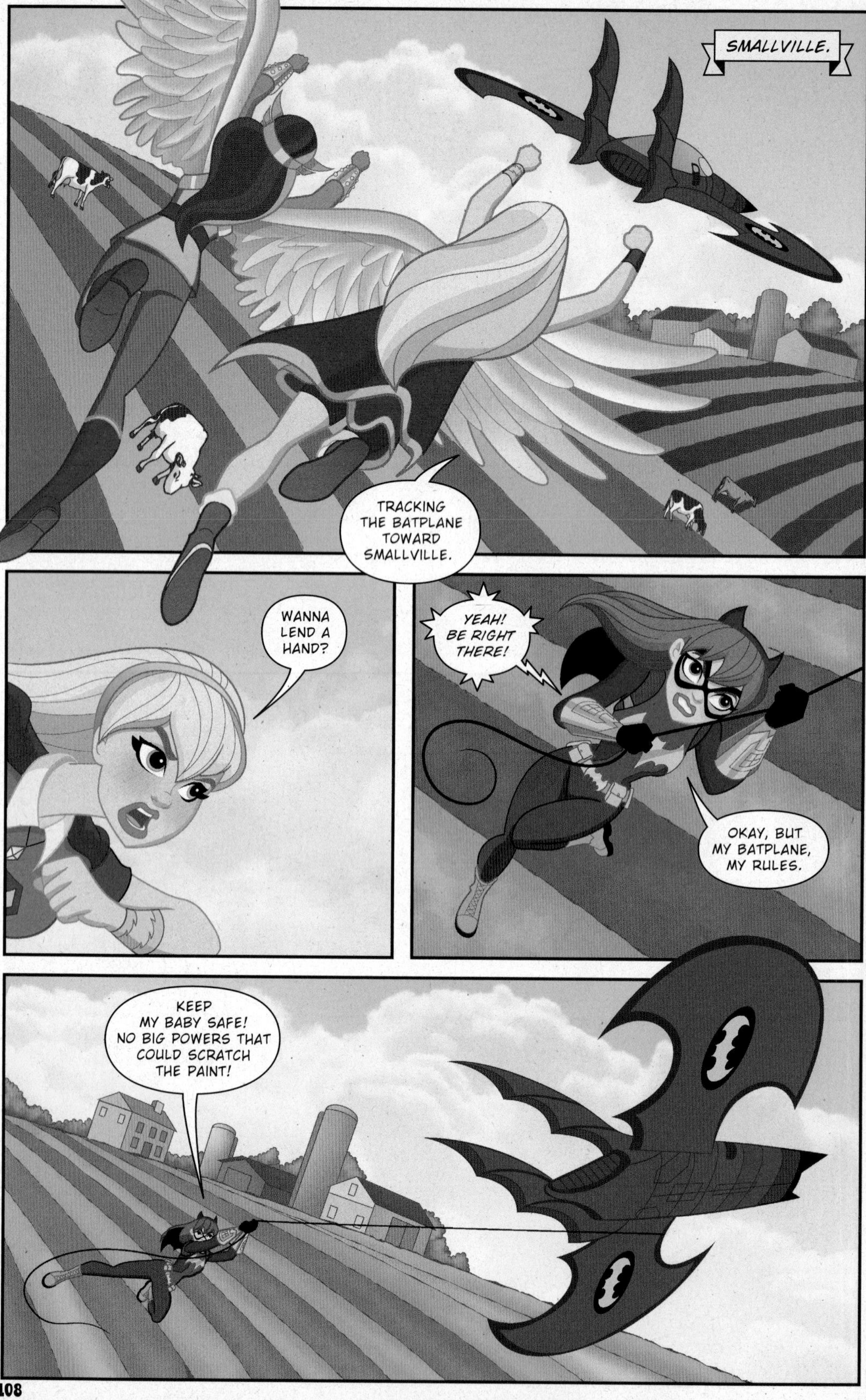
SMALLVILLE.
TRACKING THE BATPLANE TOWARD SMALLVILLE.
WANNA LEND A HAND?
YEAH! BE RIGHT THERE!
OKAY, BUT MY BATPLANE, MY RULES.
KEEP MY BABY SAFE! NO BIG POWERS THAT COULD SCRATCH THE PAINT!

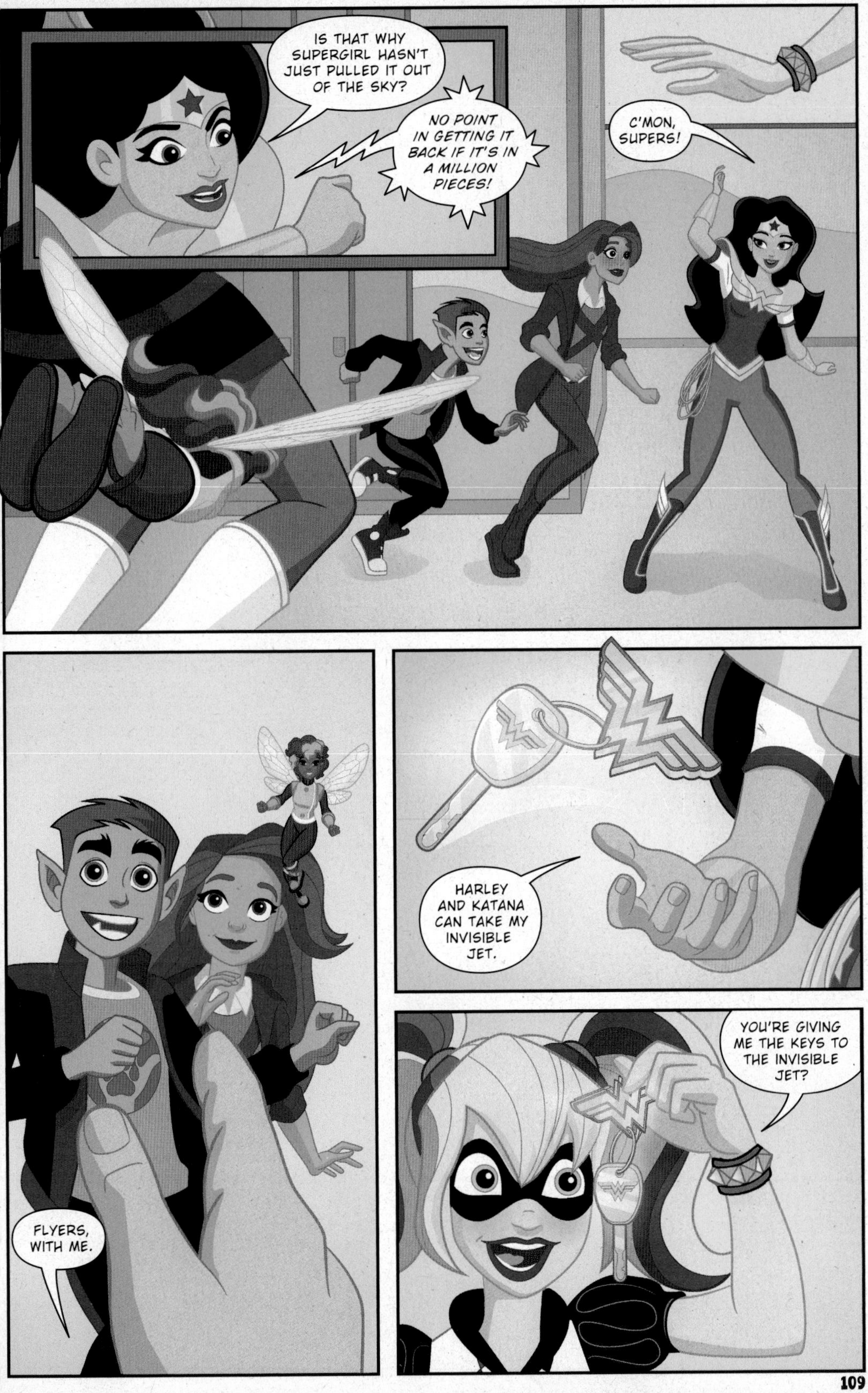
IS THAT WHY SUPERGIRL HASN'T JUST PULLED IT OUT OF THE SKY?
NO POINT IN GETTING IT BACK IF IT'S IN A MILLION PIECES!
C'MON, SUPERS!
HARLEY AND KATANA CAN TAKE MY INVISIBLE JET.
FLYERS, WITH ME.
YOU'RE GIVING ME THE KEYS TO THE INVISIBLE JET?

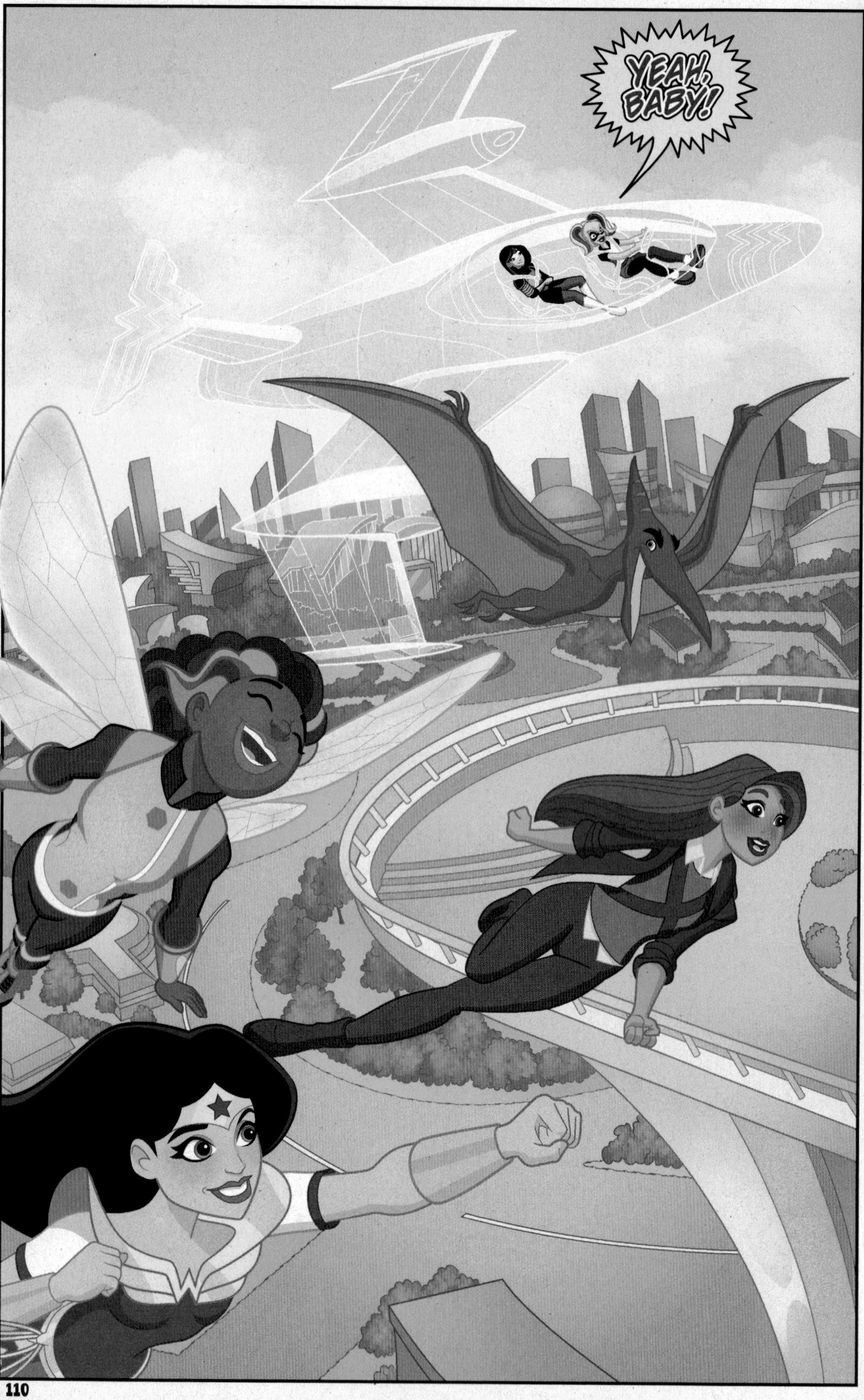
YEAH, BABY!

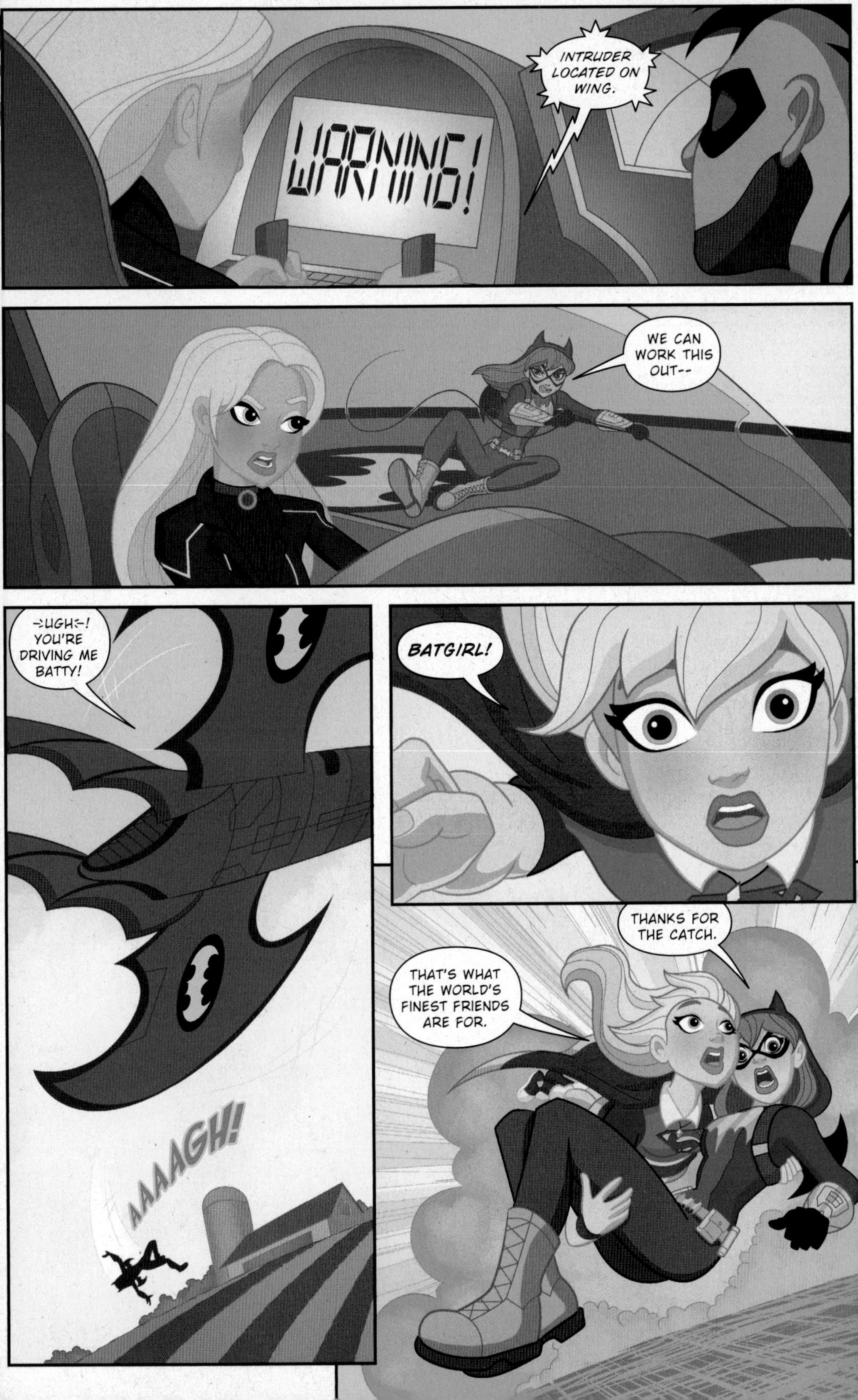

WARNING!
INTRUDER LOCATED ON WING.
WE CAN WORK THIS OUT--
-UGH-! YOU'RE DRIVING ME BATTY!
AAAAGH!
BATGIRL!
THANKS FOR THE CATCH.
THAT'S WHAT THE WORLD'S FINEST FRIENDS ARE FOR.

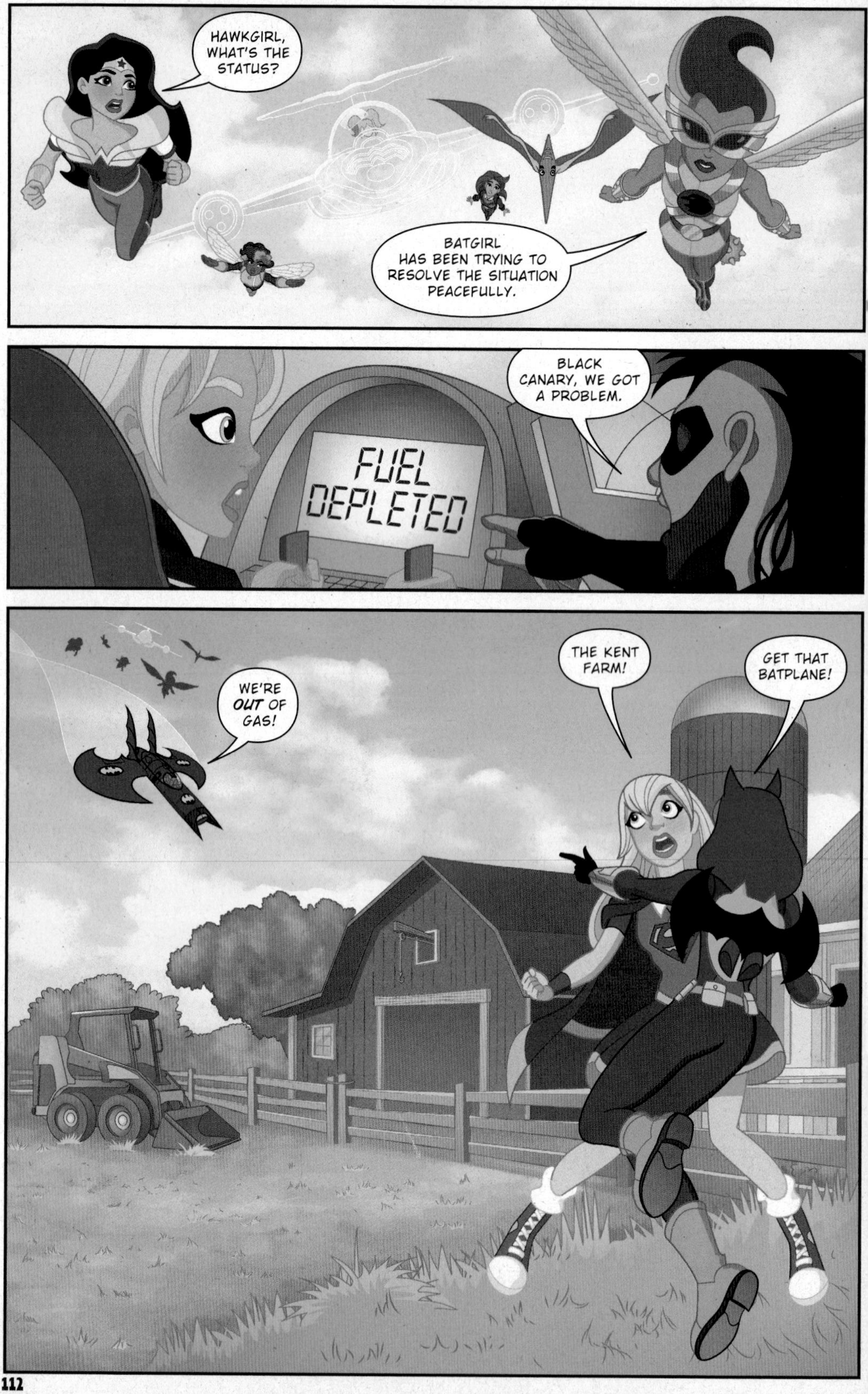
HAWKGIRL, WHAT'S THE STATUS?
BATGIRL HAS BEEN TRYING TO RESOLVE THE SITUATION PEACEFULLY.
BLACK CANARY, WE GOT A PROBLEM.
FUEL DEPLETED
WE'RE *OUT* OF GAS!
THE KENT FARM!
GET THAT BATPLANE!

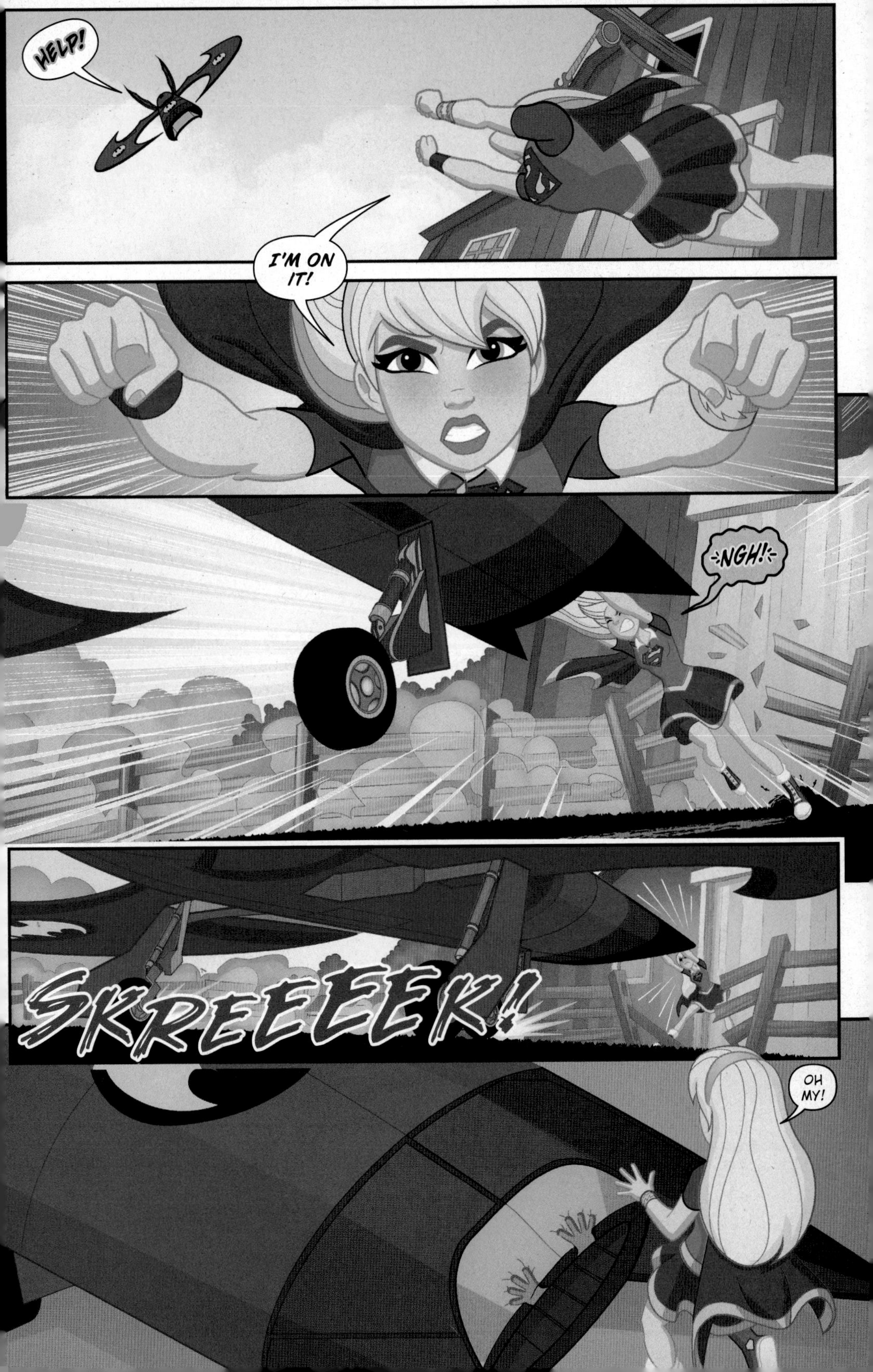
HELP!
I'M ON IT!
NGH!
SKREEEEK!
OH MY!

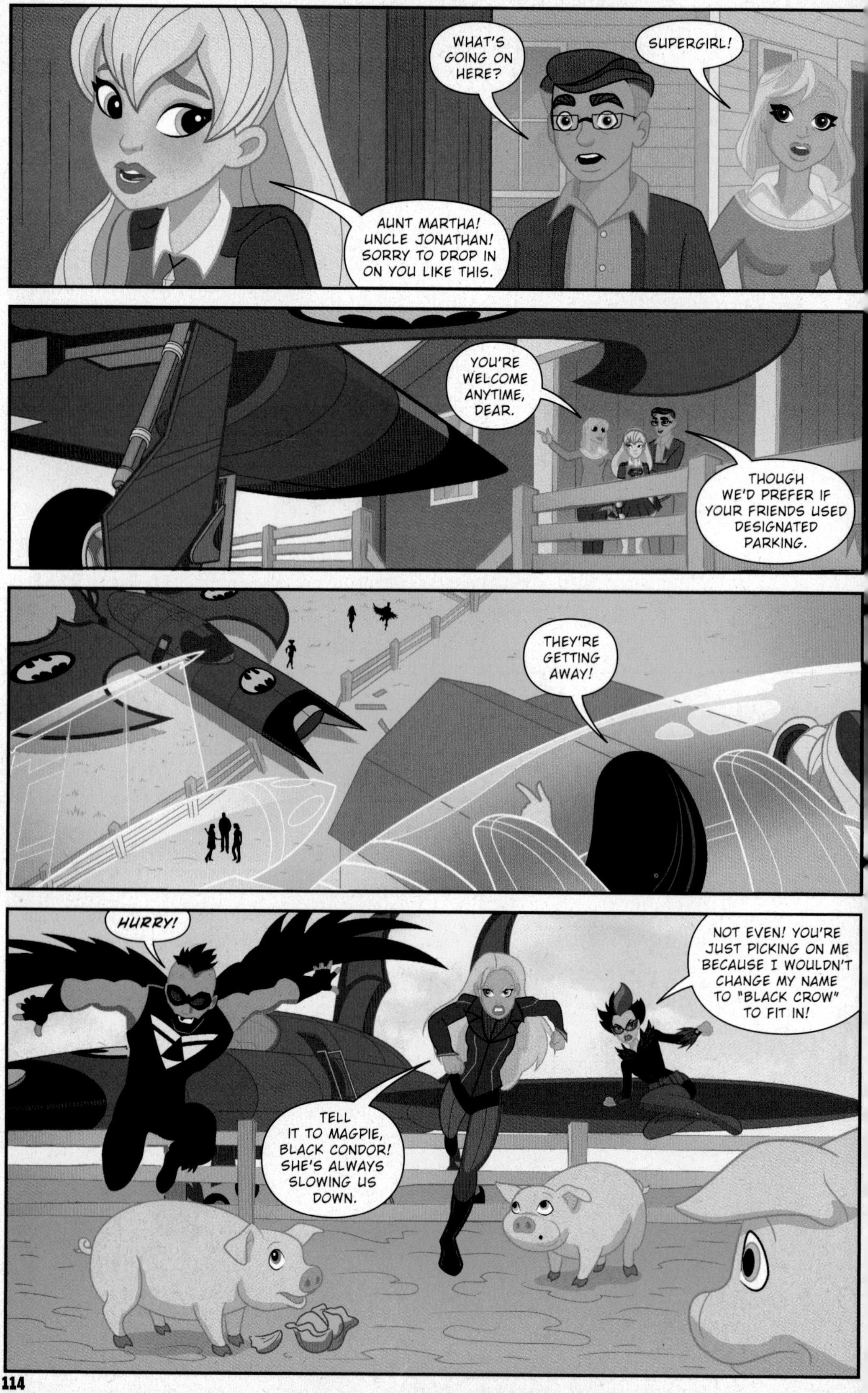
AUNT MARTHA! UNCLE JONATHAN! SORRY TO DROP IN ON YOU LIKE THIS.
WHAT'S GOING ON HERE?
SUPERGIRL!
YOU'RE WELCOME ANYTIME, DEAR.
THOUGH WE'D PREFER IF YOUR FRIENDS USED DESIGNATED PARKING.
THEY'RE GETTING AWAY!
HURRY!
TELL IT TO MAGPIE, BLACK CONDOR! SHE'S ALWAYS SLOWING US DOWN.
NOT EVEN! YOU'RE JUST PICKING ON ME BECAUSE I WOULDN'T CHANGE MY NAME TO "BLACK CROW" TO FIT IN!

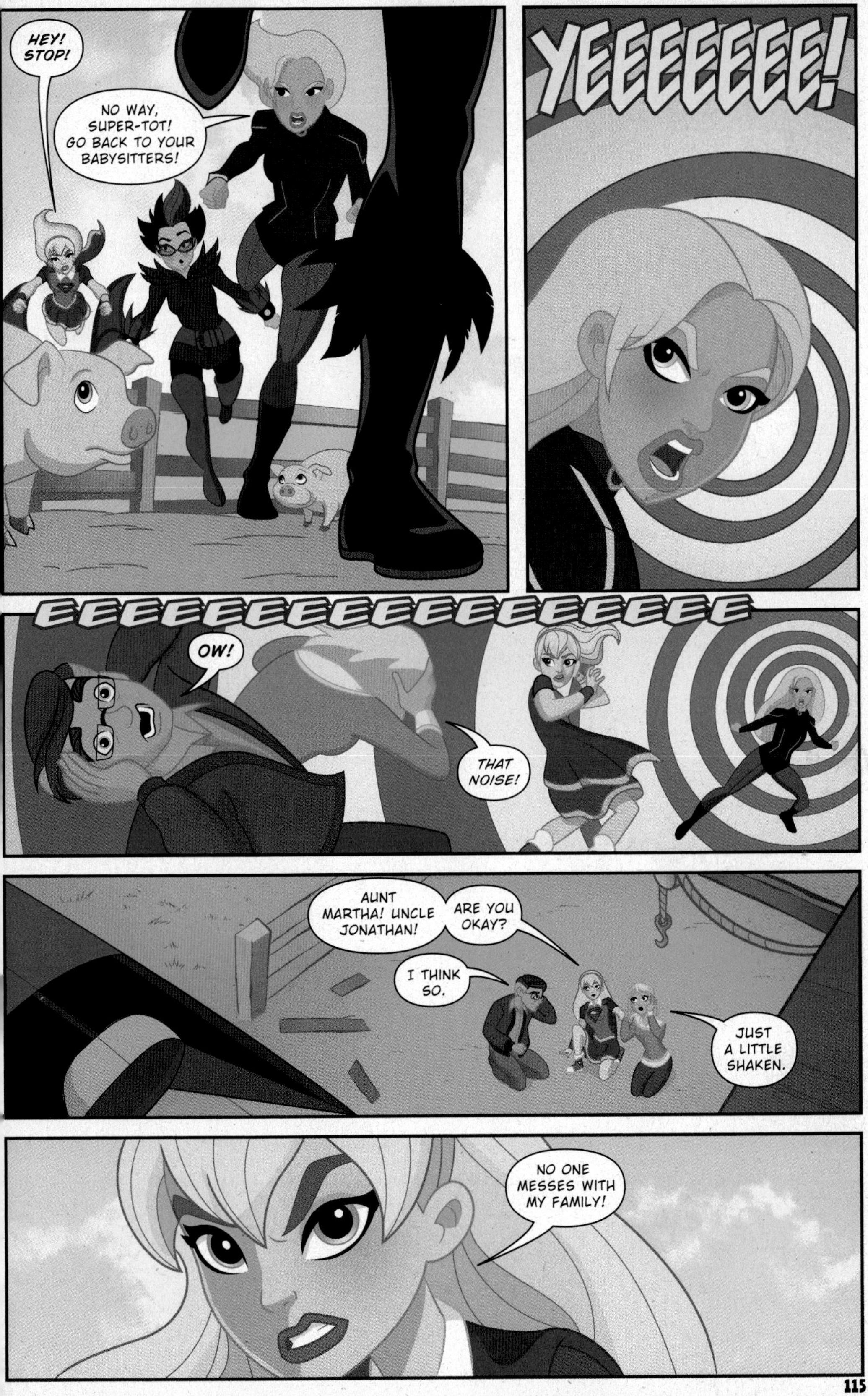
HEY! STOP!
NO WAY, SUPER-TOT! GO BACK TO YOUR BABYSITTERS!
YEEEEEEE!
EEEEEEEEEEEEEEEEEEEEE
OW!
THAT NOISE!
AUNT MARTHA! UNCLE JONATHAN!
ARE YOU OKAY?
I THINK SO.
JUST A LITTLE SHAKEN.
NO ONE MESSES WITH MY FAMILY!

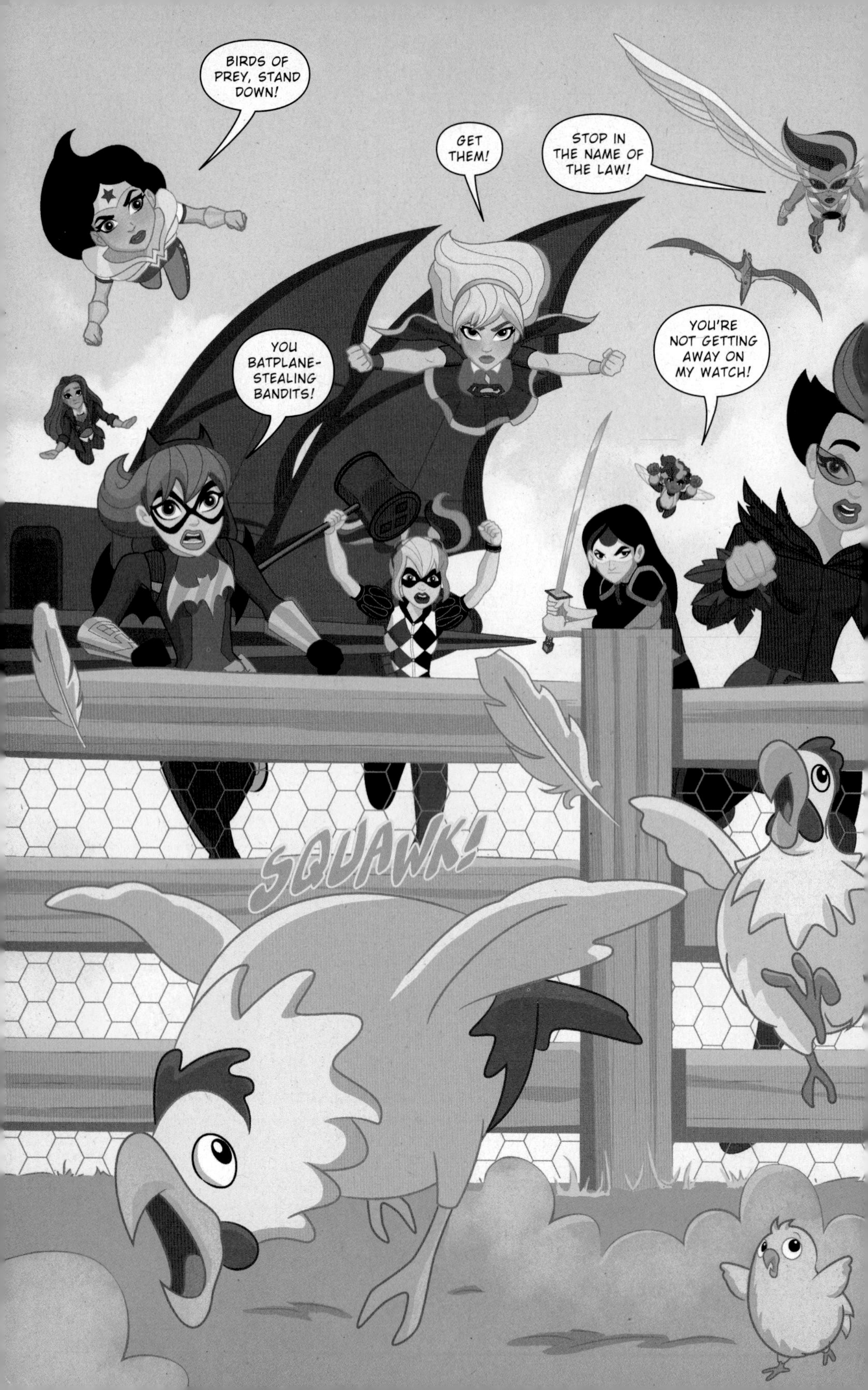
BIRDS OF PREY, STAND DOWN!
GET THEM!
STOP IN THE NAME OF THE LAW!
YOU BATPLANE-STEALING BANDITS!
YOU'RE NOT GETTING AWAY ON MY WATCH!
SQUAWK!

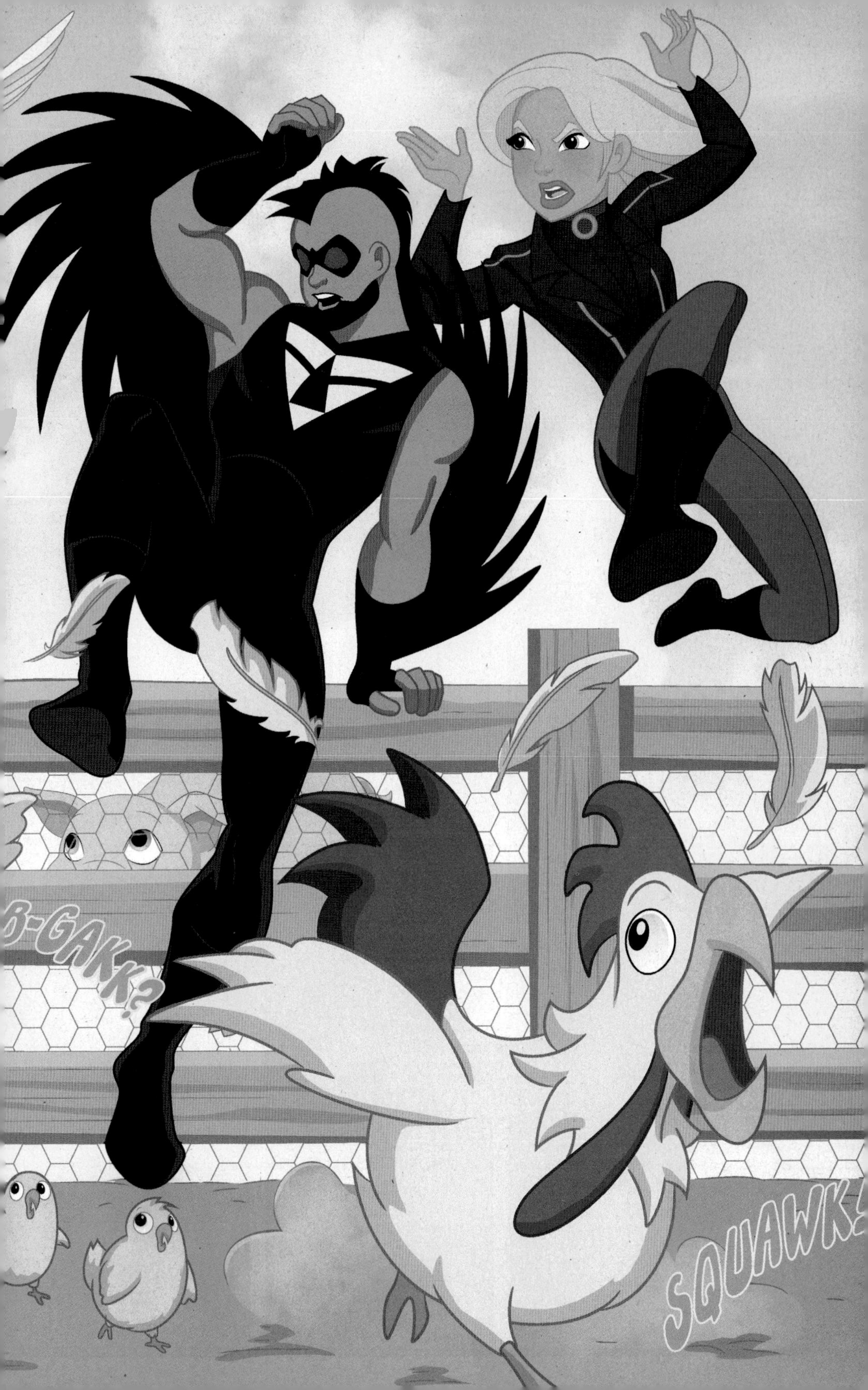
B-GAKK?
SQUAWK!

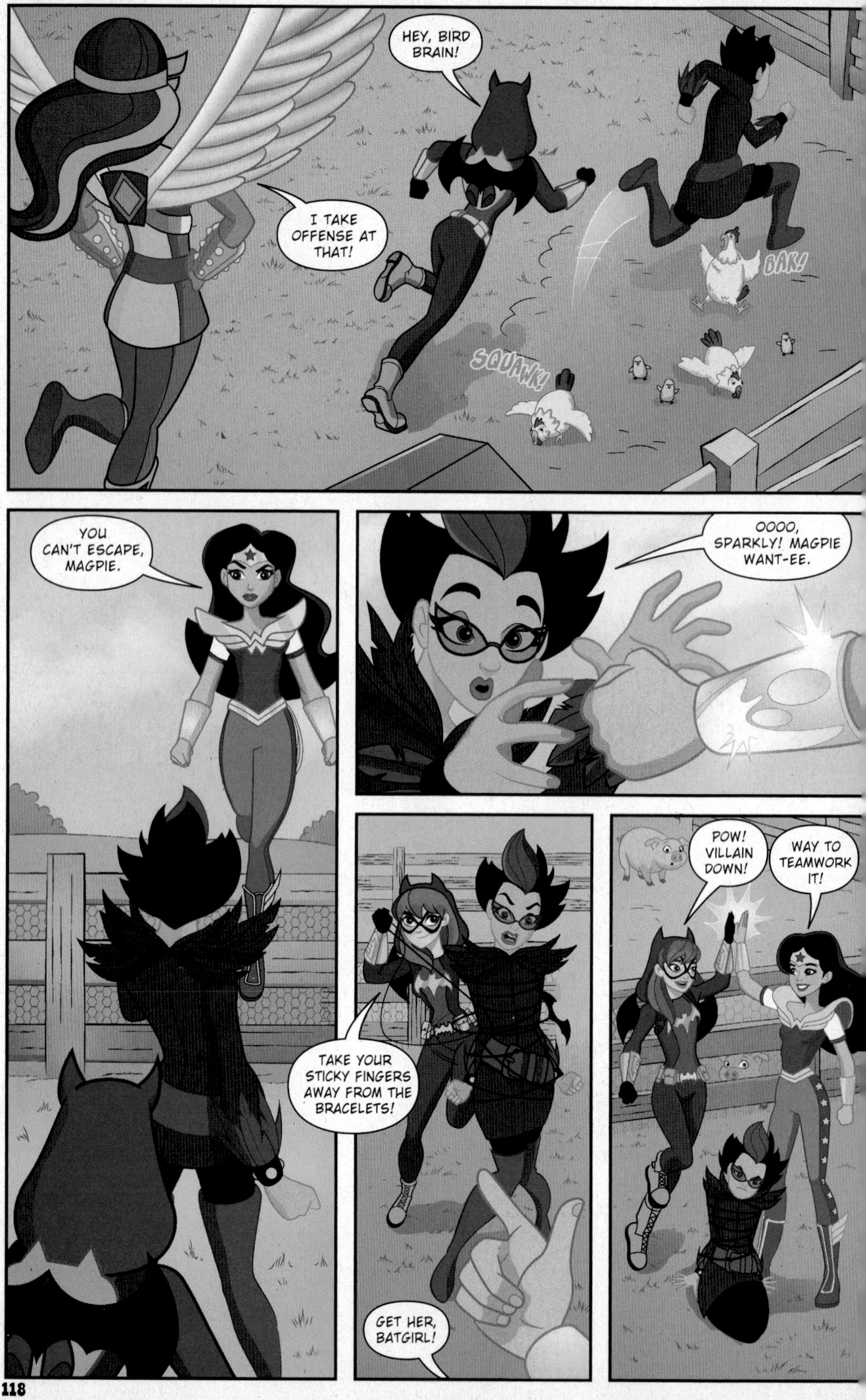
HEY, BIRD BRAIN!
I TAKE OFFENSE AT THAT!
BAK!
SQUAWK!
YOU CAN'T ESCAPE, MAGPIE.
OOOO, SPARKLY! MAGPIE WANT-EE.
TAKE YOUR STICKY FINGERS AWAY FROM THE BRACELETS!
GET HER, BATGIRL!
POW! VILLAIN DOWN!
WAY TO TEAMWORK IT!

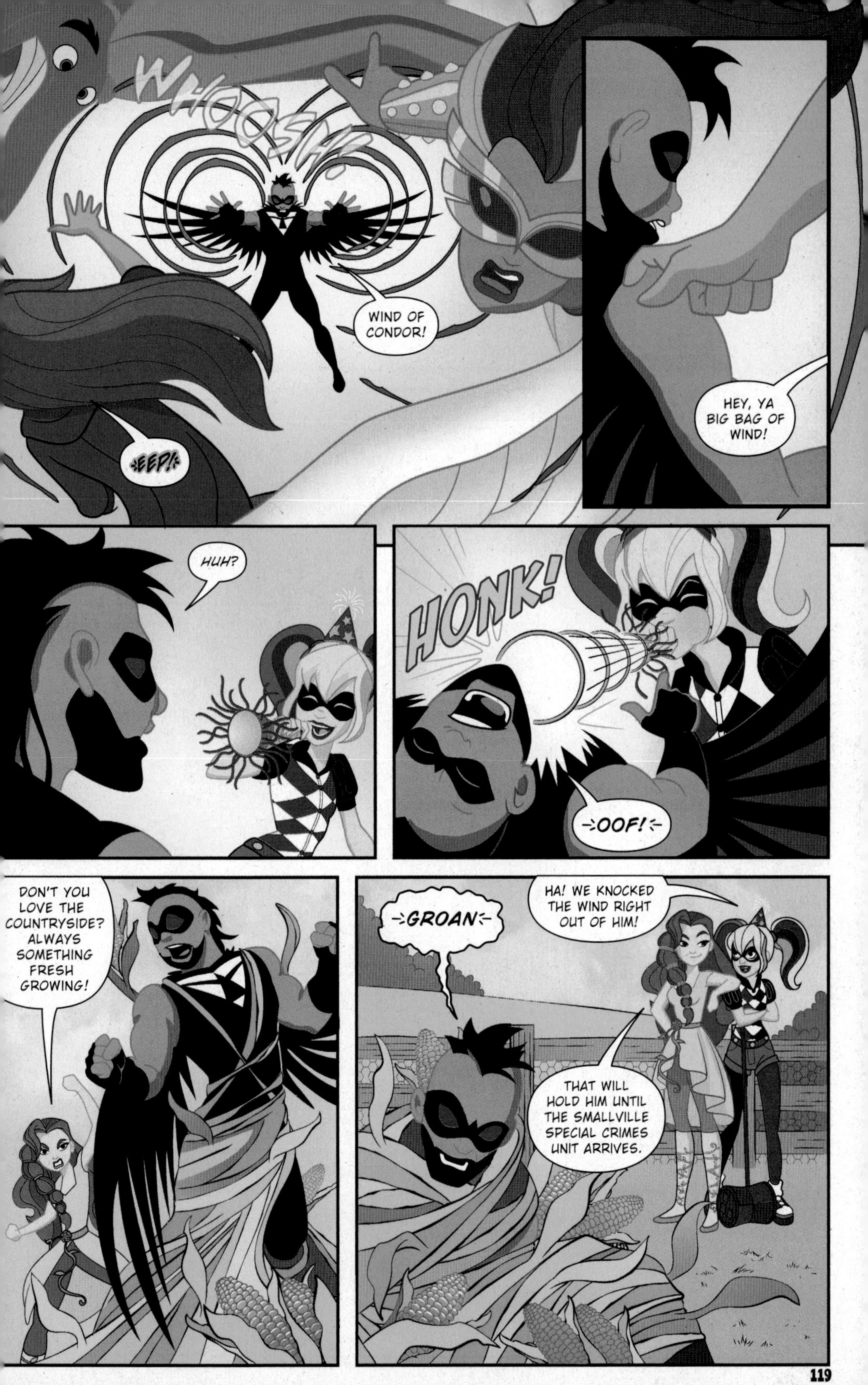
WHOOSH!
WIND OF CONDOR!
-EEP!-
HEY, YA BIG BAG OF WIND!
HUH?
HONK!
-OOF!-
DON'T YOU LOVE THE COUNTRYSIDE? ALWAYS SOMETHING FRESH GROWING!
-GROAN-
HA! WE KNOCKED THE WIND RIGHT OUT OF HIM!
THAT WILL HOLD HIM UNTIL THE SMALLVILLE SPECIAL CRIMES UNIT ARRIVES.

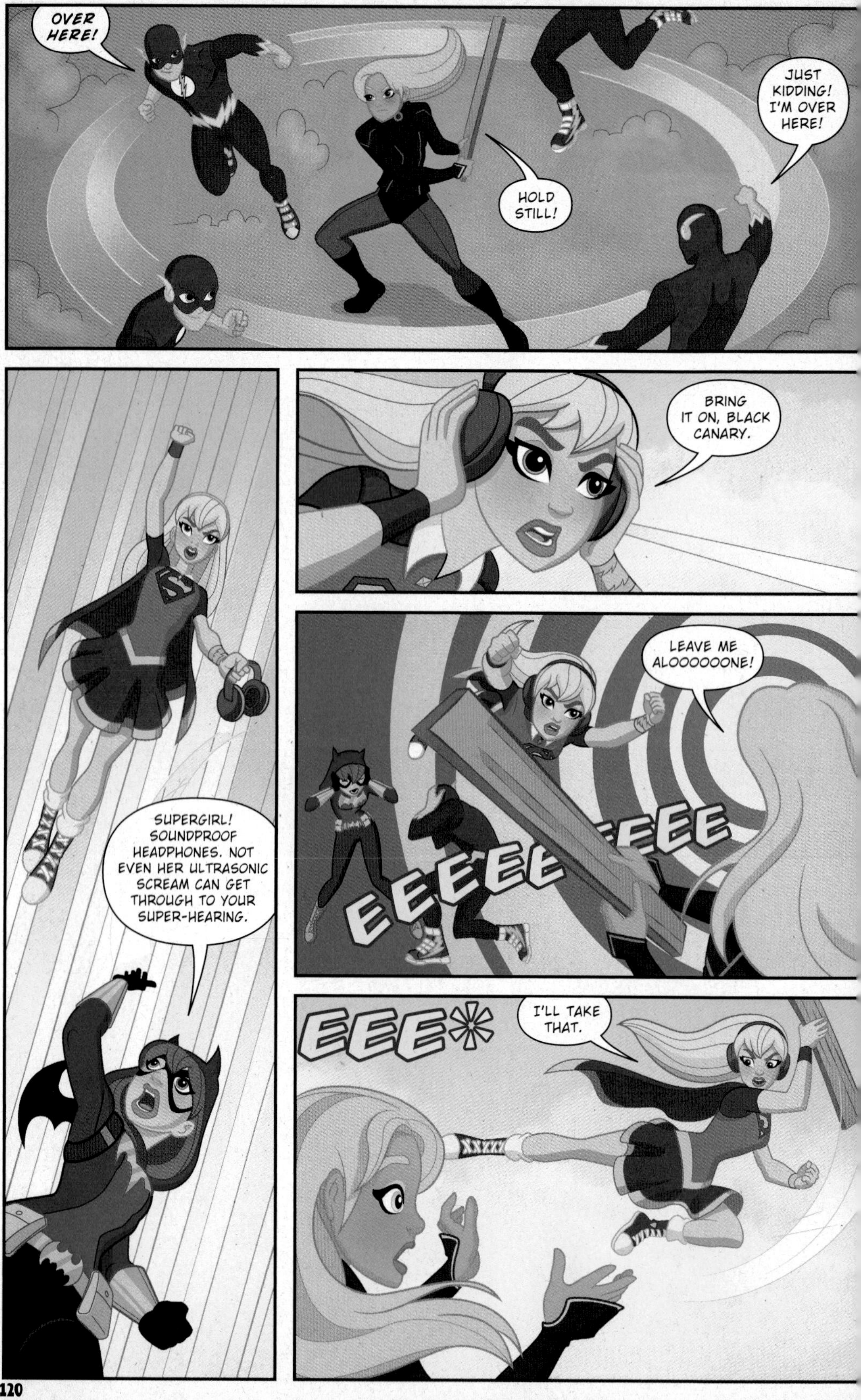
OVER HERE!
HOLD STILL!
JUST KIDDING! I'M OVER HERE!
BRING IT ON, BLACK CANARY.
SUPERGIRL! SOUNDPROOF HEADPHONES. NOT EVEN HER ULTRASONIC SCREAM CAN GET THROUGH TO YOUR SUPER-HEARING.
LEAVE ME ALOOOOOONE!
EEEEEEEEEE
EEE*
I'LL TAKE THAT.

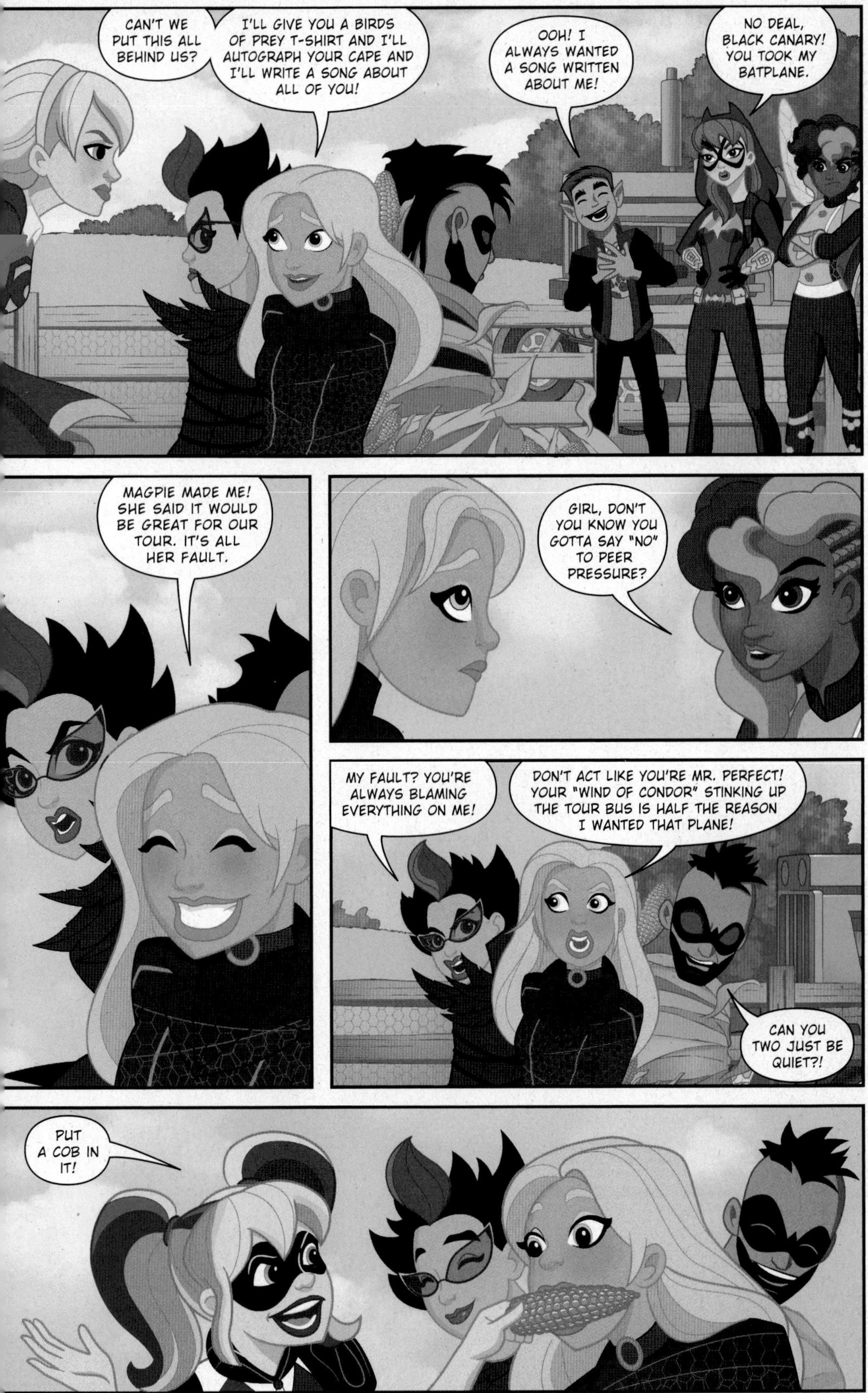
CAN'T WE PUT THIS ALL BEHIND US?
I'LL GIVE YOU A BIRDS OF PREY T-SHIRT AND I'LL AUTOGRAPH YOUR CAPE AND I'LL WRITE A SONG ABOUT ALL OF YOU!
OOH! I ALWAYS WANTED A SONG WRITTEN ABOUT ME!
NO DEAL, BLACK CANARY! YOU TOOK MY BATPLANE.
MAGPIE MADE ME! SHE SAID IT WOULD BE GREAT FOR OUR TOUR. IT'S ALL HER FAULT.
GIRL, DON'T YOU KNOW YOU GOTTA SAY "NO" TO PEER PRESSURE?
MY FAULT? YOU'RE ALWAYS BLAMING EVERYTHING ON ME!
DON'T ACT LIKE YOU'RE MR. PERFECT! YOUR "WIND OF CONDOR" STINKING UP THE TOUR BUS IS HALF THE REASON I WANTED THAT PLANE!
CAN YOU TWO JUST BE QUIET?!
PUT A COB IN IT!

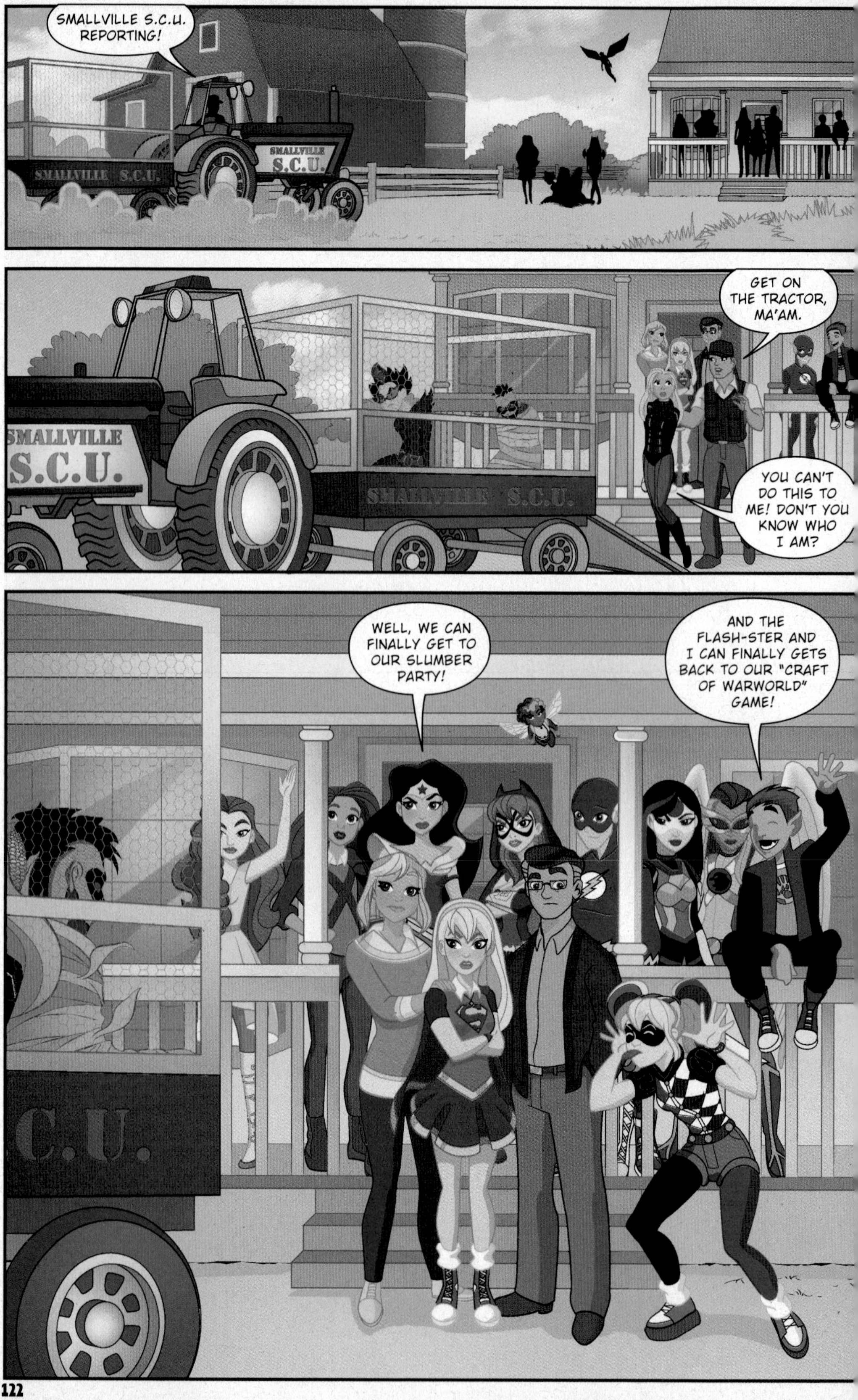
SMALLVILLE S.C.U. REPORTING!
SMALLVILLE S.C.U.
SMALLVILLE S.C.U.
SMALLVILLE S.C.U.
GET ON THE TRACTOR, MA'AM.
YOU CAN'T DO THIS TO ME! DON'T YOU KNOW WHO I AM?
SMALLVILLE S.C.U.
WELL, WE CAN FINALLY GET TO OUR SLUMBER PARTY!
AND THE FLASH-STER AND I CAN FINALLY GETS BACK TO OUR "CRAFT OF WARWORLD" GAME!
S.C.U.

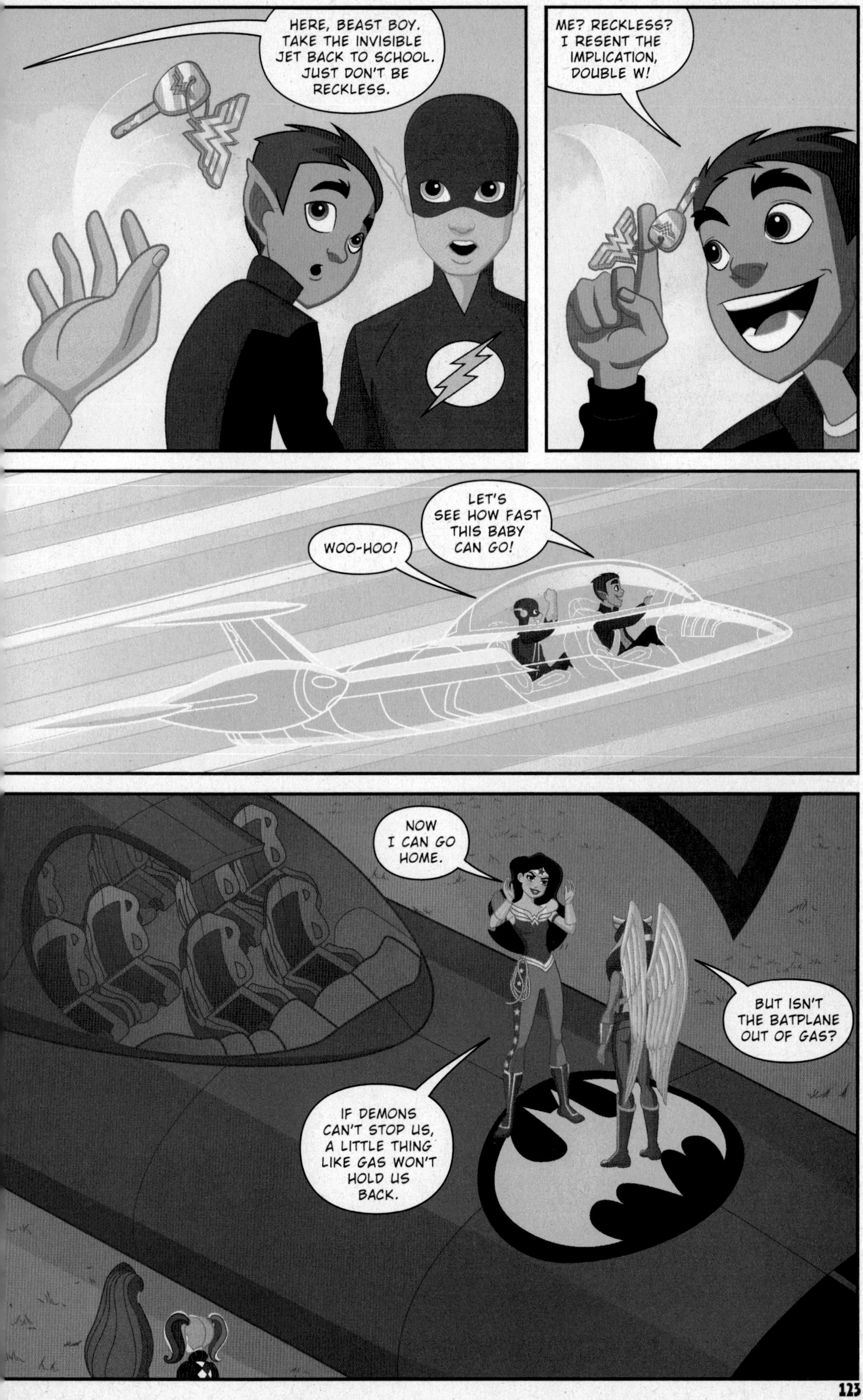
HERE, BEAST BOY. TAKE THE INVISIBLE JET BACK TO SCHOOL. JUST DON'T BE RECKLESS.
ME? RECKLESS? I RESENT THE IMPLICATION, DOUBLE W!
WOO-HOO!
LET'S SEE HOW FAST THIS BABY CAN GO!
NOW I CAN GO HOME.
BUT ISN'T THE BATPLANE OUT OF GAS?
IF DEMONS CAN'T STOP US, A LITTLE THING LIKE GAS WON'T HOLD US BACK.

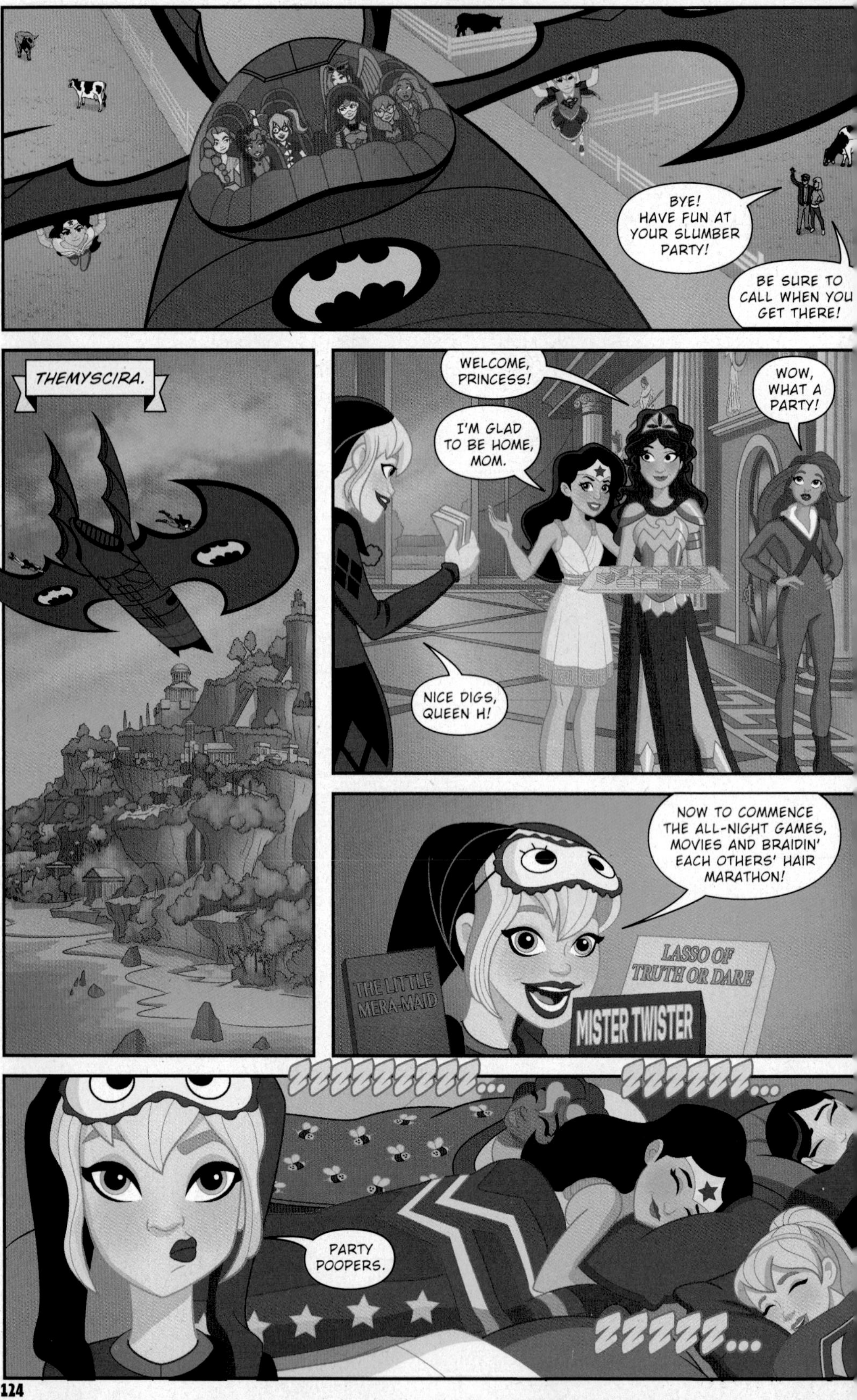
BYE! HAVE FUN AT YOUR SLUMBER PARTY!
BE SURE TO CALL WHEN YOU GET THERE!
THEMYSCIRA.
WELCOME, PRINCESS!
I'M GLAD TO BE HOME, MOM.
WOW, WHAT A PARTY!
NICE DIGS, QUEEN H!
NOW TO COMMENCE THE ALL-NIGHT GAMES, MOVIES AND BRAIDIN' EACH OTHERS' HAIR MARATHON!
THE LITTLE MERA-MAID
LASSO OF TRUTH OR DARE
MISTER TWISTER
ZZZZZZZZZZ...
ZZZZZZ...
PARTY POOPERS.
ZZZZZ...

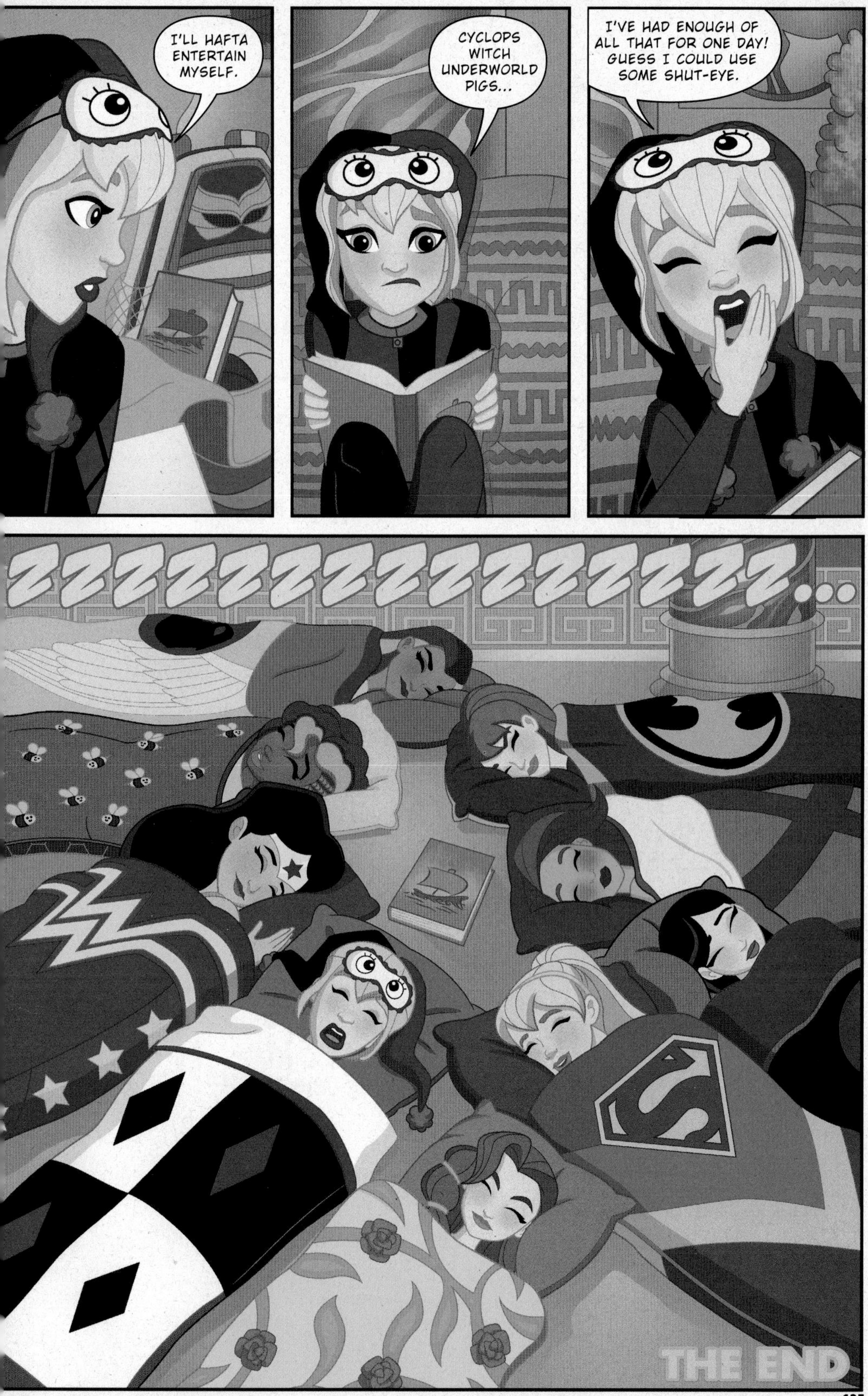
I'LL HAFTA ENTERTAIN MYSELF.
CYCLOPS WITCH UNDERWORLD PIGS...
I'VE HAD ENOUGH OF ALL THAT FOR ONE DAY! GUESS I COULD USE SOME SHUT-EYE.
ZZZZZZZZZZZZZZZ...
THE END

ABOUT THE AUTHOR

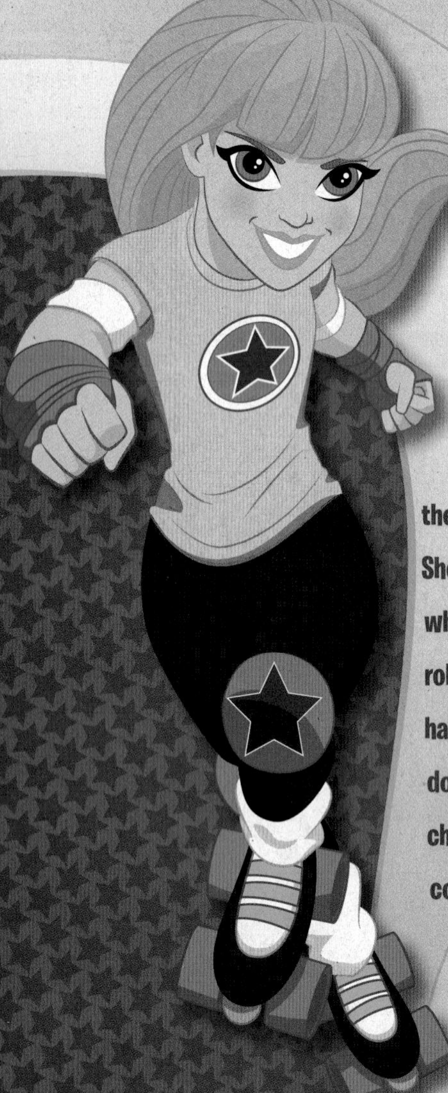

Shea Fontana is a writer for film, television, and graphic novels. Her credits include *DC Super Hero Girls* animated shorts, television specials, and movies, *Dorothy and the Wonders of Oz, Doc McStuffins, The 7D, Whisker Haven Tales with the Palace Pets, Disney on Ice*, and the feature film *Crowning Jules*. She lives in sunny Los Angeles where she enjoys playing roller derby, hiking, hanging out with her dog, Moxie, and changing her hair color. ★

ABOUT THE COLORIST

Monica Kubina

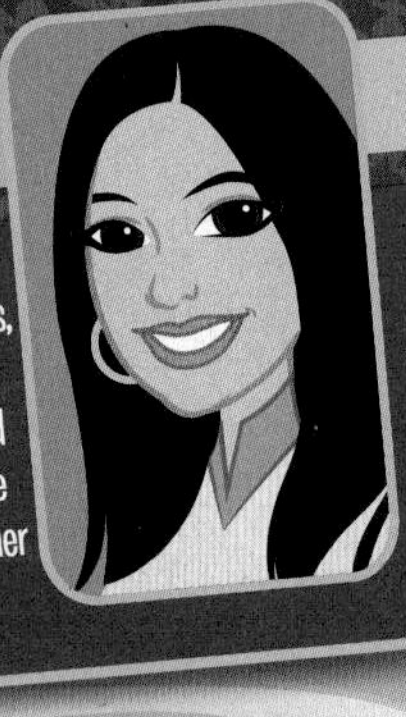

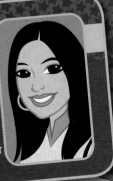

Monica Kubina has colored countless comics, including super hero series, manga titles, kids comics, and science fiction stories. She's colored *Phineas and Ferb, SpongeBob, THE 99*, and *Star Wars*. Monica's favorite activities are bike riding and going to museums with her husband and two young sons.

ABOUT THE ARTIST

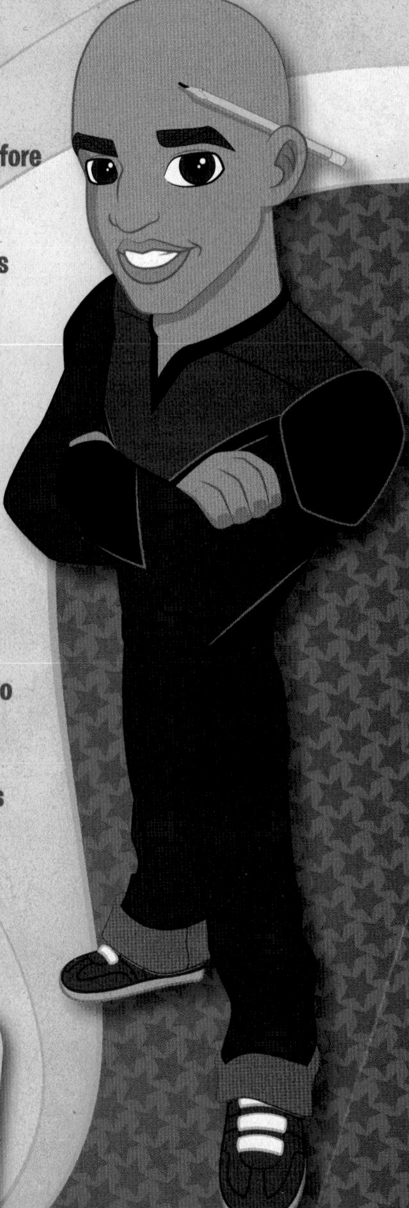

Yancey Labat got his start at Marvel Comics before moving on to illustrate children's books from *Hello Kitty* to *Peanuts* for Scholastic, as well as books for Chronicle Books, ABC Mouse, and others. His book *How Many Jellybeans?* with writer Andrea Menotti won the 2013 Cook Prize for best STEM (Science, Technology, Education, Math) picture book from Bank Street College of Education. He has two super hero girls of his own and lives in Cupertino, California. ★

ABOUT THE LETTERER

Janice Chiang

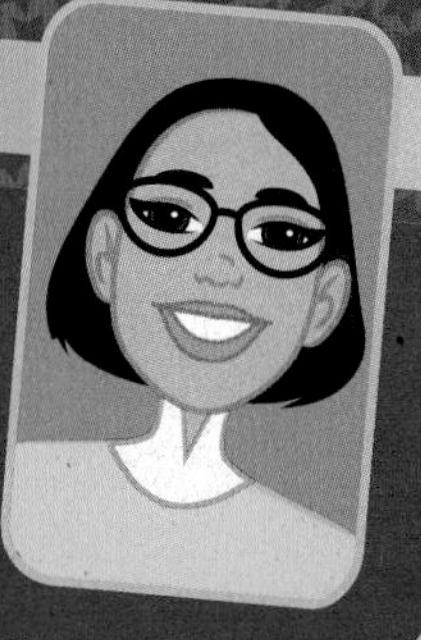

has lettered *Archie, Barbie, Punisher* and many more. She was the first woman to win the Comic Buyer's Guide Fan Awards for Best Letterer (2011). She likes weight training, hiking, baking, gardening, and traveling.

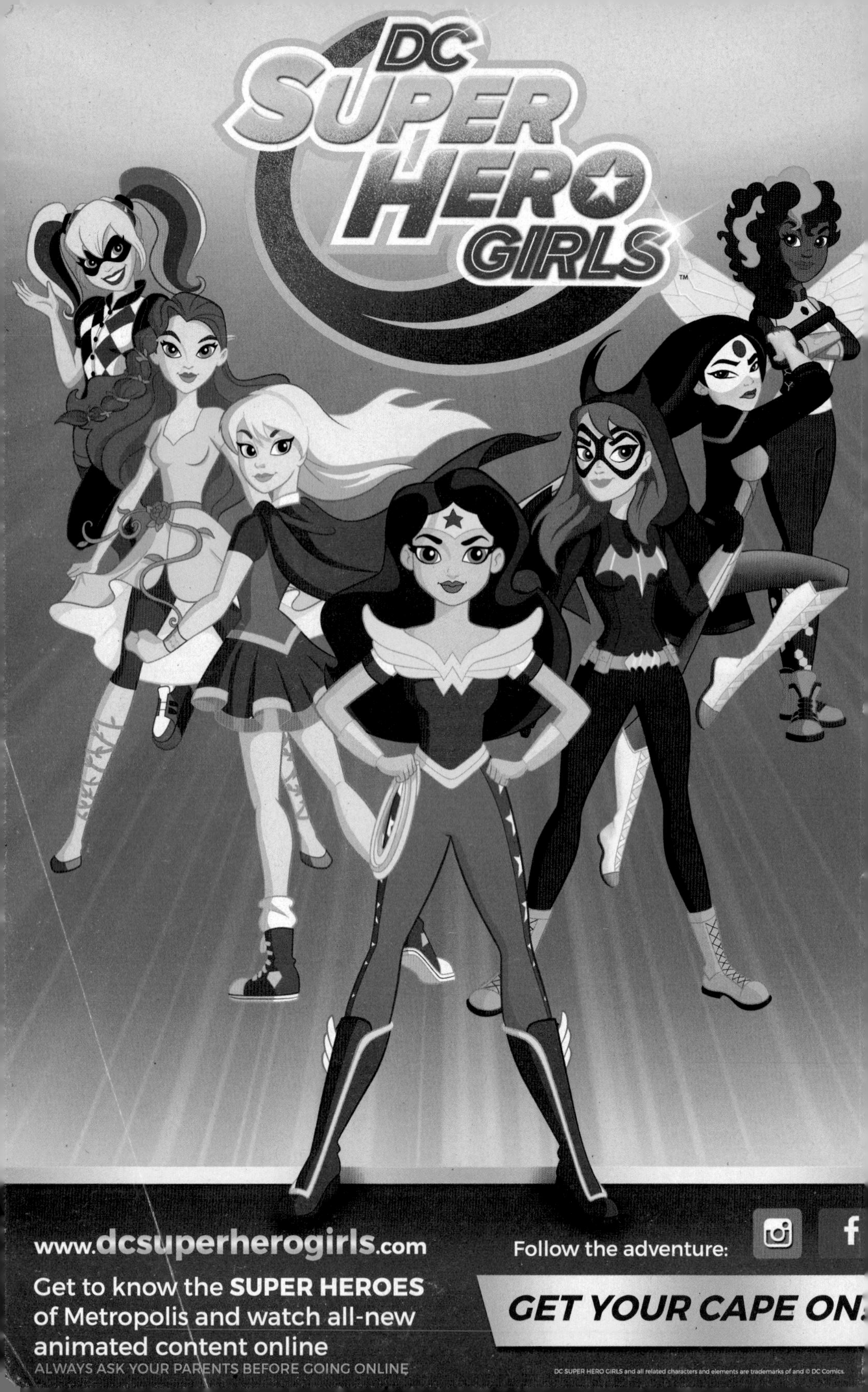
DC SUPER HERO GIRLS™
www.dcsuperherogirls.com
Get to know the SUPER HEROES of Metropolis and watch all-new animated content online
ALWAYS ASK YOUR PARENTS BEFORE GOING ONLINE
Follow the adventure:
GET YOUR CAPE ON!
DC SUPER HERO GIRLS and all related characters and elements are trademarks of and © DC Comics.